Machinations and Sacrifices

Lake Of Sins, Volume 6

L. S. O'Dea

Published by L. S. O'Dea, 2022.

MACHINATIONS AND SACRIFICES

First edition. July 7, 2022.

Copyright © 2022 L. S. O'Dea.

ISBN: 978-1942706878

Written by L. S. O'Dea.

Also by L. S. O'Dea

Chimera Chronicles
Rise of the River Man
Feeding Fersia
Breaking the Brush Men
Rage Of Rattus Norvegicus
Leaving Level Five

Lake Of Sins
Lake of Sins: Secrets in Blood
Lake of Sins: Hangman's Army
Lake Of Sins: Betrayed
Whispers From the Past
Machinations and Sacrifices
Lake of Sins: Escape

Standalone
Lake of Sins Series Box Set Books 1-3
Chimera Chronicles
A Demon's Gift

CHAPTER 1: Tuck

Tuck waited in the darkness as JD's breathing slowed and steadied with sleep before rolling away from his friend. It was late. He needed to go so he could get back before JD woke.

He put the papers he'd used to cover himself over JD. It was the best he could do to help keep him warm. The kid was so small. They needed food and protection but joining the gangs wouldn't be a good idea for either of them. In the gangs, only the strongest survived. The rest of them were used for the dangerous jobs, the ones that got them killed or arrested.

JD wanted them to join Con's gang. The kid had been talking to a few of the members, and they'd made the idea of joining sound sweet, but Tuck knew it was all lies. His mom had been in a gang when he was born, and it hadn't ended well for her or him.

"Tuck?" JD's eyes fluttered open.

Dang it. He should've left.

"Where are you going?"

"To piss." He bent, brushing the hair from JD's forehead. "Go back to sleep. I'll be right back."

"Okay." The kid's voice slurred as his eyes drooped.

Tuck waited another few minutes and then squeezed against the brick wall and slipped from behind the pile of junk where he and JD lived. It was a pretty safe setup. No one looked long enough at a pile of junk around here to see that it was stacked in a way that they had a little home. It wasn't much, but it was a few feet of solitude where they could rest without worrying about being attacked. It also had an escape route through an air vent into the building.

He checked to make sure no one was around. He wouldn't risk leaving JD alone if bigger Servants were hanging out nearby, but the alley was clear. He scurried out onto the street and then darted through a maze of alleyways, going farther and farther away from the Servant section of town.

It was risky to go so close to the Guard's part of the city, but they needed food. He'd heard rumors that Manny left the window open above his store. He stayed in the shadows, the quiet of the night putting him on edge. He should be glad he didn't see anyone, but there was something about tonight that made his skin prickle. Maybe he should go back, but then they'd be hungry again tomorrow. He had to check and see if that window was open. He crept through another alleyway. Footsteps sounded on the pavement. He hopped into a nearby dumpster to hide his scent as two skinny Guards walked by, chatting about some fight they'd seen.

He waited until he could no longer hear them and then hopped from the dumpster. He hurried to the end of the alley. Manny's sign hung over a door. His eyes skimmed up the building to the window. It was open. A cold sweat broke out across his skin. It was two stories high, but the building was brick. He could climb it. He was small but strong. Most Servants could climb to the window, but they were too big to fit through the crack. He was sure he could do both.

He glanced around, sniffing. It stank of Guard around here, but he and JD needed food too badly for him to worry much about that. He patted his pocket where he'd stuffed a bag. He'd slip in through the window, grab some food and then be back in the alley before anyone even saw him.

He glanced both ways just to make sure no one was around before racing across the street to the building. He turned, pressing his back to the wall, and checking the area one more time. Once he started climbing, there was no turning back. The street was empty. A few voices drifted on the wind, but they were muffled and in the distance. It was time.

He began scaling the wall. The brick was old and worn, but there were still plenty of toe and finger holds. He moved quickly, but that window was a lot farther away than it'd seemed from the ground. His fingers spasmed and his legs ached, but he kept going. His bag was big. He could get enough food to last them a few days, maybe a week.

He paused, his ears perking up at a soft flutter. He knew that sound from somewhere. He stared into the darkness but there was no movement on the street. He shook his head. It was just his imagination. He had to focus. He stared at his goal as he crawled up the wall. Another minute and he'd be inside the building with all that food. He moved faster, his mouth watering as the window loomed above him, getting closer and closer with each....A whoosh of air hit him, knocking him sideways. He lost his grip on the wall, his fingers scrambling for purchase and his flesh tearing from his hands as he clawed at the building.

It was no use. He was falling. He screamed, twisting his body so he didn't land on his head and then something hit him...hard, like a Grunt on a rampage. He flew forward in the air, his body bucking and spasming as something stabbed his side and back. He screamed again, louder than before, louder than he'd ever screamed as pain lanced through him. He tried to pull at the knife in his back, but his arms just dangled before his eyes. The pain, so potent before, was gone. All feeling was gone. He stared down at the street. The metallic taste of blood filled his mouth before dripping from his lips as the whoosh of giant wings carried him through the city.

They were moving fast, faster than he had, even with using the shortcuts. They were back in the Servant section of the city. His sight once clear, grew fuzzy, dimming with every labored breath. He scanned the area, finding his alley. His pile of garbage that'd been the only refuge he'd ever known. His home. "JD..." he whispered as his heart stopped beating.

CHAPTER 2: Conguise

Conguise's footsteps echoed in the hallways of Level Five. He'd been released months ago but this was his first visit back to the scene of his life's work and his greatest failure. The cameras stared down at him, still and accusing. Everything was gone. No scientists walked the halls and no whisper of movement from behind the closed doors of the now empty lab.

"Professor, I didn't expect to see you here," Gruder stepped out of his office. The younger Almighty looked haggard—his brown hair longer than normal and mussed as if he hadn't combed it that day, his clothes rumpled and hanging on his slender frame.

Conguise would've never allowed Gruder to come to work looking so disheveled, but times had changed. "I may no longer be able to perform experiments, but I wanted to speak with you."

"Yes, I heard about the terms of your release."

All he was allowed to do now was teach. He should've had Hugh killed the moment he'd realized the other Almighty had seen what he'd been doing on Level Five, but he'd trusted Jason and the system. He'd been a fool. "I wouldn't have been released if not for you."

For months he'd sat in that prison cell, waiting to die by the hands of Hugh and his Allied Classes. Oh, how he despised that name. The lower classes were as much allies to the Almightys as he was with an ant when he dropped a crumb of bread. Yet those ignorant and shortsighted imbeciles would decide his fate and destroy everything he'd accomplished.

"It wasn't just me." Gruder held open the door. "Please, come inside. I'm sure you have a lot of questions."

"I do." He walked into Gruder's office.

"Sorry. I wasn't expecting company." The other Almighty moved a pile of papers off the chair near his desk. "Would you like something to drink?" He walked to a small refrigerator.

"No. Thank you." Sitting in front of the desk of his subordinate was another new experience, but none of it mattered. He was still in charge both here and in the larger world and everyone would realize that soon enough.

"Okay." Gruder sat behind his desk. "Most of the specimens are safe and secure in facility R."

"Yes. I've seen the reports." His jaw clenched a bit. "Thank you again." He was not one for espousing gratitude, but this was deserved.

"As I said, it was a team effort."

"But you are the one who gathered the team and led them."

Gruder shrugged. "I wasn't going to let them destroy what we created."

"And they would've. They're ignorant of the future we face when our enemies come from beyond the sea."

"Of course." Gruder nodded.

The other Almighty placated him, but he didn't care because he was right. He'd read the journals from the Great Death. It was inevitable that one day the others would come to kill them as they'd tried to do centuries ago.

"Have you been to the secondary site yet?" asked Gruder.

"I was there this morning." He'd gone the first chance he'd had. Traveling through the sewers had been distasteful and dangerous, but it'd been the only way to be sure he wouldn't be followed.

"It's a bit cramped, but everyone is doing their best to keep things progressing."

"I saw that some of the specimens didn't make it." Their decomposing bodies had littered the dark corners in the sewers, filling the tunnels with ghastly odors and terrifying shadows.

"We had to make hard choices in a difficult time, but we kept the best specimens and euthanized the rest. Destroying the remains of course."

"Destroying?" Lie number one.

"We burned as many as we could, but time was not on our side." Gruder shrugged again.

"Hmm. That was true, but there's time now." There had been for months. "Send someone into the sewer to burn the rest."

"Of course." Gruder nodded, but his lips thinned a bit. He'd been in charge for a while now and it seemed he wasn't thrilled about relinquishing control.

"But..." He thrummed his fingers on his thigh. "I wasn't talking about the creatures we had in abundance who didn't make it. Those can be recreated."

"Then which creatures?" Gruder's eyes narrowed in thought for a moment. "Oh, the Accipitor." He frowned. "Yes, that was a sad misfortune. We tried our best, but as you know, she had a weak heart. The sedation was too much for her."

"I see." Lie number two. "Odd that no one remembers the destruction of her remains and she's not one of the carcasses in the tunnels." His eyes locked with Gruder's. "I looked. Checked every pile." It'd been disgusting but necessary. Now more than ever he must distinguish between those truly committed to the protection of their world and those who only pretended.

"She wasn't left in the tunnels, but"—Gruder smiled slightly—"you can rest easy knowing that no one will find a trace of her. I took care of her remains myself."

"Really?" Conguise was impressed with the other Almighty's skill at lying—no aversion of the eyes, not even a small flinch.

"Yes. She was my responsibility."

"That's right. You did inherit her, didn't you?" His fingers stilled on his leg. That was another mystery. "Still no word from Bing?"

"Bing?"

"Yes. I thought that since the war was over, she may have appeared. The two of you were close, were you not?"

"We were but sadly, I have not heard from her."

"Hmm." Good, he had the other Almighty on edge. He had every intention of keeping him there. "Ableson tendered his resignation."

"He did what?" Gruder's eyes widened. It was the first unpracticed expression the other Almighty had made.

"He met me at my house the day I was released and quit." Conguise shrugged. "First time anyone has quit Level Five." And lived was the unspoken message he wanted Gruder to hear. "Apparently, some of the scientists thought they couldn't quit. According to Hugh, Parson faked his own death to leave." He studied the other Almighty closely. He'd been sure Gruder had arranged for Parson's and Bing's death, but Parson was alive. Bing may also be.

"Unbelievable." Gruder shook his head. His face once more a mask of polite indifference.

"Exactly. The extremes some will take to leave a position when all they have to do is tender their resignation." He frowned. "It's not like Parson stole from me." He looked directly at Gruder. "Were you alone when you destroyed the Accipitor's remains?"

"What? Oh, Accipitor1. No. Silo assisted me."

"Hmm." His fingers drummed his thigh again. "Strange. No one has seen him since the lab was moved to the new facility."

"That can't be right. I'm sure I saw him the other day"—Gruder's brow wrinkled—"or that could've been a week or so ago. We've been very busy." His eyes met the professor's. "Hiding everything for you."

He'd already thanked the other Almighty for that. He would not be obsequious. "If you did see Silo, then once again you are the only one." He raised his brow. "That seems to happen a lot with you."

"I'm sorry?" Gruder's face was placid, but ice filled his tone.

"You seem to be the last one to see many. Crackderr. Parson. Bing. Accipitor1. Silo."

"I spend a lot of time in the lab, and I'm very observant." Gruder's tone changed. "My memory isn't great though, so I keep a lot of notes."

"One should be careful about that." Conguise almost smiled at the thinly veiled threat. "Paper ignites quickly. Poor McBrid learned that the hard way when his house caught on fire."

"I don't keep my notes at home. They're somewhere much safer."

"There is nowhere that's one hundred percent secure." And nothing he wouldn't do to protect his work.

"Including Facility R. Ableson assisted with the transfer from Level Five to Facility R."

"I trust Ableson." He didn't trust Gruder, and right now, he couldn't risk having anyone around whom he didn't trust completely. There were too many options in this new world. One word to Hugh and Conguise would be back in jail or dead.

"Really?"

"I know his secrets." Conguise leaned forward. "Just like I know yours." He was impressed. Gruder's breathing barely changed. "Where is she?"

"Bing? I told you. I have no idea where—"

"Not Bing. Accipitor1."

"I told you that too. She's gone."

"She belongs to me. She belongs in the lab."

"She's gone." Gruder almost snarled.

"I will find her."

"She has been destroyed. There is no trace of her anywhere."

"What do you think the public will do to her when they see her? Someone will eventually. Do you think they'll understand? Do you think they'll see her beauty? Her uniqueness?" He shook his head.

"They won't. All they'll see is a monster. A predator. She'll terrify them, and the ignorant always kill what they fear. She's safer in the laboratory."

"You were safer in prison." Gruder stood. "I forgot to mention that I've spoken with Hugh."

Conguise's heart skipped a beat. Had this been a trap? He forced himself not to look around for the ambush, not to run.

"I'll be joining the team on the alternative meat initiative. So, like Ableson, I'm also resigning. Effective today."

His heart stopped slamming against his ribs, but he'd been around too long not to know that the second threat was coming.

"I have no intention of uttering a word to anyone about what went on here," said Gruder. "If I wanted the world to know, I would've left everything as it was." He leaned on the desk. "Just like Ableson, you know my secrets, and I know yours. Let's hope neither of us are ever forced to tattle because I have proof to back my stories, and you have nothing." He strode toward the door.

"You're right. I have nothing." Conguise didn't bother to turn when Gruder's steps faltered. "That's why my life means little. Whereas, if I'm not mistaken, you have much to live for. Don't you?"

Gruder remained silent.

"If you tattle, as you say, I'll die, but if I tattle, you'll lose what you love the most." This time he did turn. "Trust me. That's worse than dying." He choked down the ball of hatred over what Hugh had done to Viola. "I'll keep your secret, but she'd be safer at facility R." He stood and strode past Gruder. He'd find her eventually. She was his creation and she belonged to him.

CHAPTER 3: Jethro

Jethro followed the line of prisoners toward the yard. Today wasn't going to be fun. He was alone for the first time since being transferred from the holding cells to the prison months ago.

Yesterday, he'd said goodbye to the last Guard in his gang. They all should've been released right away, but Hugh had made it his mission to make anyone who'd been in the Protective Services suffer. The bigger and stronger the Guards the longer they'd stayed locked up, especially if they'd served with Jethro.

He sauntered across the yard and all eyes fell on him. Everyone knew he was on his own and alone in prison wasn't the way to live long. He had to join another group, but that's where things got complicated.

He walked toward the fence, his gaze drifting over a group of Servants. They wouldn't accept him. He'd chosen the Guards over them months ago. The predatory gleam in their vibrant eyes confirmed they'd let him die before they allowed him into their group.

Joining with the other Guard gangs probably wasn't going to happen either. Those that were left were soldiers who were still loyal to the leaders of the past. Switching sides at the end of the war had sealed his fate with them.

That left the Almightys. They were also the old regime, but Wickerwood had tried to befriend him his first week of incarceration. They were all old and out of shape. He was young, strong and an excellent fighter. He'd made it clear that he wasn't interested in having anything to do with them. He still wasn't, but his choices were limited.

He leaned against the chain-link fence and stared out at nothing. Someone would approach him with an offer but hidden in that would be a beating. His blood hummed in anticipation. He needed to release his restlessness by fighting or mating, but the latter was not an option in prison.

Scratch, a Servant, walked over to him, glancing around nervously.

He was glad it was the Servants. The Guards strutted around like they ran the place, but most backed down when faced with the ferocity of the Servants, especially since they had built-in weapons. Their claws were supposed to be filed down, but for the right price, the prison Guards had a tendency to forget about that.

"I hear yous the one to talk to about getting somethings special," said Scratch.

"Like what?" They wanted contraband. He owed Indy again. His friend had been working with Tonkers, a prison Guard, to sneak booze, candy and other items into the facility. Indy refused to work with anyone but Jethro, and that made him necessary to those who were really in charge—the prison Guards.

"We wants a visit with some friends."

"Friends?" They snuck small stuff into the prison not Servants or Guards. "What kind of friends?"

"Da female kind." Scratch rolled his eyes as he glanced at his gang.

That wasn't possible. Was it? No. Tonkers wouldn't risk it. He studied the others in the yard. Scratch was a nobody. His boss, who like to be called Life, was the one who was really asking. After several minutes he looked at Scratch. "I don't see that happening."

"I don't think yous understands. We"—Scratch glanced at Life and the other Servants in his gang—"wants what we wants and yous got connections. Yous better make it happen." His claws peeked out from his fingertips in a not-so-subtle threat.

"You don't understand." This was the opening he needed. "That request—"

"It ain't nos request." Scratch bristled, his nose twitching as he searched for the scent of fear.

Scratch could sniff all day, but he wouldn't catch a whiff of that in the air. Jethro was a lot of things right now but scared wasn't one of them. He straightened, shifting closer and getting right into the Servant's face. "I don't give a Grunt's ass what *yous* call it. It isn't going to happen."

Scratch's eyes twitched slightly. "That's not gonna make Life happy and"—he glanced around again—"yous all alone." His arm flew forward straight toward Jethro's face, claws bared.

The Servant was fast, probably the fastest in the prison, but to him it was laughably slow. He grabbed the lower part of Scratch's hand, avoiding the claws. With one quick twist he bent it back against the Servant's arm. The snap of bone echoed in the yard, quickly covered by Scratch's scream.

The scent of terror overloaded Jethro's senses and the Servant's whimpers made his blood roar. It was the sound of the weak. The helpless. The prey. He reached for Scratch's throat. It'd be so easy to tear it out and let the blood cover his fingers like a glove. He could end his enemy's life so easily. His instincts screamed. *The only good enemy is a dead one.* He took a deep, shaky breath as he forced himself to drop his arm and free his prey.

Scratch stumbled backward, holding his hand to keep it from flopping around like a dying bird. Silence filled the yard. Even Scratch's screams became nothing more than soft whimpers as he scurried to the safety of his gang before he became a target for someone else.

The Guards moved closer, smelling the weak and injured. Jethro grabbed the fence to keep from charging forward and fighting them all. A major brawl in the yard wouldn't help convince Hugh to release him. Indy kept telling him that many were fighting for his freedom and that Hugh was going to have to give in to the pressure. He prayed that it happened soon because once he took his serum, he'd be weak, vulnerable and since he was alone, probably dead.

He didn't want to die in here. He wanted to live free in the forest. He was ready to move on with his life. He was done with war, with fighting, and with Trinity. Hugh could have her. He tensed as the gang of Servants headed his way. His eyes met Life's vibrant green ones as the Servant walked past him. Life wasn't happy with his answer and that meant retaliation was coming.

CHAPTER 4: Jethro

Jethro followed the other prisoners back inside. No one else had approached him in the yard and that meant the next time would be an ambush. He walked into his cell and dropped on the cot. He should try and rest, but his blood pounded, and his muscles trembled for a fight. If he'd known no one else was going to attack, he'd have pounded on Scratch a little more to ease the tension that flowed through him.

He stood and paced. He hated being locked up. He'd go mad if he had to stay here much longer. He wanted to grab the bars and pull them from the wall, but that wasn't possible. He'd tried during the first month he'd been in here. He'd delayed taking his shot and the urge to fight and to run had roared through his body like the wind before a storm. He'd been strong and desperate, but even then, he hadn't been able to bend the metal. He walked to the bars, resting his face against them. He just had to wait this out. The urge to run and fight, to kill would wane once he took his shot.

He'd be weak, but he'd also be able to relax. After his serum he still hated being in prison, but it was manageable until the medicine wore thin in his blood. It was a blessing and a curse. Things were simple before his shot. Someone was either a friend or an enemy. There were no shadowy thoughts of why someone did what they did. Nothing mattered except who they were to him. If they were his friend, he'd protect them with his life, but if they were his enemy...It was best if they avoided him because if they didn't, they'd die. Dead enemies couldn't hurt him.

The cell door opened. It was time for dinner.

He stepped into the hallway and followed the others to the cafeteria. Everything looked normal, but as he walked through the door, he caught the whisper of violence in the air—the scent of rage and battle. He spun as a fist flew in his direction. It was attached to a very large Guard. He knew this prison Guard, but he couldn't recall the male's name. It wouldn't have mattered if he had. This was simple. This was an enemy.

He caught the Guard's fist and shoved. His enemy stumbled backward from the force, surprise in his eyes and the fresh scent of fear sweetened the air. His opponent hadn't expected his strength or his speed. Besides the scuffle this morning, he hadn't fought since he'd assembled his gang. He'd had no reason to. They'd been the strongest and the best trained in here. After a few weeks, everyone had stayed away from them.

He'd been free to take his serum as ordered by Conguise and delivered by his mother. She'd sneak it into the prison in the lining of her purse and pass it to him in the clasping of hands or a hug. Now, with his gang gone he couldn't risk taking his medicine. It'd make him vulnerable. Weak like an Almighty.

He grinned as another prison Guard charged him. This would be a real fight, not one small Servant, but a group of large Guards. He welcomed the battle. His blood could rage hot and brutal, and he'd finally be able to sleep tonight.

He sent a sharp left jab, connecting his fist to the first Guard's face and knocking him down with one punch. He glared at the Guard. That was disappointing. He'd expected a fight, not a...

Someone grabbed him around his chest, squeezing and locking his arms at his side, but he didn't need his hands to fight. He squatted and threw himself backward, racing full force for the wall. The Guard on his back would be his buffer, his pillow of blood and bone. He slammed himself against the brick wall over and over. His enemy's grunts of pain in his ear fed his desire to kill. The Guard's grasp loosened, his body sliding downward, but Jethro wasn't letting this prey slip away that easily. He grabbed his enemy's arms, holding him in place as he continued his assault. He smashed into the wall again and again, fast and hard. The Guard hung limp behind him, but his pulse still throbbed in his wrists and his whimpers tickled Jethro's ear each time they connected with the brick.

"Die," he growled as he threw them against the wall again.

Two other Guards charged from the side, grabbing his arms and breaking his hold on his enemy. The Guard on his back slid to the floor in a bloodied heap. Fists landed fast and hard on Jethro's stomach and face. Another set pummeled his side, but he barely felt it. Rage and instinct controlled him now. He had one task. One desire. Kill those who tried to hurt him.

His fists flew twice as fast as the Guards', hitting one and then the other over and over. The first fell. The second scrambled backward, holding up his hands, but surrender wasn't an option. Only death. He launched himself at the Guard, taking them both to the floor. He punched over and over. Blood splattered his skin and clothes. He opened his mouth, catching the droplets and savoring the metallic, salty taste, but it wasn't enough. He lowered his face to his enemy's neck. He needed to feel the flesh between his teeth—to tear and rip. Something sharp hit his back.

Another enemy!

He jumped off the Guard, roaring as he spun to face his assailant. A dart stuck from his shoulder. He pulled it out and glared at the shocked prison Guard in front of him. That dart should've taken him down, weakened him, but it hadn't done anything but piss him off.

"Help," yelled the prison Guard as he backed away, fumbling to load another dart into the blow gun.

"No one's going to get to you fast enough to save you." Jethro stalked toward him.

The Guard fired. The dart flew through the air and Jethro flung out his hand, knocking it away before it could connect with his chest.

The Guard's eyes widened, and the sweet scent of fear obliterated every other odor in the room.

"I'm going to tear your arms off and stuff them up your..." Another sharp pain lanced his side. He stopped, yanking the dart from his body.

The Guard he'd knocked down with one punch and another prison Guard were reloading their dart guns. They stood across from each other with him in the middle. He'd never get to them both before they fired. He sniffed before facing the second Guard. Little fear flowed from his pores and that made him more of a threat. Jethro charged as the Guard raised the blow gun to his lips. The dart flew in the air, straight toward Jethro's face. He raised his hand and knocked it away, except it didn't fall. He stopped staring at the dart sticking out of his hand. He felt nothing but...dizzy. He swayed, shaking his hand to remove the dart as the room spun. He dropped to his knees as blackness engulfed him.

CHAPTER 5: Trinity

Trinity hurried through the quiet corridors of the Council Building. It was early, but her ears perked up for any sound of her mother. She didn't need another lecture about this visit to Dr. Kalper's.

She slipped out the door and waved at a young male Grunt who lingered in the streets. She'd seen him around. He was always the first one to show up in the morning and the last to leave. He deserved to get the job.

He hurried over, motioning at one of the carriages that sat outside the building. He slapped his chest and flexed his muscles.

"Yes, you're very strong." She smiled at him. "I understand a bit of Grunt-speak." She moved her hands, using the signals that she'd picked up from Cack.

His hands started flying and he grunted so fast she couldn't tell where one sound ended, and another began.

"Slow down." She touched his arm, stopping him. "I understand a little, but you have to speak slowly."

He smiled, his large white teeth looking huge in his gaunt face. He grunted softly, "Sorry".

"No need to apologize. I'm Trinity."

He nodded vigorously as he grunted, "Producer. Almighty. House Servant. Hero."

"No."

He frowned.

"I am part Producer, part Almighty and part Servant, but I'm not a hero." She felt more like a failure than a hero. The world was different now because of her and her friends, but she wasn't sure it was better. Her life certainly wasn't.

"My hero." He smiled shyly at her.

She didn't have time to argue with the Grunt. She'd like to be back when Hugh sat in court, hearing the cases of some of those still in jail, but she had to be back before the Council meeting. Jethro's freedom would come up again. It always did, and every time fewer and fewer voted on Hugh's side. She wasn't even sure she was on his side about this anymore, but she'd decide that when it was time to vote. Until then, she had things she had to get done. "I need someone to pull the carriage. Do you want the job?"

He nodded again, slapping his chest hard enough to make her wince.

"Great." She walked to the smallest carriage. It'd just be her so there was no need to make the poor Grunt pull a larger one. He may be strong and eager, but he was too thin, his clothes hanging on his large frame.

He moved into place and began fastening the harness.

"You know how to do that?" She'd never seen a Grunt work with the traces and hadn't thought their feet-like hands were dexterous enough to connect all the tiny loops.

He nodded, the strap slipping from the three digits on his front feet. He frowned, grabbing it again.

Her hands flexed at her sides. It'd be faster if she did it, but he seemed determined. Still, she didn't want to be standing here all day. If her mother or, Araldo forbid, her father saw her... "Let me help." She began fastening the traces, not waiting for his okay.

He shot her an unhappy look, his cheeks turning slightly red.

"I'm sure you can do it." She moved on to the next one, her fingers flying over the knots.

His shoulders sagged.

"I mean, I know you *can* do it but if my mom"—she glanced at the building—"sees me she's going to ask a lot of questions that I don't want to answer."

He grinned, tapping his chest and then signaling, "My mom is like that too."

She laughed. "I think all moms are like that." She finished hooking him to the cart. "What's your name?" She checked all the knots, making sure they were secure.

"Ott," he grunted.

"Ott?" Most of their names were one syllable and sounded similar. She wanted to make sure she had it right. It'd be rude to call him by the wrong name all morning.

He nodded, smiling his goofy smile.

"Great. Do you know where Dr. Kalper lives?" Most of those in the other classes were familiar with the doctor.

He nodded.

"Then let's go."

"Trinity, wait!" shouted someone.

"Travis!" She hurried over to him as he strode toward her. He looked good, thinner but good.

"I'm so glad I caught you." He wrapped his arms around her, lifting her off her feet.

"Me too." She hugged him. She saw Mirabelle at the Council meetings, but she hadn't seen Travis in months. He was always working or trying to find work. This new world hadn't been easy on them or anyone actually.

Everyone was free now, but for most of those in the other classes life was worse than before the war. Hugh's new laws required Almightys to pay their Servants, Guards, Stockers and Grunts, but most Almightys couldn't afford that or refused to pay for services that used to be free. That meant a lot more strays. No, that term was no longer allowed. Now, they were called the Released. A new word but their reality was the same—no safe place to sleep and no food. The only benefit was that no matter where they wandered, they no longer had to worry about being rounded up and killed. She didn't want to go back to executing someone simply because they existed, but that meant a lot more Released roaming the streets and starving.

He put her down, letting his arms drop to his sides. "You look great." He smiled at her, his large round face as friendly and good natured as ever.

"You too." She tapped his arm. "I don't see many Producers anymore. I've forgotten how big and strong you guys are." Her mom was full-blooded Producer but smaller than most of the others and even Mirabelle was small compared to the males.

"Yeah. I can still work dawn to dusk." His eyes dimmed a little. "If I can find a job."

"Hugh's working on that but...Have you reconsidered farming? You're good at that and we need—"

"We can't go back to the camps." Mirabelle walked over to them from the side of the building. "I have a job here. Remember? Hugh needs me on the Council to support my class. I'm the only true Producer on the committee."

"I'm Producer too. I may be mixed but I always vote for what I believe is best for Producers. I think going back to farming is best for them and everyone."

"No. Never." His eyes hardened. "I won't go back to those fields. I won't be a prisoner again."

"But you won't be. You'll rent the land. You'll earn money." This was part of the food problem. They couldn't get Producers to go back to the fields. Some Grunts, Guards and Servants had gone and attempted to farm, but they didn't have the experience and weren't cut out for the work.

"For now but how long before that rule changes and we're food again?" asked Travis.

"Hugh won't let that happen."

"Hugh won't be able to stop it if the insurgents win."

"They won't. There are hardly any left. Hugh has troops rounding them up."

"There were hardly any of us either and we won. They could too."

"That won't happen." It couldn't. If it did, then all of this, all their sacrifices would be for nothing.

"And even if it doesn't, how long before the others convince Hugh that he'd save more lives by sacrificing the few. Us. Producers." He glanced around. "This area is nice but the others...We're starving. All of us. Guards. Servants. Grunts. Someone is going to make him believe that—"

"They won't. He'd never do that, but you're right. There are too many who are hungry...starving. That's why we need Producers to go back to the fields." She didn't know why she kept talking. She'd had this argument with so many Producers, but it never worked.

"It's not going to be us." He wrapped his arm around Mirabelle.

"Why?" She turned to the other female. "Your father is there. Your siblings are helping in some of the other camps. You know it's safe."

"Like I said, I have a job." It was clear from the tightness around her lips and the way Mirabelle glanced at Travis that this was a familiar argument between them.

"Okay." She may not like the other female, but Travis was one of her best friends. She wasn't going to cause any conflict between them. "Hugh's looking to expand the school system. He wants the young from all the classes to get an education and that'll mean adding additions to the current schools and building a few more."

"Really? When?" Travis took Mirabelle's hand and kissed it. "See. I told you this would work out."

"I...I don't know exactly when. He needs investors. He's going to try to raise it at the party."

"Great. When?"

"Ah...in a few months." She shouldn't have said anything. It seemed way too close to her. She still didn't have a dress and she had no idea how to act around all the rich, powerful Almighty who'd be there, but to Travis who was hungry, months may as well be years.

"Oh." Travis' face fell.

"You can stick around for the meeting today. They always serve something for lunch."

"I don't need charity." His eyes clouded with anger. His family hadn't been rich in the camps, but they'd worked for everything they'd had. This was no different.

"I know that. I didn't mean—"

"Mirabelle," Tammie yelled and waved as she walked over to them, holding a large basket. Curtis, at her side, carried two other baskets overflowing with produce.

"Tammie. Curtis. What are you doing here?" she asked. This morning was turning into a reunion.

"I'm here to train with your mom"—Tammie put the basket down—"and to give Mirabelle a gift from her father."

"Thank you." Mirabelle hugged Tammie. "Tell him thank you."

"You should go visit him," chided Tammie. "He'd love to see you."

"I will." Mirabelle glanced at Travis.

"He's no longer a prisoner. He could come and see us." Travis took the baskets from Curtis and placed them on the ground.

"He's old and set in his ways," said Tammie. "It won't kill you to visit him."

"It might if the rules change when we're there," mumbled Travis.

"Like you don't think they'll find you and force you to go there if things change." Tammie glared at him. "If the rules change, we're all back at the camps and dead. The best way to keep that from happening is to do our part."

"I don't have to make it easy for them by living in the cages they built for us," argued Travis.

"Give it up, Travis," Curtis slapped him on the back. "You aren't going to win this argument." He stood on tiptoe and kissed Tammie. "I'll see you at home. I'm off to see if Bo has some work for me today."

"Ask him if he needs a Producer too," said Travis.

"Will do."

"Good luck." Tammie hugged him. "And be careful."

"You too," said Curtis.

"Me?" Tammie laughed. "I'll be safe in the Council Building learning the best way to heal rashes and raging bowels from Millie."

"Herbs can be poisonous." Curtis laughed as he turned and left.

"Only the good ones," yelled Tammie.

"Ah...What time are you meeting my mom?" Trinity glanced at the door.

"Well, we're off." Travis picked up the baskets.

"Wait." Tammie grabbed his arm, her eyes on Curtis' retreating form.

"Why?" Travis looked at the others.

Trinity shrugged, her gaze darting back to the door. She needed to get out of there before her mother saw her.

"I've heard of a job. For Producers," whispered Tammie.

"You have? Why didn't—"

"Curtis doesn't like it."

"Why?" asked Travis.

"He thinks it has to do with the gangs."

"That's not good." Trinity turned to her friends, forgetting her mom for a minute. The gangs of Guards and Servants had grown bigger and more dangerous with the vast number of new strays. "You shouldn't do it then. It's not safe."

"Curtis doesn't know for sure that it has to do with gangs, and money is money. They aren't asking us to do anything illegal. They need things moved. I've heard some other Producers talking about it. They said the work is hard, but the money is good."

"What did they say they had to do?" asked Travis.

"They hauled large crates out of some of the buildings at the Warehouse District onto carts and then moved the carts to the wharf."

"That doesn't sound too bad," said Travis.

"What was in the crates?" Trinity didn't trust this.

"No one knows for sure. Some say they're removing the cages from the buildings and melting down the metal."

"Oh." She wasn't at all opposed to that. Those cages had been used to imprison her kind until they were slaughtered. "The entire area should be burnt to the ground."

"I agree." Tammie's eyes darted behind Travis again. "I'm going to the next one."

"You are?" asked Trinity. "Without telling Curtis?"

"Don't look at me like that," snapped Tammie. "You're sneaking out in the early morning. Does Hugh know about this trip you're making."

"Actually, he does." She straightened. "It was his idea."

"Where are you going?" asked Travis.

"It doesn't matter." She couldn't tell them. They wouldn't understand. She didn't understand why Hugh didn't want babies with her. "We're talking about this job. There must be some reason Curtis doesn't trust it. He's not one to overreact."

"No, but it's not the job so much as me." Tammie touched her stomach. "He's been very protective lately, but we really need the money."

"You're..." Trinity almost choked on the word.

"Yeah." Tammie smiled but her big brown eyes filled with tears. "It'll be a mix. It won't be easy. We both know that, but we love each other and—"

"That's so wonderful!" Mirabelle almost squealed with delight. "Travis and I can't wait to have young."

"I'm so happy for you." Travis put the baskets back down and hugged Tammie. "I'll go with you, so Curtis won't have to worry."

"Thank you." Tammie's smile almost glowed.

"Yeah. Congratulations." Trinity hugged her friend, hating herself for the jealousy that twisted inside her.

"Thanks. Your mom is helping me with some morning sickness issues I've been having."

"That's great. I mean, not the morning sickness but...What time are you meeting my mom?" This was the perfect reason to leave before she started crying right there in front of everyone.

"She said to come early." Tammie looked worried. "Am I too early?"

"Probably not and that means, I have to go."

"You really need to give your mom a break." Tammie touched her stomach again. "We're all going to be mothers soon. We're going to make mistakes, but we'll love our babies just like your mom loves you."

"I know she loves me. I really do." She backed toward the carriage. "But I don't see any reason to start off my day with a fight and that's exactly what'll happen if I see her."

"Why?" asked Tammie.

"I've gotta run." She couldn't talk about her visit with Dr. Kalper with any of them. They were all happy couples and ready to welcome babies into their lives, unlike Hugh who wanted to avoid it.

CHAPTER 6: Trinity

Trinity stared out the window as Ott made his way through the city. She hated feeling so angry and jealous. She was happy for Tammie and Curtis. Really, she was. It wasn't their fault that Hugh didn't want a baby.

A young Servant darted in front of the carriage. Thankfully, Ott knew better than to stop. He veered around the kid and moved faster. Rocks pelted the side of the carriage, followed by yells. If they'd stopped, they would've been robbed.

The dangerous areas seemed to grow every day, encroaching and overtaking the neighborhoods that had once been decent. Shops closed and more went hungry. She'd been so naïve to think that winning the war would solve all their problems.

It'd fixed some but had created so many others. Hugh was stuck trying to come up with workable solutions for everyone's problems which meant she was stuck too—in the city. She hated it here. She missed the woods—the trees, the fresh air, the freedom, the simplicity.

She needed the forest. She needed a break from the constant problems. She didn't actually have a set time for her appointment with Dr. Kalper. She'd just told him she'd stop by this morning. There were still hours before morning ended. She leaned out the window, slapping the side of the carriage. "Hey, Ott. Change of plans."

CHAPTER 7: Trinity

As soon as Trinity saw the small hut hidden in the trees and foliage of the forest, the tension eased from her body like dirt washing away in the rain. She leaned out the window as Ott wandered around the woods as if lost. As a city Grunt, he wouldn't see anything besides bushes and trees, even if Gaar hadn't hidden his home so well.

"Ott, stop." She hopped out of the carriage as it slowed. "We'll be here a while so let's get you out of these." She walked to his side and began unhooking his traces.

He tried to help but kept losing his grip on the knots as he glanced at the grasses and bushes surrounding them. A loud rumble sounded from his belly.

"Go." She laughed as she released him from the final line. "Eat until you're full, but don't wander too far away from the house."

"House?" He looked at her in confusion.

"The one right here, you oaf." Gaar's bellow shattered the quiet, like lightning striking a tree. "Little One." The Handler moved toward her, his gait fast and graceful for someone his size.

Ott stumbled backward, grunting nervously, but she didn't have time to worry about a scared Grunt.

"Gaar!" She raced toward him.

The Handler scooped her into his arms, swallowing her with his mass. She clung to him, fighting to keep her tears of fear and frustration buried where they belonged. He was her best friend, almost like a father. She loved her dad, but Gaar had been there for her when her father had failed.

"Trinity. Welcome." Tatania, Gaar's mate, stood near the entrance to the cabin.

"Hi, Tatania." She smiled over Gaar's shoulder before he let her drop to the ground.

"Come. Let's eat." He moved toward the house. "I made some bread."

She tried not to wince. Gaar's bread was harder than a rock. "Thanks, but I ate before I left."

"Speaking of that what brings you out here?" By his tone he suspected something.

The problem with him being like a father was he knew her too well. "Ah...one minute."

She turned to the Grunt who stood several feet away, his body shaking and looking as if another loud bellow from Gaar would send him racing through the forest.

"Calm down." She walked over to Ott and patted his shoulder. "Everything's fine. These two are friends. I'll be back soon. Until then eat what you want but don't wander too far."

"And by too far, she means don't go by the brush. Stay in the clearing right around the house," said Gaar.

Ott frowned, gesturing at a patch of long, lush grass near the small river that flowed through the pasture area. He sidled toward the river and the green grass.

Trinity glanced around. The clearing didn't have a lot of grass. "There's better grazing over—"

"I know that." Gaar didn't like his orders questioned. "Another thing I know is that there's been a Tracker hanging around."

Ott ran to her, almost slamming into her side.

"The one that left Mirra and her group?" Her hand went to her knife. The move was instinctual, but it wouldn't do much good against a Tracker.

"No." He motioned for her to go inside as he glanced at the terrified Grunt. "You want to come with us?" The house had been built for Handlers. It was large enough to accommodate a Grunt.

Ott's stomach rumbled as his eyes darted between them and the grass.

"Is he safe out here?" She would've come on foot if she'd known she was putting the Grunt in danger. Of course, that would've taken her a lot longer.

"He'll be safe by the house, just don't wander," said Gaar.

"It'll be fine." She patted Ott's shoulder again. "You can stand right here." She walked several feet to the nearby brush. "And eat all this." She ran her hand over the poufy bushes of sage fronds. "It's safe here, right Gaar?"

"Yeah. The Tracker won't come too close. Tatania and I made sure of that."

She was glad she'd missed that fight. Both Handlers and Trackers were formidable. She smiled at Ott. "See. You can eat and be safe."

The Grunt nodded and moved to her side, nudging her out of the way so he could stand exactly where she'd been.

"I hadn't meant that literally." She grinned at Gaar as she followed him into the house.

"He's thin. Where'd you find him?" asked Gaar.

"Waiting outside the Council Building, looking for work." Like so many others would today and every day.

"Things still bad?"

"Yeah. More and more Released fill the streets, homeless and hungry."

"Some have been moving into the forest." Tatania poured them all tea and sat at the table.

Gaar slid the large knife from the sheath on his side and began carving the rock that he called his bread.

"May I leave the door open?" She glanced behind her. "I don't like not being able to see Ott."

"Yes. The air is cool today and the house is hot," said Tatania.

She pushed the door open all the way and Ott looked up at her, grass hanging from both sides of his mouth. She waved before sitting at the table. She kept her face impassive as Gaar dropped a hunk of bread in front of her. It sounded like a brick hitting the table. "Are the Guards and Servants who are moving out here giving you any trouble?"

None of the other classes had been too friendly with the Handlers or Trackers once the fighting had ended. Part of her hated how they'd turned on the Trackers and Handlers but another part—the part of her that was prey—understood.

Numerous members of the other classes had started disappearing. Both Gaar and Mirra had sworn it wasn't anyone from their groups but everyone, including herself, wondered. Trackers loved to hunt. Plus, they had to eat, and produce was not in their diet.

"No. They help actually." Gaar took a bite of his bread, his jaw strength obviously much stronger than hers because he made it look almost soft.

"That's great. How?" She wiggled and worked on a corner of her bread. If she could dunk it into her tea, it might make it soft enough for her to chew.

"They keep the predators full." Gaar took another bite.

"Oh." She should've known better than to hope that they could all get along.

"What color was that Tracker you saw when we were finding our territories?" Gaar mumbled around his mouthful of bread.

"That Tracker was brown with gold markings." She'd traveled with the Handlers and Trackers when they'd left the city. Hugh hadn't wanted her to go. It'd only been about six weeks after she'd been shot but she hadn't been able to stay in the city another minute. Her mom and Hugh had been fussing over her daily and although she loved them both, she'd been on her own too long for coddling.

It'd been one of her many fights with Hugh. Her mother said it was natural for newly bonded pairs to argue, and then in the next breath, Mom would tell her that she needed to defer to Hugh. He was her mate. She needed to listen to him.

She did when he said things that weren't stupid. Her not going to say goodbye to Mirra and Gaar because it wasn't safe was stupid. Hugh had finally agreed, but he'd sent Indy, Bo and a small team of his most trusted soldiers with them. He'd said it'd been to keep the citizens from harassing them, but she was pretty sure it'd been to keep her safe. Like she hadn't been safe for years without him and his soldiers around. She could take care of herself. She was tired of proving that to him but getting shot hadn't helped.

"Hmm. Definitely not the same one that's been hanging around here." Gaar cut more bread, handing another piece to Tatania and frowning at Trinity's plate. "Eat."

She nodded and worked harder to break off that corner.

"This one is gray with eyes so green they almost glow," said Tatania.

"Where did it come from?" Besides Parra who'd died later, five had survived the Night of the Trackers. Mirra, Nirankan, Sikka, Teeko and the one who'd set off on his own. None of them had produced any offspring that'd lived, as far as she knew.

"I've been thinking about that," said Gaar. "Are you sure there wasn't another one when Mirra freed them?"

"It could've escaped into the forest," suggested Tatania.

"No. There were only the eight Mirra freed."

"That place was set up similar to the Handler camp. There could've been others in the other buildings," said Gaar.

"Nirankan would've said something if there were others. He wouldn't have left any behind to be tortured by the Almightys and their Guards."

"You left with Mirra right away but Crazy and some others stayed behind, didn't they?" asked Gaar.

"Yeah." She braced herself so she didn't shiver as the memory of the screams of the Guards filled her head.

"According to Nirankan, the Almightys were making them in that shed. Maybe they'd made some but hadn't brought them into the yard yet. Crazy could've found them when looking for Guards to kill," said Gaar.

"But wouldn't he have brought them with him?" She finally managed to snap off a corner of the bread and dipped it into her tea.

"Not if they ran off," said Gaar.

"Hmm. I don't know. Crazy wasn't the only Tracker who'd stayed behind. I think one of the others would've mentioned it to Mirra. Don't you?"

"I do. It was just a thought." He ran his finger over the blade of his knife. "Because the only other explanation is that someone is creating them again."

CHAPTER 8: Trinity

"That's not possible." Trinity's hand stilled, the bread resting in the tea. "Hugh would never allow—"

"Hugh doesn't know everything," said Gaar.

"I have to tell him." She didn't want to. He didn't need another thing to worry about. Guilt slid into her stomach, making it twist. She should be at Dr. Kalper's eliminating one worry for him but instead she was here.

"How's he doing?" Gaar's dark eyes locked with hers. He knew. He always knew.

"Good." She glanced at the bread in her hand. It was full and thick, filling with water but not breaking apart. It was too strong for that, unlike her.

"So good that you had to travel for miles early in the morning for a cup of tea and bread at my house?" He patted her forearm. "I'm glad to see you, and you're always welcome, but what's wrong, Little One?"

She took a bite of the semi-soggy bread, delaying her answer.

"I can wait all day."

She swallowed, putting the rest of the bread down and finishing her tea. "It's nothing. Really."

"Nothing wouldn't send you across the city and into the forest."

"It's not that far." She'd been happy but surprised when Gaar and Tatania had chosen to stay so close to the city. The other Handlers had gone deep into the forest to make their homes.

"Far enough and answer my question."

"Hugh's good. We're both good but..." She felt so disloyal saying it. "I hate the city."

"You may want to reconsider your mate." He frowned at her. "Now, tell me the real reason."

"Reconsider my mate?" The words came out sharper than she'd meant. She lowered her voice when his eyes narrowed. "I love Hugh. I don't want another mate."

"Then you'd better figure out a way to accept the city."

"Hugh hates the city too. We'll be moving to the forest soon."

Gaar's eyes darted to Tatania who shook her head slightly as she filled their cups again.

"We will." Obviously, they didn't believe her, but it was the truth.

"You really think Hugh is going to move to the forest? Who will lead if he leaves? Who will hold that much power and still be fair?" asked Gaar.

"He's setting that up. He's making a new government. Changing the way everything is done. Once that's in place, we're leaving."

Gaar studied her, his black eyes seeing too much.

"He doesn't want this." She rambled, trying to convince herself more than him. "He doesn't like being in power."

"That's why he's the perfect Almighty for the job."

"They'll have to find someone else because we're moving once everything is settled."

"It'll never be settled. Large groups like the ones here will always have problems. Each class will see things differently than the others. They need someone to guide them. Someone honest and fair. If Hugh leaves, those with their own agenda will take his place, and you know what happens in that kind of world."

"Hugh's not perfect. He does things like that too. Makes decisions for his purposes."

"So there is more to your visit than hating the city."

"I was talking about when he made you and the other Handlers take the serum even though he knew what it did to you."

"He had his reasons." Gaar scratched his chin.

"Yes. *His* reasons." Just like why he wanted her on birth control instead of letting Araldo decide when they had young.

"His reasons were for the good of all."

"Not the Handlers."

"Immediately? No. But long term? Yes."

"How was making you infertile, making some lose their young, good for Handlers in the long term?"

"Would you rather we'd been slaughtered in the streets? Imprisoned? That's what would've happened if we'd lost the war. Even those of us who managed to escape would've been hunted and killed."

"Of course, I don't want that." She had no idea why he was defending Hugh. Gaar didn't hate Hugh, but he was supposed to be on her side.

"It's time to grow up, Little One. Life doesn't always give you easy choices."

"Do you think I don't know that? Nothing in my life has been easy. I was food."

"We're all food."

Her jaw clenched. She knew better than to use that argument with him. What others saw as abhorrent cruelties he considered a natural part of life.

"I know things haven't been easy for you, but they aren't for anyone." He leaned closer. "What I'm saying is Hugh had nothing but bad choices and he had to choose one of them. The difference between him and others is that he chose the one that'd benefit the majority, not just him." He leaned back. "The decisions we make in bad situations tell a lot about us."

"He doesn't want to have offspring with me." The words burst from her.

"What? Nonsense," said Tatania.

"It's true. I'm supposed to be at the doctor's right now getting on birth control." At their blank looks she explained. "There are things you can use and medicine you can take so the female doesn't get pregnant."

"Why would you do that? Nature decides." Tatania glanced at Gaar.

"That's what I said but Hugh..." She swallowed. "He doesn't want to risk that. None of these methods are foolproof, but they usually work."

"So it's hobbling nature?" Gaar looked at Tatania, his face scrunched up in confusion.

"Yeah. Kind of like tying her hands." She stared at her teacup.

"He doesn't ever want offspring?" asked Gaar. "You need to find another mate."

"He does. At least he says he wants them but not yet. Later when things have settled."

"They'll never settle completely." Gaar repeated his words from earlier.

"I know and he wants us to get married."

"Aren't you bonded?" asked Tatania

"Yes. We bonded before the war, but that's not enough for him."

"That's not his way," said Gaar. "You chose him. He followed your tradition and bonded; you should follow his and marry."

"I want to. I'm ready to marry him, but he wants a big wedding. We can't do that now because he's too busy. I suggested a small ceremony, but he wants to show the world that bonding between the classes is good and right and..." She stopped rambling. "Sorry."

"He's right."

"What?" She hadn't expected Gaar to take Hugh's side on this.

"The world needs to see the two of you. A mixed breed Producer and Servant bonded...married to an Almighty. They need to see it happen and accept it."

"But I...I..."

"You want young right now so badly that you can't wait a while?" Gaar frowned at her.

"No." She wanted babies eventually, but she really didn't care when it happened.

"You can't fix your problems, Little One, if you aren't honest with yourself." He tapped her forehead, none too gently. "When you're in the forest you prepare for an attack from Brush-Men, Cold Creepers and others but do you worry about the River-Men?"

"Not unless I'm near the water." That was basic training. Know the area and prepare for any possible danger.

"Exactly. You can't fight this unhappiness if you're looking for a River-Man in the trees."

She stared at him, her real fear making her throat tighten. "Do you think he doesn't love me enough?" she whispered. "Is that why he doesn't make time to get married? He's a leader now. I'm not a good mate for him. I'll never fit in with the Almightys or in the city. I hate the meetings and the politics."

"He loves you." Gaar patted her hand.

"I'm not sure that's enough." She tried to swallow the lump in her throat, but it was too big, choking her with fear and uncertainty.

"You'll have to decide that." He took a gulp of his tea. "I've seen Hugh do many things that some would consider questionable but every decision he made was for the good of the war or the other classes, except when it came to you."

"Me?"

"When you were shot, he killed for you. He killed to end the fighting. To force surrender. That turned many against him, but he did it for you."

"I..." She'd heard about him killing the female from the Council, but she hadn't thought about it this way.

"He loves you. You are the only one who can cause him to compromise his principles."

"I don't want him to do that." As annoying as his principles could be, it was one of the things she loved most about him.

"Then don't make him choose between you and them. He will choose you and then we'll all lose."

CHAPTER 9: Hugh

Hugh barely kept from laughing out loud as William, aka Bill, Vickers, the lawyer for Wilt Wickerwood, gushed about his client's importance to the community.

Wickerwood looked like a different person as he sat at the table across the room from Hugh. No one would recognize the affluent Almighty with overlong hair and wearing tattered and worn clothes, but no matter how he looked, the male was a rich pervert who needed to stay in prison.

Hugh glanced over the crowd, his eyes lingering for a moment on Professor Conguise who sat in the front row. He'd done everything he could to keep Conguise in jail, but there'd been nothing on Level Five except expensive lab equipment when he'd sent his team to raid the laboratory. All the mutated creatures he'd seen when he'd saved Tim had disappeared.

He would've still kept the professor locked up, but Conguise had been regaled as a hero for saving Trinity. He was sure that was the opposite of what the professor had been trying to do, but all the eyewitnesses had sworn otherwise.

The professor tipped his head in acknowledgement and Hugh's gaze shifted to the rest of the crowd. They had a full house today. A mixed group of many of the classes sat scattered about the room.

The lower classes waited to see if Wickerwood would be punished or if this new government would be as unfair to them as the last. The Almightys, on the other hand, feared retribution for every past action they'd taken against those in the other classes. It was a potentially explosive situation and he needed to be careful.

He had every intention of punishing Wickerwood but penalizing him for something that had been legal at the time would send the Almightys into a panic. He and the Allied Classes had won the war, but the Almightys still held a lot of power.

"As you see, my client is an asset to the community not a threat," said Vickers.

"Clarification." He held up his hand. "He *wasn't* a threat to the community before because according to the old laws the only community that mattered, the only one with rights, consisted of Almightys. His fondness is for young female House Servants not Almightys."

There were murmurs of approval from some of the crowd.

"Yes," said Vickers, a smile in his tone. "Which was not illegal at the time. My client would never dream of breaking the law."

"He was arrested with a young Servant, barely thirteen years old, in his bed." It didn't matter that it hadn't been illegal; it'd been wrong.

The murmurs from the other classes grew angry.

"Yes." Vickers pulled at his collar, glancing at the crowd behind him. "But my client performed these actions during the rule of the old law not the new. He hasn't broken any laws, current or past, and therefore should not be incarcerated."

"That's where our opinions differ."

Wickerwood wiped his forehead as he glanced uneasily at his lawyer.

"He was arrested because the Allied Classes had taken the city. We had won the war. We were in control and our rule was therefore in effect." His gaze went to Townsend in the gallery. He and the reporter had gone over this countless times. He needed Vickers to take his bait for this to work.

"But my client didn't know that." Vickers almost winced as the words left his mouth.

"Ignorance of the law is no excuse." He paused, studying the crowd. The Almightys looked nervous. Good. They should be. There shouldn't need to be laws to keep someone from raping the young of any class. "However, I'm a fair man and I can govern this case by the old rules."

Wickerwood relaxed a bit, but there were snorts and grumbles from the other classes. They'd been oppressed for too long to cause much of a scene in public—in private or on the streets was another story.

"Good. Then my client is free to go." Vickers started to gather his things.

"No." He didn't even attempt to hide his smile. "We still need to address the laws that were broken."

Vickers frowned, perplexed and then his eyes narrowed. "You can't mean..."

"Oh, but I do. Your client has admitted to having intimate relations with numerous members of a different class."

The crowd gasped and then began whispering amongst themselves.

"If you punish him for that then you'll have to punish half the Almightys not to mention the other classes." Vickers' eyes gleamed with victory. "Yourself and your soon to be in-laws included."

"I don't *have* to do anything." It was time to put the arrogant lawyer in his place.

"That's not..."

He raised his brow, stopping Vickers' argument. He had complete authority. He was setting up rules and regulations so that no one had this much power, but until everything was in place, he was the ruler. "But fortunately for your client, I don't believe anyone, including myself, is above the law. And you're right. Many of us, myself, my fiancé's parents and other close friends have participated in interclass relations."

The crowd fell silent, even their breathing seemed to stop. Vickers' eyes narrowed, sensing a trap. The lawyer was smart, but he was smarter.

"But they were all consensual." His gaze met Wickerwood's. "Can you prove the same?"

"I...I never hurt anyone," stammered Wickerwood.

"Liar," shouted Meesus.

He held up his hand, sending her a look and hoping she'd shut up and let him continue. She glared at him, seething in silence.

"So you say, but what do the Servants say?"

"Ask them." Wickerwood almost jumped from his chair. "I was kind. Gentle."

The crowd's murmurs of discontent rumbled through the hall like a gathering storm.

"Let me confer with my client." Vickers leaned by Wickerwood, hushed whispers drifting from their huddle. The lawyer straightened. "I'd like to convene until we can bring in the Servants. My client assures me that they will confirm his statement."

"All of them?" He leaned forward. "I must have testimony from all of them that it was consensual. I'm not letting a rapist of even one go free."

"Yes, they'll all agree." Wickerwood nodded, his head bobbing in his excitement.

"And you can find them all?"

"Finding them should be the responsibility of you and your government," said Vickers. "You're the ones who took them from the safety of his home."

"I know where the females I freed from his house are." He glanced at Meesus. Her eyes were bright and hopeful. She finally understood what he was doing. He lowered his gaze to Wickerwood. "I'm talking about the ones who were gone before my soldiers arrived."

"You have no proof that he did anything with anyone except those you found at his residence," said Vickers.

"But I do." His lip turned up in a sneer of a grin as Wickerwood's face paled. "He confessed to me about his"—his eyes darted to Meesus—"relations with a young female."

Vickers turned to his client, blue eyes hard. The lawyer didn't like to lose.

"I thought...I didn't know he was going to arrest me," said Wickerwood.

"Tell me who has that young female." Hugh was so close to finding Meesus' daughter he wanted to shout at the other male to answer him, but he had to stay calm. "We'll ask her if your relations were consensual. If she and the others agree that they consented, you go free."

"I...I don't know." Wickerwood's face paled even more. "I don't know where she is."

"Then tell me who took her."

"I...I can't." Wickerwood glanced at Vickers. "He'll kill me."

"Give me a minute." Vickers conferred with his client again.

Hugh leaned forward, his eyes darting to Meesus. Her hands were clasped together, her face tight with excitement. Not only would he finally be able to repay her, but he'd be one step closer—one disgusting male closer—to ending the rape of the young Servants and Guards.

Vickers cleared his throat and stood. "My client cannot answer that question."

Meesus' face fell.

Hugh was pretty sure his did too. "No, he refuses. There is a difference." One that would not be met with mercy.

Vickers tipped his head in consent. "But since the others will testify that their relations were consensual, it only leads to believe that this one was too."

"No." He was done playing. "Either he gives me that name or the deal is off."

"Hugh...I can't," begged Wickerwood. "You don't know him. He's ruthless."

"Then introduce us." He was more than willing to take on this male. "I can protect you."

"No." Wickerwood laughed a bit hysterically. "You can't. Not from him. No one can protect me from him if I talk."

This was over, for now. He'd get the old Almighty to give up the name even if he had to send in a spy. "Then it's your choice. Old laws or new?"

Vickers turned and whispered with Wickerwood before facing Hugh again. "We shall abide by the rule of the old laws."

"As you wish." He paused until the audience had silenced. "My verdict is—"

"May I speak?" Meesus stood.

"Of course." He'd hoped she'd remain quiet and let him handle this. He should've known better.

"My daughter and others like her were sold to the highest bidder. Forced to mate with these old"—her beautiful face twisted with disgust—"males. Loaned to friends. They will never recover from this. You never forget rape." She swallowed, her eyes dropping for a moment to where her hands were clutched in front of her, claws digging into her skin hard enough to draw blood. "My daughter is still missing. Perhaps still in the hands of males like him." She looked around the room. "The punishment for interclass relations varies greatly." She turned back to Hugh. "You have the authority to decide how severe or lax the punishment. I beg you, punish him to the fullest extent of the law."

His eyes met hers. She was angry and frustrated. He agreed with her, but he couldn't abide by her wishes. Punishing one Almighty wasn't enough. He wanted them all. He wanted the entire ring that trafficked young Servants and Guards destroyed.

"I'll take your plea into consideration."

She nodded and sat.

He turned toward Wickerwood who was sweating again. "I would be justified in sending down the harshest punishment." He paused, letting the Almighty squirm. "Death."

The crowd gasped. A few clapped.

They weren't going to like the rest of his speech. "But this world doesn't need a martyr, especially one like you."

Wickerwood began breathing again but the crowd's whispered outrage filled the courtroom like the hissing of a hundred snakes.

"You will spend the next thirty years in jail."

"Sir, my client is an old man. That's a death sentence," said Vickers.

"You're right." He rubbed his chin. "You can exchange years for lashes."

Wickerwood paled.

"How many?" asked the lawyer.

He looked at Conguise. "How many lashes was Jethro given for his indiscretion?" This was the first time he'd spoken about the incident between Trinity and Jethro to anyone besides close friends.

Conguise cleared his throat. The professor despised interclass relations. He was enjoying this as much as Hugh. "Twenty."

Vickers turned and began speaking in whispers to his client before facing Hugh again. "Can they be broken out over time?"

He nodded, sending a smug look to Conguise. On this one matter they were in agreement. "Yes, but let me make sure you understand. Jethro Remore was given twenty lashes for one indiscretion that did not end in mating. Your client did mate. He will be given fifty lashes for every indiscretion."

"But that's..." Vickers clamped his mouth shut, locking in his outrage.

"We can discuss with the Servants whom we freed from his house how many times they recall having relations with your client. Then we can try and track down other Servants that he'd used thusly over the years."

Vickers shook his head. Wickerwood had turned so pale the blue veins on his face looked like a roadmap.

"That's not enough." Meesus stood, her voice a harsh whisper that spread across the room like a virus, making others grumble in anger. "He should die for what he did to us. To our young."

"Meesus, please sit." The other Servants in the audience were siding with her. He didn't need another incident. He'd spent a lot of time trying to assure the Almightys that the other classes were civilized and not much different from them. A fight now could erase all the progress he'd made.

"I will not let this pass, Hugh Truent. You betrayed me."

"I did not be—"

"You promised—"

"To help you free your daughter and I will when we find her." His gaze swept the crowd. "I have Servants and Guards looking for all the imprisoned young. We are making arrests. We're putting away Almightys like him"—he sneered at Wickerwood—"daily." He looked back at Meesus. "But I never promised to kill anyone."

"Justice has not been served here today. Justice will never be served in a court of Almightys or those chosen by them." She stormed out of the room, the other Servants in the crowd standing and following her.

He stared after them. She was right, but he'd change that. He was in the process of setting up an election so that the magistrate and the council were chosen by all the classes not just the Almightys. He needed the groups behind him. He needed them to know that he was on their side. Today had not furthered that agenda. His gaze met Townsend's. He hadn't wanted to go this route, but he had no other options left. It was time to talk to Jethro.

CHAPTER 10: Hugh

Hugh waited in his suite of rooms for Townsend. He was a little surprised Trinity wasn't back from seeing the doctor yet. She'd told him she'd try to be back for the court hearings. Kalper was probably busy. A knock sounded on the door, and he opened it.

"You're supposed to check to see who it is?" Rex gave him a disgusted look from the hallway.

Townsend stood behind the large Guard, trying not to laugh.

"And you're supposed to go home at night and not haunt the halls." He'd spent over a month finding the Servants and Guards who worked at the Council Building places to live. Before the war they'd spent their free time trying not to be noticed or hiding in the tunnels and rooms beneath the main building. The area was cold, bare and depressing.

"It ain't night now, and I told you I'll start going home when you start being smart."

"Oh Hugh, you do tend to attract the best Guards." Townsend stepped around Rex.

"I'm not sure how that always happens to me," he mumbled as Townsend walked past him. He turned back to Rex. "You know I'm your boss, right?"

"Yeah, and my job is to keep you alive. I can't do that if I'm not here and no one else is either."

"What does he mean by that?" Townsend was no longer amused.

"This idiot sends everyone home at night," said Rex.

"I do not. There are teams—"

"Outside. No one inside." Rex's tone dripped with disgust.

"Really, Hugh?" Townsend shook his head. "The Guard's right. You are an idiot."

"One would never know that I'm the ruler around here." He may need to re-evaluate his dislike of yes-men.

"And we'd like to keep you in that position," said Townsend. "You know it's dangerous. Why don't you have Guards inside the building?"

"Right now, this is my home, and if I wanted my every move monitored, I'd put that tracking device back inside my body."

"I get that, but you should have some Guards here even at night."

"No one is going to be in my suite." That was the one place he and Trinity could be themselves. He ran his hand through his hair. Not that they had much time together. He was always busy, and she was unhappy. He hated that he was the reason she was sad, the reason she stayed in the city, and the reason she was going against her belief in nature and using birth control.

"Of course not, but they should be nearby. Just in case you need them."

"I'll consider it."

"Until you decide we're right, I'll keep sleeping in the chair outside your room." Rex rubbed his lower back. "Even though it pains me."

"Go home." He closed the door.

"The Guard is right." Townsend walked into the living room and sat on the couch.

"We have other things to discuss." He dropped onto a chair.

"You have no idea."

"What is that supposed to mean?" He counted on the reporter to fill him in on the hot topics throughout the community, but he was getting a little tired of all the problems.

"Something you don't want to hear."

"What now?" He dropped his head back on the chair.

"There have been sightings of...something in the city."

"What do you mean...something?" His head snapped forward.

"Something bird-like but big. Really big." Townsend pulled a notebook from his pocket.

"How big?" His blood ran cold. He hadn't hallucinated all those creatures on Level Five nor the empty lab. That meant, they went somewhere.

"Big enough to take Servants and small Guards." The reporter flipped through the pad of paper and began reading, "Several Servants near the Holstein area heard screaming and then saw a Servant in the air. Carried by a large, dark, winged creature."

"The Holstein area?" The constriction around his heart eased. "There's a lot and I mean a *lot* of gang crimes and murders in that area."

"So?" Townsend looked up at him.

"I've had troops patrolling the area and investigating the murders."

"Again. So?"

"Are you sure this isn't their way of explaining a murder?"

"By making up a story about a monster who carries them away. Why? If there's no body, there's no investigation."

"Bo reported—"

"Bo? I thought you had him harvesting the food from the Rock Islands?"

"I did. They're back. They delivered the food to the homes for the Released. We're also rounding up volunteers to go and start farming the islands. The ground is fertile. It'll produce a lot of food...in time."

"That's good news."

"Yeah. Finally something in our win column, but I think we can put the rumors of the bird-monster to rest. As I was saying, Bo reported the bodies of a couple of Servants. They were mangled pretty badly. Torn apart."

"Like by a giant bird creature?" Townsend's face paled.

"I doubt it." He laughed. "More likely by a group of Servants. Both of them were involved in the local gangs."

"I don't know." Townsend stared back at his notebook. "I interviewed them myself. They were pretty scared."

"Yeah. Of the other gangs."

"But why would they make something like this up? Where would they even come up with this idea?"

"The Exhibit." At the reporter's confused look, he added, "You had to have seen it. We all had to go when we were kids."

"No. I never...Wait. The Exhibit? That joke of a display with Servants and Guards dressed in costumes?"

"That's the one."

"No one believed those were actually creatures from the forest."

"Some did. Probably more than you think."

"No way. That was such a joke."

"The other classes aren't as educated as Almightys." He shrugged. "Most are taken from their parents at a young age. No one around to tell them it's not true."

"Still..."

"And if it's not the Exhibit it could be coming from those who lived in the forest during the war and saw those mon...creatures."

"That I can believe, but it doesn't explain a bird-like monster. As far as I know there are none of them flying through the forest."

"Except Avions, and they may not be monsters, but they are a pain," joked Hugh.

"Exactly. Avions prove that it's possible to create a creature that can fly."

"Conguise is no Araldo."

"But he's not incompetent either. He's succeeded in creating other monsters. Why are you so sure this isn't one of them?"

"Everything I saw on Level Five was focused on aquatic creatures not flying ones." He didn't want to even consider the possibility that something else had escaped the lab. He had more than enough issues with the food shortage, the small pockets of resistance, the crime due to poverty, trafficking of young Servants and Guards and more. He didn't need this to deal with right now.

"But not in the forest."

"Cold Creepers live on land, but they can swim. Their webbed feet make them very fast in the water."

"What about the Brush-Men?" asked Townsend.

"Oh...They still don't fly, and birds would be tough to create. The bones have to be light to fly and that means they have to stay small like the Avions or they'd crush their own bones."

"I don't know. The Servants I interviewed all had similar stories."

"Yeah, because they're spreading those stories to cover the murders they're committing and to keep witnesses off the streets."

"I hope you're right," said Townsend.

"I am." He prayed he was.

"I don't understand how you can be so sure."

"I'm sure because Conguise was here when we won the war. He didn't have time to set them free before the Guards and I searched his lab. He had to have moved them earlier. Maybe while I was in prison but more than likely after my escape. He couldn't risk someone believing me."

"So you think all those...experiments are sitting in another lab somewhere?"

"Yeah. I do. As much as what Conguise is doing disgusts me, I have to appreciate the amount of effort and brilliance that went into the cross-mutation of species. This is his work, his purpose. If he turns them lose, he loses control. He wouldn't do that."

"Then how did they get into the forest?"

"I'm still trying to figure that out. My guess is that those must've escaped somehow. Maybe when they were young and small."

"I hope you're right because if Conguise sets even a few of the things you told me about loose in the city, all the other problems we have will seem like nothing."

"I'm right. I'm sure of it." His eyes met the reporter's. "I pray to Araldo that I'm right."

CHAPTER 11: Hugh

"Okay." Townsend put his notebook away. "Then let's talk about today."

"Court did not go as I'd planned." Normally, the fiasco at court would've been Hugh's least favorite topic to discuss but anything was better than the idea of Conguise's creatures roaming the city streets.

"Nope. Not at all." Townsend frowned. "But I thought you were going to wait to see if you could get Wickerwood to talk before you released all Jethro's friends."

"I am. I want to give Wickerwood a few days to make sure he doesn't change his mind about telling us the name of his partner."

"You are? What do you mean? All the Guards who served with Jethro were released."

"What are you talking about? I released four of them a few weeks ago to alleviate some of the complaints about only keeping them in prison because they once worked for the Protective Services. The others are still in jail."

"Then someone goofed or...purposely misunderstood. My sources told me this morning that they released the last of Jethro's friends yesterday."

"You have sources that work at the prison?" If Townsend wasn't a good friend, he'd consider looking into the reporter. The Almighty seemed to have connections everywhere.

"I got to know them when you were incarcerated." Townsend smiled slightly.

"Really? You could've saved me from some beatings." He'd been the Guards' favorite punching bag for more years than he cared to remember.

"I wish I could've, but my sources give me info. They don't take direction." Townsend leaned forward. "And they say Jethro is all alone and that isn't good."

"No, it's not and I didn't order the release of his friends." He stood and walked to the kitchen, grabbing a bottle of whiskey and pouring him and Townsend a drink.

"Do you think it was an honest mistake or something else?"

He went back into the living room and sat, handing his friend a glass. "I don't know, but I need to find out."

"What are you going to do about Jethro? This changes everything."

"No." He took a sip of his drink. "It just expedites the situation."

"Okay. Then what are you going to do if he refuses to work with us?"

"I'll have to let him out or let him die." Martha, Kim and Jackson would never forgive him if he did the latter and he wasn't a hundred percent sure Trinity would either. "The question is when do I release him?"

"Jethro isn't safe in there alone," said Townsend.

"He can take a few beatings. I did." Hugh sipped his drink. "It might make him more willing to work with us."

"Or it might make him dead."

"The kid is strong. He can withstand losing a fight or two."

"Yeah, I know. He can handle it because you did, but you were beaten by the Guards not the prisoners."

"They weren't easy on me."

"They also weren't allowed to kill you."

"Good point." He stared at his drink. "I don't want him dead, but I do want more samples of his blood."

"You still think Conguise did more than fix his spine?" Townsend leaned back against the couch.

"I do." That was another one of his nightmares.

"You could force him to give you a blood sample. He is in prison."

"I don't want to draw any attention. I have no idea what the professor will do if he thinks we suspect."

"What can he do to Jethro if he's in prison?"

"Many of the prison Guards have worked there a long time. I don't know who are sympathetic to the old regime. I interviewed them all. They seem to be simple Guards who are happy to have a job, but appearances can be faked. Plus, many would probably be eager to make some extra money." He swirled the liquor in his glass. "It isn't worth the risk. As you said, Jethro is alone in there."

"Another reason to set him free."

"But we need him to get close to Wickerwood. We need names of those running the sex trafficking ring, and we need answers on why Wickerwood had been forcing the interclass breeding of all those he'd had locked in that nightmare of a building. We found no trace of their young and like it or not, Wickerwood is our only lead."

"Not true. We know Vickers is involved somehow."

"We think. We don't know."

"And Dresschew is also involved."

"Dresschew?" What was his friend talking about? "Serbian Dresschew died years ago, and he had no children."

"I know that." Townsend rolled his eyes. "Who was going to inherit Serbian's fortune was all anyone talked about for months."

"Then..."

"The Dresschew company name comes up way too much on the paperwork for the garbage dumpsters and buildings where we know Servants were trafficked."

"You think Francis Terbasse is behind this?" He stood and began to pace. This made no sense. "He's nothing more than an aging playboy who spends Serbian's fortune."

"Perhaps this was all in place before Dresschew died and Terbasse is letting it chug along. Serbian wouldn't have done the work himself. He would've hired a business manager."

"I don't know. My mother spoke highly of Serbian Dresschew. He was often at her fundraising parties to help the lower classes. I'd find it hard to believe he was involved in something like sex trafficking."

"People can be quite deceiving and donating to charitable causes is the perfect disguise."

"Even if his estate is involved, we can't go after Terbasse. He's too connected. He may be a good-for-nothing playboy, but he's well liked. I need his support."

"Even if he's behind the sex trafficking?"

"Of course not." He shot his friend a disgusted look. "But we don't know that. All we know is that a few of his many, many businesses were listed as owners of buildings—mostly abandoned buildings that anyone could access—where young female Servants were found."

"Found? Imprisoned is the correct term."

"Imprisoned just like those on the estate which leads us back to Wickerwood. We have no proof that Dresschew and now, Terbasse had anything to do with it. That's why Wickerwood is our only real lead. We know he's involved. We just need him to talk and that means we need someone for him to talk to."

"You really think keeping Jethro in prison, if he'll even agree to work with us, will make Wickerwood talk?"

"I do." Or he hoped.

"I don't know. Wickerwood looked terrified in court today." Townsend shook his head. "Only someone very powerful would scare Wickerwood like that."

"Powerful or ruthless."

"That usually equals money. Terbasse has money. Lots of it," said Townsend.

"I don't know that he actually does. Not that kind of money."

"I agree that Terbasse throws money around like his fingers print it but there's no way he could've gone through Dresschew's fortune."

"I don't think Dresschew was as rich when he died as many thought." He sat back down. "I remember coming home from school one day and my mom complaining to some friends that their recent fundraisers hadn't been as successful as they'd hoped. Apparently, Dresschew wasn't donating as much as in the past." He held up his hand to stop Townsend from replying. "One of the women started gossiping that Dresschew had made some bad investments, quite a few and that money was...tight."

"Tight? For Dresschew?" Townsend laughed. "I wish money was that tight for me."

"Maybe you should follow the paper trail. Perhaps Dresschew sold some of those businesses. That'd make more sense to me than he or Francis Terbasse running the sex trafficking ring."

"I'll look into it, but I think it's a huge waste of time." Townsend frowned, shaking his head. "You wouldn't believe the number of shell corporations I'll have to dig through to find the actual sale of any of Dresschew's businesses."

"And while you're doing that, our best bet is to convince Jethro to work with us."

"I'm not sure there's even a point in that anymore," said Townsend.

"What do you mean?"

"Why would Wickerwood befriend him now. Jethro has no one. Before the other Guards were released, he had friends and power. Now, he's on the bottom. Wickerwood is going to understand that."

"Jethro is young and strong. He'll be an asset to an old Almighty like Wickerwood."

"I don't know. I think it's too dangerous now that Jethro's friends have been released." Townsend's eyes met his. "It could be a paperwork mistake, but if someone purposely released them to leave Jethro vulnerable then you have to get him out of there."

"If I do that then we have no chance on finding those involved with sex trafficking, and if they started breeding young to traffic"—he ran his hand through his hair—"we have to stop it now before those kids are hurt."

"I understand that, but you can't leave him in prison to die."

He could, but he wouldn't. "Let's hold off for a few days. I'll see if I can find out how the Guards were released and then..."

"Hugh!" Rex pounded on the door.

He hurried across the room, sending Townsend a concerned look. Rex wasn't one to interrupt or to overreact. He opened the door. "What's the matter? Is it Trinity?" He tried not to let panic take over. She should've been back by now.

"No. Jethro. There was a fight. He's in the hospital."

"How bad?" The relief that washed through him that nothing had happened to Trinity, quickly twisted into guilt. It was his fault Jethro was still in prison.

"Bad enough to put him in the hospital," said Rex.

He bit back his reply. He had no idea why he surrounded himself with wise-mouthed Guards. He turned to Townsend. "I guess my decision has been made for me." It was time to talk to Jethro.

CHAPTER 12: Trinity

Trinity's carriage stopped in front of Dr. Kalper's house. Gaar was right. She refused to make Hugh choose between her and his principles. If he wanted to wait until they were married to have young, she was fine with that. Her parents wouldn't understand, but she'd deal with them later. She jumped out of the carriage. "Ott, this shouldn't take too long. Are you okay in the harness?"

The Grunt nodded, smiling his big, toothy smile.

"Great." She walked to the door and knocked.

"Trinity, glad you made it." Dr. Kalper opened the door, his eyes darting over her head to the Grunt. "There's food on the side of the house. Not much but you're welcome to it."

"Ott just ate..." Her words trailed off as he snorted in disagreement, his eyes going to the pile of cut grass by Kalper's house. He'd already eaten almost all of Gaar's shrubbery. "Uhm. Sorry. Go ahead." Her heart twisted in sympathy. It'd been a long time since she'd been hungry like that.

Ott grinned and hurried into the yard, the small carriage rumbling behind his too thin frame.

"Come." Dr. Kalper held the door, and she stepped inside the house. "Ott, holler if you need anything."

Ott looked around, his eyes widening as they landed on two skinny Guards who walked down the sidewalk on the other side of the street.

"Is he safe out here alone?" she asked.

"Yes." Kalper nodded at the Guards and then smiled at Ott. "You should be fine. We've had a few problems in the neighborhood but everyone around here knows me and leaves my house alone."

"Are you okay with this, Ott? If not, we can come back later and bring a few Guards." It wasn't like she was delaying on purpose. She was looking out for Ott.

"Nonsense," said Kalper. "Ott, would you like to wait in the garage? My Grunts live there. They took my Servant and her son shopping, but they won't mind you waiting in their room until we're done."

Ott motioned to the grass.

"No. Sorry. There's no grass in the garage."

The Grunt glanced at the two Guards who were almost out of sight and then pointed back at the grass.

"I think he wants to eat," she said. "Yell if you need me."

Ott waved his hand, not even bothering to look up.

"The office is back here." Kalper walked down a hallway.

She had no good reason not to follow him. She trusted Kalper but this would be the first time she'd be examined by an Almighty or even a male. Her mother had been the healer in their camp, but Mom didn't know anything about preventing pregnancies. The little Mom did know, she'd learned from Kim, and since Kim had ended up pregnant, Trinity didn't think that advice was good enough for Hugh.

Dr. Kalper had been secretly helping Guards and Servants minimize the risk of pregnancy for years. Although they were all Almighty at the root of their DNA, there were still significant differences especially in reproductive areas. The other classes were much more fertile than the Almightys. They'd been bred that way, especially Producers because no babies equaled death.

"How is Hugh's search for a solution to the food situation going?" he asked.

"We're trying to get Producers to go back to the camps, but that's not working very well. We've opened it up to others and...they're doing their best. Hugh does have a team of his top scientists working on meat alternatives."

"I hope they come up with something fast. Hunger can make even the best of us do things we wouldn't normally do." The doctor opened the door to his office, letting her go inside first. "Change is never easy, but with pockets of the Protective Services still fighting and the hunger and homelessness, we could slide back into the past very quickly."

"I know. Hugh knows." One of their regular arguments centered around her moving to the forest and staying with Gaar and Tatania where it was safer. If the unrest boiled over into action, Hugh and his companions would be the first to die.

"I'm sure he does. Tell him to let me know if there's anything I can do to help. I have friends from all the classes." He paused as if not sure if he should speak but then said, "I hope he's aware of the machinations of those who were once in power."

"Like Conguise?" She hated the professor and he hated her. He barely tried to hide his sneer of disgust when he had to address her at the Council meetings.

"He's one, but there are others much more powerful and dangerous than the professor." He waved his hand at the examination table. "Hop on up and let's take a look at you."

"Like who?"

"Bette Wilson's family for one." He motioned to the table again. "And Wickerwood still has many friends. They won't admit their relationship out loud, but they'll help him in the shadows."

"Even though he was raping young Servants." She climbed onto the table, her pulse racing.

"Many still don't consider that rape."

"But the Supreme Almighty's family was ostracized for the same thing."

"Jason and his wife had made many enemies over the years. The other Almightys just used his actions as an excuse to get back at him. Wickerwood, on the other hand, was a friend to many."

"What about the Supreme Almighty's granddaughter? Did she make a lot of enemies too?" She felt bad for the young Almighty. She knew how it was to be friendless.

"No. Stella was a casualty of her grandparents' ambition. Please lie back on the table."

She hesitated. She'd be vulnerable lying on the table with him standing above her.

"I operated on you after you were shot." He smiled kindly at her.

"Right." She stretched out on the table. If he'd wanted to hurt her, he'd had the chance dozens of times. "I kind of forgot about that."

"May I?" He touched her shirt.

She nodded.

He pulled it from her pants and lifted it, exposing her abdomen. "The scar from the gunshot is healing nicely."

"Ah...thanks." She wasn't quite sure how to respond to that.

"The regenerative properties of the other classes never cease to amaze me." He pressed on her abdomen. "Tell me if anything hurts."

"Okay." She stared up at the ceiling. It was worn and stained. Dr. Kalper had chosen to help the less fortunate over making money.

"How are you and Hugh doing?"

"Good." It was an instinctive answer.

"You don't sound too sure." He pulled her shirt back down. "I'm going to take some blood."

"Hugh and I are good." She sat up. "Really, we are." She flinched slightly as he stuck the needle in her arm. "It's wonderful being with him. Being in love."

"I was married for years."

"Were?"

"She passed." His face saddened for a second but then lightened. "It was the best twenty years of my life, but relationships are more work than we think. When we fall in love, everything is wonderful, but then it gets...real." He smiled and pulled the needle from her arm, pressing a piece of cloth to the small puncture. "It's still great, but it takes work."

"Yeah." She loved Hugh but living with him wasn't easy.

"I'm sure being under the constant scrutiny of everyone makes it even more difficult."

She bit her lip, trying not to cry. It was horrible. Everyone was more sophisticated than she was. They knew how to talk and how to dress and how to eat at fancy dinners. All she knew was how to survive.

"And all the pressure Hugh's under can't help." The doctor moved to a microscope.

She blinked back the tears. Her arguing with him over everything didn't help either. She was a horrible mate.

"Give it time." He glanced at her. "Hugh loves you."

"Then why am I here?" She covered her mouth with her hand, but it was too late.

"Oh. My dear." He walked over and took her other hand. "You and Hugh are different."

She gasped. She hadn't expected a jab about her class from him. She tried to pull free from his grasp, but he tightened his grip.

"I don't mean because you're Producer and Servant—"

"Don't forget Almighty. I have that in my blood too." Thanks to her father.

"From what Hugh says everyone does." He patted her hand and then let it go. "But I don't mean your genetics. I mean how you were raised."

"Excuse me." Her life hadn't been perfect, but she'd known love and happiness.

"You were raised to...produce young. Almightys are raised to only bring children into this world when they're ready to care for them."

"And Hugh's not?" That hurt.

"With everything he has to do? With all the problems that have fallen onto his young shoulders?"

He had a point. "But offspring are blessings."

"Just like love and relationships require work, so do young. Do you really think Hugh could be a good father when he's constantly called away for one crisis or another?"

"He'd be an excellent father. No matter what."

"Yes, you're right." He smiled and walked back to the microscope. "Your father is a Servant, right?"

"Half Almighty but he was raised as a Servant. Why?" She wasn't so far from the forest that she didn't sense a trap.

"I don't imagine with your mother being a Producer and living in an encampment that he was able to be around much when you were young, was he?"

"He tried."

"I'm sure he did his best, but the world made it impossible for him to be with you as much as he would've liked." He glanced at her. "Like he is with your little brother."

"Point taken." She wasn't good with words but even she should've seen that one coming. Her father was a better dad to Arthur than he'd been to her. She didn't want her young to grow up barely seeing their father.

"I love smart patients." He grinned.

The front door slammed.

"Dr. Kalper! Help!" cried a female.

"Wait here." He ran out of the room.

That wasn't going to happen. Not everyone liked the fact that Kalper treated those from the other classes, and they liked it even less that he was training other physicians to do the same. Even though they'd won the war, the world was still divided, and their side needed people like Dr. Kalper.

CHAPTER 13: Trinity

Trinity slid off the table, pulling her knife from the sheath at her side as she crept down the hallway.

"Calm down, Callie. I can't understand you." Dr. Kalper stood at the front door, his hands on a Servant's shoulders. "You're safe. No one's going to hurt you."

The female babbled incoherently. She was young—maybe ten or twelve—skinny and dirty. Another stray left to fend for herself. Her face was streaked where the tears had washed away the grime, and her clothes were covered in blood, but it was her eyes that made Trinity's heart freeze. She'd seen that look on the faces of the Producers, right after one of them from the group that'd escaped the Finishing Camp had been taken by a River-Man.

"You...Don't...They...You have to come." Callie's claws dug into the doctor's arm as she clung to him, her small body trembling.

He didn't even flinch. "Calm down and tell me what happened?"

"She's still alive..." Callie tugged on his arm. "You...you have to help her."

"Who?" asked Kalper.

"Please." Callie tried to pull him toward the door. "She won't make it long."

"I'll get my bag." He turned, spotting Trinity. "Sorry. I have—"

"Go. It's fine." She could wait. She slid her knife back into the sheath.

He nodded, grabbing a doctor's bag from the closet. She followed them out of the house.

"My carriage." Kalper stopped. "I gave my Grunts the morning off."

"Please, doctor. We have to hurry." Callie almost danced with nerves.

"I'll take you. The carriage is small, but we can all fit." She waved at the Grunt. "Ott, we need to go."

Ott's eyes widened and he stuffed more food in his mouth before hurrying to the street.

"You should stay here. I don't know how dangerous this might be." Kalper glanced at Callie who was already climbing into the carriage. "You can wait in my house. My Grunts will be back soon. They can take you back to the Council Building."

"I can take care of myself, doctor." Araldo, Almighty males thought females were helpless.

"I know but"—he lowered his voice—"Callie isn't one for histrionics. Something bad—really bad—had to have happened to cause her to act like this."

"I've seen more than my share of bad, and you may need help."

"If you're sure."

"I am."

"Thank you." He stepped aside, letting her enter the carriage before climbing in after her.

"Callie, where are we going?" He settled on the seat opposite her and the young Servant.

"Warehouse District." Callie's pale face made her bright green eyes even more vibrant.

Kalper leaned out the window. "Ott, take us to the Warehouse District. We'll give you more specific directions when we get there."

This was just great. Trinity hated that place. So much death had happened there. Remy had died in one of those buildings. She would've ended up there, slaughtered and sold for food, if she hadn't snuck out that night so long ago

"I'll show you where it...where they are." Callie's eyes were glazed as if seeing into a place that was dark and scary.

"They?" Trinity glanced at the doctor.

Callie nodded. "A lot of them."

"Tell me what happened," said Kalper.

"I...I sleep in this building...It's empty most of the time and I go there...It's safe." Callie's eyes teared up. "At least, I thought it was. Last night...I didn't go there." The young Servant began to tremble. "If I'd been there..."

"But you weren't. You're safe." He took Callie's hand. "I won't let anything happen to you."

"Th-thank you." Callie nodded.

"So, this building..." prodded the doctor.

"I...I went back this morning to sleep. I was out with friends last night and"—Callie swallowed—"when I went inside..." Her free hand shook so hard as she tried to wipe her eyes that she only smeared more dirt across her gaunt cheeks. "So many dead. I...I just stood there. Too scared to run. Too scared to move. And then...I-I heard...a noise...a sob...a whimper." Her claws dug into the doctor's hand, drawing blood. "I wanted to run. To get out of that place, but I couldn't leave her. I don't know how she survived. No one should survive that. No one."

The carriage slowed and Trinity's gaze drifted to the window.

The entire area was run down and dirty. Large buildings sat almost on top of one another. Empty windows like eyes, dark and soulless, stared out of structures that were falling in on themselves. Groups of buildings were separated by yards, barren and encircled by fences that were torn open, the sides ragged like they'd been ripped apart by prey.

"I'd heard rumors." Callie's body shook. "Stories. About this stuff but I never believed..."

"Where do we need to go?" asked Kalper. "Which building?"

The Servant's arm almost spasmed as she pointed out the window. "Last building. Over there."

The Warehouse District had died along with the old rule, but that building seemed even worse than the others. It stood alone. The windows mostly intact, and the walls sturdy. It should seem safer, but it didn't. Something about it seemed cold and evil, like it collected nasty secrets.

Servants mingled about but they stayed in small groups and none of them ventured too close to that building. Usually when a carriage approached, the strays would glide into the shadows, watching from safety to see if they should run or hunt. Today was different. They stood in the open, whispering to each other and fidgeting as their eyes darted like pendulums, away and back to that building. Some meandered slowly toward it while others scurried in the opposite direction, their faces wearing the same look that she'd seen on the Producers—pure horror.

CHAPTER 14: Conguise

Conguise sat in the parlor waiting for Meesus. He kept his hands on his lap, wanting to touch as little as possible in this vile whorehouse. Meesus glided into the room dressed in a silk robe, her hair falling free about her shoulders. She looked like the trollop she was. He kept his face impassive. It wouldn't do to offend. He needed as many allies as he could get, even those beneath him.

"My females tell me you requested to see me personally." She walked to the liquor cabinet. "Let me be very clear." She poured herself a drink and turned to face him. Her brilliant green eyes were hard like jade. "I no longer service clients. Under any condition."

He allowed his lips to glide upward a little, hoping it looked more like a smile than a sneer. "That's perfect because I do not...associate with those outside of my class."

She studied him, obviously wondering why he was there. "Would you like a drink?"

"No. Thank you." There was no way he was putting anything from this place near his mouth.

"Not to be rude, but what is the point of your visit if it is not to enjoy yourself." She sat on a chair across from him, her eyes calculating.

He'd come to the right place. She'd be perfect. "I agree with what you said at the hearing."

She continued to stare at him, her expression not changing at all. She must not have understood that this meant he'd chosen her side over one from his own class.

He needed to be more direct. Subtlety was lost on the lower classes. "Wilt Wickerwood should be executed or at least whipped to within an inch of his life, not left to live his remaining years

71

in a comfortable cell." Prison would be worse than the jail where Conguise had waited, but it was still better than the homes of many of the other classes.

"You are sincere." She tipped her head. "But I don't believe it's for the sake of my daughter and the other Servants that you feel this way."

"Does it make a difference if I'm willing to help?" He fought the urge to fidget under her perusal. Their unswerving focus was one of the things he hated about Servants. Nothing but snakes should be able to go so long without blinking.

"Motive always matters in the end."

"My reasons are my business." He shrugged. She was shrewder than he'd expected, but she was still only a Servant. "I can help you get revenge for your daughter. That should be enough." It would be for him. He'd do anything and use anyone to get justice for Viola.

"I am a cautious female." She smiled.

He tipped his head. This was not as easy as he'd expected. "I don't wish harm to you or your kind."

"Who do you wish harm?" She took a sip of her drink.

This time he studied her. How much should he tell her? "Hugh also betrayed me."

"Ah, I see. You wish to remove Hugh from power so you can step in." She started to stand. "I don't think that will benefit me or my—"

"Sit." His tone was a command and her eyes narrowed to angry slits. "Please." He softened his voice. He wanted to slap her, make her obey but that was no longer the world he lived in and to survive he must adjust.

She sat, her eyes still hard.

"Once I wanted power but no longer. I'm old—"

"Not that old." Her eyes skimmed down his frame.

He forced himself not to shudder in revulsion. "I'm tired."

She tipped her head at the concession.

"I want to be left alone with my work."

"And how is Hugh stopping that?"

"I will not rest until I've seen justice for what he did to my daughter." What had happened to Viola was common knowledge. There was no reason to keep the hate from spilling from his lips.

"And you will have that when Hugh has been removed from power?"

"No." He shook his head. "I will have that when Hugh has suffered as I have."

"You don't care that he has the power you once owned?" She took another drink.

"He can run the world for all I care." The world was ruined anyway. Hugh would just take them there faster.

"Why should I help you with your justice?"

"Because I can help you get yours. You and your kind will never be taken seriously until you stand up for yourselves. There are those whose job it was to breed and sell your kind. They won't be punished under Hugh's laws because what they did was not illegal at the time."

Her face hardened, but she nodded.

"I suggest that you punish them yourselves."

"And be locked up? How does that bring me justice?"

He leaned back, forgetting for a second that he didn't really want to touch the chair before quickly shifting forward. "What justice do you want? Justice for your daughter or for your kind?"

"I want justice for me. I want Wickerwood dead." She stood and glided to the bar.

"I may be able to arrange that."

"At what cost to me?" She watched him as she refilled her glass.

"I want to take away the one thing that Hugh values above all else."

"And what do you believe that is?" She leaned against the cabinet.

"The mixed breed. Trinity."

"I have nothing against the young female, and I won't hurt her."

"I didn't say that we hurt her." Although a death for a death had been his plan, it seemed the whore had some standards. He could modify his revenge, for now.

"Then what do you propose?" She moved back to the chair and sat.

"She has a past with Jethro."

"So I've heard."

"I believe that he still has feelings for her and her him." He could convince Jethro to see how vile she was later.

"You're suggesting that we play matchmaker?" Meesus smiled.

"They'll be happy, and Hugh will be miserable." He'd find someone to kill Trinity later, although having her tied to Hugh's half-brother for years did have its appeal. No. It was against nature and even though Jethro had betrayed them all, he still harbored a fatherly fondness for the boy. Young males made mistakes of the heart, but it shouldn't ruin their lives.

"It will not be easy." Meesus exposed her claws and studied them for a moment. "Hugh is not a male whom females easily forget."

He wanted to scream his pain. Viola had been taken with Hugh from the moment she'd met him. He'd tried to persuade her to look elsewhere—Hugh was not malleable—but she'd insisted that they were in love. His lips moved into a sneer. Love, hah. Hugh had never loved Viola. If he had he would've never forgotten her so fast. "Hugh can be his own worst enemy. He is not a trusting male."

Meesus' eyes widened. "Perhaps, but he is possessive. How do you plan on separating the two? They must not be together in order for doubt to slip between their ears."

"Leave that to me."

"What will you need me to do? Hugh will be suspicious of any rumors I spread."

"I need you to take a young, innocent Almighty under your knowledgeable wings. She'll need help in seeing the benefit of a relationship with Hugh and in achieving that goal."

"If I do this, I will expect Wickerwood's death shortly."

"I'll begin work on that immediately." He stood and walked to the door, pausing as he turned to face her. "If it can be arranged, would you like to deliver Wickerwood's punishment yourself?"

"Yes." The word hissed from her lips like a snake, slippery and deadly.

"I can't promise anything yet, but I'll see what I can do."

"Thank you." She finally gave him the look of gratitude that he'd deserved from the moment he'd deigned to meet her.

"It will take a bit more time for that...perk."

"Not too much." Her eyes narrowed suspiciously.

"No. Of course not." He smiled. "I shall be in contact soon with more information."

CHAPTER 15: Jethro

Jethro kept his eyes shut and his breathing steady, feigning sleep so he could gather as much information as possible. He was tied to a bed, but he wasn't in his cell. The smells were different. Only a slight odor of fear, no feces and no stench of sweaty, unwashed males. Instead there was disinfectant and blood, but most of the latter was coming from him.

"It took three darts to bring him down. That's not normal. Even a Grunt or Producer goes down with one," said a male.

"How much sedative was in the dart, Miles?"

That was Hugh's voice. What was he doing here? Jethro tensed but kept his mouth shut. Now, it was even more important to find out what was going on. He didn't trust Hugh.

"Three ccs in each dart. One should've knocked him off his feet, but it didn't seem to do anything but make him angry," said Miles.

"It was probably the adrenaline," said Hugh.

"You wouldn't say that if you'd seen him." Miles' voice became softer. "I've seen a lot of fights and there's something not right about him. Even if he's a mixed-breed it doesn't explain what he did."

"Please. He's just a strong male who trained with Guards," said Hugh. "We've all read about the adrenaline rush during battle. From what you've told me, he was fighting for his life. Why didn't you stop the attack sooner?"

That was a good question, but Jethro didn't think Hugh would get the real answer. The prison Guards had started this fight not the prisoners

"The Guards got there as soon as they could," said Miles.

"There should be Guards with the prisoners at all times when they're out of their cells."

"They were, but they had to leave to get the tranquilizers. They don't carry those with them."

"How do they break up altercations if they don't use tranquilizers?" asked Hugh.

"They have clubs."

"Then why didn't they use them? Why did they delay by running to get tranquilizers instead of attempting to use their clubs first?"

Jethro was impressed that Hugh wasn't believing any of the Gruntshit tale Miles was trying to feed him.

"A few did. Jethro went through them like they were nothing." Miles was scrambling but unfortunately, he was making sense. "The others ran to get the tranquilizers. It was their only option."

"Their only option?" Hugh moved closer to the bed. "I don't see any bruises that look like they were caused by a club. Only fists."

"He took them out. You didn't see him. He was fast and...brutal."

"So the Guards were afraid."

"Officially, I'm not saying that," said Miles. "But yeah, I think they were, and I don't blame them. I'm telling you there's something not right about him."

"There's nothing different about him." Hugh's words dripped with derision.

Jethro kept his breathing steady, but he laughed inside. Miles was right. He was different but he was glad Hugh didn't think so.

"Besides the fact that he spent months training and working with Guards instead of Almightys," continued Hugh. "He had to be strong and fast, or he'd never have survived."

"It's more than that, Hugh. I swear. You need to see him fight."

"Hmm. I don't agree, but I'll look into it. Even if he is a great fighter, there's still no excuse for what happened today. I can't have prisoners being attacked. It doesn't look good. Tell the Guards that there'll be a thorough investigation into this situation, but right now,

I need you to get something for his cuts. We have to clean him up. I can't let his family and friends see him like this."

"Is he getting released soon?" asked Miles.

Jethro really wanted to hear that answer.

"Get the good antiseptic. I don't want him dying from an infection." Hugh ignored the question.

"Got it," said Miles as he walked across the room.

As soon as the door closed, Hugh whispered, "Are you okay?"

Jethro continued to moderate his breathing.

"I know you're awake."

"How?" Jethro opened his eyes, staring up at the male he hated more than anyone else.

"You tensed when you heard my voice. It was barely noticeable, but I was watching." Hugh grabbed a syringe, uncapped it and then squirted the contents down the drain. He turned back to Jethro. "I need you to trust me."

That was never going to happen.

Miles came back in, and Hugh turned around, cupping his hand around the syringe.

"He's awake?" Miles stopped in the doorway. "He shouldn't be awake for hours."

"I gave him a shot to spark his adrenaline." Hugh opened his palm, showing the doctor the empty syringe.

"I don't think you should've—"

"Don't worry. I didn't give him much. Just enough to wake him. I have some questions that I need answered and I don't have all day to wait."

Jethro eyed Hugh. Why was he covering for him?

Miles nodded but stayed on the other side of the room as he opened the packages of salve for Jethro's wounds.

"Why were you attacked?" asked Hugh.

So they were going to play this game. "Don't know. Ask the prison Guards who attacked me."

"The prison Guards who attacked you?" Hugh actually sounded surprised.

"Yeah. It wasn't prisoners."

"He's delusional. The initial attack was from prisoners. The Guards tried to break it up." Miles walked over to the cot. "The tranquilizers can mess with his head for hours. Days even." His eyes met Jethro's and it was clear that Jethro had better go along with this story.

"I'll need to talk to the prisoners involved," said Hugh.

"Sure," said Miles. "As soon as they *can* talk. They're both pretty banged up. One has a broken jaw. The other we had to sedate to ease his pain."

"Then I want to talk to the prison Guards."

"They've all been sent home. Some had to go to the hospital. He did a real number on all of them. Broken ribs, fingers, arms...broken everything. It's almost unbelievable that one Almighty could do that much damage to four Guards in such a short period of time."

"It didn't seem short to me." That was kind of true. Time had slowed. Each movement and punch replayed through his mind, and yet it'd all happened fast in one glorious moment of survival. He flexed his fists. The cuts were already healing. He slid his hands under the sheet. He didn't need Hugh or Miles to see that.

"I don't want this to happen again." Hugh's gaze went to Miles and then back to Jethro.

"Gee. Me either." He didn't even try to hide his contempt. "But it never would've happened if I wasn't alone in here." He glared up at his half-brother. "Thanks to you."

"I didn't...What can I do to help keep you safe?" Hugh seemed sincere and a bit angry.

"You can turn me loose. I don't deserve to be in here and you know it." His hatred for the other Almighty seethed into something almost living.

Hugh hesitated a moment. "Setting you free isn't an option."

"What crime did I commit except that of a soldier? All the other soldiers have been released."

"You were more than a soldier. You were a leader. You instigated and organized the attacks."

"So I'm being punished for being good at my job." Jethro snorted. "Figures. You say you're different, but you seem an awful lot like those who were in charge before you."

"It's not my fault you were on the wrong side of the war."

"That's not why I'm still in here and you know it."

"That is exactly—"

"The only reason I'm still locked up is that you're afraid—"

"I'm not afraid of you."

Jethro couldn't help inhaling and testing the air. Hugh wasn't lying. The only fear in this room was coming from Miles. "I know that." At least, he did now. "But you are afraid that your fiancé will want a real male. One who can protect her. One who can fight and not just someone who spouts political drivel."

"Don't talk about her. Ever." Hugh's eyes narrowed and his hands clenched at his sides.

Jethro almost snarled. If his limbs weren't still heavy from the sedative, he'd rip through the restraints and tear Hugh apart.

"Ignore him." Miles grabbed Hugh's arm, pulling him away from the cot.

"Good luck in here." Hugh yanked free and turned toward Miles. "Let me know when he's dead."

Hugh's angry footsteps echoed down the hallway as Miles closed the door. Jethro waited. He was vulnerable, but the doctor had to get close to poison him. He'd watch for an opening because he refused to let Miles inject him with something and pass off his death as a consequence of the beating.

"If you want out of here, you'll stop taunting Hugh. He holds all the power...out there."

"Meaning, he doesn't in here?"

"You tell me. Do you think Hugh arranged for those Guards to attack you?"

"I told you. I don't know why they attacked me. Prisoners? Sure. I'm alone. Vulnerable. But the prison Guards? I have no idea why they went after me."

Miles rolled his eyes.

"Believe what you want."

"You don't think it has anything to do with you being alone in here and running a very lucrative business?"

So that's what this was about. Other prison Guards wanted in on the cut as well as Miles. "They should remember that there is no business without me. Indy won't work with anyone else."

"You think he's the only one who—"

"He's the only one who figured out how to get past the honest Guards."

"And now, we know. Why do we still need Indy? Or you." Miles walked across the room. "I'm just saying that maybe you should be nicer to Hugh. Life in here can be dangerous." He opened the door and motioned for someone to come forward. Tonkers and another large Guard entered the infirmary. "The only way you're going to survive is by making new friends."

He should've known Tonkers was behind this. The Guard had been whining about wanting a bigger cut of their business.

"Let's go." Tonkers unfastened the restraints and pulled Jethro off the table. The second Guard grabbed his other arm and they escorted him out of the infirmary.

"You have a new partner," said Tonkers.

"We don't need another partner." He tipped his head at the other Guard. "Apparently, there are already four of us."

"You aren't the boss anymore," said the new Guard.

"Then who is? You?" He laughed but none of this was funny.

"Gap? Nah. He ain't smart enough to be the boss. Are you, Gap?" laughed Tonkers.

"Nope. I'm strong." Gap's grip on Jethro's arm tightened. "And mean but not smart."

"Then who? Miles?" He was liking this even less.

"Miles ain't the boss but he's working with us. The new boss's idea," said Tonkers. "It'll be easier with him. Those who pay can pretend to be sick. I'll bring them to the infirmary and when they're done, I'll take them back to their cells."

"Our way was working fine." He was losing control and that was never good, especially in here.

"That way is over. We're branching out."

"Branching out? Indy hasn't said anything to me about this."

"Indy's out." Tonkers' lip raised a bit. "You were supposed to be out too."

"What are you talking about?" His friend had better still be alive. "Indy is the one who knows how to bypass the honest Guards."

"We learned from watching him. Now, we don't need him." Tonkers shoved Jethro. "Or you. The Almightys are our partners now. Wickerwood is the new boss."

That wasn't good at all. "Why am I still alive?" Even though they hadn't been able to kill him in the cafeteria, Miles could've finished him off in the infirmary.

"I have no idea." Tonkers shrugged. "Orders changed. You should thank Wickerwood."

"I guess I should." It made him want to vomit but he could no longer afford to be choosy about his friends.

CHAPTER 16: Hugh

Hugh stormed out of the infirmary and Rex fell into pace along his side.

"I'm guessing that went as well as I thought it would," said Rex.

"Why are you here again?" He shot the Guard a disgusted look.

"To protect you. Even when you're being a dumbass, it's my job to make sure you don't die."

"Then protect me in silence." He didn't need the Guard's sarcasm right now.

He'd handled the situation with Jethro poorly. It didn't help that Jethro blamed him for the beating he'd just received. He wasn't the one who'd let Jethro's friends out of prison, but he was going to find out who had. He turned a corner and continued to the right as Rex veered left.

"Where are you going? The exit is this way," said Rex.

"I'm quite aware how to get out of here." He continued down the hallway.

"Then I'll ask again. Where are we going?" Rex hurried and caught up with him.

"To see the warden."

"Why?"

"You're a nosy Guard." He'd never admit it to anyone, but he was glad Rex was comfortable questioning him like this. When he'd first taken over, Rex had been as silent and obedient as an abused Guard. He'd lived to serve and to only be seen when needed. It'd taken months for Rex to learn that even though Hugh was his boss, he didn't believe he was Rex's superior.

"I'm nosy because I need to know what kind of foolishness you're getting yourself into this time so I can be ready."

"Someone released all Jethro's friends."

"Someone?" The Guard gave him a puzzled look.

"Yeah."

"I thought you were the only one with the authority to release prisoners."

"I am, but I didn't sign those papers." Either his signature had been forged convincingly or the warden was involved. He opened the door that led to the reception area of the warden's office.

"Mr. Truent. It's nice to see you," said the middle-aged Almighty who sat at the desk outside the warden's door.

"Thank you. It's nice to see you too"—he glanced at the nameplate—"Gerard. I need to speak with Mr. Quarks."

"I'm sorry. He's in a meeting." Gerard smiled but there were shadows behind his eyes.

"Great. That gives me time to prepare." He'd planned on chatting with Quarks while Rex and Gerard gathered the papers, but this would work too.

"Prepare?" Gerard started to look even more nervous. "For what?" He shook his head. "It doesn't matter. Mr. Quarks will be in this meeting for quite some time. If you'd like"—he pulled out an appointment book and paged through it—"I can schedule you for—"

"That won't be necessary." He didn't like using his authority to push others around, but he'd do it when he had to. "I need to see the records for Calvin Folgrant and the following prisoners." He rattled off the names of Jethro's friends.

"Why do you need to see those records?" Gerard glanced at the door.

It was a quick flit of the eyes, but it was enough for Hugh to know he was right to suspect Quarks.

"Because..." He stopped. He had a choice right now—make an enemy or a friend. "How long have you worked here?" There were photos on the Almighty's desk of two children from young kids to young adults.

"Eighteen years, sir." Gerard stiffened as if facing his executioner.

"That's a long time. How many wardens have you seen come and go?"

"Eight, sir. Counting Mr. Quarks."

"That's a lot of bosses."

"I suppose."

"It's a testament to your skill and honesty that each new boss has chosen to keep you instead of replacing you with someone of their own choosing."

"I'm good at my job, sir." Gerard stiffened even more. "Very good."

"I'm sure you are and I'm sure you'll be here to assist the next warden when the time comes." His eyes drifted to the door and then back to Gerard. "I'd like to see those files."

Gerard frowned but said, "Yes, sir." He stood. "This way, sir."

Hugh and Rex followed Gerard to the back of the office and through a side door. They walked down a long, narrow hallway before Gerard stopped at a door, unlocked it and opened it. The other Almighty turned on a light and Hugh followed him inside.

Shelves filled the room. Each of them packed full of files. There'd been a lot of prisoners over the years. Which shelf and which box held his files? Did they have a special section for escapees? What about ones who escaped and then became the ruler?

"Except for Folgrant"—Gerard walked across the room and ran his finger along a line of folders before pulling one down"—the records that you want are of Guards who were released within the last few days and weeks." He walked to the desk near the door and dropped the file on a clean spot before digging through the stack of folders on the nearby table and chair. "They should be over here. I haven't had a chance to file them yet." He opened a box that'd been buried under a stack of papers. He searched it, pulling out two files and tossing them on top of Folgrant's folder. He opened another large box, retrieving a few other files.

"It seems you have quite a lot of work to do." That was an understatement.

"It gets done, sir." Gerard's eyes were wary as he glanced at Hugh.

"Maybe you could use some assistance." He could swing another small salary out of the budget, and it'd give one other family a steady income.

"No offense, sir, but I've been doing this on my own for a long time and I do a good job."

"I'm sure you do, but I'm also sure you could use some help. There are a lot of people out of work right now."

Gerard grabbed the stack of files he'd put on his desk and handed them to Hugh. "I need this job, sir."

"I'm not firing you. It just looks like there's a lot to be done and you could use an assistant."

"I've handled it by myself for eighteen years, sir."

"What happens when you take a day off?"

"I manage."

"What about when you take a vacation? When you come back after a week or more, is all this work piled up and waiting for you?"

"Yes, sir. Most of it." Gerard seemed to force the words past his lips. "But Mr. Quarks takes care of anything that can't wait."

"You must truly dread coming back, knowing all the work that you'll have."

"I enjoy keeping busy."

"You'll enjoy not being overworked too."

"Sir..."

Hugh held up his hand, stopping Gerard from saying any more. "I want you to place an ad for an assistant today. You can be one of the members on the panel for the interviews. I want you to hire someone you can work with, but it will be someone from another class."

"Yes, sir." Gerard didn't look happy about this.

"This individual will not be your replacement. I promise."

A bit of the hardness eased from Gerard's face.

"If they do well and are happy here, they may enable you to apply for a better position."

"The only other jobs available are ones where I'd work directly with the prisoners. I'm not interested in supervising Guards, and I'm not qualified for the infirmary."

"There's another position."

Gerard's brow wrinkled in thought.

"The current warden may decide to leave. Have you ever considered applying for that position?"

"No. You know the rules. Only someone whose family worked in the prison system or served on the Council can apply for the position of warden. My family's military."

"It's a brand-new world, Gerard. All you need is to be qualified and honest and you can apply for any job you want."

"Mr. Quarks is a good warden, sir. It's a hard job with a lot of pressure from many different places."

"I'll remember that when I speak with him."

"Thank you, sir. Is there anything else that I can assist you with today?"

"Actually, there is. I'd like my file too." He had no idea why he wanted it. He knew what would be in there. He'd heard it all in his farce of a trial. If nothing else, it'd serve as a reminder of how everything could disappear in an instant with one misplaced word in the wrong ear.

CHAPTER 17: Hugh

Hugh flipped through the files as he and Rex sat across from Gerard outside of Quark's office. It'd only taken him a few moments to search the documents. They were all signed with his name, but the signatures weren't even close to his.

"I need to see Mr. Quarks now." He stood, handing Rex his file.

"Yes, sir." Gerard left his desk and walked to the door. He tapped twice before opening it and stepping inside.

A few minutes later, Vickers came out of the room. "Hugh," he said as he left.

It wasn't that unusual for a lawyer to meet with the warden, but he was a suspicious man, and he already didn't trust Vickers.

"Mr. Truent." Gerard opened the door, stepping aside.

He stood and walked into the warden's office. Rex followed him, closing the door behind them.

"If you wanted to see me, you should've put it on my calendar," said Quarks. "I was in a meeting with—"

"If I wanted to set up an appointment with you I would've." He dropped all the files on the warden's desk except for Calvin Folgrant's. "You released these Guards."

"Yes." Quarks glanced at the names on the folder tabs. "Under your orders."

"That's not my signature."

"What? Of course, it is." The warden flipped through the top file and pointed at the signature. "That's your name right here."

"It is"—he dropped Cal's folder on the desk next to the one Quarks had opened—"but I'll repeat myself. That's not my signature." He opened Calvin's folder. "This is."

The warden looked at the two of them. "They are a little different."

"A little different? They're blatantly different."

"I see hundreds of papers a day." Quarks' face heated with anger. "That's your job."

"How am I supposed to know which one is your signature?"

"You were with me when I signed Cal's."

"But I wasn't with you when you signed hundreds of other ones. You used to come to my office, and we'd discuss the prisoners but you're too busy for that now. All I get is paperwork saying to release this prisoner or that one. I check to make sure you signed it and then follow your orders."

"You've seen my signature enough times. You should've noticed the difference and at least asked me about it."

"Who would forge your signature?"

"That's a good question. Not many have access to the necessary paperwork."

"It may have been Gerard." Quarks lowered his voice. "He has access to everything."

"I don't think it was Gerard." Almightys like Quarks made him sick. They were so fast to push the blame off on someone else.

"Then I have no idea who it might be."

"Are you sure? Everything is traceable on the computers and the cameras."

"You're welcome to look at what we have." Smugness lurked behind Quarks' eyes. "We've had some power outages lately. I was told we didn't lose anything important."

"You know what else is traceable? Cash deposits into your account paid to you for releasing those Guards."

"Search my bank account. You won't find any deposits except my paychecks."

"So they paid you in something besides cash." He may not have proof yet, but Quarks purposely released Jethro's friends.

"No one paid me anything. I made a mistake."

"Falsifying prison records and releasing prisoners without the proper approval is an offense that could mean prison."

"You have to prove it first and you can't because I didn't do it."

"But you did. You released them and my signature is obviously forged. That alone is enough to get you jail time."

"I didn't notice. I was in a hurry. I agree that I should've paid more attention. I apologize." Quarks almost snarled.

"I'd believe you except this wasn't a one-time thing. This happened eight times." He picked up each file and dropped it. "Eight. And in between those times, I released other prisoners. You went from one release form with my real signature to another with the forged signature several times and you never noticed that the two were different. That isn't a mistake."

"My wife is ill. I've been under a lot of stress."

"I'm sorry to hear about your wife, but that's not going to keep you out of jail."

"You're not going to be able to convict me on this." Quarks pushed the papers across his desk. "Like I said, I made a mistake. So unless you want to use your authority as the Supreme Almighty..."

Hugh's jaw clenched at the title. This was one of those times when it was hard not to use the power he had.

"I won't be going to jail."

"Maybe the jury will see it your way but whether they do or don't, you're out of a job."

"You're going to have a mess on your hands without me running this place for you." Quarks' face twisted with anger as he grabbed a few of his personal items off the desk.

"The keys." He held out his hand.

"I wish I'd been warden when you were in prison. You would've never escaped." Quarks pulled his key chain from his pocket and removed several keys, tossing them on the desk before he strode from the room.

"Rex, grab those files." He picked up the keys and walked to the door. "I don't want them disappearing on us." He stepped into the outer office. "Gerard, I need you to be the warden for a bit."

"What?" Gerard paled.

"You heard me. Quarks is gone." He dropped the keys on the other Almighty's desk.

"Ah..." Gerard stared at them.

"You've been an assistant to the warden for eighteen years. You know how to do this job." He picked up the keys and put them in Gerard's hand. "You probably trained most of the wardens you've worked for."

"That's different, sir."

"It isn't. Not really." He'd seen this over and over again. Everyone in their society had been raised to believe that they could only do one thing—the job their family had done for centuries. Most never even questioned it. "Give it a try. If you don't like it after a couple of weeks or a month. I'll find someone else. If you do decide you want the job, Rex will help you with hiring someone to be your assistant as well as the job we talked about earlier."

"I like my current job," said Rex.

"It's time for you to branch out too." He was tired of the Guard staying outside his suite all the time. "We can talk about hiring Guards to patrol inside the Council Building at night."

"We need to do more than talk about it," said Rex.

He ignored the Guard. "Gerard, have all the locks changed."

"Yes, sir." Gerard slid the keys into his pocket. "You may also want to have the computer access codes changed."

"That's definitely getting done."

"It hasn't been changed in years, sir. Lots of years."

"What are you trying to tell me?" The other Almighty seemed to be on the verge of saying something important.

"Mr. Quarks was a good boss."

"When I told him that my signature was forged, he blamed you." Gerard's face tightened. "Do you remember Warden Sheno?"

"Yeah. He was a warden here for years." As far as he knew Sheno had been a harmless Almighty—not doing any real good nor bad.

"He was here when I started."

"He died from natural causes on the job, didn't he?"

"Yes, sir. He was sick for quite some time. His son filled in for him a lot."

"Really?" That wasn't allowed.

"Yes, sir. That son went to college with Mr. Quarks."

"Are you saying Sheno's son—"

"The two of them also went to college with Wilson's son. They stood up at each other's weddings. Mr. Wilson, junior, was here a few times the last couple months. I hadn't seen him since Sheno was warden."

"Thank you, Gerard." That explained everything. Quarks hadn't gotten paid. He'd helped a friend try to get revenge.

"Bette Wilson was a nice lady," said Gerard.

"She was. Sometimes. Like all of us." He regretted killing her. If he could do it again, he'd find another way to end the war, but since he couldn't go back in time, he'd have to live with the enemies he'd created.

"I guess it depends on how you feel about someone. We shouldn't judge the good or the bad. We should judge the overall." Gerard headed for the door. "I need to go get the locks and the passwords changed."

CHAPTER 18: Trinity

Trinity followed Dr. Kalper out of the carriage. Ott's muscles quivered and his nostrils flared as he leaned as far away from the building as possible. She didn't blame him; the scent of blood and death permeated the air.

"Callie?" The doctor stared into the carriage where the young Servant sat, her eyes huge in her pale face.

"I can't...I can't go in there again." Callie's words were whisper soft.

"Okay, but I need to know where this female is," said Kalper.

"Back of the room." Callie swallowed.

"Which room?" he asked. "It's a big building."

It was. Big and terrifying. It stood three stories high, and it was in better shape than many of the others. This meant it'd been used recently, and the only buildings around here that'd been used before the war were the slaughterhouses.

"Callie," prodded the doctor. "The quicker I find her the better chance she has to survive. I need you to tell me where she is."

"In the back. Against the wall."

"But which room? What floor?"

"In-in-inside." Callie made a shrill sound like a tea kettle letting out steam before it exploded. "Y-you can't miss them."

"Okay. Wait here." Kalper glanced at Trinity and then at the Servants who mingled nearby. "Perhaps, it'd be better if you stay here too."

"You're not going in there alone." Whatever had happened here, it was bad. She could smell the fear that lingered in the air—not fresh but potent in its intensity and abundance.

"Callie and Ott may need your presence out here." He tipped his head at the Servants.

They were all dirty and skinny with a hardness to their faces that was a signature of life on the streets, but their eyes were filled with true fear. Something terrible—unimaginable even for them—had happened in that building.

"No one's going to do anything to them. Not today." Today, they'd seen enough horror.

"Are you sure?" The doctor glanced around the area again.

"Yeah. Look at them. They're out in the open. Scared." Horrified was more like it. When he still didn't seem convinced, she added, "They're not coming anywhere near this building."

They hovered in groups, but it was like a river kept them several yards from this building and not one of them crossed even an inch over that imaginary line.

"If anyone approaches, run." Kalper patted Ott. "Don't worry about us. Take Callie and run." He strode toward the building.

Trinity frowned at the doctor's back. Ott wasn't the bravest Grunt she'd ever met. She grabbed Ott's bridle and pulled him close. "Listen to me. If you're really in danger, run."

He nodded, pulling her arm up and down.

"But, if you're still here when we get back, I'll feed you dinner. Understand?"

His eyes lit up, but then he glanced at the group of nearby Servants.

"You only get food if you stay." She shouldn't have let him eat at Dr. Kalper's. Food was a great incentive, but it only worked if one was hungry. She had to sell this offer because she didn't want to be stranded here. "You have family? Friends?"

His eyes narrowed as he grunted, his hands flying, filled with words.

"A brother and mother? Great. You stay. I'll feed them dinner too."

Ott glanced at the Servants again but then his eyes took on a resigned look before he nodded.

"Good." She patted his shoulder. "You'll be fine. They won't come over here." She didn't blame them. She'd rather go through Brush-Men territory than go anywhere near that building, but the doctor was almost at the door. She unsheathed her knife and ran to catch up with Kalper, stopping behind him at the front door and grabbing his shoulder. "I should go first."

He turned, only the slight scent of fear giving away his nervousness. "I can't let—"

"I'm faster and stronger. Plus, I have a knife. Not to mention it's going to be dark inside, and you can't see in the dark." She dropped her hand and stepped in front of him. She wasn't arguing about this. "I'm going first."

He frowned but nodded. "Be careful. I'll be right behind you. I may be old, but I've learned a lot of tricks in my days."

"I'm sure you have." She smiled at him, but her lips trembled. She didn't want to do this, but it had to be done.

She put her hand on the door. It was open a crack. Callie may not have shut it in her haste to get out, or maybe something waited inside for them, tempting strays with easy access. Her grip tightened on her knife as she let everything slip away but the skills Gaar and Mirra had taught her. She stayed still, ears forward as she listened. She tuned out the soft whispering of the Servants, Kalper's uneasy breathing and Ott's feet shuffling on the ground and focused on the room ahead—the building before her. Silence. No breathing. No movement.

She fought the urge to gag as she inhaled. Scent—foul and dank—seeped through the thick wood of the door. She knew that smell. She took short breaths, preparing herself as she stepped into the building.

"Holy Araldo," whispered Kalper, covering his nose with his hand. "I've never smelled anything like this."

"I have." It was the Finishing Camp all over again.

The shadows danced in the building, knowing the sun wouldn't dare to enter and shine them away. The air, musty and rotten, dripped with death and fear. Only the metallic odor of blood was different from the Finishing Camp. She wanted to turn and run. She didn't want to see what was inside, but she moved forward, immersing herself into this dark cave of death.

The muted light from the dusty windows high up the wall cast an eerie glow over the room. Her eyes quickly adjusted to the dim light, but she stumbled to a halt, her hand shaking at her side. The Finishing Camp with its rows of prisoners had been bad, but at least there'd been hope. In here there was only death.

Bodies filled the room from corner to corner. Every flat space—floor, tables, empty crates—held a body. She'd fought and killed many creatures, but she'd never seen so much blood. It was splattered everywhere—the walls, the floor, even the ceiling. Puddles formed in the shallower spots of the concrete.

She forced her feet to move closer, the ghastly scene becoming clearer with each step. They were all female Servants. Their abdomens sliced open, intestines spilling onto the floor. Hunks of bloody flesh sprinkled across the room, forming pathways that the killers must've taken.

She'd come to terms with what the Almightys had done to the Producers. Everything had to eat. It wasn't right that they kept them in camps in a pretense of protecting them from predators, but the killing and eating of Producers was no different than the creatures of the forest. This was different. This was slaughter. Waste. Murder.

"Who would do this?" She looked behind her, but the doctor was making his way across the sea of bodies to the back of the room.

She followed him, trying not to look at the faces frozen in pain beneath her feet as she stepped over one then another and another.

The doctor stopped, kneeling next to a young Servant. The female's breath was labored, her eyes glassy as she stared at the ceiling. Her face was stained with dirt and blood except for trails made by her tears. He stared at the wound as he reached for his bag.

Trinity had seen death many times and it was here now. She looked at the doctor, hoping he understood.

"Everything's going to be okay." His fingers moved off his bag and he took the Servant's hand. "You should rest. You'll feel better soon." The doctor's voice was calm, trying to give comfort in the Servant's last moments.

"Who did this to you?" She knelt beside the female. Vengeance was comforting too.

The Servants eyes locked with hers, lips moving. "Proc..."

"Who?" Trinity lowered her head, putting her ear next to the Servant's mouth, but there was nothing. No words. No breath. No life.

"We need to check to see if there's anyone else alive." The doctor stood.

CHAPTER 19: Trinity

"I'll take this side." Trinity headed in the opposite direction from Dr. Kalper, this time keeping her eyes on the dead. It was the only way to ensure none still lived.

They were all young. All females. All Servants. Blue and green eyes once vibrant, now stared glassily back at her. She didn't need to bend and check them. They were all dead. All torn apart, innards spilled. She moved down the rows, counting to give her mind something to focus on besides the horror. One. Two. Five. Ten. Twenty.

The rows of bodies seemed never ending. The numbers became names for the dead. Number eighteen had black hair and blue eyes. If it weren't for the fangs, peeking from the grimace that froze her lips, she could've passed for an Almighty. Number twenty-three's eyes were a pale green like spring grass. Yet she'd never see another spring.

Trinity stopped counting at forty-two. She didn't want to know any more of them. She trudged along, no longer trying to miss the entrails. It was impossible anyway. It took too long to try and find a tiny toehold to stand, and she had to get done. She had to get out of there before she raced from the room screaming.

Doctor Kalper leaned against the wall ahead of her, exhaustion taking over his aged features.

"Who would do this?" She stopped at the end of her aisle. "It makes no sense. Why didn't they harvest the...meat?"

He sighed. It was a weary sound as if his body couldn't handle any more grief and had to expel some before it burst into sadness. "There's a lot you still don't know about this world."

"Tell me." She'd do something about this. She was no longer a helpless fugitive. Now, she had power.

"Let's go." The doctor rubbed his hand over his face. "I'll tell you everything I know on the way back."

"We can't leave them here." Like garbage. Unwanted. Unloved. Unavenged. "We need to bury them and notify their families if possible."

"You can send someone to gather the remains when we get back." He made his way along the wall. It was the clearest path to the door. "I doubt you'll find their families though. Guards and Servants are usually taken from their parents a little after birth."

"We can try." She'd forgotten how the other classes had lived. Producers grew up with their parents. Of course, they were then slaughtered and eaten, but her youth had been pleasant compared to that of Servants and Guards.

When they stepped out of the building, they both inhaled deeply. The stench, once so potent to them out here, was like the purest air after being inside.

Ott snorted, his large feet almost dancing when he saw them. He waved his arm, motioning for them to hurry. Trinity took in the crowd as they walked toward the carriage. More Servants had gathered, but none had approached the building.

"Did you find her?" Callie stood next to Ott, her legs twitching like she was ready to run. "Is she alive?"

The doctor shook his head, opening the carriage door. "She didn't make it, but thanks to you, she wasn't alone when she passed." He motioned for the young Servant to get into the carriage.

"She's dead? They're all dead?" Callie's voice took on that shrill tea kettle sound again. "What if someone saw me? What if they—"

"You can stay with me." He rested his hands on her shoulders. "You'll be safe at my place. You know that."

Callie nodded and almost flew into the carriage, squeezing herself into the corner. "It would've been me. If I hadn't stayed out last ni—"

"But you did and you're safe." Dr. Kalper climbed inside, patting the young Servant's arm.

Trinity hopped in after him, wiping her bloody hands on her pants as she sat next to Callie. "You said you'd tell me everything."

"And I shall. As horrible as it is." His eyes locked with hers—a lifetime of sadness in his blue gaze. "There are some in our culture who believe that specific organs from certain classes contain magical properties."

"Magical? There's no such thing as magic." The hair on her arms stood as an image of the Forest Witch flashed through her mind.

"Perhaps more medicinal than magical but those beliefs hold no basis in science."

"What did they take?" That explained the trail of guts spilling across the floor. Apparently, intestines weren't magical, but they were delicious, according to Mirra. She couldn't stop the shiver that danced down her spine.

"Different organs were missing from different Servants. Some seemed to be missing quite a few." He looked out the window. "I didn't examine them all. I should've, but I couldn't. Not again."

"You've seen this before." She fought the bile that threatened to rise up her throat.

He nodded. "Once or twice over the years, but not like this." He ran his hand over his face again as weariness settled over him. "Never this many. I believe it happens more often than I've seen, but the bodies aren't usually found."

"Why would someone leave so many of them like this? It's sure to cause an investigation."

"Our world has changed." His gaze met hers. "It's already impossible to buy Servants and Guards from the shelters. As soon as Hugh's programs to help the other classes start expanding, it'll be even more difficult to purchase and harvest the organs."

"They're stocking up." A cold sweat broke out across her skin.

CHAPTER 20: Hugh

Hugh sat at the head of the council table, his eyes darting to the door for the hundredth time. It wasn't like Trinity to be late. She knew how important these meetings were.

"Hugh, we need to discuss Jethro," said Jackson.

"Yes. Of course." He focused on those sitting at the table.

He'd created a council of advisors to help rule their world. Leaving all power in one Almighty's hand wasn't a good idea, even when he was that Almighty. The advisory board consisted of two from each class or at least it was supposed to. The Handlers and Trackers hadn't been interested in participating and the Avions had all bickered over the job. Each one of them had wanted it. He'd gone against every instinct he'd had and had offered the job to Birdie and another Avion. They'd both crowed their promises but neither ever showed up for the meetings.

"Let's hear the arguments for releasing Jethro," he said.

Jackson tried, not very hard, to stifle a groan. They'd gone over these points on numerous occasions over the past months.

"For the record." He nodded at the two Servants who transcribed everything said in these meetings.

"Again? Why?" asked Tim. "They haven't changed from the last time when we decided to leave him in prison where he belongs."

"Because it's the process and—"

"That you created," said Tim.

"Yes. The process that I created for the benefit of everyone. Going over the points before each decision is the right way to do this. Nothing is forgotten or left unspoken and it's all down on record." He was proud of this process and had no intention of changing it, unlike how the advisors were chosen. This time he'd picked them, and on days like today, he wondered what he'd been thinking when he'd selected these particular individuals.

He'd wanted a council filled with members loyal to their class and with their own ideas on the best way to become one society. So he'd purposefully picked some who didn't always agree with him—Trinity, Jackson and Tim to be precise. Then he'd chosen Mirabelle because her father was an important Producer at the Remore camp, so she had experience with low-level politics. Plus, she didn't see eye-to-eye with Trinity which helped balance the Producers.

Next, he'd chosen Reese, his one moment of clarity, because he could trust her. She almost always sided with him as opposed to Jackson who definitely had his own thoughts about issues. He must've been mad to select Tim. The Servant never agreed with him. Ever.

He'd also picked Barney as Tim's opposite. He didn't know many Grunts, so he'd selected Cack's wife and brother. It helped them supplement their income since Cack had died serving the Allied Classes. As for the Stockers, he'd chosen an older male and a younger one. The two seldom agreed on anything which kept them balanced.

That left the other Almighty. This was where he'd been moved by either a moment of brilliance or insanity.

"This is ridiculous." Conguise's lips turned up in a sneer.

Today, he was leaning toward insanity. He'd chosen the professor because it'd appeased the Almightys who still respected the old way, and it kept his enemy close.

"You know this is a waste of time," continued Conguise.

"Rules, Professor. None of us in this new government are above the law." His eyes locked with Conguise's. The professor was experimenting on Servants and Guards on Level Five. It was both illegal and unethical. Unfortunately, he couldn't prove it. Yet.

"Don't dance around it, Hugh. Say it out loud. Exactly what are you accusing me of doing? What law did I break besides the moral one of turning on my friend and leader to save...Trinity?" The professor's throat almost spasmed as he said her name. He more than hated her and what she stood for—an amalgamation of the classes and an end to the falsely perceived superiority of Almightys.

"You'll know if I'm accusing you of something. Just like I was aware when you and the Council accused me of treason." He yearned to spill all his suspicions to the world. Even Conguise's most loyal supporters would turn on him for what he was doing, but he couldn't until he had unequivocal proof. He'd find it. Someday. Somehow. When he did, he'd accuse Conguise with soldiers, an arrest and an execution. "Right now, I'm reminding everyone"—he glanced around the room, his eyes lingering on the door for a moment—"that the laws apply to each of us as well as those we serve. We will not have another situation like we had with Jason." His eyes locked with Conguise's again. "You know. Your good friend." He couldn't help the jab. The former Supreme Almighty's predilection for underage female Servants had come out in the investigation.

"I had nothing to do with his....non-business activities." The professor's face turned a brilliant shade of red.

Hugh held his breath. If the older Almighty had a heart-attack it'd save him a lot of problems.

"Jason's actions were despicable. It's debasing." Conguise's face wrinkled in disgust.

A soft growl rumbled from Jackson's chest. He and Kim were in an open mixed-class relationship. The Guard was loyal and even tempered, except when it came to Kim.

Although he'd love to see Jackson tear Conguise apart, he'd better calm the room because he didn't need a martyr for the old ways. There were still pockets of fighting in the woods between those who wanted life to return to how it'd been for centuries. "I'm going to assume that you mean the trafficking and rape of young Servants and not the intermingling of the classes."

"Of course." Conguise glanced about the room, his face cooling to a soft pink.

"Hugh," Cack's widow Bitt glanced at the door. "I need to get home soon."

"Again he's sidetracked the issue," said Conguise. "We cannot leave until we have his agreement to set Jethro free."

"And I'm not agreeing to anything until we follow the protocols that are in place. I want to hear the arguments for releasing Jethro Remore from prison."

"He was acting under his duties as a soldier. Following orders from his betters," said Conguise. "You've freed others, including Cal, who were more tied to the old regime than Jethro."

"You make him sound like nothing but a good soldier but was he really? Yes, he was very good at his job—hunting and killing—but he did what he wanted not what he was ordered. That's a dangerous quality especially in these times of unrest." He wasn't ready to set Jethro free. He needed the kid's help and freedom was the only thing he had to offer the other Almighty.

"He told me about the weapons," said Jackson. "Because of that information, I was able to warn you. Saving your life, I might add."

"You came at an opportune time," said Tim. "But Hugh and I would've made it into the Council Building on our own."

Jethro was the one subject on which he and Tim were in agreement.

"Right," said Jackson, his tone belying the word. "Not quite how I remember it." His gaze darted to Bitt who stared at her hands.

"Yes...uhm..." Tim glanced away. "Cack did save us but that doesn't mean Jethro should go free."

"He isn't a threat to anyone," said Conguise.

"I'm not so sure about that." His eyes met Conguise's again.

He'd spoken to the professor in private before he'd been forced by his constituents to free the Almighty. He'd questioned Conguise thoroughly on the few documents—mostly order forms, inventory records and a few papers on basic experiments—his Guards had found on Level Five, including the treatment Jethro had received that'd allowed him to walk again. Conguise had rattled on about the genome sequencing he'd created that had been able to repair damaged tissue and muscle. Although the professor had made it sound plausible, Hugh didn't believe any of it.

Conguise had injected Jethro with something new and dangerous. Something that should be beyond the realms of science. Something like what their ancestors had done to all of them before it'd been outlawed. He'd had the prison take everyone's blood at intake and he'd studied Jethro's. He had no idea what had been done to the kid, but Jethro wasn't pure Almighty any longer.

"The only reason you don't want Jethro released is because of his past with your fiancé." Conguise's voice almost purred with satisfaction. "You've released almost everyone else. Almighty soldiers. Guards. Servants. The only ones besides criminals who are still in jail are those who...dallied with the other classes and only a select few of those remain behind bars."

"Yes. The ones who dallied"—he almost spat the word—"with young females and males who didn't want what was done to them." He inhaled deeply. "Having relations outside one's class was illegal before the war, and it's illegal now if it's rape. Rape of anyone, no matter their class, will not be tolerated."

"And yet Jethro did neither of these things." Conguise's long fingers tapped on the table like a spider preparing to jump. "Well, he did the first one but so did you...with the same female as a matter of fact."

"Tim." He didn't even have to look to know that the Servant was ready to leap across the table and tear out Conguise's eyes.

"Calm down." Jackson jumped up, blocking Tim. "You know he does this to get to you. He wants you to leave. Then you can't vote."

Hugh had to hand it to Jackson. The Guard was loyal to a fault, but his loyalties were at odds. Having Tim leave the council room would've probably guaranteed Jethro's release.

"You aren't going to get that." Tim sat back down in a huff. "But one more word about my daughter and I'll catch you outside of this room. Outside of this building."

"He's threatening me." Conguise sneered. "What kind of government...What kind of leadership allows threats in its chambers? How can I feel safe casting my vote honestly?"

"You're afraid of a Servant?" Hugh leaned back in his chair. The professor had set this trap for himself.

"Of course not." Conguise stiffened. "Let's get to the vote."

"So to be clear. The only argument you have for Jethro's release is that I'm jealous?"

"No, but it's the one that matters because it's the truth."

"No, it's not." It really wasn't, but by the looks from the others no one believed him.

"Did you realize that Jethro is engaged?" asked Conguise.

All heads turned toward the professor.

"I guess not." Conguise smiled. "He was promised to Jason's granddaughter, Stella. To my knowledge this association is still in place."

"Is this true?" Hugh turned toward Jackson.

"Not that I know"—the Guard shrugged—"but he could be. Jethro and I didn't talk much before the war and still don't. He isn't allowed many visitors. Kim and I usually give our turns to his mother." Jackson was getting better and better at these political moves.

"His poor mother. It can't be easy for her with her son in prison and her livelihood gone. A strong, young male like Jethro could help care for his family." Conguise looked around the room, his usual condescending glare softened to a fatherly plea. "Don't you agree?"

"I need verification of his engagement." This was the first he'd heard about a fiancé. He'd met Stella years ago when she'd been barely a teen, but she'd be an adult now.

The professor's soft look disappeared like a shadow in the sun. "That proves that Jethro's interest in your fiancé is the only reason you're keeping him in jail."

"No, it doesn't." Gruntshit. He'd walked right into that one. "A romantic involvement settles a male down." It was the first thing he could think of and even as he said it, he felt the trap fall around him.

"Yes, a good female makes a male less likely to cause trouble, especially in troublesome times such as ours." Conguise leaned forward, ready for the verbal kill. "Once again, I state the obvious. With his engagement there is no reason to keep him in jail."

The professor had boxed him into a corner but only if this relationship existed. "I still need verification"—he tipped his head at the Servants who were writing everything down—"for the record." He smiled but it was false. The professor was not a novice at political maneuvering. Conguise never would've mentioned this without proof.

"She's waiting outside." Conguise's tapping slowed as if there was no hurry now that he'd won the argument.

Everyone turned and Cruck, Cack's brother, walked over to the door and opened it. A petite, blond Almighty stood from her place on a bench outside the door and walked into the council chambers. She was young and attractive, moving with a fluid grace. She and Jethro would make a cute couple. His large build and dark hair would make her look even more delicate.

She stopped a few feet away. Her blue eyes met Hugh's for a quick moment before she looked down at the floor. "Your sovereign highness." Even her voice was demure.

"That title no longer exists. You may call me Hugh."

Tim frowned at him, but he ignored the Servant. Tim believed Hugh needed a title—something to distinguish him from the rest of them and to show respect. He didn't want a title. He didn't want to be their leader.

She glanced up at him, a slight smile in her eyes. "Thank you...Hugh."

"What is your relationship with Jethro Remore?"

"We are affianced."

"Why hasn't he spoken of this? Not even to his family." He glanced at Jackson again and the Guard nodded.

"I believe he was trying to protect me." A slight flush covered her pale cheeks.

He leaned back in his seat. That was a possibility.

"You have your proof. Shall we vote?" asked Conguise.

"We can't vote without Trinity," said Tim.

"Not everyone needs to be present for the vote to occur." Conguise gave the Servant a smug look.

That was true. If they waited for the Avions to attend they'd never get anything done.

"She is the one most affected by the outcome of this issue," snapped Tim.

"I hardly think that's true." Conguise's voice dripped with condescension. "Jethro and Stella are surely more affected, not to mention Jethro's mother. The poor woman is quite distraught." The professor's gaze fell to Hugh.

He struggled not to shift in his seat. Jethro's imprisonment had put a strain on his relationship with Martha.

"I say we vote," said Conguise.

"I second it," said Jackson.

He nodded. He truly had no choice. "Guards?"

"Free," said Jackson.

Reese's brown eyes darted to his. "Prison."

He called the Stockers next. As usual, they voted opposite each other. The Grunts were wildcards on this issue. Cack's wife blamed all soldiers in the Protective Services for her mate's death, but she'd been treated well when she'd worked for the Remores. She seemed uncertain but when Cruck voted to free Jethro, she sided with keeping him in prison.

"For the record, I vote that he should stay in prison." He glanced at the professor.

"For the record, he should be freed," said Conguise.

"Servants?" This was his one hope. This was the one issue where Tim sided with him.

"Prison," said Tim.

Barney studied Conguise for a long moment and then sighed. "Free."

"What?" He hadn't expected that.

"Congratulations, Hugh. Your system does work." Conguise didn't even try not to sound smug.

"I think you're forgetting that we're tied, and I break the tie."

"I think you're forgetting about the Producers." Conguise nodded at Mirabelle. "As is the case most of the time, isn't it my dear?"

His dear? What in Gruntshit was going on? Conguise was barely civil to the other classes even when he needed something from them, but right now, he was being...kind.

"I didn't forget." He turned toward the lone Producer. The empty chair next to her a reminder that Trinity had not yet arrived. Had Conguise arranged for her to be delayed?

"I...I think he should be set free," said Mirabelle.

"There we have it." Conguise stood.

"Not yet." He felt like he was dancing on a wire over a lake filled with River-Men. "I can overturn the vote." That was another thing he wanted to change...later. Until more laws were in place to protect this government he was creating, he had the power to overrule his council. He held up his hand at the unhappy mumbling. "I'm not going to do that, but I do want to hear Trinity's opinion on this. She was the one..." What Jethro had done to her—keeping her as a prisoner, touching her—made his heart explode in anger but he had to stay calm. "I want to hear Trinity's opinion on this."

"This is a ploy to get your way. At least we knew our place with the old rule. Just call yourself the Supreme Almighty and be done with it." Conguise's words dripped with disgust.

"It's not a ploy, but I believe she should have a say in this."

"She's your fiancé. Your opinion is her opinion," said Conguise.

The door burst open, and Trinity strode into the room. "That's not true." She was filthy, her clothes smeared with blood.

"Are you okay?" He hurried toward her, Tim and Jackson right behind him. "What happened?"

"The blood isn't mine." She held up her hand, stopping him from wrapping her in his arms.

"Are you okay?" he asked again as he tucked a strand of hair behind her ear. Nothing mattered but her.

"I'm fine." Her golden eyes met his, fear and sorrow lurking in the shadows. "But you need to come with me." She swallowed. "You need to see what...You need to see this."

He turned toward the Council. "We'll reconvene tomorrow."

"That's unfair," said Conguise.

"Too bad." Hugh took Trinity's hand and headed for the door.

"Dad, Jackson, you may want to come with us," said Trinity.

"There they go again," said Conguise. "Running off for adventures when there's business to attend to. It's no wonder there's no food and nothing is getting done."

"Ignore him," whispered Trinity. "This is bad. Really bad."

"Newsworthy?" If not, he couldn't ignore the professor's outburst. He couldn't afford to let the other members be swayed by his lies, especially since everyone was hungry.

"Yeah." Her gold eyes were huge in her face. "Unfortunately, I don't see this not being a headline."

"Jackson, go get Townsend and meet us..." He looked at Trinity.

"In the Warehouse District."

"Got it." The Guard started to walk away. "Which section?"

"Straight through to the back. You can't miss it. You'll see a group of terrified Servants standing in front of the building."

"Gruntshit." This had to be bad if Servants from that area were scared. They were usually the ones who terrified others.

CHAPTER 21: Hugh

Hugh sat in his private suite with Trinity, Jackson, Tim, Dr. Kalper and Townsend. He was exhausted—physically and mentally. They'd been at the Warehouse District well into the night, investigating and then arranging for the transportation of all the Servants to a vacant shelter until they could examine the bodies.

He struggled with the fact that someone could do something like that. He couldn't even imagine the pain the Servants had endured. They'd been butchered without any form of anesthesia or pain killers. They'd been tied or held down and cut open while alive and cognizant. Only the blood loss or the removal of a necessary organ had alleviated their suffering.

"This can't keep happening," said Kalper.

"Keep happening? It's happened before?" He'd never heard about anything like this, but something about it was familiar somehow.

"Yes." Kalper's face was pale and haggard. "It's been going on for years."

"Wait." His gaze darted to Townsend. "The Chapman."

"Wickerwood's estate," said Townsend.

"Yeah." He turned to the doctor. "Have you ever heard of The Chapman?"

Kalper frowned. "No. Is that a title or a person?"

"I'm not sure, but when I was undercover at Wickerwood's estate there were crates of illegal drugs and organs in a large walk-in cooler. Parson told me they were for The Chapman."

"I've never heard of him...or her," said Kalper. "Did you question this Parson about him?"

"A little, but when we raided Wickerwood's estate after the war, Parson promised to come to the Council Building and talk, but he never showed up." Trusting Parson had been a big mistake on his part. "And now, we can't find him. The only thing I know for sure is that Chapman has a Handler working for him."

"A Handler?" Kalper's eyes widened. "You'll need to be careful."

"Yeah, very. I still find it hard to believe that no one reported this when it happened before." Jason and the former Council had been corrupt, but he found it hard to believe that all of them would've ignored something like this.

"It was never on this scale. A body here and there. I believe it happened more often than that, but I can only speak of the bodies that I saw."

"Are you sure this is the same thing? I've seen a few reports over the years of mutilated Servants, Guards, Stockers and even Avions," said Townsend. "The articles always stated that the deaths were due to gang wars."

"That was the government covering up what was really going on." Kalper's voice raised. "Gangs have no reason to remove organs. Murder is enough for them."

"Not Producers or Grunts?" asked Trinity.

"No," said Kalper. "But it doesn't mean it didn't happen to the Grunts. We may just not have found the bodies."

"What about Producers?" she asked.

"I'm sorry." Kalper looked around the room before meeting her gaze. "There would've been no reason to harvest organs from Producers. Any parts wanted could be bought. Those who weren't butchered by the owners of the camps were sold at auctions."

"I'd like to see all your notes on those other cases." Hugh took her hand. The fate of Producers had been horrible, and he hated any reminder of what his kind had done to hers. "I can't believe no one ever looked into this. Everyone from the other classes was supposed to be accounted for and their whereabout known at all times."

"You know as well as the rest of us, that even though it was the law, it was seldom enforced," said Townsend.

"Yes, but I would've thought they'd have to investigate crimes like these. If for no other reason than to pretend that the law mattered."

"They did...sometimes...but never thoroughly"—Kalper glanced at the others in the room—"because no one cared."

"I can't believe I missed this," said Townsend. "You said you believe there were more than the ones you found. How many more?"

"I don't know," said Kalper.

"A guess. Two a week? Ten a week?"

"I really have no idea. I've seen"—Kalper paused—"about twelve of these deaths over the last eight years."

"Twelve." Trinity squeezed Hugh's hand. "That's twelve too many."

"Agreed." He leaned closer to her, finding comfort in her nearness. She was safe and he was going to make sure she stayed that way.

"Yes, but don't forget that those from the other classes used to disappear all the time," said Kalper. "Most Almightys assumed they ran away. They didn't report it because then they'd have to admit that they didn't monitor them. Instead, they purchased a new Guard or Servant."

"The shelters were supposed to track the purchases and keep track how many Guards and Servants were in each household," said Hugh.

"They do," said Townsend. "But the shelters don't communicate with one another, and no one monitors the purchases. An Almighty could rotate through all the shelters, taking one or two at each before making their way back around to the first shelter. No one would remember that they'd purchased a Guard or Servant several months ago, and if someone did, the Almighty could say the Servant or Guard died." He shrugged. "No one ever investigated those deaths either because, once again, no one cared."

He started to argue that he'd cared, but he hadn't. If his sister hadn't sent for him because she'd noticed that Tim was gone and then if Tim hadn't admitted that Trinity was his daughter, he wouldn't have cared about an escaped Producer or a wayward Servant. Guilt washed over him. Trinity squeezed his hand, her golden eyes sad but filled with understanding. She was too good for him. He didn't deserve her, but he wasn't letting her go.

"I suspect that there will be an increase in these kidnappings and killings due to the new rights given to the other classes," said Townsend.

"It certainly seems that way," said Dr. Kalper. "I've never seen a slaughter of this magnitude before. The most had been three. Sisters. The youngest had been nine." His voice cracked. "Unless you need me for something else"—he stood—"I'm going home. If no emergencies come up, I'll resume the autopsies tomorrow."

"How long before you've examined them all?" The sooner they knew what had been taken the sooner they could maybe have an idea of who had done this.

"Too long if I have to do it alone, but I'll talk to some doctors I know. We'll do our best to get them done quickly."

"I know you will," he said.

"Can we bury those you've finished?" asked Trinity.

"I should keep them until I'm done," said Kalper. "In case I need to reexamine them." He turned toward Hugh. "We'll need some sort of refrigeration."

"The storage rooms at the shelter were built to stay cool."

"I don't think cool is going to be good enough. Even if I get help, it's going to take time to examine them all."

"Jackson, round up as many portable solar generators as you can find as well as air conditioning units."

"Okay," said Jackson. "I'll check the hospitals. They should have some."

"I can talk to Ray," said Tim.

"Wait and see what Jackson can find first." He was already indebted to Ray for the Servant's help during the war. He didn't want to owe him anything else unless absolutely necessary.

"I'll gather a team to start digging the graves," said Trinity.

"We can't bury that many." He squeezed her hand. "We don't have the room in the city, and we can't haul them to the forest."

"We aren't going to toss them in the trash like—"

"Of course not." He paused, pretty sure she wouldn't like this either. "We'll cremate them." It was one of the reasons he'd chosen the shelter to house the bodies.

"Hugh..." She swallowed but nodded. "Okay. I understand...but I want their ashes."

"Of course."

"I'm going to set them free in the forest." She leaned against his shoulder. "I think they'll be happy there."

He put his arm around her, but his gut twisted. Just like she'd been happy in the forest. She didn't say it, but it was obvious that she wasn't happy in the city.

"I'll send you the reports on exactly which organs were removed when we're done," said Kalper.

"Thank you for your help." Hugh stood and shook Kalper's hand.

"Anything you need." The doctor's blue eyes were like ice. "I'll do whatever is necessary to stop these atrocities."

"And so will we. This is my number one issue, after the food shortage."

Kalper nodded and left.

He sat back down. "We need to collect the records from the shelters. We can tally the sales and speak to the Almightys who had more Servants and Guards than seem necessary for their businesses and homes."

"Why?" asked Townsend. "That won't mean they were involved. Their Guards and Servants could've been stolen, and if someone were moving from shelter to shelter, adopting to collect organs, they would've used a fake name."

"True." His mind scrambled. "We need to start the census now." He drummed his fingers on the arm of his chair.

Jackson nodded. "I'll send out some Guards—"

"Not just Guards. I want teams going. I want an Almighty, Guard, House Servant, Producer, Stocker, and Grunt in every team. Throw in an Avion if you can get one to show up."

"If we split them up, they can cover more ground," said Jackson.

"No. It's important for them to learn to work together. It'll help to remove their biases against each other." It'd worked for his army; it'd work for this.

"You think that's more important than getting a count of everyone, so we know if someone disappears?" Jackson obviously didn't agree with him.

"In the long run, yes. Plus, many of the groups have started to segregate themselves. It won't be safe for a Guard to go alone into a Producer establishment and vice versa."

"Okay, but it'll take longer." Jackson still wasn't a fan of this plan.

"I know." He ran his hand through his hair.

"I think a census is a good idea," said Townsend. "But how are you going to get them to comply."

"They all won't. I understand that, but if they want to vote, they need to comply."

"Vote?" Townsend's eyes widened a bit.

"Yes. What Meesus said at the hearing was right. The other classes will never get a fair shake even with a council made up of their peers, if the council is handpicked by an Almighty. So we're going to have an election."

"Do you really think that's wise?" Townsend's gaze darted around the room to the others.

"I do, or I wouldn't be setting it up."

"Would the election just be for the council?" asked Townsend.

"Nope." He squeezed Trinity's hand. "My position too."

"You can't do that." Townsend shook his head. "Someone like Conguise could get elected and then we're right back to where we were."

"Calm down. It won't be until after I put some checks and balances into place so that when someone like Conguise is eventually elected, they won't be able to do too much damage."

"Why Hugh?" asked Townsend.

He sighed. "No one should be in power forever. Not me. Not you. No one. We, as a coalition of groups, need to learn to govern ourselves. I'm going to set that up. Will there be mistakes? Of course, but even those mistakes will be better than having one person with all the power."

Townsend frowned, still not happy with this news.

"Besides the census, how do we fight this?" he asked.

"I'd be willing to bet that this market for...goods is either run by the same individual who organizes sex trafficking, or they know each other," said Tim.

"I agree. They have to at least be aware of each other," he said.

"In all my years looking into the trafficking of Servants," said Townsend. "I haven't been able to find out much. Just whispers and a few who are linked through businesses."

"You need a spy," said Jackson.

"But who?" asked Trinity. "They can't be associated with Hugh, but they have to be someone we trust."

Townsend looked at him.

"Hugh?" She stared at him, her golden eyes suspicious. She knew he was hiding something.

He needed to tell her. He should've told her before. Since he trusted everyone in this room there was no reason to wait any longer. "Jethro."

"Jethro?" Jackson almost choked on the word.

"Yeah. Wickerwood knows who delivered his Servants to him. He just refuses to name names. We need to convince Jethro to get close to Wickerwood."

"You're letting Wickerwood go free?" Jackson sounded appalled. "After what he did?"

"No." His eyes met the Guard's. "I'm not setting either of them free. Not yet anyway. I need Jethro to stay in prison until he gets the information we need."

"We just voted to release him. You're going to overrule that vote?" Jackson almost growled.

"No, I'm not, but paperwork can take time."

"This isn't right," argued Jackson.

"Neither is disemboweling almost a hundred Servants." He took a deep breath. "Jethro is the only shot we have to get information from Wickerwood."

"Oh. Gruntshit," groaned Jackson. "Kim and Martha aren't going to like this." He dropped his head onto the back of the couch.

"I don't think Jethro's going to be thrilled either." He wasn't looking forward to trying to convince his half-brother to work for him.

CHAPTER 22: Jethro

Jethro walked into the yard. As he'd expected, last night had been quiet. If Wickerwood had wanted him dead, he'd be dead.

He strolled across the courtyard, subtly sniffing for any hint of fear, anger or any indication of where an attack would originate, but the wind was strong today. The scent of smoke from the Mile of Fire obliterating everything else. He leaned against the fence, protecting his back.

Gap walked over to him. "You need to come with me."

"Why?" Right now, he wasn't too keen on going anywhere alone with Gap or Tonkers.

"Because I say so." Gap's hand moved to the club at his side.

His blood raced and his skin tingled. He should press the situation. Make the Guard attack him. He needed another fight, but he was pretty sure his new partner wouldn't appreciate him killing one of the prison Guards who worked with them. He clenched his fists, the cuts from yesterday already gone.

"Be a good boy and come on." Gap grabbed his arm, leading him across the yard and into the building.

Jethro's teeth almost ground to powder as he struggled not to shatter the Guard's face with his fist. As soon as they were inside and away from the eyes of the other prisoners, he yanked free. "What's this about?"

"You'll see." Gap grabbed his arm again.

Jethro trembled with the need to feel flesh tear. Gap turned down the hallway and escorted him toward the visitor section.

"Who's here to see me?" His mother wasn't due for another few days. He glared at the Guard. If something had happened to Indy, he'd kill them all—Tonkers, Gap, Miles, Wickerwood and anyone who tried to stop him.

"You'll see." The Guard opened the door to one of the private rooms and escorted Jethro inside.

An older male Almighty sat at the table. He wore a very expensive suit. Jethro would guess he was a businessman or a politician, but since this was prison, he had to be a lawyer. His hair was a dull iron gray, but his eyes were sharp.

"Jethro Remore." The other Almighty half-stood and held out his hand.

Jethro accepted the handshake. The other guy's grip was firm and his arm muscular. He was older but obviously kept in shape. Jethro sat on the chair across the table from his visitor.

"You can wait outside," said the older Almighty to Gap, and the Guard left without question.

Jethro glanced at his uncuffed hands and feet. This wasn't normal. Even when he was with his mom, they insisted on restraining him.

"We don't need cuffs, do we?" The other Almighty stared at Jethro's hands.

"No." He had no reason to attack this male, at least none that he knew about yet. However, if he changed his mind this guy would learn a hard lesson.

"Good. My name's William Vickers. You can call me Bill."

"You're an attorney, right?"

"Yes, sir. One of the best."

"Did my mom hire you? If she did, give her the money back. She doesn't have it to spare."

"I don't work for your mother." Bill smiled, showing perfect, white teeth.

"My last pro bono attorney didn't dress as well as you." Jethro leaned back, crossing his arms over his chest. A lawyer wasn't going to convince Hugh to release him, but at least this guy looked like he'd seen the inside of a courtroom.

"I'm sure he didn't." Bill laughed and then sobered. "I can tell you're wondering why I wanted to see you."

"No. I'm wondering how you think I can help you." A guy like this wouldn't do anything for anyone, unless he got something out of it. Jethro didn't have an issue with that. It was the way the world worked. He just had to decide if he were willing to make the deal.

Bill's eyes widened in surprise for a quick second before he said, "Why would you think that?"

Jethro leaned forward. "Because that's the only reason someone like you would come to see someone like me. You may say it's to help me, but it's really to help you." He leaned back. "Package it up however you want. I know the truth. So just hurry up and tell me why you're here. I'm missing my outside time."

The lawyer's eyes turned brittle.

"Don't get upset." He had no idea why others wanted to lie and pretend. He preferred to keep things simple. "I'm fine with a trade. If you can help me, then maybe I'll be willing to do whatever it is you need me to do."

"You're smarter than I'd expected." Bill smiled again, but this time it was veneer over anger. "That's good. It'll make things easier."

"Now that we've sized each other up, do you want to get to the point?" He may as well push the other male. He needed to know if it made the guy attack or flee.

The lawyer stared at him for a long moment. "Direct, aren't you?"

"No reason not to be."

"What would you say if I told you that I could get you out of here?"

"Heard that before, but I'll play. How are you going to do what no one else has been able to? Hugh, my loving brother, wants me to stay right here."

"Yes, but even Hugh has to follow some of the laws." Bill tapped the folder on the table in front of him. "But even more important than the law, he needs to do what his constituents want."

"And what do they want?" He was definitely listening.

"According to these signed affidavits, many of them want you set free." Bill opened the folder. "You have a lot of friends in all sections of society." His eyes met Jethro's. "In that, you are similar to your brother."

Jethro grabbed the folder. It was filled with letters, some from his family and friends, but others were from Townsend and his family and many of the Guards who he'd served with in the war. His throat tightened. They'd risked a lot by signing these. "Has Hugh seen them?"

"Nope." Bill shook his head. "I went and collected them myself." He grinned. "Well, I sent my employees to do it."

Jethro closed the folder and slid it back to the lawyer. "It's not going to work. Hugh made it very clear the other day that he intends on keeping me in here. Probably until I die or get killed."

"He'll bow to the pressure of what society wants. All I have to do is make these public."

"He'll drag his feet."

"I don't think so. Hugh is a political animal. He's walking a tightrope, trying to keep both sides happy. This is an easy win for him, releasing you makes everyone happy."

"What's in it for you?" He wanted to believe that this would work, but one thing he knew was that nothing in life was free.

"Since we're being direct, that is the question, isn't it?" Bill's grin was nothing but gleaming white falseness.

Jethro waited, a sense of dread filling him. This male reminded him of Jason—all smiles and favors paid for with pieces of his soul.

"I have a job for you once you're free."

"Doing what?" He didn't even try to hide the disgust in his tone.

"Fighting."

"Fighting who?" He had no interest in fighting for the Protective Services again.

"Whoever challenges you."

"I don't understand." But the lawyer did have his full attention.

"There's a circuit, so to speak, of fights and fighters." Bill leaned back. "You'll be great."

"Who are these fighters?" He'd heard about the underground fighting rings; he just hadn't expected to participate.

"All sorts of different folks."

"Almightys?" He already knew that answer. Almightys ran the fights. They didn't participate.

"You'll be the first."

"And you'll make a fortune off that." Everyone knew Almightys couldn't win in a fight against Servants or Guards. He'd be a ringer. The important question was who'd told the lawyer about him?

"We both will." Bill leaned forward. "You'll be rich."

"What percentage of the winnings do I get?"

"Ten."

"I don't think so." He'd love to beat the crap out of anyone and everyone, but he wasn't going to make this guy rich by doing it.

"Ten percent may not sound like much, but we'll pay all your expenses and you'll be out of jail."

"I'm fine in here." He stood.

"Twenty percent."

Jethro shook his head. He wouldn't mind fighting for a while. It soothed him, but he was done being used by rich, powerful Almightys.

"Sit down. I can offer you more."

Jethro twitched at the command but sat back down. Someone had told this lawyer about him. It might help to find out who.

"I know that you have certain...proclivities." Bill leaned forward, lowering his voice. "Things that were hard to find before are almost impossible now."

"What have you heard about me?" A tingle danced down his spine and his fists clenched on his lap. He was pretty sure those whispers were lies.

"I've done my research. I know you received a certain...gift from Jason."

"I received no gift from Jason."

Bill's smile was almost a leer. "Don't try to hide this from me. Like I said, I always do my homework." It was a warning clear and simple.

"What gift do you think I received?" Jethro itched to reach across the table and show Bill how he handled threats.

"Tee."

Jethro laughed to hide his agitation. If Bill tried to drag Tee into this, he'd kill the other Almighty right here in this room. "She wasn't a gift. I paid for her."

Bill stared at him a moment and then laughed. "Jason did have a tendency to overstate his generosity."

"If he said he gave her to me, then he certainly did in this case." He'd paid with his freedom to choose his own mate.

"I hear this Tee is living with your mother."

Jethro's eyes met his and held. Bill was in very dangerous territory by mentioning both his mother and Tee.

Bill squirmed under his scrutiny. "I imagine that will make your...situation with her a little difficult."

"There is no situation with her."

"Of course. How could there be with her at your mother's house and you in here? When you're released will she live with you again?"

"What business is it of yours?"

"It isn't. I just wanted to let you know that the relationship between you and young Tee is a little more difficult now than it had been in the past. Everyone is watching for things like that, and if you like your freedom, you'll have to be more circumspect. A young female Servant living with a single male...You should get married. No one thinks twice about young female Servants in a home with a wife."

"I have no intention of doing that anytime soon." He'd have to break that news to Stella when he was released. Even though she was still writing to him on a regular basis, he was sure she'd be relieved. A former soldier as a future husband had been distasteful enough to her, but now that he'd added prisoner to his resume, she must be ready to faint every time she heard his name.

"You're engaged, aren't you? Jason's granddaughter, right? She'd be perfect for you. She was raised to expect certain...appetites to be met elsewhere."

"I told you. I won't be marrying anytime soon."

"Ah. Of course. Jason is dead. That contract is void. Doesn't matter. I can help you disguise your relationship with Tee."

"Like I said"—Jethro leaned forward, trying to make this as clear as possible—"there is no relationship between us."

"Of course." The lawyer's eyes sparkled. "You were together for some time. Same dinner every night, so to speak." Bill's grin was sly. "I can help you find a new dish. Perhaps one a little fresher. Dinner stales so quickly."

That was all he needed, another young Servant with whom to pretend to have sex. "I think that this time, I'll explore my options by myself."

"Even better. I can help with that too."

"You sure are a helpful guy." He wanted to smash the lawyer's skull between his hands. Vickers was as vile as Jason had been. He should kill the lawyer and remove one pervert from the world. "Thirty percent."

"Twenty." The lawyer smiled again, but this one was genuine, a meeting of like minds and comradeship.

He didn't try and hide the gleam in his eyes. The lawyer would misunderstand and think that the anticipation in his gaze was for the young females when in reality he'd caught the scent of his prey. "Thirty or no deal." He leaned back. "Jail isn't so bad, and no matter what he said, I'm sure Hugh will let me out eventually. I have faith in my mother's badgering skills."

"Thirty it is." Bill held out his hand.

Jethro hesitated. "One more thing. I'll only fight two weeks a month. I need downtime. Time to recoup or I won't be my best."

The lawyer's eyes narrowed but he said, "Deal."

"Great. When do I get out?"

"I'll go see Hugh today. You'll be out before the sun sets."

CHAPTER 23: Jethro

Jethro paced in his cell, wanting to rip through the walls with his hands, or better yet, he'd tear Bill Vickers apart piece by piece. It'd been two days since their meeting, and he was still locked up. He should've taken his serum days ago, but he'd waited to be released. It was a good thing because the last two days had been nothing but fights. Each group had targeted him again and again. He wasn't getting any protection from the prison Guards, not even Tonkers. Apparently, Wickerwood hadn't wanted him dead...yet.

He had to figure out a way to get the gangs to leave him alone because he really needed to take his serum. The thought of it already made his skin crawl. If he waited any longer, he wouldn't take it, and then he'd lose the use of his legs. The prisoners would kill him slowly if that happened. They enjoyed playing with the weak.

The prison Guards walked onto the block. It was time to go into the yard. His muscles quivered in anticipation of the coming fight. Today, he wasn't waiting for someone to attack him. It was time to go on the offensive. If he went after the bosses, it might make them think twice about sending their gang to ambush him, and that might buy him the time he needed.

"Come with me." A prison Guard opened the cell door.

Jethro followed him down the hallway, another Guard behind them. They were in charge, in power. He'd love to knock that confidence down their throats. He could take them both. Snap their necks in an instant. His hands fisted at his sides. He really, really needed to release some steam because it was the only way he was going to fit in his skin, but these two were decent guys. They never harassed the prisoners. They just did their jobs. He had no good reason to attack them, except for the one word that echoed through his head—enemy.

The Guard in front turned down the hallway that led to the visiting rooms.

"Visitors again? I'm a popular guy lately." If it was Vickers, he'd better be ready to release him, or Jethro would probably beat the shit out of the lawyer.

"Apparently, very popular," said the Guard as he opened the door to one of the rooms.

He moved inside and sat at the table. He fidgeted in his seat. He needed to run, swim, fight. Something. One of the Guards bent to hook his feet into the restraints attached to the table when the door opened.

"Leave us." Hugh strode in, taking the seat across from him.

"As soon as we get him locked in, sir," said the Guard.

"We don't need that, do we?" Hugh looked at him, his brow raising.

"Of course not." His dear brother wasn't happy. Jethro wanted to grin right in the pompous ass's face but instead he lowered his head. If he continued to look at the other Almighty, he'd attack. On a good day, everything about Hugh got under his skin, and today was far from good.

"You heard him. We're fine. You can go," said Hugh.

"But...but I—" stammered the Guard.

"Leave us," ordered Hugh.

The Guard left and Jethro raised his head, his eyes meeting Hugh's. His enemy was here. Alone. Vulnerable. He'd love to take his time, killing Hugh slowly, but the Guards wouldn't be too far away. He'd have to be quick.

"I have an offer for you."

"An offer? Shouldn't you be discussing this with my lawyer?"

"Your lawyer?"

"Yeah. My lawyer." If he put his fist through Hugh's face, would it make him look less surprised or more? He glanced at the door across the room. "Where is he anyway?"

"I don't know anything about your lawyer."

"Vickers is going to get me out of here." He refused to let Hugh see his disappointment that the lawyer hadn't already spoken to him.

"Out of jail? No." Hugh frowned. "I need you to stay in here for this job. Not forever. Just for a little longer."

"Stay here. In prison." Jethro's desire to punch the other Almighty in the face over and over again was almost palpable. Hugh's nose would look better flat anyway.

"Yes. I need you to get close to Wickerwood. He's involved..."

Jethro saw Hugh's lips move, but he didn't hear anything, as waves of hatred surged through him. This male was the reason he was in prison. This male had Trinity. She was his mate, not Hugh's. His instincts screamed for him to attack. They were alone. The Guards were outside the door—close but not close enough to stop him. He could kill the other Almighty in a flash.

"Are you listening to me?" Hugh leaned closer.

Jethro could smell the anger on the other Almighty, and it made his blood roar through his veins. This was his competition, his enemy. It'd only take a slight movement to send Hugh's face into the table and his brains out his ears.

"The government that I envision is not in place yet. I'm still the final law. I can keep you here forever. So I suggest you pay attention." Hugh leaned back, some of his anger dissipating. "I know staying here even a little longer isn't ideal but..."

Jethro lowered his head, trying not to look at the other Almighty. His arms shook as he struggled not to move, not to attack. Hugh deserved whatever he got. He was the reason Jethro was in here, instead of being in the yard beating some Guard, Almighty or Servant to a pulp. It was Hugh's fault that he was still inside the prison instead of at home with a female or two in his bed—Servants, long and lean with claws.

"Are you okay?" Hugh leaned closer again. "Are your injuries from before bothering you? Do you need to see a doctor?"

He started to reply, but the words wouldn't form in his mouth. He shook his head, trying to clear the sound of his blood pounding through his ears, but all he could think about was kissing Servants like Trinity but not her. She'd never be in his bed because she was with Hugh.

"Are you answering my first question or second or third? I can't tell by the head shake." Hugh's light tone, sobered. "Seriously. Are you okay?"

Jethro raised his head, letting his enemy see his hatred and rage. Hugh immediately leaned as far back in his chair as possible, his concern quickly turning to fear. Jethro inhaled the sweet scent. He fed on fear. It made his enemy weak.

"Jethro, what's wrong?" The fear was still there, but instead of growing stronger, it became weaker as Hugh ignored his instincts.

It was a mistake. Jethro started to reach for him but stopped. Those eyes looked just like his mother's...filled with concern. He swallowed. "I...need..." He couldn't tell Hugh about the serum, but he had to take it. Now. Before he did something he'd regret. "Sick. Need..."

"Get a doctor. Quick!" Hugh stood, yelling for the Guards.

"No. No doctor." Jethro shook his head, pushing himself to his feet.

The two Guards charged into the room. He couldn't let them take him to the infirmary. His shot was in his cell. If he didn't get it, he'd tear them all apart. He glared at Hugh. This was his fault.

"Calm down," said one of the Guards.

"Jethro, it's okay. Help is coming." Hugh stepped toward him.

"Stay back." The warning rumbled from deep inside his chest. He'd kill Hugh if he got any closer. His blood called for him to do it now. He had to get away. He shoved the closest Guard, sending him flying into the wall, and raced toward the door.

"Wait!" shouted Hugh.

He couldn't do that. He flew out of the room. The other Guard and Hugh followed him, but he was too fast for them. He ran, leaving the visiting area before they made it even halfway down the hallway. Another prison Guard stepped into his path. He didn't bother to slow down. He plowed into the Guard, lifting him up and over his shoulder as if the burly male weighed as much as a dried stick. The Guard toppled to the floor behind him. Jethro's instincts screamed for him to stop and finish the job. It'd only take a few seconds. Injured enemies could still attack, but dead ones would never bother him again. He forced himself to keep moving, killing that Guard wouldn't fix anything. His answer waited in his cell. He raced around a corner and then another until he was on his block. It was empty. Everyone was in the yard.

He flew into his cell, digging through his bedding. He had to hurry. Their footsteps sounded heavier. They were getting closer. His fingers grasped the syringe, pulling it from the crevice in his mattress and plunging it into his arm. The liquid burned cold and his body spasmed, betrayed by him once again. He shoved the needle back into its hiding spot and collapsed on the floor as the medicine took control, calming him and making the harsh blacks and whites of the world a lovely shade of grays and blues.

He smiled, his eyes drifting closed. Why had he fought this? It was beautiful. Peaceful. A sharp pain, like a knife so cold it burned hot, sliced through his gut. Pain he was used to, but this was different. Something was wrong. He crawled to the toilet, his stomach twisting and heaving. His breakfast burned up his throat, splashing into the bowl, but it didn't do any good. The pain rolled through him, his body spasming as it tried to expel the poison, but it was in his blood not his stomach. He clung to the toilet, staring at his arm where he'd injected himself. He could tear his skin with his teeth and bleed it out.

"Get a doctor, quick," shouted Hugh as he stormed into the cell and dropped to the floor, awkwardly patting Jethro's back. "Help is coming. It's going to be okay."

He rested his head on the toilet, the cool of the rim soothing his heated flesh. Hugh might try, but he really didn't think anyone could help him now, except maybe Professor Conguise.

CHAPTER 24: Jethro

When Jethro woke his fever was gone, and so was the anger in his blood. The room was white and clean. It was some kind of hospital, but it was too nice to be the infirmary.

"You're awake," said a female.

He turned his head and a female Guard, probably in her early thirties, stood in the doorway, smiling at him. She was pretty. This definitely wasn't the infirmary.

"Where?" His voice cracked from disuse and lack of water.

She moved to his bed and lifted his head as she held a glass to his lips. He took a small sip. The first drop made his thirst hit him like a carriage. He grabbed the cup, gulping the water.

"Slow down." She tried to pull the glass away, but he couldn't let that happen. He needed this water like he needed air. He wrapped his hand around hers, holding it in place.

"Ouch." She tugged. "Let me go." A hint of panic crept into her tone.

His body clamored for him to snatch the glass or break her hand, anything to keep the water, but instead he let her, and the glass go, his arm shaking. "Sorry," he mumbled. He wasn't sure if the apology was for hurting her or for letting her go.

"It's okay." She stepped away, but the friendliness from before was gone. She feared him now. It was in her voice and in the air. "I'll get the doctor."

He started to ask her again where he was, but he'd lost his chance to befriend her. He'd get nothing from her unless he forced it. She left the room, and he closed his eyes, listening and trying to prepare for whatever came next.

The door opened a few moments later. Sure and steady footsteps headed toward him. He opened his eyes. A middle-aged male Almighty stared down at him.

"How are you feeling? I'm Dr. Kalper." There was no fear or hesitation in the doctor's voice. "I was getting a bit worried about you." He prepared a needle.

"What's that?" He didn't want any more medication.

"I need a bit of your blood." The doctor tied a band around Jethro's arm.

"Why?" He studied the Almighty. The male didn't seem to be aggressive.

"To figure out what poison they used on you."

"Poison?" He grasped the doctor's hand before the man could stick him with the needle. No one had poisoned him, but it was better that the doctor believed that.

"That's what we think." The doctor's eyes were sad as he gently removed Jethro's fingers before sticking the needle in his arm.

"Where am I?"

"My home office." Kalper capped the needle and put a small cloth on the wound, pushing Jethro's arm up to stop the bleeding.

"Why am I here?"

"Hugh was very concerned." The doctor smiled. "He's a good male. He lets his anger get in the way sometimes...but who doesn't?"

He didn't want to admit it, but Hugh *was* a good male. He understood why Hugh was angry with him. He was angry with Hugh for the same reason. Hugh had touched Trinity. His lips turned up in a sneer. The other male touched her on a regular basis. He gritted his teeth. He had to stop thinking about that.

"I know you don't see it now, but Hugh is on your side. You should mend fences, so to speak."

"How long before I go back to prison?" He closed his eyes. He didn't want to talk about Hugh.

"You're free." Kalper patted his shoulder.

"Free?" He opened his eyes and sat up, swaying a bit as the room spun.

"You need to rest for a little longer." Kalper gently pushed him back down. "Eat something. You've been unconscious for almost five days."

The breath left his body in a whoosh. Five days. He'd never slept that long before. He couldn't be late taking his serum again.

"We weren't sure you'd make it. By the time Hugh got you here, you were burning with a fever. I've never seen anyone that hot before."

The door opened and the nurse came in with a tray of food—soup and bread. His stomach rumbled.

"You're in for a treat," said Kalper. "Pepper is an excellent cook."

"Thank you, doctor." She smiled, but it was guarded as her gaze darted toward him. She put the tray on the table next to his bed.

He grabbed the bread, frowning when she jumped. If he wanted to hurt her, he would've done so already. The warm, yeasty smell of the bread teased his nose. He took a huge bite. He was so hungry. He dropped the bread and picked up the bowl, tipping it to his lips.

"Easy." Kalper touched his arm. "Make sure you can keep it down. It's been days since you've eaten."

"He has visitors." Pepper gave him a disgusted look as she stepped away.

"Hugh?" asked Kalper.

"No. His sister and her mate." She headed for the door. "Shall I send them in?"

"Are you ready for visitors?" asked Kalper.

He paused from eating for a second. He hadn't seen anyone but Indy and his mother in months. "Yeah. I'd like that." His throat closed up with emotion as he waited. It'd been so long but he was finally, truly free.

CHAPTER 25: Jethro

Jethro laughed as Kim finished another story about Tee and their mother. It seemed the little House Servant wasn't quite ready to conform to his mother's mothering. He loved his mom, but he knew firsthand how much she could smother with her love.

If it hadn't been for his dad, he never would've had any freedom once he'd hurt himself and had ended up in the wheelchair. His smile slipped from his face. His father hadn't been perfect, but he hadn't deserved to die like that. Now that he was free, when the serum ran thin in his blood, he should hunt down Mirra and kill her—slowly. When she'd taken her last breath, he'd skin her and wear her as a cloak. Trinity would hate him, but what did that matter? She was with Hugh now. *But was she happy?* He could make her happy. They were alike. Wild. Creatures of the forest.

"I'm so glad you're okay"—Kim's blue eyes filled with tears—"and free." She took Jackson's hand. "We were getting really worried that you'd never wake up."

"Have you been stopping by every day?" His chest tightened, making it hard to breathe. It'd been so long since he'd felt the love of family.

"Of course." Kim took his hand and squeezed it. "So has Mom." She hesitated. "And Hugh." His disgust must've shown on his face because she continued, "You need to get over your dislike of him. It makes no sense."

"He kept me in prison for no reason."

"You tried to kill him." Jackson touched his stomach where Jethro had accidentally stabbed him instead of Hugh. "I think that counts as something."

"I'm sorry that I hurt you, but we both know that had nothing to do with why he kept me in prison." He glanced away and then back at them. He hated this weakness in himself, but he had to ask. "Has she visited?" His heart slowed as he waited for one of them to speak, even though by the pity on their faces he already knew the answer.

"No." Kim's voice was soft. "She's with Hugh now. You know that. You have to let it go."

"I have." He was trying. "I thought..." He shrugged. "I thought we were still friends. That's all." He'd just wanted a small bit of hope, but apparently, that was gone too.

"You need to move on," said Jackson.

"Like you did?" He stared at where the Guard clasped Kim's hand.

"He did," said Kim. "But I didn't. That's why it's different. Trinity is with Hugh."

"You were with Davies."

"I was never really with him. Not like that." She leaned against Jackson. "I never loved Davies." Her eyes filled with pity. "Trinity loves Hugh. You have to accept that."

She'd loved him once too. Part of him screamed that he could make her love him again. He could fight Hugh and win, but the part of him that was in control now, didn't want to fight. His sister was right. He'd lost Trinity to Hugh. It was over and he needed to move on.

CHAPTER 26: Jethro

Jethro stood at the door to his mom's house, his heart racing. He'd finally convinced Kalper that he was well enough to leave. All he'd wanted was to go home. It was what he'd dreamed about in prison, but now that he was here, he had no idea what to do.

So much had happened in this house. Memories of his childhood—happy and sad—surged through him. He'd had his family, but he'd been friendless and lonely until he'd met Trinity. His world had changed that fall. He'd lost his father, but he'd gained the use of his legs. He wanted to go back in time, to see his dad again, but no matter how much he wanted it, that wasn't possible. The only way was always forward. He opened the door and walked into his childhood home.

"Jethro!" His mom rushed into the room, wrapping her arms around him. "You weren't supposed to be here until tomorrow."

"Are you complaining?" His legs shook as he sank into her embrace. Through all the changes, she'd remained his constant. His arms tightened around her, and he couldn't stop the tears as her warmth and love filled him.

"You're home, my baby boy. You're finally home." Her grip tightened almost painfully before she pulled away, smiling through her tears. "Let's get you something to eat."

"Jethro! I missed you." Tee stood near the refrigerator, holding a casserole dish. She'd gained some weight and she looked happy. She took a step toward him but stopped as her eyes darted to his mother. "I mean. I'm glad you're home." She glanced away, her cheeks flushing a bit.

"Please set another place at the table." Mom walked over to the refrigerator and pulled out a jug of iced tea. "Sit. We have a big dinner prepared for tomorrow."

"You don't need to do anything special." They'd never been rich, but their refrigerator had never been that empty.

"Nonsense." Mom filled a glass with tea and put it on the table. "You're home. You're safe. We're going to celebrate."

"Jethro!" Kim hurried into the kitchen and hugged him, Jackson trailing behind her.

Tee put the casserole dish on the table.

"I thought Dr. Kalper was releasing you tomorrow." Kim grabbed a loaf of bread and dropped it next to the dish of food before pulling out a chair and sitting.

"I persuaded him to let me leave a day early." He glanced around the table. "It looks good."

"Please." Kim nudged his shoulder. "We all know what you think about a meat-free dish."

"Kim," Mom chided. "That was before. Things are different now."

"Seriously"—he looked at his sister—"it all looks better than you know." He wasn't lying, but he also wasn't talking about the food. He picked up the casserole and ladled a small amount into his bowl, noticing that it was mostly broth. He passed the dish to Tee who'd taken the chair on his other side.

"Thank you." She handed it to his mother, not taking any.

"What's the matter? You don't like it?" he asked.

"It's good, but I'm not very hungry." She wrinkled her nose.

"Nonsense." Mom put some in Tee's dish. "You need to eat." She put a bit in her bowl before passing it to Jackson.

"I'll get a job. Soon." He took a bite of his food. The flavor was okay...for vegetables.

"It won't matter." Kim put some in her dish. "Jackson has tried but there's no food to buy." Her hand drifted to her stomach.

"No food?" His eyes went to his sister's abdomen. Her belly was rather large for someone who'd been eating like this for months.

"No. No food in the stores." Jackson's gaze was concerned as it went to Kim's stomach. "Producers are, of course, no longer...meat but—"

"And they shouldn't be." Kim's voice held a hint of steel that made it clear, arguing wasn't allowed on this topic.

"I wasn't saying they should be," said Jackson.

"Sorry. I know you didn't mean Producers should be food." Kim's fingers caressed her stomach. "I'm just cranky." She took his hand. "The problem is that since the Producers have left the camps, there's no one to grow the food either."

"Hu..." Jackson cleared his throat. "We've gotten some Guards, Servants and Grunts to move into the camps, but they know nothing about farming. Trin..." He cleared his throat again. "We're trying to train them but there's barely any food coming into the city." He touched her stomach. "Something has to change."

"Is there...What's going on?" Jethro stared at the two of them. He really didn't have to ask. He knew they were together as mates. The rest was inevitable.

"We've started our own small garden in the backyard," said Mom, looking around the table nervously.

"Kim." Jackson squeezed her hand. "I think we should tell him."

She turned toward Jethro, her eyes glowing with more happiness than Jethro had seen in years. "We're going to have a baby."

His heart twisted. It'd be a mix breed. Even with the new laws their baby's life would be filled with hatred and prejudice.

"I knew you wouldn't be happy. You're so much like Dad." Kim's eyes hardened.

"It's not that." He loved his father, but he'd never agreed with Dad about the way the other classes were treated. "I'm happy for you." He glanced at Jackson. "Both of you."

"But..." Kim gave him that older sister look that still made him bristle.

"But nothing." There was no reason to tell her how hard this was going to make things. She wasn't stupid. "I'm just surprised. I've been gone a long time." He smiled. "I am happy for both of you."

"Thank you." Kim leaned against Jackson. "We know this won't be easy, but together we'll make it work."

"We will." Jackson's face filled with so much love that Jethro wanted to puke.

"So back to the food issue." Any topic was better than watching the two of them simper at each other. "There has to be food somewhere. I'm sure the rich aren't going hungry." Everything had a price in this world.

"I'm sure not, but we're far from rich," said Kim. "Even further than before the war."

It made sense. They no longer had Producer camps to bring in money.

"But we're doing fine," said Mom.

"I'll start looking for a job today." He took another bite of his food. It was better than what he'd had in jail.

"Speaking of that"—Mom stood—"an Almighty stopped by a few days ago." She walked to the counter and dug through some papers. She grabbed a letter and handed it to him as she sat back down. "He said this was for you. He wore a very expensive suit."

Jethro opened the envelope. It was from Vickers.

"Is it a friend of yours from college?" asked Mom.

"No." Vickers wasn't a friend. "It's from the lawyer who was going to help me get out of jail, but Hugh beat him to it." Which meant he didn't need to have anything to do with Vickers. He didn't want to fight, not now that the serum had cooled his blood. He'd do whatever he had to do to help feed his family, but he'd do that without going into business with Vickers.

CHAPTER 27: Jackson

Jackson sat at the kitchen table, praying to Araldo that this meeting between Hugh and Jethro went well, or Kim would have his hide. He wasn't thrilled with Hugh's plan, but it really was the best chance they had of stopping this killer.

Jethro fidgeted in his seat. The kid seemed unable to sit still, a nervous energy coursing through him. Since his release from prison, besides when he went looking for a job, Jethro had been in the woods. It was normal...or at least not that odd. Jethro had always loved the outdoors and being locked up for months must've been a complete nightmare for him.

A knock sounded on the door.

"I'll get it."

"If you have to." Jethro shifted on his chair, his gaze going to the window where the moonlight made the damp grass sparkle.

He walked across the house and opened the door. "Hey."

"Is everything...ready?" Hugh stood in the doorway, looking a bit uneasy.

"As much as it can be." This meeting wasn't going to be easy on any of them. "This way." He turned and walked through the living room.

"Jethro." Hugh nodded slightly as he entered the kitchen.

Jethro glanced at them and then turned back toward the window, dismissing Hugh.

"Jethro, you agreed to this meeting. Stop being a Grunt's ass." Jackson shot Hugh a look, hoping the other male would understand that Jethro was still pissed—about the length of his imprisonment but more because he'd lost Trinity. If Hugh let his jealousy take over, it wouldn't do anyone any good.

"I agreed to meet because I figured"—Jethro glanced at Hugh again—"I'd end up back in jail if I didn't."

"That won't happen," said Hugh.

"Like I'm supposed to believe you." Jethro spun on his chair, facing them. "Why did you let me out anyway? And don't tell me it was because I was sick."

Jackson braced himself when Hugh's eyes gleamed.

"I let you out because the Council voted for your release."

"I'm surprised you didn't overrule it."

"I may not agree with the decision, but I'm not above the law. No one is, not anymore."

"Sure. Whatever you say." Jethro looked back out the window.

"Look. I don't want to be here either and—"

"Oh, poor Hugh." Jethro turned toward them again. "It's so unfair when you have to do something you don't want to do...like stay in jail for no reason."

"I had my reasons for keeping you there."

"You're right. You did. How is Trinity anyway? Has she tired of you yet?"

"Jethro, stop." If Jackson didn't do something this situation would explode.

"No. If he wants to waste time by sending childish insults let him." Hugh sat at the table. "It's exactly what I expected from someone like him."

"Someone like me?" Jethro's face hardened with anger.

"Calm down." Jackson pulled out the chair between them and sat. "I don't want to get stabbed again."

"Don't worry. I won't miss a second time." Jethro glared at Hugh.

"I'm going to need more than that"—Jackson touched his side—"because your soon-to-be nephew or niece would like their father around."

"Gruntshit." Jethro leaned back on his chair, grinning slightly at Jackson. "Kim will kill me if I stab you again."

"I'll kill you," mumbled Jackson. "That hurt like a—"

"We need your help," interrupted Hugh.

Jackson held back a smirk. When he wanted to be Hugh was the consummate politician. This was the perfect time to approach Jethro for a favor. The kid was feeling familial bonds.

"My help?" Jethro's eyes flew to Hugh, obviously, not expecting that. "I'm not helping you with anything...inside or outside of jail."

"Come with me before you make that decision." Hugh stood.

"I don't need to go anywhere."

"I'll admit that I don't think much of you, but I did think you were the kind of male who protected those weaker than him," said Hugh.

"I am."

"Apparently not if it means working with someone you hate." Hugh walked to the kitchen door and paused. "Since your mind is made up, you have no reason not to come with me...unless you're scared you might change it." He strode out of the room.

Jethro didn't move.

"I'd never admit it to him"—Jackson stood—"but even though he can be an ass, I'd follow him anywhere." He walked out of the kitchen and out of the house, climbing into the carriage and sitting next to Hugh.

"Do you think he's coming?"

"Yeah." But he wasn't sure. The boy he'd known would be here, but Jackson was still getting to know the man Jethro had become. "He's a good guy, and he has to be curious about what you said."

"I hope so. On both counts."

"Give him a break. He's been through a lot. I still don't think we have to do it this way. No one needs to see what we've seen."

"Trust me. He does. You saw him in there. He hates me." Hugh stared out the window toward the house. "It's understandable, but he's not going to agree to do anything for me. Unless—"

"Unless something else is more important than his anger." Jackson refused to believe that these two Almightys, who he respected and were his friends, would hate each other forever.

"I don't think he's coming." Hugh continued to stare at the house.

"Give him another minute. He's young and angry. He wants to make you wait. Piss you off if possible."

Jethro stepped out of the house, closing the door with a slam.

"This ought to be pleasant." Hugh leaned back against the seat.

"Can you blame him?" Jackson smirked. "You kept him in prison longer than Conguise."

Hugh looked at him out of the corner of his eyes. "You forgot to mention the real reason for the animosity."

Jethro climbed into the carriage and sat. "I'm only here because if Jackson is involved then Kim knows about this too. I don't want to listen to her nag at me for not going."

"Your reason doesn't matter to me." Hugh stuck his head out of the window and gave the Grunt directions before leaning back against the seat as the carriage started moving. "I'm just glad you're here."

Jackson was surprised. That had actually been pleasant. They were both just angry. They didn't really hate each other.

"Yeah. Don't be. I'm not going to change my mind about helping you, no matter what. I'd sit and eat cookies, while you gasped your last breath."

Jackson groaned. He should've known it wouldn't be that simple.

"Cookies?" Hugh laughed. "Just like the boy you are. I'd toast you on your way out." He pretended to raise a glass. "Good riddance."

"The one good thing about me dying is that I won't have to see your face anymore." Jethro smirked.

"Perfect for both of us." Hugh grinned.

"Yeah, too bad for you that I don't plan on dying anytime soon. You should go ahead and do it though. That way we still won't have to see each other."

"I guess it's too bad for both of us then." Hugh sobered as the Grunt turned into the parking lot of the large crematory. "They weren't so lucky." He hopped out of the carriage.

"Why are we here?" Jethro's face seemed whiter in the shadows as he stared at the square brick building, his nose quivering as if taking in the scent.

"Follow me." Jackson didn't even want to think about why Jethro was sniffing like a Guard or Servant. The odor of decay wasn't strong enough out here for an Almighty's nose to catch.

He climbed out of the carriage, Jethro behind him as they walked to the door. Kalper had finished the autopsies yesterday. The cremations would start tomorrow. That's why this meeting had to be tonight.

"I don't know if you're aware of items sold on the black market." Hugh pulled a set of keys from his pocket and opened the door.

"Like what?" Jethro rolled his eyes. "Stolen jewelry and drugs."

"Not exactly." Hugh stepped inside, turning on the light.

Jackson braced himself, wanting to give the kid some warning, but that time had passed. Hugh was right. They needed Jethro's help and seeing this would ensure they'd get it. He followed Hugh into the room.

The scent of death filled his head—blood and decay, dank and strong. Bodies were piled against the walls, stacked three to five high. All covered with sheets. The cloth eerily white in the dim light of the room.

Hugh walked to one group and pulled off a cover, unveiling the body of a young female House Servant. She was almost as white as the sheet. Her eyes, open and chalky, stared at nothing. Her torso had been torn so badly that they hadn't been able to sew it back together.

"What happened to her?" Jethro hadn't moved from the doorway.

"To them." Hugh removed another sheet and then another, showcasing similar wounds on similar bodies. All young. All females. All Servants and all ripped apart.

Jethro paled and Jackson instinctively moved closer, trying to give him comfort by his presence. He'd felt an overwhelming feeling of hopelessness and fear when he'd first seen the bodies. A monster prowled their streets, preying on the weak and vulnerable. They had to catch him, and the only way they'd succeed was by working together.

"Who did this?" Jethro's voice was harsh with anger. It seemed that Hugh's plan was working.

"We don't know. That's why we need your help," said Hugh.

"What do you need me to do?" Jethro stared at one of the females.

Jackson wanted to sigh in relief and pat the kid on his shoulder. Jethro was going to help. He never should've doubted it. He'd always been a kind boy. Even though he'd fought for the Protective Services and had done some questionable things, kindness and selflessness were in Jethro's genes.

Plus, this job would be the perfect distraction for him. Jethro could submerge himself in the underground and right the wrongs being done. Hopefully, it'd help him forget about all he'd lost.

Jethro's face was half-hidden by the shadows, but his eyes were hard and determined. This wasn't the boy he'd known. Jethro was an adult. He had been for quite some time, but Jackson hadn't wanted to see it because that meant that his feelings for Trinity weren't those of a child. If Jethro loved Trinity like Jackson loved Kim, the distance between them wouldn't matter. There'd be no peace for Jethro without her.

CHAPTER 28: Conguise

Once again, Conguise sat in the parlor of the whorehouse. He was almost growing accustomed to the tacky opulence of the décor. "I need your assistance with Stella. She's proving to be more stubborn about leaving her apartment than I'd expected."

He'd dropped whispers in all the right ears. The girl was now totally alone—ostracized from the little polite society that was left—and yet she hadn't once asked for help. Jethro had been released from prison. He couldn't have her clinging to him. The boy was softhearted enough to end up ensnared by her and that wouldn't do at all.

"What we need is for someone to scare our little Stella right out of her home," said Meesus.

"That would work." He studied the Servant. "But she mustn't be hurt."

"Of course not. She is an Almighty." Meesus' eyes gleamed with challenge.

Conguise didn't miss the sarcasm but nodded anyway. The other classes thought they were equals in this new world. Let them believe that, at least for now. Within time, the natural order of things would straighten out, but right now, he needed his revenge more than his pride.

"But how will we get our little Almighty to Hugh?" Meesus glided across the room. "She is engaged to Jethro, is she not?"

"I'll take care of that. All I need from you is to scare her. She cannot remain at her home. She must flee to me or to Jethro."

"How about both?"

"What?"

"Tell me when Jethro will be at your home, and I can make sure that she arrives there." She shrugged. "She'll flee to both of you."

"Yes. That'll work." He didn't want to admit it, but he was impressed. He stood. "I need this done as quickly as possible."

"Is tonight soon enough?" Her eyes were bright with amusement. "We can wrap her up and deliver her to your door."

He was not amused by her flippancy. They weren't friends; they were temporary allies. He'd received a letter from Jethro earlier that week. "Jethro will be at my home in two days. Make sure to drop her off near my property but not too close."

CHAPTER 29: Hugh

The next day, Hugh and the others sat in a meeting room in the Council Building. He hadn't wanted to invite Jethro to his and Trinity's personal suite. He glanced at the door. Ray was late as usual.

"So," said Townsend. "Since it seems we're going to be waiting awhile, let's go over some other items."

Hugh's eyes darted to Jethro. There was a lot that he wasn't ready to say in front of his half-brother.

Townsend pulled out his notebook, ignoring Hugh's glance. "There's been another disappearance in the Holstein area."

"That's a really bad part of town," said Jackson. "Servants and Guards disappear from there all the time."

"Yeah, but this one was carried away through the streets," said Townsend.

"The gangs are usually a little sneakier than that." Jackson turned toward Hugh. "Do you want us to send more troops to patrol?"

"Not yet."

"You can't keep ignoring this," said Townsend. "Someone—"

"Have you gone there and interviewed the residents? I'm not talking about the kids in the gangs on the streets but the business owners and others who are...more respectable and less prone to make up stories to—"

"I still don't think they'd make up a story like this." Townsend flipped through the pages. "There'd be so many things more believable than a creature that flies and carries Servants away in the middle of the night."

"Whoa." Jackson glanced around at the others. "You said carried through the street, not picked up by a giant bird."

"Because we don't think it's true." He hoped it wasn't.

"*You* don't," said Townsend.

"*You* actually, truly believe this?"

The reporter shrugged. "I think it warrants further investigation."

"I agree but later. We have more important things—"

"Important things like me." The door opened and Ray glided into the room with two large male Servants.

"They should wait outside." Hugh had to bite back a groan when he realized one of Ray's companions was The Victor. He hadn't seen the Servant since he'd ditched him at Wickerwood's estate.

"They stay with me." Ray smiled but it was the grin of a Tracker who was about to catch its prey.

He raised a brow. He was the ruler here, at least for the moment. He didn't mind when those close to him disobeyed or questioned his authority, but Ray was not one of them. Still, the Servant was there as a friend. "I think you'll prefer that this conversation remains private."

"And you still think that leaving them outside the door will accomplish that?" Ray laughed.

"It will in this room." He enjoyed watching Ray's smug expression turn curious. "I had it improved. Nothing said in here, spoken in a reasonable tone, will be discernable outside."

"Really?" Ray's brow wrinkled as his eyes gleamed with challenge.

"Yes. I understand and appreciate the similarities and the differences between the classes."

Jethro and Townsend looked at him. They hadn't been aware of the improvements. He'd used Jackson, Tim and Trinity to test. None of them had been able to hear a word from inside the room, even with their ears pressed against the door. All he needed now was a Tracker and Handler to test it, but they weren't quite as cooperative. It didn't really matter anyway because they all lived in the forest.

Even if one were to come into the city, he'd know about it before they got close enough to this room to hear anything.

"I guess we'll see." Ray tipped his head, and his escorts left the room, closing the door behind them. He sat, crossing one long, lean leg over the other. "So what do you want?"

"Straight to the point. I like that about you." The sooner they were done; the sooner Ray could leave. The Servant made him uneasy, especially since Ray and Meesus had a history.

"Time is for business and business means money." Ray exposed his claws and tapped them systematically across his thigh. "I like money."

"Then let's get to it." He leaned forward. "It has come to our attention that there is a market for...certain items that are not readily available."

Ray's face tensed a bit, but his fingers continued drumming against his leg.

"It has also come to our attention that a lot of your money is made in acquiring and moving these products." The Servant had supplied the Allied Classes with many items that had been difficult to obtain during the war. Hugh hoped Ray wasn't involved with gathering or distributing organs, but it made sense that if he wasn't he knew who was.

"Who's spreading that rumor?"

So Ray was going to play innocent. This wasn't going to be easy. He didn't have any leverage over the Servant.

"Ray, someone's killing and harvesting the organs of House Servants, young females mostly," said Trinity.

He didn't think that pleading with Ray's sense of decency would get them far, but Trinity was always hopefully naïve.

"These things have been happening for a very long time, my dear." Ray smiled sadly at her. "The world is a cruel place. I would've thought you'd learned that lesson by now."

"I was supposed to be food." Her eyes narrowed. "I know firsthand about the cruelty of our world."

Ray continued to stare at her for a long moment before he turned back toward Hugh. "I assume that I won't be inconvenienced by anything that I tell you."

"Tell me you're not involved in this, and I'll ignore everything else illegal that you say."

"As you know, I'm in the business of finding certain items for others and delivering them. Like the serum for the Handlers and Trackers that I obtained for you."

Trinity shifted in her seat, her eyes darting to him.

"And I appreciate your help." He'd used Ray for quite a few things in the past and he refused to feel guilty about it. He hadn't purchased anything that had hurt anyone. Well, he hadn't known at the first what the serum did to the Handlers and Trackers.

"But you want more." Ray's green eyes gleamed. "You're tallying up quite a bill."

"I think looking the other way on your illegal activities should wipe that slate clean."

"Hardly." Ray laughed but there was a hardness to his eyes.

"Tell me that you don't kill our kind and harvest their organs." Tim's voice was clipped. "I know you've done a lot of...questionable things but no amount of money is worth that."

"It's not just our kind, Dad," said Trinity. "Dr. Kalper said this happens to Guards, Stockers, Grunts...everyone."

"But Almightys." Ray's eyes hardened. "They seem to get a pass on this desecration too." He tapped his lip with one long claw. "I wonder why?"

"You're saying an Almighty is behind this." He wasn't surprised.

"I didn't say that, but"—Ray looked at Tim—"I am saying that I'm not in the business of harvesting organs. They are available on the market though."

"We were recently made aware of that," said Hugh.

"Yes. I heard about the warehouse. Sad. Truly sad." Ray didn't seem upset at all.

"What do you know about the ones who do deal in organs?" he asked.

"Nothing really." Ray looked at his claws, cleaning a bit of dirt from under one of them.

"But something. Possibly?"

"No." Ray shrugged. "I don't deal with that, nor do I allow my people to work in that market, although it is lucrative."

"Do you know anyone who buys or sells organs," he pushed. Ray knew something but apparently, he had to ask the exact right question to get a useful answer.

Ray pursed his lips. "There is a club where you can get *anything* you want."

"Yes, Club Gall," said Jackson.

"You're better informed than I'd thought." Ray's eyes widened.

He would've preferred that Jackson had kept quiet about the club. Ray may have been going to mention a different one, but it was too late for that. "Can you get—"

"You inside the club?" Ray laughed. It was a rich, deep rumble from his chest. "Oh, no one would talk to you. You are Hugh Truent. The wise and benevolent. The freer of all." His words dripped with derision.

"I wasn't going to ask that you get me into Club Gall."

"Who then? Your Guard?" Ray looked at Jackson and laughed even harder. "Everyone knows the Hairless Guard is Hugh Truent's sidekick and most trusted ally." He turned to Tim. "And don't even offer. They know you're his friend too."

"I wasn't going to offer," said Tim. "I thought you knew me better than that. I don't stick my neck out unless absolutely necessary."

"That was the old Tim. My friend for years." Ray studied him. "Now...let's say that Truent has been a bad influence on you. Take my advice and stop being so helpful. It'll get you killed one day."

"Is that a threat?" Tim's fangs peeked from his lips.

"No." Ray's eyes were sad. "A warning but not from me."

"Then from who?" asked Tim.

"Just whispers," said Ray.

"Ray, who's threatening my father?" Trinity almost bristled with anger.

"No one, my dear. He's just known now. His name comes up too often with Hugh's." Ray turned to him. "You've made many enemies as well as friends."

"That's how it works," he said. "But I wasn't going to ask you to get Jackson or Tim into the club either." Holy Araldo, Ray must think he was an idiot.

"No. Then who?" Ray's eyes fell on Trinity.

He'd just opened his mouth to give a very emphatic no when Jethro spoke.

"Me. Can you get me inside Club Gall? Everyone knows I hate Hugh."

Ray stared at him as if just realizing that he was there. Then he nodded slowly. "Yes, you'd do well there. You fought for the other side in the war so those sympathizers will accept you, but you also helped the winning side and were imprisoned"—his eyes slid to Hugh—"for a long time. Both groups can accept you or hate you, depending on the tale you tell." His eyes narrowed and he sniffed before shaking his head. "And something about you reeks of dark, unfulfilled desires. You'll fit right in."

Trinity's lips tightened but other than that she remained impassive. Jethro only smiled at Ray.

"Will you help him?" Hugh asked.

"Hang out with him? Introduce him around?" Ray's eyes twinkled with merriment.

"Yes." He pushed down his annoyance at the Servant's odd sense of humor. Nothing about this was funny.

"No." Ray chuckled. "Absolutely not."

"Why?" The Servant's games were another thing he disliked.

"That'd look suspicious, but unlike Tim, I don't like you enough to make enemies." Ray smirked. "However, since I also don't like what they're doing to young female Servants, I may know of someone who might be able to help—unwittingly, of course."

"Who?" Hugh had to admit he was surprised that Ray was being this helpful.

"Terbasse."

"Francis Terbasse?" His gaze darted to Townsend. Perhaps the reporter had been right and Terbasse was involved.

"That's the one," said Ray.

"How can he help? He's nothing but a pampered playboy." He didn't want Ray to think they were even remotely suspicious of Terbasse.

"Who is well known in those circles."

"But why would this rich guy help me?" asked Jethro.

"He wouldn't."

"Then why—"

"Unless he considered you a friend"—Ray waved his hand—"of sorts."

"How do I become his friend?"

Hugh shrugged when Jethro glanced at him. He had no idea, but he did like that Jethro had looked to him. Maybe the two of them could learn to get along, at least a little.

"By entertaining him or giving him something he wants."

"I'm a fun guy but I don't know that I'll be that entertaining."

"But you do have something that I believe would appeal to Terbasse," said Ray.

"Me?" Jethro pointed to his chest. "I don't have anything but bills."

"As Hugh said, Terbasse is a...connoisseur of females. He has a weakness for helpless females in distress."

"What females do you know who are distressed?" His gaze went to Jethro who was as confused as he was. "Sassy is mourning Bruno, but I don't feel—"

"I don't have any sway over Sassy," said Jethro. "Indy is the one who's watching out for her."

"Terbasse prefers Almighty females," said Ray.

"Oh. I don't know any..." Hugh's eyes went to Jethro and then to Jackson.

"No. Kim is not going undercover," Jackson almost growled.

"She'll kick your ass for even thinking she's helpless," laughed Jethro.

"I didn't," he said. "Not really. She was the only Almighty female that I know who's associated with you and in the right age group." His sister certainly wouldn't catch Terbasse's eye.

"He knows someone who's perfect." Ray turned and stared at Jethro. "He's just not thinking hard enough."

"Me?" Jethro pointed at himself again. "I don't know any—"

"Your fiancé. The lovely, abandoned Stella. Pure as snow. Born and bred to marry the next Supreme Almighty, only to have everyone turn on her, painting her with her grandfather's sins." Ray smiled. "Terbasse would trip over his tongue if you brought her to Club Gall."

"No." Jethro's tone was firm. "We're not involving her."

"She is Terbasse's type," said Hugh.

"She's innocent," growled Jethro.

"So was I." Trinity glared at Jethro. "But that didn't stop anyone from trying to kill me and my family."

"We were wrong. I said it. Are you happy?" Jethro snapped. "But that doesn't mean putting Stella in danger is right."

"She's perfect." Ray purred. "With her by your side, you'll be in Terbasse's group in no time."

"No. He's right," said Trinity. "We shouldn't involve this Stella."

"Suit yourself. It was only a suggestion." Ray stood. "But there will be more killings. A lot more. Not everyone is ready to accept the equality of the classes, especially when it means their lives have to change." He headed toward the door.

"Wait," said Hugh. "There has to be another way to get Jethro inside the inner circle of the black market." He looked at Ray. It almost killed him, but for this he'd beg. "Please. Help us stop this from happening to any more young Servants."

Ray's eyes narrowed but he strolled back across the room. "He needs to live the life. Just visiting the club isn't going to fool anyone." He leaned against the wall, watching them. "What are you doing for work?"

"I...I'm doing this." Jethro glanced at Hugh.

"Yes, but what's your cover story?" asked Ray.

Silence filled the room.

"You're kidding, right?" Ray looked at all of them.

"He'll have a cover." He should've thought about that.

"He'd better because they will look into it before inviting him anywhere. It'll also be the only thing that'll keep him alive at Club Gall." Ray's eyes were brittle. "I'm not kidding. This isn't a place for amateurs."

"We're not amateurs. He'll have a job that fits the crowd." He glanced at Townsend, hoping the reporter had an idea of what kind of job that was.

"Being an unemployed, former member of the Protective Services who was kept in jail for...an exceedingly long time"—Jethro glanced at Hugh—"and who hates the new Supreme Almighty isn't enough?"

"I'm not the Supreme Almighty." That type of rule was over.

"You may as well be." Jethro shot him a disgusted look.

"I agree," said Ray. "But no, that's not enough. It might keep you alive at Club Gall, but it won't get you invited into The Sin."

"The Sin?" Townsend glanced around the room.

"Yeah. It's the club you don't know about." Ray smirked. "They take a lot of members from Club Gall but not everyone."

"The Sin? I never heard of that place. Where is it?" asked Trinity.

"You sound like you know all the clubs." He knew she'd gone to the Howling Hut but what other clubs had she frequented. He'd always thought she'd spent her time in the forest with Gaar and Mirra, not hanging out at clubs.

"There is no set place but everyone who buys top product from the market knows the location of the next...party."

"What kind of job do you suggest I get?" asked Jethro.

Hugh's attention darted to Jethro. He was impressed. He hadn't expected him to be so focused and determined.

"Theft. Blackmail. Robbery," said Ray. "Anything outside of the law. The further outside the better." He turned to Hugh. "How committed to stopping this are you?"

"Very. What they did to those females..." Bile rose in his throat.

"Then have Jethro kill someone." Ray said it as if it were as common as choosing fruit from the market. "If you can't pick the target, I'd be happy to suggest someone."

"Kill?" He almost choked on the word. "No. That's not going to happen."

"What about almost killing someone?" asked Jethro.

"Like stabbing them but not killing them?" Ray seemed affronted. "What's the point of that, except to make an enemy?"

"No. Killing someone, or even almost killing someone, will land him back in jail." Hugh had to put a stop to this line of conversation.

"Only if you catch him," said Ray.

"He just admitted—"

"That's not what I'm talking about." Jethro stood. "I mean fighting. Street fights."

"That"—a smile broke out across Ray's face, exposing his long, sharp canines—"would be perfect. Club Gall loves fighters."

"Then we're set." Jethro looked around the room. "I was approached by a lawyer in prison. He said he could get me released if I agreed to fight for him."

"What lawyer?" asked Townsend.

"Vickers. I don't remember his first name."

"Bill Vickers? I mean, William Vickers." Hugh glanced at Townsend.

"Yeah. That's him," said Jethro. "You know him?"

"That's Wickerwood's lawyer," he said.

"If Vickers wants to hire you, take the job. Wait." Ray's face scrunched up in confusion. "Why would Vickers want to hire an Almighty to fight?"

"Because I'm a damn good fighter."

"You're an Almighty. You can't be that good, but it doesn't matter. The crowd will love seeing you in the ring, getting your pretty face pummeled."

"I don't plan on getting pummeled."

"No one ever does." Ray's tone was amused. "But win or lose, being a fighter will get you into Club Gall."

"I'll go see Vickers tomorrow." Jethro stood.

"Are you sure about this?" It was perfect...too perfect, and Hugh didn't like it.

"Yeah. I can handle myself. I trained with the Protective Services, and it wasn't easy. I wasn't an officer. I lived with the Guards. I know how to fight."

"I know all that." But he didn't know exactly what Conguise had done to Jethro, but the professor had done something. He'd studied the sample Kalper had taken, and he had no idea what was happening inside Jethro. The only thing he knew for sure was that his blood was different than anything he'd ever seen.

CHAPTER 30: Jethro

After the meeting Jethro headed straight to Stella's apartment. He needed to end their engagement. He didn't want anyone thinking they were still involved. It wasn't safe for her.

A shadow shifted and disappeared around a corner. He stopped, checking the address on one of the letters that she'd written to him while he'd been in prison. He'd been completely surprised when he'd received the first one. He hadn't expected anything from her. It wasn't like either of them had cared for one another. They'd both been pawns in her grandfather's schemes.

He continued down the street. This area had never been affluent, but it had been full of decent, hardworking Almightys, but that had changed.

Many of the houses were in shambles—doors missing, windows broken, roofs that looked like the next strong wind would cause them to crumble. The businesses weren't much better, big locks on the doors and bars on the windows. Servants and Guards meandered along the streets, staying in the darkness as much as possible. They eyed him but didn't approach. He was young and strong. They'd find easier prey.

He continued walking, following the numbers on the stores that still had them, until he found the address that matched the envelope. He made his way up the stairs of her building, passing a drunk Guard who was passed out in a corner.

He stopped in front of her apartment, feeling guilty. She had no one. Her grandfather's depravity had robbed her of her friends, and his poor financial choices had taken her money. Then her grandmother had killed herself. Stella had no one except him, but Ray's comment today had convinced him that the best thing for her would be if he ended their fake relationship. The fact that he was getting rid of a fiancé who he'd never wanted wasn't a factor in his decision. He knocked on the door.

Stella opened it slightly, peeking through the crack. "Jethro!" She exclaimed, shutting the door for a second and unhooking the chain before opening it again. "You're out of jail." Her blue eyes were alight with surprise and her blonde hair was pulled back in a ponytail. She looked way too young to be living here alone.

"Finally." He grinned. She was cute but not his type. Even in prison, without any female companionship, he'd never fantasized about her. She was too pale, too blond, too typical Almighty for his taste, but maybe he could end their engagement without abandoning her completely. He'd already talked to Kim, and he still needed to see Conguise. The professor knew a lot of people. Perhaps he could help her.

"Come in." She stepped aside, closing and locking the door behind him. "Are you hungry?" She walked to the table near the kitchen.

The apartment was basically one big room. A bed was pushed in the corner, a chair sat by the window with a blanket tossed across it and a book lay on a nearby table. There was a small refrigerator, stove, and sink next to the table, and a door to the side of the kitchen area that was probably the bathroom.

"No." He was always hungry, but he wasn't taking any of her food. Her clothes hung on her frame and her cheekbones were sharp in her face.

"Something to drink?" She dug through one of the cabinets. "I bought this last winter." She held up a bottle of very cheap bourbon. "Someone at the store recommended it to help get rid of the chill. I tried it twice, but I'd rather be cold." She wrinkled her nose and then her eyes widened. "Not that it's bad. I mean...I just don't like bourbon. You might like it though or—"

"I'd love some." He sat at the table.

She poured some in a glass and handed it to him as she sat across from him.

"Thanks." He tried not to grimace as he took a sip of the bourbon.

"When did you get out of jail?"

"I got home a few days ago." There was no reason to mention his extended stay at Kalper's house. That'd bring up more questions than he wanted to answer.

"Your mother and sister must be so happy." She smiled at him.

He felt like a jerk. She was as innocent as Tee, and she had no one...except him. He couldn't do it. "I've been talking to Kim about you."

"You have?" The friendliness in her tone slipped a notch.

"Yeah. She's been working at Mike's Pub."

"And?" Stella's smile was completely gone now.

"And she meets a lot of people there. She's going to find you somewhere else to live." He took another sip of his drink, wincing slightly. This stuff was nasty.

"I like it here." Her eyes shone with hurt.

She had to be lying. This place was a dump and dangerous. "This area isn't safe."

"It's not bad during the day." A slight blush spread across her cheeks which was actually kind of cute.

"Don't worry about the expense. I'll take care of it." He stared at the bourbon. He hadn't meant to say that. Sure, Hugh was paying him for this job, but he couldn't afford three households. He still had his place in the Warehouse District, and he was, of course, helping his mother.

He could sell his place. Tee had moved in with his mom, but he'd need somewhere to live, especially when undercover. He was pretty sure the people who frequented Club Gall and The Sin didn't live with their moms.

"I don't know what to say." Her eyes met his, warmth replacing the uneasiness.

He smiled, and she blushed a bit more. He took another drink. This stuff wasn't that bad after the first few swallows. "Consider it payback for everything that you've done for me."

"Like what?"

"The letters." He shrugged. "I liked getting them." It wasn't a lie. It'd been an escape. The only one he'd had. His sister, Jackson and his mom had written but Stella's letters had been full of day-to-day things, ramblings mainly and they'd helped him pass the time.

"I didn't write to you, so you'd owe me." Her eyes hardened.

"I know that." He wanted to slap himself. He didn't understand females. "I just...Sorry. I don't know what to say to you."

"You don't have to be uneasy around me." She flushed more and stared down at her hands, before glancing at him from under her lashes.

His eyes traveled down her body as he finished his drink. A few weeks after his serum he could drink as much as he wanted without a fuzzy head, but right now, alcohol hit him fast and hard. It'd been a long time since he'd had a female. Her breasts were nice—firm and a good size. Her hips were lean and her legs long. Soon he'd be undercover. He wasn't sure how much opportunity he'd have to mate. She was female and by the look she was giving him, she was willing. He smiled at her again and took her hand. "Come here."

She stood and walked around the table, stopping in front of him. He dropped his hold and ran his hands down her sides feeling her soft curves. She was female. She'd do.

He took her arm and pulled her onto his lap. "Much better," he murmured in her ear. She shivered as he trailed kisses down her neck while his hands wandered toward her breasts. She stiffened. "Shhh," he whispered. "Trust me. You'll like this."

"I've never..." She put her hand on his, stopping his progress.

"Never?" He hesitated, his mouth still on her neck.

"No." Her voice was barely a whisper.

He placed a kiss on her lips, soft and coaxing as he pushed his guilt aside. Everyone had to have a first. He'd go slow. He'd make it good for her. She opened her mouth, accepting his kiss. He lifted her and stood, walking to the bed. He laid her down and began unbuttoning his shirt. She was so small and pale. Her face was flushed, and her eyes were...worried.

"Are you sure about this?" His arms dropped to his sides, but his body screamed at him for asking that stupid question. She hadn't said no, so that meant proceed, but he couldn't ignore the doubt in her eyes.

"Yes. We're engaged." She smiled, her lips trembling. "This is what engaged couples do."

If that was the payment for these services, then he couldn't continue because he wasn't going to marry her. Ever. He started buttoning his shirt.

"Did I do something wrong?" She sat up, her face worried.

"No. Nothing." He walked toward the door.

"I'm sorry." She followed him. "I didn't mean—"

"Don't." He turned, grasping her thin shoulders. "Don't be sorry. I came here to tell you that I'm leaving."

"Leaving? Where are you going?" Her face paled.

"I can't tell you the details, but I have a job. I'll be gone for a while."

"How long?" She wrapped her arms around her torso, protecting herself.

"I'm not sure." He hadn't meant to hurt her.

She turned away from him and then spun around. "If you want to break our engagement, tell me. I'll be fine on my own." She glanced around the apartment, worry in her gaze.

"That's not it." He mentally kicked himself for not taking that opportunity.

"Is it another female? I know I'm not your type."

"There's no one in my life." The only one he wanted was engaged to his half-brother.

"Grandfather and Father both preferred the other classes. If that's what you like, then tell me. I won't settle for a life like my mother and my grandmother had." Her tiny chin jutted out. "This is a new world, and I want more."

"Good for you." His lips twitched. "You deserve more." He wasn't lying. No one deserved to marry for anything but love.

"So you really aren't leaving because of another female?"

"No."

"Then why did you..." She glanced back at the bed, a small frown teasing her lips.

His jaw clenched. He should tell her right now that he didn't want to marry her, but she had no one...absolutely, no one but him. "This job I'm doing isn't completely safe and if something happens to me, I don't want to take..." His gaze darted down her body. "You should save that for someone who'll be around."

"When you come back then?" She flushed. She was beet red now and he couldn't stop the smile from spreading across his lips.

"Okay. When I come back." He'd tell Kim to introduce her to some other males. Hopefully, by the time he finished this job she'd be in love with someone and dump him.

CHAPTER 31: Jethro

Jethro sat in the waiting room of the offices of William Vickers, trying not to fidget. Yesterday's visit with Stella had been uncomfortable but today was going to be a lot worse. After this meeting he had to visit Conguise. He wanted to ask the secretary how soon Vickers could see him, but he'd already asked twice, and the answer had been the same.

Mr. Vickers is very busy. He'll see you as soon as he can.

The lawyer may be busy, but he wasn't that busy. This was a punishment. He'd come to the office to schedule an appointment, but the secretary had said that Vickers had instructed her to have him wait. At first, he'd been pleasantly surprised that Vickers had said anything about him to anyone. He shouldn't have been. He'd been waiting for over two hours.

This was nothing more than the lawyer paying him back because Jethro hadn't run to Vickers' office as soon as he'd been released from prison. The lawyer thought he was teaching Jethro that all the power belonged to him, but this lesson proved the opposite. The fact that Vickers still wanted to talk to him showed Jethro that he had the power, not the lawyer.

The secretary glanced at her watch and then looked at him. "Mr. Vickers will see you now." She stood and walked to the door.

No one had gone into or out of that office since he'd been there. Vickers could've seen him a long time ago. He wouldn't forget this, but he plastered a pleasant expression on his face and stood, following the secretary across the room.

She tapped on the door.

"Yes?" said Vickers from inside the room.

"Jethro Remore to see you, sir." She smiled at him as if he hadn't been ready to see Vickers two hours ago.

"Send him in."

She opened the door, wearing a false smile that Jethro wanted to shake off her face, but he just walked past her into the room.

"Jethro." Vickers sat behind his desk, his smile as fake as his secretary's. "How can I help you?" He motioned to the chair in front of his desk as the secretary closed the door behind her.

"I'm here about the job." He sat, seeing no reason not to be direct.

"The job?" Vickers gave him a perplexed look. "I assumed you weren't interested when you didn't come to see me." His tone was pleasant, but a lecture lurked in his eyes.

"I was only released a few days ago."

"A little over a week."

"I spent time with family." He wasn't in the mood for a lecture, but he'd put up with it. He needed to get in with the crowd that frequented the black market and he needed to fight. His blood was already beginning to stir.

"I understand." Vickers smiled but his eyes were hard.

Jethro waited but the lawyer only stared at him. He should ride out the silence. Make the lawyer talk first, but he wanted to be done. He still had his meeting with Conguise to get through. "Is the job still available?

"Hmm." Vickers frowned as he pulled a manilla file out of his desk drawer. "Let me see what I have open." He flipped through the papers. "When you didn't come by the office, I thought you were no longer interested." He glanced at Jethro, his blue eyes hard, before looking back down at the papers. "I filled that position."

"I'll make you more money than whomever you hired." He was done with this game.

"I doubt that." Vickers' eyes met his. "You'd have to win big to make up for the thirty percent I agreed to give you." He looked back down and tapped the top paper. "I can get you in for one fight, but—"

"When?"

"Now, you're eager?" Vickers' tone dripped with derision.

He shrugged. It probably wasn't the time to remind the lawyer that he'd only fight two weeks each month.

Vickers frowned. "Friday."

"Great. Where do I need to go?" It wouldn't be quite two weeks since his shot, but it'd be close enough.

"*Great.* That's all you have to say?"

"Thank you." He forced the words past his lips. He hated this Almighty already, but he needed him.

The gratitude seemed to appease Vickers a little, at least his lips lost the sneer. "It's a small crowd. I'll pay you ten percent."

"Ten percent? No." He wasn't giving the lawyer ninety percent.

"That's all I have available." Vickers pushed the papers aside. "I had jobs lined up for you, but you weren't interested."

"I was spending time with my family."

"You've been out of prison for over a week. You couldn't take a few hours out of one day to come and see me?" Vickers' eyes narrowed. "Why were you released anyway? From what I'd heard Hugh had no intention of setting you free...ever."

Jethro had to be careful without looking like he was being careful. He didn't want to admit that he'd had an issue in jail. Being weak wasn't going to get him this job...or would it? "Hugh came to see me. I still wasn't feeling great after being jumped." He paused. "I'm sure you heard about that." It'd probably been the reason Vickers had approached him in the first place. "Hugh felt bad for me." He smirked. "I am his brother after all."

"Brothers can hate each other more than anyone else."

"But they still appease their mother."

"Sometimes." Vickers shrugged. "So Hugh changed his mind because you were injured." He paused. "I don't have a job for a fighter who's hurt, and I certainly don't pay them thirty percent."

"I'm fine now."

"The incident at the jail wasn't that long ago."

"I heal fast." The other Almighty had no idea how quickly he could mend.

"Not thirty percent fast."

"I'll tell you what." Jethro leaned forward. "I'll fight this one for free, but after I win, you pay me fifty percent."

"Fifty percent?" Vickers laughed but his eyes shone with interest. "No."

"What do you have to lose? This is a freebie. Even if I win you don't have to hire me"—he leaned back in his chair—"but you will. I'll even go so far and say that you'll be happy...no, thrilled...to pay me fifty percent because I'm going to make you rich."

"I love confidence but arrogance...That can get you killed."

"Knowing your abilities is not arrogance."

"You don't even know who or what you're fighting."

"It doesn't matter. I'll win." He could beat any Guard, Servant or Stocker out there. "And if you don't believe me you can bet on my opponent." He grinned. "Of course, then you'll lose."

CHAPTER 32: Conguise

Conguise drew a sample of blood from Jethro's arm. Even after months in prison, the boy looked strong and healthy. Good, because he needed this experiment to work. Once he had a successful prototype nothing would stop him. He locked the vial of blood in his desk drawer and glanced at Jethro. "Do you have enough serum? It's important that you continue to take it on schedule. Your body needs to learn to accept the foreign bodies and incorporate them into itself."

"Yes, I have enough, and I know." Jethro stood. "You've told me this a thousand times."

"It's important." The boy didn't understand how special he was, and that the future of their world rested on his shoulders.

"I know. Trust me. I want this to work more than you do." Jethro's eyes grew dark. "I can't go back to being in a wheelchair. I just can't."

"Don't worry." Conguise sighed and walked around his desk, clasping Jethro's shoulder. "That isn't going to happen." Losing the use of his legs would be better than what would actually happen if something went wrong, but he'd never explain that to him.

"I thought you said you weren't sure when I asked you before."

"I wasn't."

"But you are now?"

He hesitated. He should let Jethro worry about losing the ability to walk.

"Professor. Please. I need to know what will happen. I had to delay taking it in jail."

"You shouldn't delay. You need to take it on time. Every month."

"I understand, but sometimes things happen. If I'd taken it on time in jail, I would've been killed, beaten to death. What will happen if I don't take it? Will I lose the ability to walk?"

"No," he said. Jethro's DNA was past the point of reversal.

"Then what will happen?"

"Right now, it's hard to say."

"Try. Please," said Jethro. "I need to know."

"You'll be fine as long as you take the serum on schedule."

"But what if something happens and I can't take it like when I was in jail? Or I lose it? What will happen if I'm late? And how late is okay? A week? Two weeks? I really need to know."

"I understand your concern, but I can't give you an exact answer." He gave Jethro his most fatherly smile when all he really wanted to do was rush the boy out of his house so he could take a look at the blood. Through his contacts at the jail, he'd managed to get a few samples of Jethro's blood—tiny bits from fights and arranged attacks. The boy's cells had changed dramatically in prison—merged and mutated. The foreign DNA had become more cohesive with the Almighty genes, closer to becoming one. He'd been concerned at first, but Jethro was still more Almighty than beast. He'd have to incorporate stressors like those faced in prison into his subjects in the lab.

"Then give me your best guess. Give me something. Some idea of what's going to happen to me."

"If you take—"

"Yeah, I know. If I take it on schedule, I'll be fine but what if I can't?"

He sighed. "It depends."

"On what?"

"On how your body is adjusting with the serum."

"I don't understand," said Jethro.

"The...medicine that I used to heal your injuries is still seen as foreign by your body."

"My immune system is attacking it?"

"Yes." Or something like that. "But your body is starting to merge with it, accept it. Like I said before, the hope is that one day you may be able to stop taking the serum all together."

"So I might be fine if I can't take it."

"Or you could be dead." He couldn't...wouldn't let Jethro compromise all he'd achieved.

"Oh." Jethro's face paled.

"That's why it's so important that you continue to visit me so I can monitor your blood, and that you take the serum on time." He patted Jethro's arm. "Don't worry. I'll let you know if you can discontinue taking it."

"Thanks. It's not that I don't want to take it. It's just that sometimes things happen and—"

A rapid tapping sounded on the door, as if from a small fist.

"I wasn't expecting anyone tonight." He glanced out of his office as his House Servant walked toward the door.

Stella burst into his house. Her clothes were torn and dirty, her blond hair messed and falling loose. Her blue eyes were large with fright and her pale face was ghostly white. She hesitated, staring from Conguise to Jethro, her lips trembling.

"Stella, what happened?" Jethro jumped from his chair and hurried to her side.

"It...was horri...horrible." She fell into his arms, clinging to him and sobbing.

"Bring her into my office." He held the door open while Jethro half-carried, half-dragged Stella inside the room. He poured a small draught of whiskey into a glass and handed it to her. "Drink this."

She obediently swallowed the liquor, coughing slightly.

"What happened?" Jethro placed the glass on the end table and helped her to sit on the couch.

She blushed, pulling her clothes together to try and cover her pale breasts, but the shirt was too badly ripped.

"Here." Conguise handed Jethro a blanket and he wrapped it around her shoulders.

"Now, tell us what happened," said Jethro.

Conguise sat on a chair across from her. It seemed Meesus had been successful in her attack. He studied the girl. Her clothes were torn, but she didn't have the shocked and haunted look of one who'd been violated. If he were wrong, Meesus would pay. He had warned the Servant that Stella was not to be harmed. Of course to a prostitute, rape might not be considered harmful.

"I...I was on my way home from the grocery store when t-two House Servants started following me." Her eyes teared as her hand clutched Jethro's. "I walked faster, and I thought it was okay. They kept walking when I got to my apartment."

"But..." prodded Jethro.

Her hand trembled. "I shouldn't have answered the door. I shouldn't have—"

"This wasn't your fault." Jethro was more than furious.

Conguise stood, taking her glass from the table and adding a little more whiskey to it before handing it back to her. He'd have to make sure Jethro never found out about his involvement.

"They pushed their way inside." She stopped, her eyes glazing over in memory. "One of them tied me up while the other..."

A muscle ticked in Jethro's cheek and Conguise held his breath. The next words out of her mouth would seal the fate for Meesus and her Servants.

"Searched the house. I don't know what they were looking for, but they tore up everything—my clothes, the couch, my bed."

"Did they hurt you?" Jethro's body tensed, waiting for her answer.

She let go of his hand and rubbed her wrists before touching the bruise on her cheek. She'd been hit, slapped by the look of it. Normally, he'd want the Servant responsible to die for touching an Almighty, but this time he'd let it go. The attack did have to appear real.

"Stella." Jethro took her hand again. His voice was calm but serious. "Did they *hurt* you?"

She looked at him, confused until his eyes dropped to her breasts where the blanket had fallen slightly open. She flushed as she pulled it closed.

"No. I got away before they could..." Her voice trailed off for a second and then she cleared her throat. "When they didn't find whatever they wanted, they untied me and forced me out of the house." Her eyes teared up again.

"Go on." Jethro squeezed her hand.

"They made me get into a carriage. Th-they put something over my eyes. I thought they were going to..." Her voice cracked.

"It's okay. You got away. You're safe," said Jethro.

"Yes." She nodded. "The carriage stopped, and they both got out, arguing about something. They'd forgotten to tie me back up, so I tore off the blindfold and slipped out the other side. Then, I ran. I didn't know where I was going. I just ran. I was so afraid that they'd find me."

"But they didn't," Jethro said, calmly. "You're safe now," he repeated.

"Yes." She smiled slightly, her lips trembling.

"How did you end up here?" asked Conguise. He'd better join in the questioning or Jethro would be suspicious.

She looked at him and he felt a pang of regret. She was so young and innocent. He remembered Viola at that age—her life ahead of her. He shook off the unease. She hadn't actually been hurt and in the long run this would work out well for her. He was helping her obtain the future she'd been promised since birth—to marry the leader of their world.

"When I was running through the woods, I made myself slow down and look around. I realized that I wasn't that far away from your house. You were the only one who I thought would help me." She glanced down at the floor.

He leaned forward and patted her hand. "You came to the right place, my dear." He lived in a very rural area, but there were others nearby that once would've helped her. However, since the discovery of her grandfather's harem of young Servants, along with his whispers of lies, the world she knew had turned its back on her. "Why don't you go clean up. You'll feel better." He needed to talk to Jethro alone. The boy would be ripe for suggestions.

"I'd like that, thank you." She stood.

"Afar," he called his Servant.

"Yes, sir." The Servant appeared in the doorway, obviously lurking nearby.

"Take Stella to Viola's room." He turned to Stella. "I still haven't cleaned out her closets. There are some clothes of hers from high school..." He swallowed. He didn't want to part with anything that'd been his daughter's, but he could hardly have Stella wash and then put on her filthy garments.

"Thank you." She clasped his hand. "I'll have them cleaned and returned."

"Nonsense." He shook his head. "They aren't doing any good hanging in her room. I need to donate them, but I haven't found the time." It was a lie and the other Almightys knew it, but he didn't care. He needed to say the words to protect himself from the truth of his weakness.

"Thank you," she said again before following Afar from the room.

As soon as she was gone, Jethro started to pace. "I told her that apartment wasn't safe. She needs to move."

"She does." This was going well.

"Kim is looking for another place for her."

Oh, that wouldn't work at all. "I doubt any place Stella can afford will be safe."

"We'll find something." He sat down again. "Kim knows a lot of people from working at Mike's Pub. She's already found a couple of apartments in decent areas that might—"

"They may be safe areas, but they won't be safe for Stella."

"What do you mean by that?"

"Her grandfather had many enemies, especially after his proclivities were discovered. She did say it was Servants who attacked her."

"You think they blame her for her grandfather's actions." Jethro frowned. "She had nothing to do with what Jason did. She's innocent."

"So were her grandfather's...special Servants." He drummed his fingers on the desk. "She's the only one left in her family to pay for his sins."

"That's not right. She had nothing to do with Jason's perversion."

Conguise had to literally almost bite his tongue to keep from asking Jethro how Jason's interest in House Servants was a perversion when Jethro himself lusted after a mixed breed, but that argument wouldn't serve his purpose tonight.

Stella came back into the room, looking much better although the bruise on her pale skin was more pronounced now that she was clean. The Servant had hit her hard. He should bring that up with Meesus, except it did add credibility to the attack.

"Feeling better?" Jethro stood.

"Yes. Thank you." She nodded slightly, wringing her hands.

Jethro went over to her. His protective instincts were going to get him into trouble one day. The sooner Conguise got this damsel in distress away from Jethro the better. If the boy wasn't careful, he'd cross a line that he couldn't uncross, and then he'd be saddled with this conniving harpy for the rest of his life. She looked sweet and innocent, but it was an act. She'd make Jethro miserable in the long run. He knew. He'd married a woman just like her.

"What's the matter?" asked Jethro.

She looked up at him, her blue eyes wide. "Where am I going to stay? I can't go home. I just can't."

Conguise remained silent, watching. It was quite interesting from a scientific point of view. Instinctively, she understood that Jethro wanted to protect her, and she was setting the trap with her young, supple body and beautiful face.

Jethro hesitated, obviously not prepared for that question. "Ah. I don't..." He turned toward the professor.

"I'm sorry, but it wouldn't be appropriate for her to stay here. Although I'm old enough to be her father or even her grandfather, I am a bachelor." He'd let Jethro sweat this one out for a moment.

"I don't mean to be a bother." She lowered her head. "Don't worry about me. I'll find somewhere to go." Her voice cracked on the last word.

He wanted to applaud her performance. Just as he'd expected, she was an expert at manipulation. She may have had no part in her attack, but she'd use it to her advantage. Once she was Hugh's wife, he'd have to remember that she could be a dangerous enemy or a priceless ally. He'd make sure she appreciated his helping her become the wife to their new leader.

CHAPTER 33: Jethro

"You're not a bother." Jethro touched Stella's arm.

"Thank you." She leaned against him. "I feel so safe with you."

"Ah..." He dropped his hand and took a step away from her. "I can't let you stay with me either. It wouldn't be right."

"Oh." Her shoulders sagged as she glanced at him from under her lashes. "Are you sure? We are engaged."

"Uhm. Yeah, but—"

"I promise I won't pester you. You can do whatever you want. I won't even ask you where you're going when you leave." She moved closer to him. "I can cook and clean. Please. I'm scared to go back to my apartment." She shivered.

Jethro felt the blood rush from his face as his chest tightened. He was caught. Trapped. If he let her move in with him, he'd have to marry her. Society already hated her. They'd use this as a reason to hate her even more. He glanced at the professor, hoping Conguise would help him and come up with another solution. Any solution.

"Perhaps it'd be better if she stayed with your mother," Conguise suggested.

"Of course, that's perfect." Jethro almost collapsed in relief.

"Oh." She didn't sound happy. "If that's what you think is best."

"You should probably get some rest." Conguise walked over to them. "You've been through a lot."

"Yeah. Right." And he had to tell his mom that they had another guest and another mouth to feed. He took her arm and led her to his carriage.

Conguise followed them, stopping in his doorway. "Jethro, I need to speak with you for a minute."

"Okay." He turned toward Stella. "I'll be right back." He closed the carriage door and walked to the house.

"What happened to Stella is inexcusable," whispered Conguise. "It never would've happened before Hugh came into power. You may not agree with how everything was before the war, but you have to admit that some things were better."

Jethro's jaw clenched, but he remained quiet. He truly doubted that Conguise had called him back to the house in order to vent about Hugh's new laws.

"Right now, we need to take every opportunity that's given to us and"—Conguise nodded at the carriage—"this is an opportunity."

"What do you mean by that?"

"Stella needs somewhere to stay."

"I'm taking her to my mother's." He thought that problem was solved.

"You want her to stay there indefinitely?"

"Uh..." He didn't. Actually, she couldn't. He was going undercover. He couldn't have her overhearing things that were said between him, Jackson and Kim. He didn't trust her to keep quiet. He barely knew her.

"Am I wrong in my assumption that you don't want to marry her? If I'm wrong, then by all means, let her stay."

"No." Jethro's frown deepened. "You're not wrong. I'm not marrying her."

"Have you told her that?"

"Ah...not yet. I was going to but—"

"Why you didn't doesn't matter. What does is your need to find somewhere else for her to stay."

"Then why did you suggest my mom's house?"

"It was a first thought. A first reaction." Conguise shrugged. "I was trying to help. You didn't seem to know what to say."

That was completely true. "Okay. I agree she needs to live somewhere else, but where? You said she wouldn't be safe in another apartment."

"She won't be safe alone. You need to find her another male. A husband."

"Who?" He threw up his hands. "I don't exactly know a ton of guys looking to get married."

"It can't be that hard. She's young and beautiful. She was raised to be obedient."

"Then you find her a husband."

"I've tried," snapped Conguise.

"You have?" Jethro's jaw almost dropped to his chest. He'd never pictured the professor as a matchmaker.

"Yes. I never felt it was right that she lost everything due to Jason's...poor choices."

"Good. Then it's settled. You find her a husband." He wanted to race to the carriage before it somehow became his problem again.

"As I said, I tried. Those I know have judged her and found her guilty."

"Gruntshit. That's not right. She didn't do anything."

"I know that, and you know that. What we need is someone else. Someone eligible to be her husband who understands that she isn't to blame. Someone fair." Conguise frowned. "He should be an Almighty. I don't know that Stella is ready for a spouse from another race."

"I agree, but who? I don't know anyone. I didn't keep in touch with guys from high school or college. I was in the Protective Services and then jail. Not exactly great places to find an eligible husband for Stella."

"True. She does deserve an upstanding male, but a common soldier won't do. She should be paired with someone who could utilize her abilities. She was raised to be the wife of the next Supreme Almighty."

"Yeah, but there aren't..." The words died in his throat. This could fix a few of his problems. It wouldn't be easy but...

"Did you think of someone?"

"Maybe." If he could figure out how to make it work, it'd be perfect for her and for him. His eyes darted to the carriage.

"Who do you have in mind?"

"Hugh." He almost whispered the name.

"Hugh?" Conguise seemed perplexed. "But he's with—"

"I know who he's with, but Stella would be a better wife for Hugh. You said it yourself. She is a politician's child. She'd fit in Hugh's world well."

"Hmm. I don't know. He seems quite taken with his current fiancé."

"I'm sure he is." He almost choked on the words. Trinity was his. "But she won't be a good wife for Hugh. She was born to live in the forest." Wild and free. Just like the first time he met her.

"You think she won't do well as—"

"She'll do great, but she won't be happy."

"You think she's unhappy?"

"I think she could be happier." With him. Living in the forest together like they had on the other side of Harbor Point. "And I think Stella would be a better wife for Hugh." He stared at the carriage. This would work. Stella was young and pretty and...His shoulders sagged. No, it wouldn't work. Hugh wasn't a fool. He wouldn't turn from Trinity to Stella.

"You're right. Stella was taught from birth how to entertain, and how to raise money for causes. She'd be an asset to Hugh and...she'd be safe. There is nowhere safer than the Council Building."

"I agree." That was a good point. Even if Stella and Hugh didn't end up together, she would be safe and not living with him or his mother.

"Good. Then it's settled."

"Settled? What do you mean? I can't just drop her off at Hugh's bedroom door."

"Of course not." Conguise gave him a disgusted look. "We need someone to suggest to Hugh that Stella would be better living at the Council Building than at your mother's house."

"It can't be me." Jethro held up his hands. "Hugh would never agree to anything I suggest, but I may be able to get Jackson to say something to him."

"That's a brilliant idea, but you can't ask the Guard. You have to let him think it's his idea, or Hugh will never accept it or her."

"He nodded. I think I can do that." No, he *would* do it. He'd do whatever he had to do to get Stella out of his house and into Hugh's.

CHAPTER 34: Jethro

Jethro's carriage stopped in front of his mom's house. He stared at Stella who sat across from him, hands folded in her lap. None of this was her fault, but for some reason he felt manipulated. He didn't want her staying here. His mom would see this as a sign that he was serious about Stella.

"Are you sure this will be okay?" She glanced up at him. Her voice was quiet, as if afraid to ask the question.

His eyes landed on the bruise on her cheek. She had no one and nowhere to go. He smiled. "Yeah. It'll be fine. My mom will love having you stay, and you and my sister will get along great." He hesitated. "Uhm...I should've told you that her mate is a Guard. If that bothers you, I can see about finding a room to rent for you." If Conguise was right, she might not be safe, but she should be fine for one night. He could figure out something else tomorrow.

"It doesn't bother me." The words seemed forced and knowing her grandfather and father's predilection for the other classes he understood.

"Jackson and my sister are both adults and both consenting."

She flushed slightly. "Of course. I never—"

"I know you didn't." He took her hand. "I just wanted you to know."

She nodded, staring down at their clasped hands.

He dropped his hold and opened the carriage door. "Shall we?" He jumped out, offering his hand to help her.

She climbed out of the carriage and stared up at him, her blue eyes filled with gratitude. "I-I...Thank you."

He nodded, feeling even more like a Grunt's ass for scheming to get rid of her, but she'd be happy with Hugh, and he'd be happy with

Trinity. He headed for the house. He should go inside first and warn everyone, but he wasn't going to ask her to stand outside alone. He opened the door and walked inside, Stella behind him.

Jackson sat on the couch next to Jethro's mom. Kim came out of the back room followed by Tee who shot him a quick friendly smile. He winked at the young Servant and her smile widened. At least he'd done something right. She was happy living with his mom and sister.

They all stared at him, the expressions on their faces ranging from curious to confused. He glanced at Stella who stood with her head bowed.

"Jethro?" His mother looked at Kim, but his sister only shrugged.

"She was attacked." The best way to get his mom and Kim on his side was to play to their sympathy. He placed his finger under Stella's chin and raised her face to the light. The bruise was darker now, a sharp contrast to her pale skin. It looked perfect.

"Oh my! You poor thing." Kim hurried over to Stella, taking her hand and leading her to the couch.

Jackson stood, giving Stella his place on the sofa.

"What happened?" Mom examined Stella's face. "Who did this to her?"

"Servants." He stayed by the door. "They broke into her house looking for something and then kidnapped her."

"It's getting so unsafe...everywhere." Kim's eyes were wide as she stared at him.

"She managed to get away." He'd leave the part out about her finding her way to Conguise's house. The more he thought about it, the more it seemed a little strange. The professor did live in a rural area but why would city Servants take her way out there? There could be some kind of market for Almighty females, but Conguise's area wasn't that rich or that poor.

"That's horrible," said Kim. "Do you have any idea what they wanted?"

"No." Stella shook her head. "I don't have anything of value. Not anymore."

"I think it may have been because of who she is." He went and stood by Jackson.

"It isn't fair." Stella's large, blue eyes filled with tears, but she blinked them away. "I"—she stressed the word—"never did anything to anyone."

"This isn't your fault." Mom patted her hand.

"She can't go back to her apartment." It was time to drop the news. "It's a mess. Unlivable."

"Don't even think about it," Jackson muttered quietly for Jethro's ears only.

He ignored the Guard. "I'd let her stay with me, but..."

Kim's eyes narrowed as his mother said, "Of course she can stay here."

"Thank you." Stella's shoulders sagged with relief. "I won't be any trouble."

Kim glared at Jethro over Stella's head and mouthed. "We need to talk."

"You'll be a welcome guest." Mom took her hand and led Stella up the stairs. "We'll put you in Jethro's room." She stopped, sending Jethro a proud look. "Come with us, please."

It was not a request. He frowned as he followed them to his old bedroom. This was exactly what he'd feared. Mom was probably already seeing Stella in a wedding dress and him in a suit.

"You can sleep in here. Feel free to rearrange anything." Mom glanced at him. "I know Jethro won't mind."

"Nope. Make yourself at home. I haven't lived here for a long time." He needed to put a stop to his mother's train of thought.

"It hasn't been that long." Mom moved over to the dresser and opened a drawer. "You can wear one of his T-shirts to bed tonight and..." She turned to him. "She's going to need her things."

That was his cue. "Good idea. I'll go to her apartment right now." He raced out of the room before his mom could stop him.

"Jethro," Kim hollered as he barreled down the stairs toward the door.

"Can't talk now. Have to go get Stella's things." He almost ran out of the door, his feet stumbling to a halt when he saw Jackson leaning against his carriage.

"This is not going to work," said the Guard.

"She had nowhere to go. What was I supposed to do? Leave her and let her get kidnapped? Raped? Murdered?"

"Of course not." Jackson stepped closer, lowering his voice. "We can't have her here. Not with you undercover and us meeting here, using the tunnels to come and go."

"I know but where should I take her?" This was going perfectly. He just needed Jackson to think of Hugh or at least the Council Building. "If she were attacked because of what her grandfather did, she won't be safe anywhere. Not alone anyway."

"There's no one that'll take her in. No old friends of the family?"

"If there were she wouldn't have been living in that dump."

"True." Jackson sighed. "Hugh isn't going to be happy about this."

"Then let him come up with another idea." Like marrying her himself.

"He's got enough to worry about."

"Yeah, so do I." He pushed past the Guard.

"I didn't mean that you didn't. I just meant—"

"I know." He opened the carriage door. "But I hadn't expected this either." In the heat of the moment with Conguise he'd forgotten one very important fact about Jackson. The Guard was exceedingly loyal...to Hugh. Even if Jackson thought about the safety of the Council Building, he'd never suggest it because it might make Hugh's life more difficult.

"We'll think of something."

"I hope so." He made himself sound depressed. "But right now, I've gotta go and get Stella's stuff. Mom's orders." He wasn't going to get any help from Jackson or Kim, but he knew exactly who would help him. It was time to call in a favor.

CHAPTER 35: Jethro

Jethro followed Townsend into his study.

"Have a seat." The reporter shut the door behind them and walked to his desk. "Since you're here late and alone, I'm assuming you've come to collect your pound of flesh."

"I've always appreciated intelligence. It saves so much time." Jethro smiled as he sat. "And I can't stay long." He still needed to go to Stella's apartment.

"What do you want?" Townsend sat behind his desk.

"Nothing much."

"In my experience, that always means it's a lot."

"All things considered, what I'm asking is nothing compared to what I did for you."

"I'll be the judge of that."

"Fair enough." He didn't care what Townsend thought about this favor, as long as he did it. "Stella was attacked tonight. She needs somewhere to stay."

"Is she okay?" Townsend's expression changed from guarded to concerned.

"Yeah. She's a bit bruised and scared, but she's okay."

"What happened?"

"She was attacked in her home and kidnapped by Servants. She got away, but being she had nothing worth stealing, I'm afraid they went after her because of who she is, and what her grandfather did."

"That's very possible." Townsend frowned. "Many want revenge, and some don't care who pays."

"She can't go back to her apartment. She needs somewhere to stay. She's at my mom's house but—"

"Good. You can't take her to your place."

"Ah..." He'd been prepared to explain why he couldn't take her to his house, not to have the reporter tell him he shouldn't. "Why?"

Townsend opened one of his desk drawers and pulled out a notebook. He flipped through the pages. "From what I've learned the party at Crosnics Manor is being organized by Vivian Vickers, Bill's wife."

"Great. I met with Vickers today. My first fight is Friday. Once I win a few fights I'm sure to get invited."

"Not if you're engaged to Stella."

"What?"

"Calm down. I'm not suggesting that the two of you really break up, but you need to pretend to. I'm sure Stella won't be thrilled but there is no way you'll get invited to the party if she's your fiancé."

"That's such Gruntshit. They need to stop blaming her for what her grandfather did." He didn't want to marry her, but he didn't like seeing her ostracized either.

"I agree, but that's not the reason."

"It's not?" Now, he was confused.

"No. Vivian has hated Jason's wife for years. Actually, she hated their whole family."

"Then I better make it known that Stella and I are no longer engaged." This was working out better than he'd planned. He'd been prepared to explain that he didn't know Stella well enough to trust her being there when they met to discuss the black market, but Townsend coming up with his own reason was better.

"Good idea and you're right. She can't stay at your mom's house. It'd look suspicious for your former fiancé to live with your mother, and you can't afford to look suspicious."

"No, I can't." The reporter owed him, but Townsend was friends with Hugh. Jethro wasn't a hundred percent sure the reporter would agree to suggest that Stella move into the Council Building if he thought Jethro was trying to break up Hugh and Trinity.

"I suppose that she can stay here." Townsend didn't sound all too excited about it. "I'll have to talk to Libby first."

"That won't work." He scrambled for a reason as the reporter stared at him. "She is...uhm...She isn't too accepting of interclass pairs." Guilt stabbed him but he pushed it aside. Being with Hugh would be better for her in the long run. "You know...with her grandfather and all."

"Oh, yeah." Townsend's face which had hardened, softened a bit. "I suppose she might see my relationship with Libby as similar, even though Libby was an adult when we first..." He cleared his throat. "And she was definitely consenting."

"I know, but it's hard for Stella right now. Time will help."

"Of course." Townsend nodded. "What her grandfather did was...Well, we both know what that was. There's no need for us to discuss it."

Time to broach the subject before Townsend came up with another place for Stella to live. "I was thinking that she might like to stay at the Council Building. She did kind of grow up there."

"You want her to move in with Hugh and Trinity?" Townsend's eyes narrowed. "I'm not sure Trinity is going to be okay with another female living with them."

"Why? There are plenty of rooms there. It's not like a private house. A lot of others live there too—Guards, Servants, Trinity's parents and brother."

"I suppose. Still, she's your fiancé."

"And I trust her." He did. He trusted her to see the opportunity and take it. Abandon a large, rough Almighty for a polished one.

"And you need me to do what exactly?"

"To suggest this." He stood and began to pace. "Hugh and I...We're working together but we're not exactly friends. I'm not asking him for this favor. He'll turn me down out of spite."

"I don't think he'd do that."

"I can't take the chance. I need to know that Stella isn't in danger while I'm working. The Council Building is the one place where I know she'll be safe." Hopefully, safe in Hugh's arms.

Townsend studied him for a long time. "I'll talk to Hugh."

"Do not let him know that this was my idea, or he'll find some way to refuse."

"I won't."

"It has to be soon."

"I'll take care of it." Townsend wasn't happy.

"Thank you." He headed for the door.

"Now, we're even."

He stopped and turned to stare at the reporter. "If she moves into the Council Building, then we're even."

"Agreed."

It was fair. He'd saved Townsend's family and the reporter was giving him a chance to make one of his own. He'd heard rumors that Hugh and Trinity fought a lot. She couldn't be happy living in the city. Add some jealousy to their already unhappy relationship, and hopefully, it'd fall apart. Once Hugh was out of the picture, he could make Trinity remember how much she'd loved him.

CHAPTER 36: Jethro

Jethro crept into the house and put a load of boxes by the door. Stella hadn't been kidding. Her apartment was a disaster. He'd spent hours trying to pack up everything that was worth saving. He hurried back outside to get the rest of her things. The house was quiet, and he wanted to keep it that way. He grabbed the last few boxes and took them to the house. He put them on top of the others and turned to leave when Kim darted out of the back room.

"Hey," he whispered, hurrying toward the door. "Goodnight."

She touched her finger to her lips to silence him as she grabbed his arm, pulling him down the hallway. She quietly closed the back door and dragged him across the yard, stopping under the tree where Jackson paced.

"What were you thinking?" She dropped his arm.

"What else was I supposed to do? She was attacked in her home. I couldn't leave her there."

"I understand but did you have to bring her here?" asked Kim, exasperation in her voice.

"Where should I have taken her? Everyone she knows disassociated themselves from her after Jason's...What he did."

"She can't stay here," said Jackson. "It's not safe. She might overhear something."

"I hadn't even thought about that." He lied.

"Unless you trust her to keep quiet." Kim watched him.

"Ah...I don't know her that well."

"She's your fiancé," said Kim.

"Not by choice." He shrugged.

"How nice." Trinity wandered out of the bushes, her hand clasped in Hugh's.

He glared at the heavens for a moment. It was just his luck to have her show up at that exact time. It didn't matter that he'd become engaged in order to save Tee. Of course, he hadn't told anyone about that or his flogging. Talking about those things didn't make it any better. It'd only cause his family pain. Plus, Tee was working really hard to forget about what Jason and his friends had done to her. His mom suspected something had happened to the young Servant, but he wasn't saying anything unless she asked. Once others knew the truth, it was somehow more real. Right now, Tee was regaining a bit of her youth and happiness. She'd never regain her innocence, but this would have to do.

"Hugh, what are you doing here without any Guards? It's not safe for you to travel at night alone," said Jackson.

"I'm not alone." Hugh pushed back the hood of his cloak and kissed Trinity's hand.

"Yeah. He has me." She leaned against him.

Jethro looked away, wanting to puke.

Jackson wasn't amused. "If you aren't going to take this seriously then you—"

"I'm taking this very seriously." Trinity's humor fled.

"And that's supposed to make me feel better?" Jackson rolled his eyes. "You aren't known for your levelheaded decisions."

"Hey. My decisions haven't been that bad." Trinity looked to Hugh, who averted his eyes. She glared at him before turning to Kim.

"Uh..." His sister looked away.

"Why didn't you use the tunnels?" asked Jackson.

"And creep into your basement?" asked Hugh. "You weren't expecting us. We would've had to find you and—"

"It would've been better than coming here through the streets. The two of you could've been followed," said Jackson.

There was a rustling in the bushes. It was large but too noisy to be anything dangerous. Only Kim looked worried.

"Sorry." Townsend stepped out of the brush and into the backyard. "This was my idea. I'd heard about your houseguest and told Hugh and Trinity that we all needed to meet."

The reporter must've gone directly to see Hugh after Jethro had left. Was it to tell Hugh about their conversation or something else? He watched Townsend, but the reporter kept his eyes on the others.

"How did you hear about that?" asked Kim.

"Did you really think her attack would go unnoticed?" Townsend ignored her question.

"Who was attacked?" Hugh looked around their group. "What are you talking about?"

"Do you want to tell them or should I?" Kim's gaze fell on her brother.

"Tell us what?" Hugh's voice was guarded.

"It seems both of my brothers are idiots," said Kim.

"Hey," said Hugh at the same time that Jethro said, "I had no choice."

Kim shook her head and when Jethro didn't continue, she explained about Stella.

"She can't stay here," said Hugh. "We agreed that meeting at your house was the least risky. If discovered, we all"—he glanced at Townsend—"except you, have a reason to be here that has nothing to do with our mission."

"And even though Stella has been ostracized from everyone she's ever known"—said Townsend—"there are many, like Bette Wilson's family, who'd do and promise anything to see Hugh fail...and die."

"She has nowhere else to go." Jethro's eyes met Townsend's for a second. The reporter wasn't happy, but he was doing what he needed to do.

"What about renting her a room?" asked Hugh.

That had been his suggestion at one point too, but now, seeing Trinity with Hugh, he knew he'd do anything to break them up. All he had to do was steer the conversation the way he wanted without being obvious. "She's afraid. She doesn't want to stay alone." He frowned. "I don't think the motivation behind the attack was robbery."

"Was it Servants who attacked her?" asked Hugh.

"Yes. They targeted her, followed her, and attacked her."

"I agree. I doubt it had anything to do with money. It was probably due to who she is. What her grandfather did," said Hugh.

"What about friends?" asked Trinity.

"She has none," he said. "No one will speak with her or help her. They all abandoned her after her grandfather's appetites were revealed."

"That wasn't her fault." Trinity's face hardened.

"Doesn't matter. No one wants to be associated with her, especially now that the entire class system is in upheaval," he said.

"She should stay here then," said Trinity. "We'll be careful not to talk around her."

The generosity of Trinity's spirit touched his heart like nothing else ever had. Even his body's desire for her, his true mate, paled in comparison to what his heart felt. He tore his eyes away before anyone saw the longing on his face, and his gaze met Townsend's.

The Almighty shook his head, a look of pity in his eyes. Jethro turned away. It was bad enough having these feelings for her, he didn't need pity too. Now that Townsend suspected the real reason behind his request, he wasn't sure the reporter would honor their agreement.

"It's too risky," said Jackson.

"Is she that untrustworthy?" Trinity's eyes fell to him and for once there was no anger, only a question.

"I really don't know," he said truthfully.

Townsend looked like he was struggling with a decision and then he said, "Perhaps she should stay at the Council Building. It's large enough and there are others there."

Trinity's face paled a moment and she glanced at Hugh. He was slowly shaking his head, but it was clear that he was pondering the suggestion.

"She'd be safe there," said Townsend.

"I suppose it'd be okay." Hugh nodded. "It'll send a message that I'm...That this government isn't just for the other classes. We're here to help everyone...everyone who's innocent."

"But if we can't trust her, she can learn more at the Council Building than anywhere else," said Trinity.

"I disagree," said Hugh. "We're always careful about where we speak secrets in the Council Building. There are too many ears around for us not to be."

"But if she's persuaded by friends, like Townsend said might happen, she could be dangerous," said Trinity.

Jethro laughed and all eyes turned toward him. "Have you met Stella?"

Trinity shook her head.

"She is the least dangerous person I know." In the way that Trinity meant. Stella would never harm Hugh, not physically. No, she'd see the benefit of being his wife and she'd lure him, trap him and marry him.

"Jethro's right," said Hugh.

"You've met her?" He was surprised that Stella hadn't set her sights on Hugh already.

"Years ago. Before I was imprisoned. She was a sweet child and she's innocent in all that has happened to her."

"And she's not stupid. She'll appreciate your kindness in letting her stay with you," said Townsend. "If one of your enemies approaches her, she'll more than likely stay true to you."

"She is quite loyal," he added. "Even though our engagement was arranged by her grandfather, she wrote to me in prison."

"She did?" asked Kim.

"Yeah."

"Plus, like you said, it should help your standing with the Almightys," said Townsend. "There are some middle-class folks like me who feel what happened to her was completely unfair."

"It might hurt your relationship with the Servants though," said Jackson.

"Not if we tell the truth," said Hugh. "Stella had nothing to do with her grandfather's perversions and she shouldn't be punished for them." He turned to Townsend. "You can write a piece about her. Explain how we're helping the granddaughter of my enemy because she's been unfairly treated. We'll make sure they see that I stand for justice for everyone."

He wanted to clap and shout bravo. Hugh was a politician born and bred. He and Stella would be perfect together. "Then I guess this is all settled." He fought to keep the grin off his face.

"It seems to be." Kim watched him closely. "You can tell her tomorrow."

"I can't." He tried to look unhappy. "I have my first fight scheduled. I have to get ready. You'll have to do it."

"You are such a jerk."

"Is there anything else we should discuss?" Hugh looked around but no one said anything. "Then we'll be going." He tugged on Trinity's hand.

"Goodnight," she said as the two of them walked away.

"We should get some rest too." Jackson put his arm around Kim as they headed for the house.

"Goodnight." He glanced at the reporter as he started across the yard. "My carriage is out front."

"We're even," whispered Townsend before disappearing into the brush.

Apparently, the reporter wasn't happy about his involvement, but the deed had been done. Now, all he could do was hope Stella was as persuasive and persistent as he thought she might be.

CHAPTER 37: Jethro

The next evening, Jethro ducked behind a building near the location of his first fight. He waited, listening for footsteps or any sign that he was being followed. This wasn't a good part of town, and he didn't trust Vickers.

He continued down the alley. No one would expect him to follow this route. If the lawyer was setting him up it'd be a big mistake. It'd been almost two weeks since he'd had his shot, and he felt like he could take anyone. He paused, his nose twitching at the scent of bodies, a lot of them. The sounds of voices drifted toward him with the evening breeze.

He moved farther into the shadows. There was no shame in running from an ambush. Right now, he wasn't strong enough to take on a group. He waited but the voices didn't get any closer. He stayed in the shadows as he continued down the alley, stopping at the end and peeking around the corner.

The street was blocked off by multiple carriages and filled with members from all classes. He scanned the area, his gaze stopping on Vickers. The lawyer stood at the front of the makeshift ring, talking to a huge, older Guard with a vicious scar from temple to chin. Vickers searched the crowd, probably looking for him.

This all looked legitimate. It was time to step out of the shadows and into his new life as a paid street fighter.

CHAPTER 38: Jethro

No one paid much attention to Jethro as he made his way through the crowd. They were all focused on placing bets and filling up their drinks while they waited for the next fight.

As soon as Vickers saw him, the Guard by his side waved his hand and several other big Guards pushed through the crowd, heading in his direction. He kept walking, ignoring the instinct to find a place near a wall or building—anywhere that he could better defend himself.

This wasn't a trap. They weren't preparing to attack. They were going to escort him to the lawyer. He shifted his shoulders, trying to shake away the tension as they circled him and herded him toward Vickers. He'd been heading this way anyway. Nothing was happening that he didn't want to happen.

They stopped in front of Vickers who was talking to a well-dressed Servant. They spoke for several more minutes before the Servant disappeared into the crowd.

"You're late." The lawyer turned toward him, eyes hard with anger. "I thought you got scared and changed your mind."

"Hardly. I thought you might be planning some payback for my tardiness in answering your summons."

"Don't talk to your betters like that." The old Guard at Vickers' side stepped forward, his chest almost brushing against Jethro's chin.

"He's not my better." Jethro stared up at him. The Guard was big and ugly with a scar covering one side of his face from chin to temple, but he could take him easily. "I'm an Almighty too."

"He's still better than you."

"Sovee. Enough." Vickers held up his hand and the Guard growled but moved back to the lawyer's side. "The crowd grows restless. They're excited to see the next fight."

"They can't wait to see an Almighty get the Gruntshit kicked out of him." Sovee smiled, the scar on his face almost making his one eye nothing more than a slit.

"Then they're going to be disappointed." Jethro glanced around. "Where can I place a bet?"

"The fighters don't bet," said Sovee.

"This one does." He looked at Vickers. "As long as I bet on myself to win, there's no question that I'll throw the fight."

"True." Vickers waved his hand and the Servant from earlier appeared from the crowd, book and moneybag in his hands.

"This will be even more fun," said Sovee. "You're going to get beat up and lose your money." The Guard held out some cash. "On the other guy."

"Your loss." Jethro handed the Servant his money. "Me to win."

"Got it." The Servant took the money from them both, jotting down their names, the amounts and their bets in the book.

"What are my odds?"

"One hundred to one"—the Servant's green eyes almost glowed with amusement—"that you lose."

"Good. I need the money."

"You should've looked at your opponent before betting." Sovee laughed as he pointed to the center of the crowd.

A giant of a Guard stood in the makeshift ring. He was young and had large, strong features, long arms and fists the size of dinner plates. There was no way this guy was all Guard. He had to have Grunt or Producer in him.

"It won't matter. I'll beat anyone you put up against me." And he would. This Guard was big and didn't look bright. Plus, his size would probably make him slow. It'd be an easy win. He turned to

Vickers and the Servant. "I'll be back in a minute." He headed for the ring.

"Ha. In a minute, you'll be lying in the center of the road unconscious," shouted Sovee. "And I'll be richer and happier because I got to see an Almighty get the snot beat out of him by a Guard!"

The crowd cheered at Sovee's taunts, but Jethro ignored them all. His focus was on his opponent. His enemy. The males around the center barely moved as he pushed through them. They sneered at him. Here, in this place, being an Almighty held no value...unless you were rich. He was fine with that. He'd had to earn respect from the Guards in the Protective Services. He'd earn the respect of this crowd too...or their fear. Either would work for him.

He stepped into the open area and the Guard who was refereeing waved him to the other side of the ring.

"What are the rules?" he asked as his opponent snarled at him. The Guard was trying to make him nervous, but it wouldn't work. Jethro wasn't scared, but he was looking forward to the scent of his enemy's fear in the air. Right now, there was nothing but the sharp scent of anticipation.

"Rules!" The referee shouted, "This Almighty wants to know the rules."

The crowd burst into laughter.

Apparently, there were no rules.

"No. No." The referee held up his hand, silencing the crowd. "Let's help this Almighty." He turned to Jethro. "For you, the rules are simple. Try not to die." He pointed at the large Guard. "For him, punch until the Almighty drops to the road."

The crowd roared at the joke.

"Got it." He was tired of this. He wiggled his fingers to coax his opponent closer. "Let's get this over with, shall we?"

"You wanna see dark that much, huh?" The large Guard moved forward, talking to the crowd as the referee stepped aside. "Fine by me. Don't let anyone say I'm not an obedient Guard. I'm gonna give the Almighty exactly what he wants. A close up of the road. I'll even make him kiss it." He swung one of his huge fists.

The air whooshed with the force of the Guard's punch, but Jethro had no problem avoiding it. He ducked and then took two steps forward, his knuckles slamming into his opponent's stomach. The Guard grunted in surprise and Jethro hit him two more times—fast hard punches—before darting to the side and sending one quick uppercut to his opponent's jaw.

The giant stumbled backward, and Jethro followed, hitting the Guard on the shoulder, the chest, the gut—anywhere he found an opening. His enemy was weak and on the run. It was time for the kill. The Guard threw a punch, but his aim was wild. Jethro easily dodged the blow, landing one of his own to the Guard's torso before following it with another punch to the jaw. This time the Guard fell to his knees, swaying slightly before hitting the road face first.

Silence filled the street.

Jethro's arms trembled at his sides as he forced himself not to follow his enemy to the ground and finish him off. The Guard wasn't really his enemy. He was just an opponent. He took a deep breath. The sweet scent of fear filled the air from the Guard and the referee. He tipped back his head and inhaled again. More fear trickled toward him from the crowd. He wanted to shout, to roar his triumph, but instead he straightened. His eyes met the referee. "He hit the road. I think you declare me the winner now."

"Ah..." The referee just stood there.

"Or do I have to kill him first?" He raised his hand and licked some of the blood from his knuckles.

"No. No." The referee walked over to him, lifting his arm. "The winner. The Almighty."

No one cheered.

"Good enough for me." He turned and walked toward Vickers and Sovee, grabbing the Servant who'd taken his money by the arm and pulling him along with him. "I want my winnings."

"Ah...right. Yeah." The Servant opened his bag and counted out a wad of cash before handing it to Jethro.

"Thanks." He smiled at Sovee. "And thank you for your donation. Loser." He turned to walk away. He'd fought. He'd won. Now, it was time for a drink and a female.

"Wait," shouted Vickers.

His spine stiffened at the command, but he needed the lawyer. He had a job to do. He turned around.

"Training. Tomorrow at six a.m."

"Training? I don't need—"

"It's part of the deal." Vickers wasn't kidding about this.

"I don't need—"

"Trust me. You do. Now that they've seen you fight, the matches are going to get harder and harder." Vickers grinned. "I owe Wickerwood for telling me about you. I hadn't believed him, but...I was wrong. And I never...almost never say that."

"Fine. I'll train but I want another fight...soon." He needed to remind the lawyer about his two weeks on and two weeks off rule.

"Oh, it'll be soon." Vickers eyes went to the crowd behind him. "They won't stand for anything else."

The lawyer was right. Only soft murmurs trickled from the once rambunctious crowd. They were still in shock that an Almighty could take out a Guard...a big one. Soon that shock would turn to anger for some, fascination for others, and disbelief for most. He was going to have to prove himself again and again, and he couldn't wait. He'd show everyone that he could beat anyone and anything they put in the ring with him.

CHAPTER 39: Trinity

Trinity headed for the courtyard. It was the one place in the Council Building besides their suite of rooms where she could relax without worrying that others were watching and judging her. The gardens weren't the wild forest that she loved, but it was the closest she was going to get. They were peaceful and quiet, and she needed a moment of peace before her appointment with the seamstress.

She was having a dress made for the big party that Hugh was arranging to raise money for the new schools. Before her first meeting with Mrs. Champfur she'd been both nervous and excited. She'd never had a fancy dress. She'd dreamed of looking lovely and elegant, but those dreams had died a quick death after her first fitting.

The Almighty seamstress had put her in a gown that'd made her look like a bale of straw with arms and legs. The female swore the next dress would be better, but Trinity wasn't so sure. She didn't belong in the city wearing a dress. Her place was in the forest, wearing pants and throwing spears, but she wanted to do this for Hugh. She opened the double doors and inhaled the crisp morning air as she stepped outside and froze. An intruder was in her garden.

Stella sat on the bench under a tree reading a book. She wore a light blue dress and had her pretty blonde hair pulled back with a barrette. The same kind that always tangled in Trinity's hair and made her look like she was accessorizing with a beetle, but of course, Stella looked perfect.

Trinity glanced down at her stretchy pants and long shirt. She looked like a tall, gangly giant. Peace and patience would have to wait because the only thing she'd accomplish by staying out here was the bolstering of her own self-doubt and insecurities. She turned to go back inside.

"Trinity," said Stella. "Good morning."

"Ah." Her day kept getting better and better. She turned back around. "Good morning."

"Did you want to sit out here? It's lovely this time of day. Cool and fresh." Stella wrinkled her cute little nose. "I don't know why I think it's fresher in the morning, but it just seems that way. Don't you think?"

"I guess." She'd always thought that too, but she really wasn't in the mood for company.

"Oh. I'm sorry." Stella closed her book, the smile fading from her face. "I'm sure you came out here for some solitude and here I am chatting away." She started to stand. "I'll go back to my room."

"No. It's fine." She didn't want to chase the other female away. She knew what it was like to feel like she didn't belong.

"Are you sure?" Stella sat on the edge of the bench as if ready to bolt.

"Yes. Of course. There's plenty of room out here for both of us to enjoy the morning." She smiled as she walked over and sat next to the other female. Of course, Stella was in the perfect spot. It was shaded with just enough sun to make it warm but not hot.

"It'll be nice to have some company."

"Yeah. Nice." That wasn't the word she'd use to describe this. Trinity had been avoiding the other female ever since she'd arrived. Stella was everything she wasn't—petite, polite, demure and she fit into city life. Whereas Trinity was tall, blunt and would sooner stab someone than make chitchat over tea.

"I want to thank you for letting me stay here. I know this can't be easy," said Stella.

"Please. This place is so big. We barely even know you're here. I grew up in a hut. My bedroom was smaller than the bathrooms in this building." She tried to make light of the situation, but she wasn't particularly thrilled to have a perfect Almighty female living here. It made Trinity's flaws that much more obvious, at least to her, and it was another reason for arguments and lectures from her mom.

"If you don't mind my asking, what was it like where you grew up?"

"It was fine until they killed us." Trinity glanced at her. She wasn't going to amuse the perfect Almighty with tales of her childhood.

"I'm so sorry about that. Really, I am. Most of us didn't know what they did to your kind. I had no idea. I thought meat was like an apple or any other fruit or vegetable and Producers just grew it."

"I know. I was told that most of those in the other classes, including Almightys, didn't know." Sometimes she thought that made things better but other times she feared how everyone had been fooled by a few. Still, it'd been nice of Stella to try and explain. Most of those from the other classes didn't bring it up at all—as if not talking about it made the past disappear. She should try and be nice too. "Not everyone is against you." She cringed when Stella flinched. "I thought you might like to know that most of those who I've met don't blame you for what your grandfather did."

"I think you know better people than I do." Stella looked away, blinking, and then cleared her throat. "I can't believe they all turned on us. At first everyone supported us—my grandmother and me—but then rumors spread that we were involved. They said that Grandmother hired Servants for Grandfather and that I went to the shelters and picked out ones specially for him." She looked at Trinity, her eyes filled with confusion. "When would I have done that? I was never allowed to go anywhere."

"I heard the rumors. They didn't make sense to me either. I'm sorry this happened." It brought back so many bad memories for her. "When I was growing up Travis was my only friend. All the other

Producers either stayed away from me or picked on me because I was different."

"I can't believe they didn't see how kind you are," said Stella.

"They had other friends. They didn't need kindness from a freak." Her throat tightened as the loneliness of her past washed over her again.

"Did you ever get used to it? You know, not being liked."

"Honestly?" She took a deep breath. "No. Even now, I don't have a lot of friends, but the few I have are the best kind. I know they'll stick with me through anything."

"You're lucky to have found friends like that." Stella's blue eyes sparkled with tears.

"I am and I don't worry about those who don't like me." She smiled. "If I keep telling myself that, maybe one day it'll be true."

Stella laughed. "I'll have to try—"

"Ms. Trinity." A Servant stood in the doorway.

"No," she groaned. "Please tell me she's not here already."

"I'm sorry, miss. Mrs. Champfur is waiting for you in the Tea Room."

"Mrs. Champfur the seamstress?" asked Stella.

"Yes." Trinity stood. "She's making me a dress for the fundraising event Hugh is throwing in a couple of months."

"How lovely." Stella's eyes were wistful. "Mrs. Champfur is always so nice, and she has the funniest tales to tell."

"Maybe to you." Unless Hugh was with her, the seamstress barely spoke to Trinity. When they were alone and Mrs. Champfur did speak, it was always proceeded or followed by a "tsking" sound of disgust. She hated meeting with the Almighty, especially alone. "Actually, since you're staying here now, you should come with me. We can get you a dress too."

"Oh, I don't think that's a good idea."

"Well, I do." She grabbed Stella's hand. "We want everyone to know that we support you and that you're not to blame for what your grandfather did." She really hoped Hugh would be okay with this. "And I could use some help because I don't know what's fashionable outside of the forest."

"You don't need me for that. Mrs. Champfur knows everything about fashion."

"She's obviously never dressed someone like me because the last one she had me try on made me look like a haystack."

"It couldn't have been that bad." Stella's lips tipped slightly upward for a second, but she quickly frowned.

"It's okay. You can laugh. I did." She had...after she'd cried a bit.

"I'm sure it wasn't that bad." Stella grinned.

"It was absolutely that bad, but she's bringing something else today. You can tell me what you think." She pulled Stella toward the door.

CHAPTER 40: Trinity

Trinity stood in the Tea Room while Stella and the dressmaker spoke about fabric, stitching, colors and a whole bunch of other things that were foreign to her. She was so glad she'd dragged Stella with her.

The young Almighty had argued with Mrs. Champfur that it didn't matter if everyone else wore white and pastels, Trinity would look better in darker colors.

At first, Trinity had wondered if the other female was trying to make her look foolish, but she liked those shades better. They were the colors of the forest in the fall—rich and dark, a vibrant display before the sparsity of winter.

"Trinity. We need..." Tim walked into the room, stopping when his eyes landed on the two Almighty females.

"Hey, Dad." She'd have to explain Stella's presence later, but right now, she'd ignore the look her father was giving her.

"When you're done. Come to your suite. We need your help."

"With what?"

"Ah..."

She glanced at Stella who quickly turned away and started talking to Mrs. Champfur.

Tim grabbed her arm and pulled her into the hallway. He lowered his voice to barely a whisper. "We're going over some maps. We're trying to figure out where you-know-who took you-know-what."

"What are you talking about?"

"You know who I'm talking about and what he did to...others." He exposed his claws and made a face, showing his teeth.

"I really don't." She tried not to laugh. "Just say it. She can't hear us out here."

215

"You never know."

"We do know. She's an Almighty. But it doesn't matter because I'm done. Give me one minute." She walked back into the room. "I'm sorry, but I have to help my dad with something."

"But what about the dress?" asked Mrs. Champfur.

"I trust Stella. She'll pick out something perfect."

"Are you sure?" asked Stella.

"Absolutely." It had to be better than the last two. The dress the seamstress had delivered today had been worse than the haystack. It was a soft pink, poufy thing with so much lace and frills that she looked like a giant, pink milk thistle.

"Okay, but what about dancing and what to do at dinner?" asked Stella.

"Yeah. Uhm." She did need help with that stuff. "We'll do it later."

"When?" asked Stella.

"Ah...I'll find you." She darted out the door. She didn't want to learn to dance or to know what piece of silverware to use with what dish. That was all boring. Whatever her dad was doing had to be more exciting. She grabbed her dad's arm. "Let's get out of here." She pulled him down the hallway toward her suite of rooms.

"Are you sure? This can wait until you finish. I know you're nervous about this party."

"I'm positive. I can't stay in there another minute. I'm not meant for that kind of stuff." Give her the forest or farming any day.

"Okay, but you don't need her help. I'll teach you to dance and how to get through dinner." He smiled at her. "Sarah entertained a lot, and even though I couldn't attend as a guest, she made sure I knew how to do all those kinds of things."

"Thanks, Dad." She kissed his cheek before glancing at the empty chair outside the door to their suite.

"Where is the hulking Guard?" asked Dad.

"Hugh gave Rex a job at the jail."

"Tell him to give him another one because the Guard was sleeping on this chair last night."

"I know. Hugh found him an apartment, but Rex insists on staying here."

"He should stop. It's creepy how he basically lives outside your suite."

"I don't know. I kind of miss seeing him." She opened the door and stepped inside.

Hugh sat on the floor surrounded by maps. One of the city and one of the forest were spread out in front of him, while others were scattered on the couch and nearby chairs.

"This is so unfair." She walked over to him, her heart melting a little when he looked up at her and smiled. "I've been wasting my entire morning getting fitted for a dress and listening to two females argue about color, fabrics, and a whole bunch of other things that I don't care one bit about, while the two of you are having fun."

"I told you not to bother with a dress." He grabbed her hand and pulled her to the floor by him. "You look great in whatever you wear."

She kissed him. "I love you for saying that, but you know it's not true."

"It is true." His face grew serious. "I want the world to see the female I love. The warrior. The girl who can't be tamed." His hand cupped her cheek.

She fell into his dark blue eyes. She loved him so much it hurt. He leaned forward to kiss her.

"I'm sitting right here," said Tim.

She grinned at Hugh but didn't move.

"Aren't there more maps you need to go get?" Hugh's eyes sparkled.

"No. There's not. So get your hands off my daughter and look at the maps."

"If I have to." He winked at her.

"You do," said Dad.

"Okay." His face became serious as he pointed to a spot on one of the maps. "This is where Conguise lives, and the lab is right next to his home."

"Are you sure they didn't turn the creatures loose?" She ran her finger along the map. "These are canals, and they flow right into the forest. It'd be the perfect thing to do with the experiments. You said the ones you saw were aquatic. They could drop them in and let them swim away." The idea sent fear skittering through her blood. The River-Men were bad enough. If the things her dad and Hugh had seen had free range of the waterways, nothing would be safe trying to get a drink."

"That's an extraordinarily terrifying thing to say." Dad shivered.

"I know, but it makes sense. They could also use it to get rid of the dead. The current would take the bodies. They'd either rot or get eaten."

"It's a possibility, especially for the dead, but I don't think the professor would turn them loose. That'd be losing his life's work."

"But he wasn't there," she said. "He was under arrest at the time."

"Yeah, but he would've had a plan for evacuation in case of an arrest or suspicion from the Council."

"And you think his employees followed that?" asked Dad.

"I do," said Hugh. "I'm guessing they would've started the evacuation at the first sign that we might win. They wouldn't have waited to know for sure if we won or if we could hold the Council Building. They definitely wouldn't have wanted to fail if the old rule was successful."

"You think they were really that scared of Conguise?" asked Trinity.

"Parson faked his own death to escape. Rumors are that the professor would feed anyone who wanted to quit or didn't get results to those creatures."

"I saw those things," said Tim. "I agree. They've would've done anything to avoid that fate."

"Okay." She sat back on her feet and studied the maps. "The creatures that you saw were all aquatic, right?"

"Yeah," said Hugh.

"Were they like the River-Men and Cold Creepers who can breathe air or like fish that need water?"

"The fish-creature that was in the tank with Tim definitely needed water to live."

"But that tentacled thing in the room Laddie took us to when he freed Scar wasn't in water," said Tim.

"So we should assume that there were both kinds. The air breathers would be easier to move. That fish thing that was in the tank with Dad was little, right?"

"Yeah," said Hugh.

"But it had a lot of teeth," said Tim.

"I didn't mean it wasn't dangerous." She sent Hugh an amused look. Her father had a very fragile ego. "I just mentioned the size because in order to transport fish you have to take water. Do you think it was the only one?"

"I doubt it," said Hugh. "From a scientific point of view, it'd be better to create many because most of them probably wouldn't survive."

"Did your soldiers search the surrounding area as well as Conguise's property?" She stared at the map.

"Yeah. Why?"

"They would've had to have used carts and carriages to transport tanks of water. If they went into the forest, they would've left big indentations on the ground. Plus, navigating something that heavy through the brush and trees would've been next to impossible."

"There were no tracks leading into the forest." He trailed his finger along the map. "They had to travel by roadway, but we interviewed everyone who lived nearby. No one saw anything. Maybe a carriage or two but not a whole bunch of them or even one going back and forth over and over again."

"Then they didn't travel by road." She tipped her head, staring at the map again. "And they didn't go by forest."

"They could've traveled the road at night," said Dad.

"I don't think so," said Hugh. "Any other time I'd agree but we'd just taken the city. Those out here would've been watching the roads to see if anyone came for them."

"When did you send the soldiers?" They were missing something, but she had no idea what it was.

"About a day and a half after we knew for sure we'd won and could hold the city," said Hugh.

"And *nothing* was in the lab," she muttered to herself. This didn't make sense. The creatures didn't just disappear.

"Nothing but regular lab equipment," said Hugh.

She stood, moving some of the papers off the couch before sitting down. She stared at the maps from above to get a better perspective. "What are we missing?"

"I don't know," said Hugh. "But those creatures are out there somewhere."

"Why? Why did you have to say that?" Tim gave him a disgusted look.

"I didn't mean they were out there running loose." He glanced at Trinity and smirked.

"I know that, but I don't want to hear it. The fact that we have absolutely no idea where they are keeps me up at night. I still have nightmares about that tank and"—he made a face—"the tunnels. Araldo, I don't think I'll ever forget the tunnels."

"The tunnels." She looked at Hugh.

"That would explain everything. All they would've had to do was move the creatures and equipment into the sewer. They could've transported them to another place later."

"Or," she said. "They could've even taken them back into the laboratory."

"You think they're still there?" Dad's face relaxed a bit.

"No," said Hugh.

"I hate you," said Dad. "I really hate you sometimes."

Hugh looked at her and rolled his eyes before saying, "I'm sorry to upset you, but it'd be too risky to take them back to Level Five. We can search the facility at any time."

"Then they took them somewhere else through the sewer. Do we have those maps?" She started helping her dad who was already sorting through a stack of maps when someone knocked on the door.

"I've got it." Hugh walked over and opened it. "Townsend. Great timing. You can help us look through the ma—"

"No time. We have to go. They found another body in the Holstein area."

CHAPTER 41: Hugh

"He's just a kid." Hugh stared down at the mangled body of the young Servant. Blood had oozed out of his nose and mouth as if from an impact. His eyes had popped from the sockets and his torso and limbs were twisted at odd angles. "How old do you think? About ten?"

"Eight would be my guess," said Townsend.

"Shit." He hated that the other classes suffered like this. So many were taken from parents and then abandoned. Their only chance to survive was to join gangs.

"Hey." Jackson nudged Hugh's arm. "Isn't that one of your scientists?"

Hugh and Townsend had picked Jackson up on their way. Since he really didn't think this death had anything to do with a giant bird, he'd convinced Trinity and Tim to stay behind and continue sorting through the maps.

"What?" He turned. "Yeah. That's Ableson."

"What's he doing here?" asked Jackson.

"I have no idea." This had been a bad part of town for many years. No Almightys should live in this area.

Ableson either felt their stares or noticed their small group because he changed direction and walked over to them.

"Hey." Ableson nodded as he stopped next to Hugh. "What happened here? Did the kid jump or get pushed?"

"Still trying to figure that out." He glanced at Townsend and Jackson, hoping they'd both keep their mouths shut about the other possibility. "What are you doing around here?"

Ableson glanced away from the body, looking a little guilty. "I was meeting with Wasee."

"Who's that?"

"He's a Servant. He's helped me out a lot." Ableson pointed to his arm. "Wasee's prosthetics are a lot better than Dr. Baggerly's."

"Really?" He was surprised. Servants were intelligent and capable, but they didn't have the background or education that Almightys had.

"Yeah. Unbelievable but true. When I was first injured, I went to Baggerly. He sold me a new arm that was...It was like a mistake on my shoulder. It just hung there, and the way it was attached hurt. My Servant suggested that I go and see Wasee. His work is fantastic."

"Makes sense," said Townsend. "Guards and Servants are more likely to lose limbs than Almightys."

"And be killed because of it," said Jackson. "I've heard of this guy. He helps Guards too."

"Yes, he does," said Ableson.

"Does he have a business around here?" asked Hugh.

"Kind of. He works from his home." Ableson pointed in the direction he'd come from.

"He should open a shop. Make it a legitimate business. After the war, there are a lot more who need this service."

"Wasee doesn't have the kind of money to set up a shop," said Ableson.

"I'll give you an invite for him to come to my fundraising event."

"Why? No Almighty is going to invest in a Servant's business," said Ableson.

"It's a new world. Bring him to the party. I'll be collecting for the schools but there's no reason your friend can't mingle and try to raise some funds too."

"Do you really think someone might invest in his business?" asked Ableson.

"When they see how well you're doing and they realize how much money they could make, yeah. I think you'll get a few to invest."

"Okay. I'll see if I can convince him to come, but you have more faith in rich Almightys than I do."

"If nothing else, it's a free dinner."

"True." Ableson looked down at the kid. "I hope you catch who did this. Poor Servant was way too young to die."

CHAPTER 42: Hugh

"Grab the bag from the carriage and let's get him covered," said Hugh. On the way, they'd stopped to get Dr. Kalper, but he'd been out seeing patients. His assistant, Pepper, had given them supplies so they could bring the body back for the doctor to examine. "And then I need to talk to the witnesses." He was sure this wasn't death by giant bird, but he needed to do his due diligence.

"Got it." Jackson walked to the carriage and retrieved the bag.

"What are you going to do with him?" asked one of the teenage Servants who lingered in the shadows.

"We're taking him to Dr. Kalper," said Hugh

"JD don't need no doctor. JD's dead." The oldest of the young Servants strutted out of the shadows. He went by Con, and he was probably the leader and therefore the one responsible. He may not have killed JD, but he'd caused the kid's death by bringing him into the gang.

"I'm quite aware that he's dead." He was ready to toss all the kids into jail. "But we need to check your story."

"Nothing to check. Some monster flew through the sky and grabbed JD." Con's voice cracked a little, giving credibility to his story. "Picked him right up off the street. We were all there. It could've attacked any of us, but it grabbed JD. Carried him away. JD screaming and fighting but you can't fight air and that's all that he could reach. Air and claws."

"Where did this happen?" He now understood why Townsend wanted to believe this tale. Con's name was fitting because the kid could tell a good story, but Hugh had been around a lot more politicians than the reporter. The ability to sound convincing didn't make the lies true, just more believable.

"Right there." Con pointed down the street.

"Show me exactly where."

He and Townsend followed the teenagers a few yards.

"Right here. Lady-Bird grabbed him right here." Con stopped on the sidewalk.

"Lady-Bird?" He looked at Townsend.

"They say it's a female," said the reporter.

"Why do they think that?" The sex organs of birds were inside the body.

"We know it's a female because it is a female," said Con.

"She's beautiful," said Gray, one of the other young Servants. "Dark and deadly and her eyes—"

"Shut up." Con punched the other Servant's shoulder. "Lady-Bird ain't beautiful. She's the monster that killed JD."

"Pretty or not, are you sure this is where JD was grabbed?" He wasn't in the mood to listen to their squabbling.

"I knew no one would believe us." Con actually sounded hurt. He was a very good actor.

"It doesn't matter what I believe because I'm going to check the evidence."

"What evidence?" asked Con.

"You said this Lady-Bird had claws. What kind of claws? Like a Servant?"

"No." Con stared at his hands. "They weren't like ours. They were like a bird's feet with claws, but I don't think they slide back in like ours do but"—he shrugged—"they might. It wasn't like she hovered in the air for us to study her."

"Okay. This creature probably has talons then and she grabbed JD with those, right?"

"Yeah. That's what we said. She swooped down. Her legs tucked in. She moved so fast and then those cla...talons were out, and she grabbed him, pulling him right up into the air." Con shivered.

"Where did she grab him? His head? Arms? Neck?"

"Ah..." Con paused, his eyes narrowing in thought.

"Back," said Gray. "She grabbed his back. We were all running and"—he looked at Con—"I remember looking up at JD's face. He was so scared." The kid's voice grew soft. "And those screams. I'll never forget those."

Hugh wanted to clap. It was a moving performance but that's all it was. "I've got a problem with that part of your story." He had a problem with all of it, but he'd start there. "Come with me."

He walked back to Jackson who stood by JD's remains which were now encased in the body bag. He bent and unzipped it. "I don't see any claw marks or talon marks." He looked up at the Servants. "Do you? You said the creature grabbed his back." He moved the clothes to reveal the kid's skin. "There's blood and cuts, places where the skin split, but no puncture wounds."

"You got to believe us," said Gray.

"I'll believe the evidence." He pulled JD's shirt back down and zipped the bag. "And we'll get that from Dr. Kalper."

"I told you this new Almighty wouldn't believe us. He's no different than the old Almighty." Con looked at Townsend.

"That's not true," said the reporter. "Hugh needs evidence. You know Kalper. He's been helping the other classes for years. He won't lie."

"Even Kalper can be bought," said Con. "Let's go." He and the other Servants slipped back into the shadows and disappeared.

"This is not the way for us to get information or help around here." Townsend gave him a disgusted look.

"They weren't giving us information. They were feeding us lies."

"You don't know that," said Townsend. "Maybe this Lady-Bird grabbed JD's clothes. The shirt is shredded."

"The shirt is so worn that a slap on the shoulder would've caused it to tear."

"That doesn't rule out Lady-Bird," said Townsend.

"Fine but Servants can fall pretty far and not get hurt. Nothing could've gotten him high enough from where it supposedly grabbed him"—he pointed down the street—"to where he landed that'd cause the kind of damage this kid had to his body." He glanced up at the apartment building. "I'd guess he was pushed from the roof."

"Did either of you notice that his ear isn't cut?" asked Jackson.

"Yeah. I saw that too," said Hugh. Servants used different cuts on their ears to distinguish which gang they belonged to.

"It doesn't mean they lied," said Townsend.

"No, but it could mean that they were initiating him into the gang and maybe it went wrong. It could also mean that JD refused to join with them, and they killed—"

"Hey." Jackson nudged Hugh. "Isn't that another one of your scientists?"

"No way." He followed the Guard's gaze. "What in the name of Araldo is going on?"

Gruder walked along the sidewalk on the other side of the street, heading in their direction. His head was down, and his coat pulled up, partially concealing his face.

"Is he missing a limb too?" asked Townsend.

"I don't think so," he said.

Gruder must've felt them staring at him because he stopped and looked in their direction. His face paled before he dropped his head again and walked over to them.

"Oh my. What happened?" Gruder stared at the body bag. "A kid?"

"Yeah, and we're not sure what happened," said Hugh.

"There are a lot of gangs in this area." Gruder's eyes saddened. "They seem to be recruiting them younger and younger." He looked away from the body. "Did this kid refuse to join?"

"That's what we think," he said.

"This part of town is getting worse every day. Hopefully, the new schools can help."

"It is a rough area. Why are you here? You don't live around here, do you?" he asked.

"I'm visiting a friend." Gruder's eyes locked with his, and Hugh was pretty sure he was being sized up.

"I see." Only Servants lived in this area. Maybe Gruder had a girlfriend and wasn't quite ready to admit to interclass relations.

"I do need to get going though. I'm on my way to work. You should stop by the lab. We have a few new meat substitutes for you to try. One is actually pretty good."

"I'll come by later today or tomorrow." He had to get more food out there. A full belly went a long way to help minimize crime.

"I'll see you then and"—Gruder glanced at the body again—"good luck. I hope you find out who did this to the poor kid."

"Me too." As soon as Gruder left, Hugh turned toward the others. "We should get JD's body to Kalper."

"You two go ahead," said Townsend. "I'm going to stay here and see if I can repair the damage you did."

"I'm not going to apologize for letting those kids know that I'm looking for facts backed by evidence, not tales." He hoped it'd stop the rumors about this bird-creature.

"Good thing you're not a reporter. Those who come to tell us what they saw or heard don't appreciate being called liars."

"Then they shouldn't lie."

"Just send the carriage back for me." Townsend turned and walked away.

"He's not too happy with you." Jackson bent and lifted JD's small body, placing it into the carriage before climbing inside.

"He'll get over it." Hugh followed him and instructed the Grunt to go to Kalper's house.

"You really think gangs are doing all these killings?" asked Jackson.

"Yeah, I do."

"Good." The Guard paused and then said, "Don't you find it a bit strange that two of your scientists, both who used to work for Conguise on Level Five, are in this area?"

"Yeah, and I don't like that at all." He wasn't a fan of coincidences and two in one day were two too many.

"Ableson's story seemed true to me," said Jackson.

"Yeah. Me too." Neither said a word about Gruder's.

CHAPTER 43: Hugh

Hugh stared at the brown, shapeless lump in front of him.

"It tastes better than it looks." Ableson shifted nervously.

"I hope so." He cut off a piece and hesitated with the fork halfway to his mouth. The last samples had been worse than bad.

"I promise, this one is good," said Ableson.

Gruder mumbled something under his breath.

"Ignore him," said Ableson.

Hugh was starting to sympathize with Conguise. He'd imagined killing both Gruder and Ableson a couple of times just today. He stuffed the food into his mouth before the two scientists started bickering again. He chewed.

"So?" Ableson leaned closer. "It's good. Isn't it?"

He started to nod. The flavor was decent but...He chewed and chewed.

"Spit it out before you choke," said Gruder.

"It's not that bad," said Ableson. "I think it just needs to be cooked a little less."'

He swallowed the hunk of food and then picked up his glass and took a gulp of water. "It's not bad. Chewy but the flavor is pretty good."

"See." Ableson gave Gruder a superior look.

"Try cooking it less like you said, but even if that doesn't help, get it made and sent to the markets." It wasn't perfect, but they were desperate to get any kind of food out there. "Keep working on it though."

"Ah..." Ableson made a face. "How much should we make?"

"As much as you can. It's chewy but people are starving."

"The few batches you can make aren't going to solve anything," muttered Gruder.

"What's he talking about?" He looked from one scientist to the other.

"He's just jealous," said Ableson.

"Hardly," said Gruder. "I have no reason to be jealous of your failure."

"What's the problem?" This had been the first one that had tasted like something other than a punishment.

"We can't make it," said Gruder. "Not in the quantity that you need."

"Why?" His eyes went to Ableson.

"The main ingredient is wheat," muttered Ableson.

"Wheat? You know we have a wheat shortage."

"We have an everything shortage," snapped Ableson. "I can't work with imaginary ingredients."

Unfortunately, he had a point.

"You should be a little more creative"—Gruder grabbed the plate he'd prepared from a nearby table and slid it in front of Hugh—"like me."

"Both of you, listen carefully. I'm not Conguise. This is not a competition. We need food. Share your secrets and work together." He cut into the brown blob on his plate and stuffed it into his mouth. He almost spit it out.

Ableson snickered.

"Don't," he said around the food. It was cold and wet. "It tastes good." It did. Kind of. He swallowed and then took another bite. It was actually tasty once he got past the texture. "What is this made out of?"

"Mushrooms," said Gruder.

"Mushrooms?" That explained the texture. "Do we have a lot of dried mushrooms?"

"The dried mushrooms were what I used the last time," said Gruder. "These are fresh."

"Oh. Don't use dried again." That had been like death in his mouth. "Do you have a way to grow the amount of mushrooms we'd need to feed everyone?"

"We can grow some, but I hired Servants to harvest these near Lazaretto Falls."

"Not this again." Ableson shook his head.

"Yes, this again," said Gruder.

"What are you arguing about now?" he asked.

"Harbor Point," said Gruder.

"What about it?"

"I heard that there's a way to the other side besides going over the waterfall."

"There is, but no one remembers exactly where that opening is." They had a general idea, but that was still a long wall of rock that had to be searched.

"That could be our answer," said Gruder. "There may be a lot of food over there, and if not, it's more land to grow crops."

"Land isn't our problem. We need farmers." He stood. "But you're right. We should look into what's on the other side now that we know there's a way through the rock wall." He turned to Ableson. "Make several batches and distribute them to the food kitchens with bread. We'll see which is preferred."

"This is higher in protein than bread so it should keep them feeling full longer," said Ableson.

"Good. Experiment with the product. See if you can cut back on the wheat."

"And replace it with what?" Ableson gave him an exasperated look.

"I don't know. Use your imagination." He turned to the other scientist. "Fix the texture of your dish, and I'll get a team together to find that opening through Harbor Point. Good job both of you." He left and started down the hallway.

"Hugh, wait." Gruder followed him. "May I have a word with you?"

"Of course." He followed the younger Almighty into an office.

"I want to explain about the other morning." The other Almighty closed the door.

"Okay." He'd known there was more to the story.

"This isn't easy to say." Gruder walked over and sat on the edge of his desk. "I've been hiding this for...well, forever."

"Hiding what?"

"I was in the Holstein area visiting my mom." Gruder's chin jutted out, but his expression was tense like he was expecting a blow.

"I thought your mother passed away when you were in college." It's what the other male had told him.

"That was my father's wife, not my biological mother."

He studied the other Almighty. He had an idea where this was going. Gruder was slender with intense blue eyes and was very graceful. His gaze dropped to the other male's hands.

"Filed down daily." Gruder took a deep breath, relaxing a little.

"You don't have to hide anymore."

"As they say, old habits die hard." Gruder shrugged. "And to be perfectly honest, I'm still not sure that this new world of yours will last. I don't want to be a casualty if it doesn't. So I'll keep filing my claws." His eyes met Hugh's again. "And I'd appreciate it if this stayed between us."

"Of course." He understood. "I'm doing everything I can to make sure that we don't slip back into the past."

"I know and that's why I'm helping you." Gruder's eyes darkened. "None of us should have to hide because of who we are."

"I agree. I hope you can feel safe enough to stop hiding one day soon."

"Me too." Gruder smiled slightly. "It would be nice."

"Have you considered moving your mom someplace safer. No one would need to know that she's your mother."

"I spoke to her about it several years ago, but she's lived in that area all her life. Her friends are there."

"Has she said anything about the gangs?"

"Like what? The gangs have been a part of that neighborhood for years."

He wasn't sure how much to say. "Like anything strange. More deaths. Rumors of...new gangs. Anything abnormal."

"No. Not that I remember." Gruder frowned. "She said something about a body they found a couple of weeks ago in the trash, but that's nothing unusual in that area. Unfortunately."

"Okay. Thanks." That pretty much closed the Lady-Bird situation for him.

Kalper hadn't found any wounds on JD that had been made by talons. The scratches and cuts on the kid's body had been consistent with Servant claws. Now, he also knew that an elderly House Servant who'd lived in that area her entire life hadn't even heard rumors about this flying nightmare. This meant the only ones telling those tales were the ones talking to Townsend—the ones in the gangs. The reporter could continue to look into it if he wanted, but he was done wasting his time.

CHAPTER 44: Jethro

Jethro made his way through the growing crowd toward Sovee. He needed to collect his money from his last fight because it was time to take his shot and for once he was happy about it.

He could use a break. He'd been fighting for Vickers for several months now. Things had started great. After his second fight, he'd received an invitation to Club Gall with his payout. He'd closed the place down more evenings than he cared to admit but no one had approached him about Club Sin or the black market.

He hadn't even managed to get an invitation to the party at Crosnics Manor. The betting books at Jar, the rundown bar where a lot of the fighters frequented, were filling up with bets on the fights that'd take place there. It didn't make any sense that he hadn't been invited. He was winning his matches and raking in money for Vickers.

He pushed his way through the large Guards who surrounded Sovee. He was tired of waiting for that invitation. He wasn't shy. He'd ask the lawyer except besides his first fight Vickers hadn't been at any of the other matches. He'd never imagined that it'd be this difficult to learn something about the black market.

"Hey." He stopped next to Sovee. "You got my money?"

"Yeah. Walk with me."

He followed the old Guard through the crowd to the gym where they trained. They walked into the building. Sovee nodded at the three burly fighters who stood in front of the office door. They stepped aside, allowing him and Sovee into the back room.

"You need to make your fights better." Sovee closed the door and walked to his desk.

"What do you mean better? I win. It doesn't get better than that."

"Yes, it does." Sovee unlocked the desk drawer.

"How? It's a fight. I win. I get paid, and I get more fights." This was the one thing in his life that was simple.

"It's not just about winning." Sovee handed him an envelope. "The crowd comes to see a fight, not a beating. They want to be entertained, and you're not entertaining."

"If they bet on me, they win money. That should be entertaining enough." He opened the envelope, counting the cash.

"It isn't." Sovee sat on the chair behind the desk. "Let me give you some advice. Make the crowd wonder if you're going to win. Take your time. Hold back on a few punches. For Araldo's sake, take a hit or two and act like it hurts."

"Get me better competition and I will. The fighters you put me up against are so slow. What am I supposed to do? If I wait too long, it'll look fake."

"Clyde is one of the fastest Guards on the circuit." Sovee eyed him warily. "Your last fight should've been a good match. Instead you had Clyde down in under two minutes."

"He must've had a bad day because he was slow." When the serum was thin in his system, everyone was slow.

"I didn't think I'd like you, but I do. I'm telling you, the novelty of an Almighty beating the crap out of Guards, Servants and Stockers is going to wear off soon. At first, they'll still come to bet on you, but when everyone is betting on you, no one is making any money—even Vickers. When that happens, you're out." Sovee leaned forward. "But if you entertain the crowd they'll continue to come to the fights. The Almightys want to like you. They want to believe that they could take Guards, Servants and Stockers in a fight. You have the chance to become a favorite. You can go far with this, but you have to entertain them."

"I'll think about it, but if I have that much potential then I need a bigger cut."

"You're already getting paid more than any other fighter."

"I don't care about what anyone else makes. I want more." He needed to talk to Vickers and demanding more money should take care of that.

"You don't deserve more."

"Says who? You? It doesn't matter what you say. I want a meeting with Vickers." He turned and walked toward the door.

"Or what?" yelled Sovee. "Where else you gonna go and make this kind of money?" The old Guard laughed. "I'll see you in two weeks for training."

Jethro kept walking, but Sovee was right. Even if he hadn't been doing this to catch those responsible for killing the young Servants, he needed the money too badly to quit.

CHAPTER 45: Jethro

Jethro hesitated outside the gym. The crowd was loud, and anticipation filled the air. He tipped his head and inhaled, his nose twitching at the faint scent of blood. He wanted to push through the swarm of bodies and force them to make way for him. He was strong now, really strong, but even though it'd be the fastest path through the crowd it wouldn't be the smartest.

He ducked down a side street. Maybe he'd head over to the Howling Hut and find a female to keep him company. It'd be nice to hang out somewhere that he wasn't hated.

The fighters at Jar didn't like him because he was an Almighty, and he'd been in the Protective Services. It didn't matter that many of them had also served. They'd had no choice. Since he was an Almighty, they believed he'd enlisted because he'd chosen the old way of life. The way that had been built on their enslavement. Club Gall had more Almightys as patrons, but they were all rich and he wasn't.

He left the side street for the main road, having avoided most of the people. He moved along the outskirts of the crowd, passing the less important matches. The sharp odor of fresh blood drifted to him on a breeze. He stopped, staring at the fighters. His eyes fastened on the blood as it slid down a Guard's face and dropped onto the road. It seemed to move so slowly that he probably could run up there and catch the next drop before it hit the ground. Then he'd follow the trail and make the fighter bleed more—a lot more. His stomach rumbled and he turned away. He needed to eat.

He continued through the crowd. When he was due for his shot, the urge to run until he couldn't run anymore or to camouflage himself and wait for his prey was almost unbearable. Fighting helped ease the tension, but he didn't want to just win. He wanted to tear into his opponents with his teeth, to feel their pulse slow as the spurts of blood splattered his face and filled his mouth.

He shook his head, trying to wipe away the image. It was too tempting. He'd mention these urges to the professor, but he wasn't sure what Conguise would do. Even though the other Almighty assured him that he wouldn't lose his ability to walk, he wasn't risking it, especially since the odd fantasies disappeared as soon as he took his serum.

He left the crowd and headed down the sidewalk. The city grew quieter with each step. A few teenage Guards gathered on a shadowed stoop. He wasn't worried. There were four of them, but they were all young and skinny. They'd leave him alone. He wasn't easy prey, especially tonight. Tomorrow would be a different story, but fortunately for him, he'd be home.

"Hey, you!" shouted one of the teens. "Did you win?"

"Win? Win what? He ain't no fighter, idiot. He's an Almighty." The tallest kid slugged the one who'd shouted at Jethro.

"He did fight. I saw him last night. He had Clyde down before anyone could blink." The first kid wiped his dirty black hair out of his face.

"No way. Clyde's my man and he's fast. No one beats Clyde," said the tall kid. "He's the best fighter around. He's in all the big matches."

No, he was the best fighter. His fight with Clyde last night proved that. Yet he still hadn't been invited to the party at Crosnics Manor like the other top fighters, including Clyde. Maybe his problem was he worked for the wrong trainer and Almighty. If Vickers wouldn't agree to meet with him, he'd find another team of fighters to join. Right now, he was pretty sure any of them would take him. Hugh might be pissed but it wasn't like Jethro was making any progress on the black market anyway. This might be exactly the threat he needed to get Vickers to invite him to that party.

He stopped and the teens fell silent. "Who manages Clyde?"

The kids didn't say a word. They just slipped farther into the shadows by the building.

He pulled the envelope from his pocket. The four kids were all too thin. Their clothes almost nothing but torn fabric. He pulled out five bills, shoving the rest back into his pocket. A larger shadow moved away from the building across the street. Two Guards, both adult males, made their way toward the fights.

He watched them for another moment. They seemed harmless enough. They were adults but skinny. They'd avoid him, unless they'd seen his money. Then they may decide he was worth the risk. He'd be glad to show them how wrong they were.

He turned back to the kids. "Tell me who Clyde works for?" He waved two of the bills. "The first one to speak gets this."

No one moved for about a half of a heartbeat and then the kid with black hair scurried forward. "Clyde is managed by Mosquer." He held out his hand.

"If you're lying to me, I will find you." Jethro bent so they were eye level. "You saw me fight. You saw what I did to Clyde. He didn't lie to me or take my money. Understand?"

"Yes, sir." The kid gulped. "I mean, no, sir. I ain't lying."

"Good." He gave the kid the cash.

The teen darted back into the shadows by his friends.

Jethro held up the other three bills. The other teens stared at him with wide, hungry eyes. "If he's lying, you tell me right now." He took one of the bills and held it out.

No one moved and then the smallest one darted out of the shadows to snatch the money. Jethro smiled as he easily captured the kid's wrist. The bones were so tiny. He could crush them just by tightening his grip, but he wouldn't.

"You weren't trying to steal from me, were you?"

"N-n-no, sir."

"Is he"—he nodded at the kid with the black hair—"lying?"

"No, sir. Mosquer trains Clyde. Mosquer and Sovee they train the best fighters."

"I'm the best." He winked at the kid as he let go of his wrist.

"Yes, sir." The Servant ran back to his friends, money already tucked safely in his pocket.

"What about you two?" He held out the other bills. "Are they lying to me?"

"No, sir." Both teens charged up to him, their hands out.

"Good." He handed them the money and then turned and continued down the street.

The area became even more run down and quieter. It was as if everything that lived around there feared to make a sound, but someone moved on stealthy feet, trailing him. He kept walking. He didn't need to turn and look. He could tell by the quiet steps that only one...Guard followed him. It might be a Servant, but he didn't think so. The steps were heavier and not as fluid as a Servant's.

He flexed his fingers, itching for a fight although it wouldn't be much of one with only one Guard as his opponent. He turned down an alleyway, slowing his pace a little. It may not be much of a fight, but it was better than no fight. He took the next corner, following his usual route. He strained to hear the footsteps but there was nothing now. Maybe the Guard had only been going in the same direction and hadn't actually been following him. He sighed. So much for a fi...Someone rushed into him from the front, shoving him backward.

Gruntshit. He hit the brick wall and before he could do anything his assailant punched him in the gut. He hit the wall again, grunting as he pushed his opponent away. Someone else moved out of the shadows and then another. This was an ambush. He was surrounded and these weren't stray Guards. These were fighters—big and burly. This was the fight he'd wanted.

"Hello, Clyde." He grinned. "I see you brought reinforcements this time."

"I don't need reinforcements." The Guard strode toward him, snarling.

"You're going to need something because there's no referee to stop me this time."

CHAPTER 46: Jethro

Jethro got out of the carriage and headed into the building where Vickers' worked. Every inch of his body hurt from the beating he'd taken last night. Clyde and his friends had been out for revenge, but they'd picked the wrong night to mess with him. If they'd found him today, they would've killed him.

He'd considered waiting for his body to heal before taking his shot, but Conguise had drilled into him the importance of following the schedule. The professor was right. Even though he felt sluggish like he was carrying an extra hundred pounds in every cell of his body, he was no longer wiped out for days after taking the shot.

The first day was always bad, but it was the one day he gave himself to do whatever he wanted. Tomorrow, his mom would expect his help at the Producer camps. Unfortunately, since he didn't want a lecture, he was going to have to avoid seeing her until his injuries were healed. He hated ditching on the work. She was fixing up the camps in hopes of attracting someone to come and farm. Repairing and sometimes rebuilding the huts was a lot of work but being outside and near the forest and river soothed his soul in a way he couldn't explain.

His plans to sleep the day away had been derailed when an Almighty had shown up at his house with a summons from Vickers. He walked into the office.

"Are you all right?" The receptionist gasped when she saw him.

"I'm just great." He stared at her out of the one eye that wasn't swollen shut. "But I need you to listen very closely. I'm not sitting here all day like I did the last time. Tell Vickers he can either see me now, or he can see me in two weeks."

Her look of concern hardened. "*Mr.* Vickers is expecting you." She stood and stepped out from behind her desk.

"I got it." He walked past her and opened the door.

Vickers glanced up, his jovial smile turning to shock. "What in the name of Araldo happened to you? This didn't happen during the fight. Sovee would've told me."

"No. It didn't." He dropped onto the chair in front of the desk, not bothering to wait for an invitation. "I got jumped. Clyde didn't appreciate me making him look like a slow fool the other night."

"That shouldn't have happened. I'll have Sovee talk to Mosquer."

"Don't bother. He's got enough problems. He's going to be short staffed. The three that jumped me won't be fighting for a while."

"The three?"

"Yeah. Clyde and two of his friends." There could've been a dozen of them, and he would've won. They were lucky he hadn't killed them.

"You fought three fighters and won?"

"Yep." He grinned, wincing as his smile pulled the cut on his face.

"I'll talk to Sovee." The lawyer's eyes gleamed. "I don't think there's ever been a two against one fight in the ring."

"And there won't be. At least not with me working for you." This was the time to push. He was tired, cranky and Vickers was impressed.

"I heard you weren't happy." The excited look on the lawyer's face, shifted to disgust.

"Then I'm sure you also heard that my novelty is wearing thin."

"It won't if we put you up against two fighters."

"I'm not doing a fight like that for what you're paying me."

"For what...I'm paying you fifty percent. No one else gets even close to that much."

"No one else is me, and you're also denying me the biggest fight of the year."

"You've been in every important fight since you started."

"But I won't be in the biggest one. The one at Crosnics Manor."

"That's what this is about. Hurt feelings for being snubbed." The lawyer laughed. "I didn't know we were in grade school."

"Keeping me from making double what I'd make in ten fights isn't something I find funny." He stood. He was in no mood for this.

"Sit down." Vickers motioned at the chair. "I wanted to invite you."

"Then why am I not going." He sat. "I find it hard to believe that I did something to offend Terbasse because I only saw the guy once when he was leaving Club Gall."

"No. You didn't offend him. Francis would love to see you there."

"Then what's the problem?"

"My wife." Vickers leaned back against his chair and sighed. "Terbasse organized the party last year and it was a disaster. My wife told me that we were never going again unless a female was in charge. Terbasse is a confirmed bachelor, so my wife offered to do it." He ran his hand over his face. "The damn party is costing me a fortune, but even worse than that we had to move there. Vivian swears she can't manage the party from our house. I hate it. I have papers there. Papers here. Papers at my house. It's a mess." He paused. "You're single, right?"

"Yes. I have no plans to get married. I recently broke up with my fiancé."

"I heard about that. Smart move. I highly recommend you stick with your plan and don't get married."

"If your wife is organizing the party and you and Terbasse want me there, then why am I not attending?" This didn't make any sense at all.

"Numbers." Vickers frowned, shaking his head.

"What do you mean by that?"

"Last year you could've come. It was basically a wild bachelor party. It was great." He grinned and then sighed. "My wife was not pleased about any of it, especially the limited number of...acceptable females as she put it."

"I don't intend on bringing an acceptable or unacceptable female."

"That's the problem. It's just you. This year it's an even number of men and women."

"Okay. I'll find a date." He wasn't sure who, but he could find someone.

"It's not that simple." Vickers shook his head. "Your date would have to be approved by my wife. Plus, at this point she has everything planned. Throwing another couple into the party would upset everything, according to her." He shook his head. "You should've heard her a month ago when she thought one of the couples was going to back out." His face paled a little. "I'm not listening to that again. Next year, I'll make sure you get invited."

"I don't think my popularity will last into next year." He didn't have a year to wait. Whomever killed those Servants would strike again before then.

"You might if you start fighting more than one opponent."

"Even that will lose its appeal."

"Then we change it again." Vickers studied him. "Some of those cuts don't look like they came from fists."

"Because they didn't. When Clyde and his friends couldn't take me down with their hands, they used whatever they found in the alley, including metal pipes."

"People would pay to see that." That gleam crept back into the lawyer's eyes.

"I'm sure they would, but it'll cost you a lot more."

"I'll give you sixty percent."

"Sixty percent gross not profit."

"I can't do that." Vickers sounded appalled. "I have expenses. Advertising. The building overhead. Train—"

"I don't care. I want sixty percent gross, or I go to Mosquer and offer my services."

"You don't want to do that. Mosquer will never agree to give you as much as I already do."

"I think he'll give me more. He's down three fighters who I just beat." Jethro stood. "But since we're friends, I'll take fifty percent gross, or fifty percent profit and one invite to the party." He walked to the door. "I'm going home. You have two weeks to decide."

CHAPTER 47: Hugh

"Are you sure you don't need to see a doctor?" Hugh had expected Jethro to get some bruises and cuts while fighting but this was too much. The kid looked like Hugh had after being beaten by the prison Guards—one or two punches away from permanent damage or death.

"I told you. I'm fine." Jethro glared at him out of his one good eye as he lounged on the couch.

"You don't look fine," said Trinity. "You really should see Dr. Kalper."

"It's nothing. You should've seen me last week."

"This happened a week ago, and you still look like this?" It was even worse than he'd thought.

"Yeah, but it's all superficial." Jethro touched his cheek and winced. "No reason to see a doctor."

He walked to the bar and poured a liberal amount of whiskey in a glass before handing it to his brother.

"Thanks." Jethro took a drink and sighed. "See, I'm feeling better already."

He ran his hand through his hair as he sat back down next to Trinity. Tonight, he'd invited Ray to this meeting so they could talk about additional steps they could take to get Jethro invited to The Sin, but it looked like that wasn't going to be necessary. He didn't want to pull Jethro from the undercover work, but it was obviously getting too dangerous. "I think it may be time to stop."

"No." Jethro sat up, wincing again.

"Stop denying how badly you're hurt." He understood better than Jethro knew.

"I'll be fine, but—"

"Fine?" He stood and began to pace. "I never liked the underground fights but this"—he waved his hand toward his brother—"is ridiculous. Those cuts weren't all caused by fists. What weapons are they making you use?"

Jethro took another long swallow of the whiskey. "We aren't using weapons, and this didn't—"

"Those don't look like claw marks," said Trinity.

"There's no way the damage to your face was caused by fists." The slice across Jethro's cheek was long and deep. He couldn't imagine the damage to Jethro's body but by the stiffness in the other male's movements it was extensive. This was all his fault. He'd sent his brother undercover. It was for a good reason, but even that wasn't worth this.

The door opened and Tim, Jackson and Ray entered.

"Holy Araldo, what happened to you?" Jackson headed across the room toward the couch. "Now, I know why you've been avoiding your mom."

"It's nothing." Jethro shifted away from the Guard.

"That is not nothing." Jackson turned toward Hugh. "This has gone far enough."

"That's what I said," said Hugh. "He's done. No more fights. We'll find another way."

"That didn't happen at the fight." Ray smirked at Jethro as he glided across the room and took a seat in the sun near the window.

"What do you mean by that?" asked Hugh.

"I was there for his last fight." Ray's green eyes remained on Jethro. "He won."

"I did do that," muttered Jethro.

"Yes, you did and somehow, during the fight you managed to avoid being hit." Ray cocked an eyebrow.

"Not completely," corrected Jethro. "I took one to the jaw."

"Barely a glance. Nothing that'd cause that." Ray waved his hand.

All eyes turned toward Jethro.

"I was getting ready to tell you when they came in," said Jethro.

"If it didn't happen during the fight, when did it happen?" Hugh liked this even less.

"Like Ray said, I won the fight. I went back the next night to collect my winnings and the loser...Let's just say he and his friends weren't too happy about losing." Jethro smiled. "Believe it or not, I won the second fight too."

"That is hard to believe." Hugh splashed more whiskey in Jethro's glass and then poured a drink for everyone else before sitting on the chair across from his brother.

"I still think it's time to end this," said Jackson. "It's getting too dangerous."

"I agree." Trinity took Hugh's hand.

"Yes," purred Ray. "No one likes losing. It can mean life or death."

"Life or death? They don't..." He had no real idea what anyone in the underground or black market did and he'd sent his half-brother in there alone. His eyes darted to Jethro. "I didn't know they—"

"Calm down." Ray sounded bored. "They don't actually kill the fighters...usually. They send them to the shelters...at least that's what most of them used to do. Now, they fire them." His eyes darkened with anger. "And they die from starvation, freeze on the streets or die of some other way. Results are the same. Only slower."

"Oh." That shouldn't make him feel better, but it did.

"And they especially don't like losing to an Almighty," Ray continued. "If they can't beat an Almighty then who can they beat?"

"They'd better get used to it." Jethro shrugged.

Hugh studied his brother. Jethro was more muscular than most Almightys but that didn't explain his ability to fight. He was up against strong, healthy males from the other classes who were trained to fight. Yet he was able to hold his own. Vickers had to be raking in the money on Jethro's matches. No one knew that Jethro wasn't pure Almighty. He wasn't even sure if Jethro knew it. He hadn't yet been able to decipher exactly what Conguise had spliced into Jethro's DNA, but there was something there, and it wasn't Almighty.

"They're not going to," said Jackson. "Our physical abilities are all we have ever had over the Almightys and now you're taking that away too. You're making a lot of enemies."

"I've never needed a lot of friends." Jethro took another sip of his drink.

"Jackson's right. We have to find another way to catch the black-market butcher," said Hugh.

"Jethro said he's fine," said Tim. "Let him decide when to stop."

"I'm not going to let you send him to his death," said Jackson.

"I'm not sending him anywhere," said Tim. "I said it was his choice."

"Stay out of it." Jackson strode over to Tim.

"It wasn't your daughter he tried—"

"Dad. Stop." Trinity's face heated, but her eyes were hard. "What happened is over. Done." She glanced at Jethro and then Hugh. "We don't need to talk about it. Ever again."

The room fell silent. Trinity had told him everything and Hugh had accepted that what'd happened or had almost happened between them had been consensual. He didn't like it, but he'd accepted it. However, it didn't mean he wanted to talk about it. He and Jethro had grown a bit closer over the last few months and bringing up the past wouldn't help that.

"It may not matter much longer." Jethro sat forward on the couch. "I'm not getting invited to the party at Crosnics Manor."

"How is that possible?" asked Hugh. "They have fights there. You're the lawyer's ringer."

"But I'm single," said Jethro.

"So is Terbasse and—"

"Vickers' wife is arranging this party and she wants couples this year or an even number of males and females. Something like that."

"Terbasse can't go to his own party?" asked Hugh.

"Apparently, she found him a date or a female to sit with him. I don't know exactly how it works, but I talked to Vickers and I'm out."

"You are engaged." Tim's face was blank, but his green eyes gleamed with amusement.

"Stella is persona non-grata," said Jethro.

"He's right," said Ray. "Vivian Vickers used to tolerate Jason's family because they were in power. Now, she wouldn't be caught dead in the same room with the girl." Ray took a sip of his drink. "If you want him to go to that party, you'll have to find another female."

"What about Sassy?" asked Hugh.

"With how much she's been drinking lately?" Trinity shook her head. "It wouldn't be safe for her or Jethro."

"Let me rephrase," said Ray. "You need to find him a female who'd meet Vivian's approval."

"Wait a minute," said Jackson. "I thought we agreed that Jethro should stop."

"Jackson's right." Hugh filled his glass. He wanted the killer caught but he couldn't keep sending his brother into the ring.

"No." Jethro stood, wincing as he walked across the room and took the bottle from Hugh. He refilled his glass. "I want to finish this." He walked over to Ray, filling his glass also. "If we can find someone, that is."

"You can't keep fighting," said Jackson. "You're going to get killed."

"I can handle myself," said Jethro.

"So far, yes, but you have no idea what they'll throw at you," argued Jackson.

"I've already fought every combination of Guards, Servants, Producers, Stockers and Grunts that there is...and won." Jethro's eyes gleamed in triumph, his smile crooked in his swollen face.

"You're not invincible," said Hugh. "Thinking like that will get you hurt, maybe killed."

"Like I said, I've fought and won against everything so far. What else can they throw at me? I fought mixes that you can only imagine." Jethro glanced around the room, drawing everyone into his story. "There was one guy, I swear he must have been part Grunt by his size and Stocker by his attitude. It was brutal."

"That was a great fight." Ray stood in his excitement. "I almost bet on the other guy."

"You would've lost," said Jethro.

Ray tipped his glass to the young Almighty.

"This is all moot unless Ray knows someone who Jethro can"—Hugh held up his fingers and made air quotes—"date."

Jackson frowned. "I still don't think—"

"Too bad," said Jethro. "It's my choice and I'm going to finish this if it's possible."

"Your sister is going to kill you and then me." Jackson sighed and dropped onto the couch.

"I'll let you worry about Kim." Jethro chuckled.

"Are you sure?" He didn't want to see his brother hurt, but if Jethro said he could handle it then it was his decision. Jethro was an adult, not a child.

"Yes." Jethro nodded.

"Then we need to find him a girlfriend." Hugh turned toward Ray.

The Servant stared at his drink as he slowly swirled the glass. "She can't be just anyone. Vivian is very particular about who is invited to her parties."

"Does she have to be an Almighty?" He wasn't sure that Ray had too many contacts in that realm, but the Servant hadn't failed them yet.

"No, but she does have to be...special. Especially since adding two more people to Vivian's party is going to require her to make modifications."

"Like what? It's just two more guests," said Jethro.

"This isn't a college keg party." Ray shook his head in disgust. "There are arrangements—sleeping, seating, activities, arrivals, departures, and don't forget that there will be additional accommodations needed for your carriage and Grunt, as well as—"

"Okay. Okay. I get it." Jethro sat back down. "This is going to be a lot of work for her."

"It will," said Ray. "If we can wait until next year, there are plenty who I can set him up with who'll work."

"He isn't going to be able to last a year on the fighting circuit," said Hugh.

"Hey," said Jethro, offended.

"They're already attacking you after the fight. Do you think that's going to get better?"

"I'll handle it."

"We can't wait." Hugh turned away from his brother. The kid was too cocky. "Not only will there be more murders, but we don't even know that he'll be invited next year."

"That's true," said Ray. "Your name is already becoming well known in the circuit. In another year, either you'll be dead, or no one will bet against you. Either way, you won't be too popular with Vickers and that means you won't be on the list of names that he gives to his wife."

"It's over. We can't wait another year." Hugh tossed back his drink. This was a disaster.

"Perhaps." Ray's eyes were alight with mischief.

"What do you mean, perhaps? We can't wait for a year, and we don't have anyone that Vivian Vickers will invite last minute." He didn't like the look of amusement on Ray's face.

"You don't listen very well." Ray swirled the liquor in his glass again as his eyes darted to Tim and then to Trinity. "What I said was that there were plenty of candidates if we waited. I never said there were no candidates now."

"You have someone in mind." Hugh leaned toward Ray, hope sparking to life again.

"Yes." Ray's green eyes locked with his. "Someone who is so famous or infamous that Vivian will piss her pants at the opportunity to invite her to the party."

Ray couldn't mean...but Hugh could see in the Servant's eyes that he did. "No."

"Then it's over." Ray shrugged.

"No, what?" asked Tim. "Ray didn't say who this female—"

"He doesn't have to." Cold sweat trickled down his back because he knew Ray was right, but he still wasn't going to do it.

"She'd be perfect." Ray's eyes locked on Trinity.

"Me?" She pointed to herself.

"How can you even suggest that my daughter go with this...this..." Tim waved his hand at Jethro.

"She's the only one who'll work," said Ray.

"Absolutely not," said Hugh. "I won't ask this of her."

"Hugh." Trinity touched his arm. "We should—"

"No." He glared at her.

"Then you're right." Ray stood. "It's over."

"Yes, it is." Hugh's words were clipped. Ray could've kept his mouth shut about this but instead he'd started problems.

"Let me know if you require my assistance in anything else." Ray put down his drink and left.

Hugh re-filled everyone's glasses before sitting back down next to Trinity. She stared straight ahead, her face tight with anger. They could argue later. Right now, they had bigger issues. "Can anyone think of some other way to get into the black market?"

"Can we break into Crosnics Manor?" asked Tim. "There should be a lot of strangers coming and going during that party. We can slip in—"

"No," said Jackson. "We already looked into that option. The estate is too well-guarded, even during an event."

"What about the lawyer's house? He may have information there," said Tim.

Trinity still didn't speak. That wasn't good. Usually, she was one of the first to throw out suggestions.

"We looked into that too," said Jackson. "Vickers' Servants are extremely loyal, and he has a lot of them. He's retained all of them after the war. Apparently, he pays them well and treats them well. We'd never be able to get anyone inside."

"Do we really need the papers?" asked Jethro. "I know Vickers is involved, at least in the sex trafficking. The first time I met him he offered to find someone for me."

"Why would he do that?" Hugh didn't think that those in that kind of business made offers like that unless they suspected the other Almighty would be receptive.

Jethro hesitated but then said, "Because of Tee."

"Tee?" Jackson frowned. "You told us you found her on the street. Hurt and alone."

"I lied. This can't leave the room." Jethro took a sip of his drink.

"Of course not." He glanced around and the others all nodded.

"She belonged to Jason. I convinced him to give her to me."

"For free?" This was even harder to believe.

"No. I had to do a favor for Jason." Jethro's eyes hardened.

"What favor?" he asked.

"It doesn't matter now. He's dead."

"Fine." He'd rather know exactly what Jethro had done for Jason but by the look on the other male's face, he wasn't going to get an answer. "But we can't arrest Vickers without proof. We need the paper trail."

"And we can't get it without getting into Crosnics Manor," said Jackson.

"There may be nothing there," said Tim.

"That's true, but it was our best shot. It'd be unbelievable that at least a few of those present weren't firmly entrenched in the black market as either buyers or sellers." He glanced at Trinity. Her jaw was tense and her eyes hard. Tonight when they were alone wasn't going to be fun. "Can anyone think of any other option?"

They sat in silence for several moments.

"Then it's over. Done." He sighed. "But we aren't giving up. We'll figure out some other way to catch the black-market butcher."

"Good night, Dad. Jackson." She stood, glaring at Hugh and Jethro before leaving the room.

She could be as mad as she wanted. He wasn't going to put her in danger—he glanced at his brother—and he definitely wasn't going to send her to a house party to pretend to be Jethro's girlfriend.

CHAPTER 48: Trinity

Trinity crept down the hallway to their suite of rooms.

"You're late," mumbled Rex from where he sat outside their apartment.

"You really need to get some sleep." The poor Guard looked exhausted. "You know Hugh doesn't like you staying out here all night."

"He doesn't like you leaving by yourself either." He frowned at her. "And I agree. It's stupid."

"I can take care of myself." She punched in the keycode to their room. "Go to bed."

He crossed his arms over his chest.

"I'll tell Hugh you're out here."

"He knows."

"Seriously, Rex. Go get some sleep. I'm home. You know I can fight."

"I've been sleeping in the Council Building for years. No reason to change now." He closed his eyes.

"You are so stubborn."

"Like you can talk," he muttered.

"True." She smiled as she entered their apartment. It was the first time she'd smiled in hours. After leaving the meeting, she'd gone into the city park to try and sooth her temper, but it hadn't worked. Hugh had no right to dictate what she could and could not do. Her anger flared hot again when her eyes fell on him.

He sat at his desk, working on something. He glanced up, his face hard with anger. She walked into the kitchen and grabbed a slice of bread. Her mom had given them some of her apple cinnamon bread. It was one of her favorites, but tonight it tasted like dust in her

mouth. She put it aside and went into their bedroom to change for
bed.

"Where were you?" He stood in the doorway.

"Out." She dropped her nightgown on the bed. There was no
way she was undressing in front of him tonight.

"Out where?" His tone was laced with restrained anger.

"I needed to clear my head and cool down."

"Did running away instead of staying here and talking to me
help?"

"No, and I didn't run away."

"We are a couple. When we get mad at each other we talk about
it."

"You want to talk. We'll talk." She crossed her arms over her
chest. "You cannot tell me what I can and cannot do. You are not my
owner."

"No, I'm your fiancé."

"Being my mate doesn't give you the right to make decisions for
me." She used the term mate purposely because every time she did,
he cringed. He preferred fiancé and husband, like he was ashamed of
what they did that bound them together.

"It does when you'd decide to put yourself in danger."

"I can take care of myself." She was getting tired of telling him
this. He should know it by now.

"Like you did when Jethro captured you?" His blue eyes
darkened with anger. "I'd prefer that my *mate* doesn't put herself in
positions where she has to offer herself to another male in order to
stay safe."

"I guess you lied when you said that was in our past and that
you'd forgotten about it."

"I never said I'd forgotten about it. I'll never be able to forget
about it. I don't blame you for what happened, but I don't want you
in a position so that it happens again."

"I won't be in that position."

"You want to run off with him, pretending to be his mate." He almost spat the last word. "How does that not put you in exactly the same position?" He paused, his brow wrinkling. "Oh, you're right. This time you won't be trying to escape."

"I never said I wanted to do it." Her hands came to her hips, claws peeking out.

"Then why are we arguing?"

"Because you said I couldn't do it."

He took a deep breath, and she could see his lips move as he counted to ten. "Let me get this straight. You don't actually want to go undercover...with Jethro. You're only angry because I said that you couldn't."

"Yes and no." It made perfect sense to her, and she wasn't letting him twist it and make her feel stupid.

"What exactly does that mean?" He was truly pissed at her now.

"You didn't even give me a chance to answer. You spoke for me. In front of everyone. Even though I don't want to go, I should've been the one to decide." She moved closer to him, the anger slipping away. "I don't *want* to go, but the longer it takes to capture this monster, the more killings there will be."

"So you do want to go." His face was like stone.

"No, I want to stay with you, but I can help stop this."

"With Jethro." His eyes were blue ice.

"It would be pretend. We wouldn't really be a couple."

"Pretend? Okay. Then how about while you're away, pretending to be Jethro's mate I'll pretend to date another female. She can share my bed, but don't worry, we won't really be a couple."

"I will not share his bed." She wanted to shake him. He was purposely being obstinate about this.

"How do you know? You may spend the night somewhere and be forced to sleep with him."

"I won't mate with him."

"And I won't mate with her." He rubbed his chin. "I should contact Meesus. One of her girls could stay here with me." He began to pace. "I don't want to look like I'm a lovesick fool when the public finds out that you left me. In order to appear strong I need to move on." He stopped, tapping his finger against his lips. "Yes, I'll pick one of Meesus' girls. It has to be one who isn't known for her profession. She'll move in with me." His eyes fell on her, hard and cold. "But don't worry, even though we'll sleep in each other's arms we won't mate."

"It is not the same thing." She swore she was grinding her teeth to a pulp.

"Explain to me how it's different."

"You'd be doing this out of spite. I'm doing it to save others."

"Oh, that's right. You're the great savior. You saved the Producers. You saved Travis. You saved me, and let's not forget Jethro. He was your first, wasn't he?"

"No." She bit back her temper. He'd used those terms on purpose. "Christian was the first that I saved unless you count the rabbits and birds."

"But Christian doesn't really count, does he?" His voice softened. "I may have been your first mate, but Jethro was your first love."

She stared at him, seeing his hurt under the anger for the first time. She touched his cheek. "No. He was my second crush. You are my first love."

He pulled her to him, his mouth covering hers. There was no softness in this kiss, only anger and fear, but she melted into him. He needed her right now, and she'd do anything for him.

A little while later, she lay in his arms, her fingers skimming over his heart, scraping softly with her claws. "I won't go."

His hand trailed up and down her spine.

She leaned up. "I think I should, but for you I won't."

"Good." He stared into her eyes.

There was a knock on the door.

"What now?" He groaned as he crawled out of bed, pulling on his clothes and leaving the room.

She stared after him. She'd wanted him to tell her that he trusted her. That he was okay with her going if she wanted to.

Jackson's voice was hushed. She sat up and tipped her ears forward. They'd found another mass killing. She quickly got dressed and was putting on her shoes when Hugh came back into the room.

"You heard?" he asked.

She nodded.

"I think you should stay here." He grabbed his shoes and sat on the bed.

"Why?" She stood.

"You don't need to see this."

"It's worse than the other one? How many Servants? What could they have possibly done to them that'd be worse?" She really didn't want to know the answer to her questions, but she couldn't stay here and wait. She had to see what obeying Hugh was going to cost the others.

He took her hands. "It's not House Servants this time. It's Producers."

CHAPTER 49: Trinity

Trinity prepared herself as she followed Hugh and Jackson toward one of the buildings. This was her first trip to the section of the Warehouse District that had been used by the Remore family. These were the buildings where her neighbors, her friends and her family had been slaughtered.

"I'm going to ask again. Please, will you wait out here?" Hugh squeezed her hand.

"No. I need to do this." Plus, the outside wasn't much better. There were buildings everywhere but no sign of life—no grass, no trees, no plants, or birds. It was a dirty, foul place.

Kalper leaned against the brick wall by the door, looking even older than he was. His gray hair was messed and his skin ashen.

"How many?" asked Hugh.

"Not sure yet." Kalper swallowed. "They're cataloging everything now." His eyes fell on her. "Why don't you stay out here and keep me company?"

"I can't." Her words clawed at her throat like they didn't want to come out. "I need to see this."

"No one needs to see that," said Kalper.

"I do." Her stomach twisted as the stench of death and machines seeped through the brick walls, assaulting her senses and making her instincts scream for her to run.

She followed Jackson and Hugh inside and down a long hallway, gagging on the sweet, sickly scent of fear that clung to the air. It was dark. The lights were on, but they didn't reach the far corners. She moved closer to Hugh. Death lived here.

"Are you sure you want to see this?" Jackson halted in front of the double doors.

She wasn't but she nodded. The Guard sighed and opened one of the doors. Servants scurried about, cataloging the details. Townsend walked slowly around the room, videotaping the scene. Hugh stepped forward, his fingers still entangled with hers. Her arm lifted and stretched as he took another step, but she didn't move. She couldn't.

A Producer hung upside down in the middle of the room. A chain wrapped around one of his ankles. Most of his flesh had been hacked from his bones. His other leg lay on the floor, nothing but bone and blood and little hunks of flesh.

"Wait here." Hugh tried to pull free from her grasp.

She clutched his hand, her only security in this nightmare. This was what happened to her kind. This should have happened to her. It had happened to Remy. Bile rose in her throat. Remy who'd never hurt anyone. And Adam. Oh, Araldo this had happened to her baby brother. Her throat closed, her chest freezing. Almost everyone she'd known had ended up here...like this.

"Trinity." He clasped her shoulders and tried to turn her toward the door. "Go outside."

"No." She jerked away, her gaze on the floor. "The blood..." She'd never seen so much. It flowed across the concrete to a grate. "Is it all from him?"

"Please." His eyes drifted to where Townsend stood and then he shifted a little, blocking her view. "Go outside."

She stepped to the side, looking around him. Tossed against the wall in the shadows was something round. She moved closer. There were lots of round,...things. Except, they weren't...things. She stopped. They were heads. Some were piled like someone had tried to stack them. Others were tossed to the side. They were everywhere. Their eyes glassy and unseeing, their faces wearing expressions of pain and horror. "So many." Her knees buckled.

Hugh grabbed her arm, and she let him lead her outside. The air, once overburdened with death and machines, now a fragrant relief.

"Why would they cut off their heads?"

"Let's talk about this later." He pulled her close.

"No." She pushed away from him. "Tell me." She needed to know. He couldn't protect her. No one could protect anyone from the monster who'd done this.

"Trinity..." Hugh's blue eyes filled with sorrow.

"Tell me." She knew that hardness to his jaw. He wasn't going to say anything. She turned to Kalper. "Why did they leave the heads?"

The doctor looked at Hugh and then sighed. "They aren't easy to sell. Not many eat them. They have to be cooked for hours and then ground up."

She struggled to keep from throwing up. How did he know this? Was this something everyone knew? Something everyone did to her kind?

Mirabelle ran up to them. Her shirt soaked with sweat and her big, brown eyes wide with fear. "Is it true?" She stared at the door. "Are there Producers in there? Dead?" Her hands shook at her sides. "Butchered?"

"I'm sorry, but yes. How did you hear?" asked Hugh.

"A Guard." Mirabelle's eyes met Trinity's. "Travis didn't come home. He was coming for a job. He—"

"No." She shook her head but denying it wouldn't change anything.

"Here?" asked Hugh.

"Yes. No. I don't know." Mirabelle almost cried.

"What do you mean you don't know? Was Travis coming here or not?" She wanted to shake the other female. Travis couldn't be in there. He couldn't be dead.

"Mirabelle, calm down and tell us what you know." Hugh grabbed Trinity's hand, squeezing it.

"There was a job." The other Producer looked at her. "Remember? Tammie told us about it the other morning outside the Council Building."

"This was that job?" she asked.

"I don't know. They were going to a job in the Warehouse District." Mirabelle glanced around. "This is a big place. They could be somewhere else, right?"

"Yes. That's right. There are a lot of sections here. Travis and Tammie might be somewhere else." She clung to that idea.

"What job are you two talking about?" Hugh looked at her. "You never said anything to me about this."

"I forgot. It was the day that we found the Servants." Guilt hit her like a wave. She should've looked into this, but she'd gotten busy and now her friends were dead. No, she didn't know that for sure.

"Let's start from the beginning." He took a deep breath. "What do you know about this job? Do you know who hired him?"

"No. Not really. Tammie told us about it," said Mirabelle. "She visited a lot of Producers to help them. Some of them had done this job before. They said it was good money. Hard work but good money."

"Okay. That's good," said Hugh.

"How is that good?" asked Mirabelle.

"Those who'd worked that job before had lived," he said.

"Right." Mirabelle took a deep breath. "That's right. They'd lived."

"Who are these other Producers?" asked Hugh.

"I don't know. Tammie knew them. She'd treated them. Travis went with her and talked to them."

"Where did he meet them?" Hugh was trying to keep his voice calm. "If we can find them, we may be able to find Travis."

"I don't know. I tried to find Tammie, but she wasn't home. Neither was Curtis."

"Jackson, come here," yelled Hugh.

The Guard stepped out of the building, his face grim.

"I need you to send two Guards to Curtis and Tammie's place. If they aren't home, find them. Also, have Guards search every building in the area and interview anyone that you find. Someone had to see something. They had to either bring the Producers in as a large group together or hold them here. We need to discover which. Plus, they had to take the mea...remains out of here in a carriage. Have someone track down any carriages seen leaving this area."

"Got it." Jackson nodded. "I've already put Bo in charge of searching the other buildings. I'll let him know what else to do." He headed across the lot.

"We'll find them. I promise." Hugh's voice was calm as he took Mirabelle's hands and gave them a quick squeeze before turning to Trinity. "Take her home."

She started to argue, but the look on his face stopped her. "Okay."

"I can't leave"—Mirabelle shook her head, her eyes on the doorway—"not until I know."

A shiver danced across Trinity's skin like a spider. The only way to know for sure was to identify the heads. Her breath came in short pants. She wasn't sure she could do this.

"I understand." Hugh touched Mirabelle's arm. "Wait here."

Trinity grabbed his hand. "Do you want...I should..." She didn't want to go back inside there and search the horror filled faces for her friends, but he shouldn't have to do it by himself either. Jackson was busy and no one else here knew Travis or Tammie.

"No." His eyes met hers. "You wait with Mirabelle."

"Are you sure?" She didn't know why she was asking when her entire body sagged with relief.

He nodded before turning and walking back inside the slaughterhouse.

She stared after him, seeing nothing but the horror inside. Her knees shook so she dropped to the ground. Mirabelle sat next to her. For a long time, neither of them spoke. There were no words for something like this. Nothing would make it better and nothing could make it worse.

"We fought about this yesterday." Mirabelle's voice was hoarse. "I thought...I thought he'd agreed with me. I should've paid more attention."

"This isn't your fault. Travis is stubborn. When he gets an idea in his head, no one can stop him." She sure hadn't been able to before the war when he'd wanted to talk to his brother. No matter the danger, Travis had refused to listen to her.

"He is that." Mirabelle took her hand. "I'm scared. I don't know what I'll do if—"

"He's fine." She squeezed the other female's hand. "I know it. He's not in there. We'd feel it." She looked at the other Producer. "Right?" But she hadn't felt anything when Remy had been killed. "You'll see. He'll be fine and when you see him, you'll hug him and then hit him."

"That's for sure." Mirabelle's laughter died as Hugh came out of the building.

His face was ashen, and his eyes were shadowed with sadness. Both she and Mirabelle stood. Hugh shook his head, as he approached. She glanced at Mirabelle, not sure what he meant.

"I didn't see Travis in there."

"I knew it." Mirabelle wrapped Trinity in her arms. "I knew he wasn't dead."

"Me too." She lied. She'd hoped but she hadn't known. She hugged the other Producer for one quick second.

Mirabelle dropped her arms and stepped away. It was awkward for both of them. They really didn't like each other, but they were joined in their relief.

"You should go home and wait for him," said Hugh.

"Right." Mirabelle smiled back at Trinity, but her eyes were still filled with fear. "I'll give him a hug from you too."

"Take our carriage," said Hugh.

"Thanks." Mirabelle headed across the lot.

"Give him a smack for me too," she yelled. She should be happy, but she knew that look on Hugh's face too well. She kept telling herself that it was just the horror of looking at all the heads, but her gut knew better.

She braced herself as Hugh moved closer to her, his eyes sad. She straightened her shoulders. This was forest-time again. Time to be strong or die. Time to face what was there and not what she wanted to be true. It was the only way to survive. "What did you not want to say in front of Mirabelle?"

Hugh cleared his throat. "Tammie is...was..." His eyes met hers. "I'm so sorry."

"No. She can't..." Her heartbeat slowed and she could hear every thud in her ears. If Tammie was here than Travis was here too. They just hadn't found him yet.

"Trinity, I'm sorry." Hugh moved toward her, but she backed away.

Panic filled her chest and her heart raced. "Tammie was with my mom today. I haven't seen Mom."

"Calm down. Your mother is not in there."

"Wait! Mirabelle! Wait!" She ran across the lot and the carriage slowed to a stop. She had to see her mom. Talk to her. Make sure that her parents were okay and her baby brother. She hopped in the carriage.

"What's wrong? Did Hugh lie to me?"

"No." She wasn't saying anything about Tammie. Hugh hadn't seen Travis. There was no reason to tell the other female, not yet. "I need to see my mom. I-I haven't seen her today and—"

"I understand." Mirabelle leaned out the window. "Go to the Council Building first," she yelled to the Grunt.

"Thank you."

"It's on the way," said Mirabelle. "And Travis is okay. I know it."

"Yeah." She wasn't so sure anymore. She wasn't sure that any of them were safe. She turned and stared out the window. The shadows the building made with the moon seemed to move, obliterating all light as they consumed the land. This place was dark and evil. Nothing good ever came here. It should be razed to the ground.

"Trinity, thank you."

"For what?" She turned and looked at the other Producer. "The carriage? The streets aren't sa—"

"No. I mean, yes, but I want to thank you for more than letting me use the carriage."

Whatever the other Producer was about to say, it wasn't easy for her.

Mirabelle took a deep breath. "If it weren't for you, I...All of us would've ended up in that building." She took another deep breath. "I'm sorry for the things I said and the way that I treated you. I didn't know. I didn't believe. It was too horrible."

"It's okay." She turned and looked back out the window. "None of us knew the depths of their lies."

CHAPTER 50: Hugh

"Hugh. We need you outside." Jackson waved at him from the doorway.

He looked away from Kalper and nodded at the Guard. He should be thrilled to get out of this nightmare but by the look on Jackson's face whatever waited for him was worse.

"I'll start identifying the remains," said Kalper. "But I doubt I'll recognize too many. I wasn't allowed at the encampments, and few have come to me for help. Most continue to see the healer from their camp."

"I understand. Just do the best you can." He strode across the room. He'd quit trying to avoid the coagulated puddles of blood. There wasn't a spot on the floor that wasn't spattered in blood or bloody footprints. He stepped outside and his eyes landed on Curtis. He'd been right. This was worse.

Memories assaulted him. He was in the Remore house again. Conguise was talking. The cart rolled into the room—blood stained and ominous. He knew it'd be bad, but he'd had no idea how bad. None of them had.

"Tell me it's not true," said Curtis.

"I'm so sorry." He walked over to his friend.

"No. You made a mistake. It's not her. It can't be her." There was a fear in the Guard's brown eyes that Hugh knew too well.

"Curtis, I'm so sorry."

"No. No." Curtis' voice cracked.

"I saw her too," said Jackson.

"It can't be." Curtis' eyes filled with tears. "She can't be...I need to see her."

"You don't need to see her like this." He knew better than anyone the regret, guilt, and nightmares a sight like that created.

"I do. I have to know. I have to be sure." Curtis pleaded with them.

"I am telling you...from experience...you don't want this image in your head." He tried to remember Viola laughing and smiling, staring up at him in bed, and sometimes he did...for a minute. Then the memory morphed and changed, and she was on the cart...her eyes glassy and unseeing. Her face drained of blood.

"I have to. I have to know it's her."

"I'm so sorry, but it is her." He took the Guard's arm and tried to lead him away from the building.

"I have to see her." Curtis pulled free.

"I understand. I do but..." He may be able to save his friend from this memory. "First, can you help me."

"What?" Curtis stared at him in disbelief.

"There are others. We haven't identified all the remains. Townsend will publish his article soon. At the end of the piece we're going to ask anyone who knows of a Producer who's missing to come to the police station to identify the remains. You went with Tammie when she visited Producers to help them, right?"

"Sometimes."

"Will you look at...the others. If you know them, we can contact the families. No one needs to see their loved one like this. No one." He prayed that Curtis would help and after seeing the others would realize that he didn't want to see Tammie like this.

"I need to see her."

"You will. When you're done looking at the others." That'd give him nightmares but nothing like seeing his mate's head.

"No." Curtis' tone was firm. "I need to see her first. Then I'll help you."

He looked at Jackson. They'd both do the same thing. "Okay. Jackson, please bring her remains out here." At least he could spare his friend the horror of seeing her head laid out with the others.

Jackson nodded and walked into the building.

"You need to know that...the remains..." He'd do his best to prepare the Guard. "All that's left...is her head."

"They...they killed her for meat."

"I'm sorry." Those words were so empty and yet they were all he had.

"They...they...ate her and..." Curtis turned, bending over and vomiting, the liquid splattering on the pavement.

"You don't have to do this," he repeated as Jackson came and stood next to him, a box in his hands.

Curtis straightened, wiping his mouth. His eyes widened in horror as he touched the lid almost reverently before lifting it. "Tammie." He sobbed. "Oh, Araldo. No." He clasped her head in his hands. "No...Araldo...no."

Hugh pried his hands away from her head. The Guard fell to the ground, crying. Jackson closed the box and walked away, disappearing into the building.

"Tammie." Curtis' body shook from his grief.

Hugh sat next to his friend and wrapped his arms around him, trying to absorb some of the sadness, but it'd never go away, never.

"She...she was pregnant." Curtis sobbed. "I told her not to come here...but she wanted the money. Oh, Araldo. Tammie!"

Hugh's heart broke all over for the Guard. He had no idea what to say or do, so he repeated the only comfort he had. "The doctor doesn't think she suffered. He believes they were knocked unconscious first. I'll find whoever did this. I promise. I'll find him and—"

"Let me kill him." Curtis' fingers clasped Hugh's shirt. "You have to let me do it. I'll tear him apart. Piece by piece."

"Okay. Yeah." That'd be fitting but he wasn't sure he could allow it.

"Swear." Curtis shook him. "Swear you'll let me have him."

"I...I can't promise that."

"You owe me. I risked everything to help you. You'd be dead if I hadn't."

"I promise I'll catch him and then we'll talk." He gripped the Guard's hands. "That's the best I can do."

"It's not good enough," snarled Curtis.

"Are you okay?" Jackson walked back over to them.

"Yeah." He pulled Curtis' hands from his shirt and stood. "We're good."

Curtis got up and started for the building.

"Where are you going?" He followed the Guard.

"To identify the others."

"Are you sure?" He grabbed the Guard's shoulder, stopping him at the doorway. "This won't be easy."

"Tammie would want me to help."

"Thank you."

"Let's get this done." Curtis pulled free from Hugh and strode into the building, stopping as he entered the kill room.

It was still a mess, but the piles of heads had been placed one after the other on the floor. The ones they'd identified had been put in bags or boxes and set to the side.

"Holy Araldo," whispered Curtis. "So many. Who would do something like this?"

"I don't know, but I will find him."

"And when you do, I'll kill him." Curtis walked across the room, not waiting for his reply.

CHAPTER 51: Hugh

It was early morning by the time Hugh arrived home. Servants moved through the Council Building, cleaning and organizing. The day had just begun, and he was already exhausted—emotionally and physically.

He walked down the hallway. Rex's chair sat empty, but a note was taped to the door to his suite.

Hire Guards. Soon.
Rex.

"I know. I will." He tore the paper from the door and went into the apartment. He tossed the note in the trash on his way to the bedroom. He needed a shower and at least an hour of sleep. He quietly opened the door and slipped inside the room, stopping as his gaze landed on the bed. It was empty.

"Trinity," he called out as he hurried into the kitchen area and then the spare room. She wasn't there. He took a steadying breath. She was safe. She had to be. He left the apartment and headed for Tim and Millie's rooms. Trinity wouldn't have gone off on her own. He picked up his pace until he was running down the hallway. Who was he kidding? That was what she always did. He slid to a halt and pounded on the door.

"Hugh. What's wrong?" Millie still wore her robe, Arthur wiggling and fussing in her arms.

"Is Trinity here?"

"No. She came by late last night. I was putting the baby down so I couldn't talk. She hugged me and left." Worry filled Millie's eyes. "What happened?"

"Yeah. What's going on?" Tim came up behind his mate.

"Trinity isn't in our suite."

"So?"

"There was another..." His eyes drifted to Millie.

"More Servants," said Tim. "Jethro has to—"

"Not Servants." His eyes darted to Millie again. "I'm sorry."

"What?" She stared at him and then looked at Tim. The baby cried harder as she instinctively pulled him closer. "What aren't you telling me?"

"This time it was Producers," he said.

"Murdered?" ask Millie.

"Yes. Tammie was one of them."

"Oh...no." Millie's face paled. "Does Curtis—"

"I told him last night."

"I have to go see him." She looked at Tim. "He'll need us. Need friends. Oh, this is terrible."

"It is." Tim wrapped his arm around her. "We'll go right away."

"Travis is also missing."

"Does Trinity know?" Tim's arm tightened around his mate.

"Yeah, and she's not in our apartment."

"Gruntshit." Tim kissed Millie. "Stay with Arthur."

"Find her." She clutched his arm.

"I will." Tim kissed her again and then stepped out of his apartment. "Have you searched the building?"

"No. I came here first." They headed down the hallway.

"I'm sure she's here somewhere," said Tim, although his voice betrayed his words.

"I'll check the courtyard."

"Good idea." Tim followed him.

"You can check somewhere else."

"Yeah, but I'm sure she's in the courtyard." Tim continued walking alongside him.

"We'd make better time if you looked for her in a different location than I am." He kept walking. Tim could be such a pain.

"You check somewhere else. I know my daughter. She's in the courtyard. It's the only place that doesn't reek of city around here."

"This is the city." He didn't need to be reminded that Trinity hated living here.

They stepped around the corner and his knees almost buckled in relief. Trinity sat on a bench beneath the trees in the yard.

"I'll go tell Millie." Tim patted him on the shoulder as he left.

"Thanks." He took another deep breath and opened the doors to the courtyard.

She looked up. Even when they were sad, her golden eyes made his heart skip a beat. He walked across the grass and joined her on the bench.

"Did you find him?" she asked.

"Who? Travis? I told you last—"

"You weren't in there long enough."

He sighed. "I didn't lie. I looked at...some and none were Travis. I didn't think Mirabelle should be forced to wait as long as it'd take to look at all of them."

"I understand." Her eyes searched his. "Did you find him?" she asked again.

"No."

"Thank you." She leaned against him, her entire body sagging as if someone had removed her bones.

"For what?" His arm went around her, pulling her close.

"For looking. I...I couldn't."

"You shouldn't have to."

"And neither should you but thank you for doing it." She kissed him softly before saying, "Are you hungry?"

"No, just tired."

"You should go to bed."

He rested his face against her head and took her hand. "I was worried when I couldn't find you."

"Why? Where did you think I'd gone?" She stiffened.

"To save someone." He'd meant it as a joke. Kind of.

"I wouldn't run off without telling you." She straightened, moving away from him

"That'd be a first."

"We were not a pair when I did that. I didn't owe you any kind of explanation for anything I did then."

"I know. I'm sorry." He ran his hand through his hair. "I'm just tired."

"Me too." She entwined her fingers with his. "Let's go to bed. I couldn't sleep last night. I needed you to hold me." Tears threatened to spill from her eyes.

"I need that too." Holding her was the one thing that might allow him to sleep without nightmares. As he stood, something big whizzed past his head. He threw himself to the ground, pulling her with him and covering her with his body. Whatever it was hit the ground with a thud a few feet from them.

"Birdie!" She shoved at his chest and wiggled out from under him. She stumbled as she ran across the lawn, dropping to her knees and pulling the Avion onto her lap.

He hurried over to them. Birdie was hurt. Bad. Most of his feathers were gone. Pulled out forcefully by the blood that spattered and dripped from the Avion's small, soft body. "Give him to me. We need to get him inside." He shouted. "Call doctor Kalper."

"No. No," squawked Birdie, his wings flapping at his side. "Birdie wants to die outside in the air and trees."

"You aren't going to die." She stroked the feathers on his head, but her voice cracked.

"Sir? You called." A Servant stepped into the courtyard.

"Get Dr. Kalper. Now. Tell him it's an emergency." He turned back to Birdie. "Trinity's right. You aren't hurt that badly. You're just whining again." He kept his voice firm and a bit rough. It was sure to annoy the Avion and might put a spark back in Birdie's dull and listless eyes.

Birdie lifted his wing, but it dropped to the side as if too heavy for him. "High Hugh is wrong again. Birdie hurt bad."

The breath caught in his throat. Five large gashes streaked across Birdie's small torso directly under his wing as if something had grabbed him and had tried to keep him from flying away.

"Oh...Birdie." Her voice was a whisper as she pulled off her shirt, pressing it to the Avion's side to stop the bleeding. She glanced up at him as he squatted next to her.

"House Servant?" They all knew it was too late. Avions couldn't lose much blood without dying.

"Yes. Birdie find them when Birdie go home." The Avion's tongue flicked against his beak.

"Shhh," he said. "Save your strength. The doctor will be here soon."

"No, they have...my family and friends...a net." Birdie coughed, sending small flecks of blood to paint his face. "Birdie couldn't move net. Birdie wait for...chance." He coughed again, his wings spasming at his sides as he gasped for breath. "They grab them...one-by-one...by their feet." His black eyes, so dim earlier, sparked with anger. "The screams. They scream help. Stop. But Servants didn't listen."

"Oh, Birdie." She shifted him, helping to make it easier for him to breathe.

Birdie took a deep, rattling breath. "They took them. Stuffed in bags." He closed his eyes for a moment. "They put them in a carriage. Birdie couldn't wait any longer. Birdie had to do something." He opened his eyes and turned to look at Trinity. "They took our babies too."

"Oh Birdie, you should have come for us. We would've helped." She stroked his feathers again, as tears streamed down her cheeks.

"No time then"—Birdie shook his head—"but I come now. Save my family, Little Producer." His eyes turned to Hugh. "You…"

"Yes." He leaned closer and Birdie flailed his wing, hitting him right in the face. He shifted away, pulling a feather from his mouth. Birdie was watching so he didn't want to throw it on the ground. It seemed disrespectful somehow, so he stuck it in his pocket.

"You…owe me favors, Hugh Truent." Birdie coughed, spattering them all with his blood. "Birdie collect now." His eyes turned back to Trinity. "You tell Handler that Birdie collect. Send Handler after the Servants."

"What do you remember about them?" he asked. "I need anything at all."

"They were Servants. Vile creatures." Birdie's breath wheezed in his chest and his gaze drifted back to Trinity. "Tree. Birdie want to die in tree. Not safe on ground for an Avion."

She nodded and stood. She carried Birdie to the tree she'd been sitting under.

"I'll hold him while you climb." He took the Avion from her, surprised at how light he was.

She climbed to the closest branch.

"Promise me, Hugh Truent," gasped Birdie, staring up at him.

"I'll do whatever it takes to save your family." He meant it.

Birdie's hard, black eyes locked with his and then peace pushed away the anger. "You okay, Hugh Truent. Just like your mother."

"I'll take him." Trinity leaned down from where she was perched on a branch.

"We'll save your family. I promise." He handed the little Avion to her.

"Higher," said Birdie. "I'm going to fly away. Never get tired. Always have food."

She tucked Birdie carefully under her arm. Hugh's breath froze in his chest as she climbed, the branches getting thinner and swaying from her weight. He was about to yell that it was high enough when she stopped and straddled a branch.

The wind blew her hair and a few of Birdie's feathers drifted on the air and settled near his feet. He took the one from his pocket, caressing the softness as he stared up at them. She was so different from him and so far away. His heart stuttered at the thought of losing her. She was leaving. Going undercover. He didn't need her to say it, and he was smart enough to know that if he fought her on this, he'd lose her anyway.

CHAPTER 52: Trinity

Trinity ran her hand over her dress for the party. With Stella's help it'd turned out beautiful. It was gold with green trim. She'd looked like someone else when she'd tried it on—someone elegant and worldly, someone who belonged here.

She and Hugh had decided that she should take it and wear it at Crosnics Manor, but it didn't feel right. This had been made for Hugh. She'd suffered through the dressmaker and the fittings for him. "Are you sure about the dress?"

"Yes. I don't need to see you in a dress to know how beautiful you are." Hugh stood near the door, fidgeting with Birdie's feather in his shirt pocket.

Her heart twisted and her throat tightened as she pulled it from the closet. She stuffed it into her suitcase before flinging her backpack over her shoulder and walking over to him. "I'm the lucky one to have found you." She touched his face. Araldo, she was going to miss him.

"Be careful." He captured her wrist and kissed her palm.

"I don't want to leave you." She tried not to cry, but the tears came anyway.

"Then don't." He pulled her into his arms and kissed her like he was never going to see her again.

She clung to him, trying to store everything into memory—his strength surrounding her, his scent, his taste.

He pulled back, keeping his arms around her. "Stay with me. We can find another way."

"I wish that were true"—she rested her head against his chest—"but any other way will take too long. We need to find

Birdie's family." She looked up into his blue eyes and brushed the hair off his forehead. "I just hope we aren't already too late."

"We aren't." His arms tightened around her. "We have to believe that Kalper is right about this and that means we have time."

The doctor had arrived shortly after Birdie had died. He'd told them about the Graining of Avions. Berries were fermented and then left in areas frequented by a flock of Avions. The creatures would feed on the fermented berries until they were too drunk to fly. Then the hunter would come in and collect them. As far as Kalper knew, the Avions usually weren't killed right away. They were kept in cages and fed so they'd gain weight. At some point, their captor would then kill and eat them, or sell them for consumption.

"If they all eat as much as Birdie did, we don't have much time." She ran her finger over the feather. "He was a good friend."

"He was." Hugh kissed her forehead and then dropped his arms, setting her free. "I love you."

"I love you too." She picked up her stuff and left their rooms, tears streaming down her cheeks. If anyone saw her, their breakup would look real, but it wasn't. She'd be back as soon as she found Birdie's family.

Rex nodded to her. His face even more dour than usual.

"Take care of him," she said.

"You should stay and do that yourself." The Guard wasn't happy with her.

"I can't." Her breath hitched in her chest. She had to tell the lie they'd concocted.

"He needs you."

"I can't stay here." More tears ran down her face. She'd live in Brush-Men territory if it meant staying with him, but this was their story. "I don't belong here. He'll be better without me."

"That's Gruntshit."

"I've gotta go." She hurried down the hallway toward the door. She had to get out of there before she changed her mind. She burst out of the building and slowed when her eyes landed on her mom who was waiting for her at the carriage. She'd expected her father. "Where's Dad?"

"He's staying with your brother."

"Oh." Great, now she was going to get a lecture. She followed her mother into the carriage. Her parents weren't happy about her decision to go undercover, especially her mom.

"Are you sure about this?" asked Mom as Ott took off down the road.

"No." She stared out the window. She wasn't sure about anything.

"Then stay here with your mate. Have babies."

"I can't." Her hand drifted to her stomach and then she fisted it. This wasn't the time to think about babies with Hugh.

"You can." Mom took her hand. "Don't ruin your life to save others."

"How can you expect me to do nothing?" She turned toward her mom. "They killed Tammie and—"

"I can't undo what they did to Tammie." Mom wiped a tear from her eye. "But I can stop you from doing something that's going to make you miserable."

"I have to help."

"Let someone else do it this time," snapped her mom. "You've done enough."

"I can't." She pulled her hand free from her mom's grasp. "I'm perfect for the job." Her voice caught in her throat. "Everyone knows me. I'm famous." Her lips trembled as she forced a smile.

"You're going to lose Hugh because of this."

"No." She shook her head. "We love each other."

"Yes, you love each other but that love is fragile." Mom's eyes pleaded with her. "You have young love. Filled with passion."

She blushed.

"There is more to passion than mating. There is anger and jealousy." Mom took both of her hands. "Please. Listen to me. You've let a beautiful, single female—an Almighty female—move into your home."

"The Council Building is not my home."

"It's Hugh's home and he'll be there alone with her."

"He's not alone with Stella."

"He will be if you leave."

"No. She's staying in a different section. We hardly even see her."

"She'll be around more once you're gone." Mom let go of Trinity's hands and crossed her arms over her chest. "Trust me on that."

"She won't do that." At least she hoped. The young Almighty female was everything Trinity wasn't—educated, petite, beautiful and worldly. She'd be the perfect mate for Hugh and Trinity tried hard not to hate the other female because of it.

"Why? Because the two of you chat over dresses?" Mom shook her head. "Don't look so surprised. I saw you talking on numerous occasions." Her eyes hardened. "You being her friend will not stop her from trying to take your mate."

"She's not going to do that and"—she hurried on before her mother could interrupt—"even if she does, I trust Hugh."

Her mom snorted.

"Plus, you and Dad are still living there." Trinity and her mother's disagreements were well-known. Having her parents take Hugh's side in this fake argument wouldn't surprise anyone, and it was the perfect way to keep them safe from the monster that was killing the other classes.

"Yes, but who's going to make sure you don't do something stupid?"

She dropped her head onto the back of the seat. "How many times do I have to tell you? I don't have feelings for Jethro anymore."

"Don't you see?" Mom sighed. "That doesn't matter. Hugh will believe you do, no matter what you say, and you won't be able to prove that you never mated with him."

"I wouldn't do that. Hugh and I are a bonded pair."

"He'll never believe that you didn't mate at least once. He is a male. He's suspicious and jealous by nature."

"Hugh trusts me."

"For the moment, perhaps"—Mom studied her—"but what about when he receives reports about you and Jethro. Words leaked about how quickly you found a new mate."

"Pretend mate, not real mate. Hugh knows this." She spoke through clenched teeth.

"But those rumors will scatter doubt like dandelions scatter seeds in a windstorm." Mom grabbed her hands again. "Even if one day you can convince him that nothing happened between you and Jethro, the scars of his suspicion will remain. Your relationship will never be the same."

"Stop. Okay. I have to do this. Travis is missing. Birdie is dead. Tammie is dead. I have to do whatever I can." She turned and stared out the window.

Mom was right. Jethro already stood between her and Hugh in many of their arguments. This was going to tear Hugh apart, but she couldn't sit by and do nothing. She'd be dead if others had done nothing when she'd needed help.

CHAPTER 53: Stella

Stella sat in one of the chamber rooms sipping tea and studying the female Servant across from her. Meesus was pretty in a wild and untamed way. She had the most gorgeous eyes and hair Stella had ever seen. No wonder the males, including Almightys, were fixated on female Servants.

She tamped down her anger at the unfairness of it all. She'd been raised to be demure and polite, and no one liked her. She'd heard Jethro come back to the house the night she'd been attacked. She'd watched the group of them outside in the yard. She hadn't been able to hear them, but she'd seen the way Jethro had studied Trinity. She knew that they had a history, but her grandfather had promised her that it was exactly that—history. It shouldn't surprise her that Grandfather had lied about that too.

"I'm sure you're wondering why I called upon you." Meesus placed her cup of tea on the table.

"I am." Stella kept her face a blank, impassive mask of politeness.

"I haven't had many dealings with the females of your class in a long time." Meesus' eyes sparkled.

She almost choked on her tea. That was obvious. Meesus ran a brothel. "I imagine that's true."

"I'm sorry about what those from my class did to you."

"Thank you, but it's not your fault. You didn't attack me." She wasn't going to blame the innocent like those hypocrites who she'd once thought were her friends.

"Still. I am sorry. Males of all classes can be brutal." Meesus' eyes locked with hers. "They did not...hurt you, did they?"

"A few bruises that's all." The worst part was that they'd taken her independence. Her entire life had been planned from the day she'd been born. Her lessons regimented as strictly as any soldier or prisoner...until her grandfather's death. She'd been betrayed and ostracized, but she'd also been freed.

"That's good." Meesus smiled. "Males can be particularly aggressive when faced with one who is young and innocent."

She had nothing to say about that. She was young and she was an innocent. Her grandfather had guarded that well. It was her only commodity according to him.

"You are not happy." Meesus tipped her head, studying Stella.

That was an understatement. She was engaged to a male whom she barely knew. He seemed kind, but there was something wild about Jethro that scared her. She was pretty sure she could get past that if she got to know him better, but he didn't care for her at all. Yes, he'd taken her to his mother's, but he'd wasted no time dumping her at the Council Building where she'd spent most of her youth.

When her grandfather had died, she'd lost everything, but that hadn't bothered her because she hadn't wanted any of those things. She'd never asked to be the sole heir to her grandfather's legacy.

Oddly, she'd been happy in her little apartment. She'd been at peace there. She'd had the security of having a fiancé without the bother of one. It'd been almost perfect until the attack. Now, she was a burden to Jethro and to Hugh Truent. He and Trinity had welcomed her, but she'd grown up around politicians. She'd seen through the welcome to what it was—a way to promote himself. He alone had accepted the tainted granddaughter of the perverse former Supreme Almighty. Plus, by taking her in he was mending his relationship with his brother who many considered a hero for switching sides and helping the Allied Classes win the war.

"I think"—Meesus continued to study her—"that you need a friend."

"I've never found them to be worth the effort." That struck a chord, and she covered her reaction with a sip of tea. She did miss having friends. She and Trinity had been on their way to friendship, but the other female was gone now.

"Ah, so naïve. A good friend is worth everything."

"I have yet to find one of those." She lowered her teacup.

Meesus laughed. Of course, it was as musical and lovely as the Servant. "You have spirit. I was not sure. You hide."

"Excuse me?" She'd never hidden in her life. She'd never been allowed to. She'd always had to make an appearance with her grandparents. Stand or sit quietly through the parties. Smile politely but remain silent.

"You hide." Meesus waved her hand. "Your hairstyle is meant to hide your beauty, not enhance it. Same with your clothes." Her lip curled. "Expensive but bland like a beige wall."

She touched her hair. It was pulled back in a neat chignon. Her grandmother had taught her to dress so that she was attractive but not overly so.

"If you like, I can teach you not to hide." Meesus leaned forward. "I can show you the power of being a female."

She eyed the Servant's clothes, rich and vibrant like their owner. No male ever looked past Meesus without noticing her. "I-I'd like that." Her grandmother would hate it, but Grandmother no longer got any say in Stella's life. Her grandmother had chosen to leave her alone and invisible in this world. She wanted someone to see her, to desire her.

"We shall go shopping, you and I." Meesus smiled, taking a sip of her tea.

The blood drained from her face. So much for wanting something. "I don't have any money." She did miss having money.

"Don't worry about that." Meesus flipped her hand as if this was inconsequential.

The offer touched her. "No, I couldn't ask you—"

"Oh, I won't pay." Meesus laughed. "Not in the end, anyway."

"I-I don't understand."

"I will collect my money from your husband."

"Jethro doesn't have any money." She may not want to marry him, but he was the only offer she had. She looked down at her teacup, staring at the bland brown liquid. It was like her and her life—tepid and barely tolerable.

"You will not be marrying Jethro." Meesus touched her hand as she stood. The other female's skin was warm and soft.

"I won't?" She looked up, her eyes locking with Meesus' vibrant ones. She shouldn't be surprised that he'd moved on to someone else, but she'd thought he'd at least tell her.

"Oh, no. We will find a bigger catch than him for you." Meesus tugged on her hand, making her stand.

"A bigger—"

"Yes. You don't know your worth." The Servant walked around her. "You are the perfect Almighty. Pale, thin and blonde."

She swallowed. It wasn't a compliment.

"And we will take those qualities and improve on them."

"We will?" She wasn't sure how. She burned in the sun and her hair just got lighter.

"Yes. We'll make you the perfect temptress. A wild, untamed Almighty in a pretty package."

Her heart raced at the idea. She'd never been wild or a temptress. She wasn't sure how Meesus was going to do that, but she was willing to let the other female try.

CHAPTER 54: Hugh

Hugh stared at his oatmeal, his day looming gloomily ahead of him. No, that was incorrect. It wasn't just his day. His life loomed gloomily ahead of him. He pushed his bowl aside. Sue had come into town last night to deliver some food. They'd had dinner and had talked late into the night, reminiscing about Laddie. He'd gotten sidetracked with other issues but finding where Conguise had moved his unholy experiments was exactly the kind of thing that'd help him not think about Trinity.

The professor had to have had a contingency plan in place for an emergency evacuation that didn't include destroying everything. That meant the experiments had been moved and every trail left some evidence. He just had to find it. The maps in his apartment were the perfect place to start. He finished his coffee and stood, suddenly a little excited for the day ahead.

Millie strode into the room. Tim shot him a commiserating look as he trailed after his mate. Hugh sat back down. Millie had something to say and by the pinched expression on her face it wasn't going to be pleasant.

She stopped in front of him, hands on her hips. "If you think I'm not going to tell my daughter that you're already having dinner with her replacement—"

"Trinity left me." He pointedly looked at the open door as he poured more coffee in his cup. "Whom I have dinner with is none of her business."

Millie flipped her hand at her mate and Tim quickly closed the door. She sat on the chair next to Hugh.

"It was no big deal. Sue and I were in the library," he whispered. "We decided to have dinner and catch up. We'd just started eating when Stella had come in for a book. It would've been rude not to invite her to join us."

"Then be rude." Millie glared at him. "That female has eyes on you."

"No, she doesn't." He held up his hand to stop Millie's argument. "And even if she does, I have no interest in her. I have no interest in anyone besides your daughter."

"Then stay away from her."

"I'm not going to seek her out, but I'm also not going to purposely avoid her."

"You really think that her living here won't cause issues?"

"It won't. Trinity trusts me, and I trust her." He wasn't so sure about trusting Jethro though.

"My daughter is a young, naive fool. She doesn't understand males." She shot Tim a glare.

"Millie, that's ancient history," said Tim.

That was interesting. It seemed Tim hadn't been loyal their entire relationship.

"It happened," she said through gritted teeth.

Tim shot him a help me look. He sipped his coffee, letting Tim take his punishment. The Servant glared at him, and he smiled over his cup.

"A long time ago." Tim sounded like they'd had this argument way too many times. "We were kids."

"Trinity is a child and he"—Millie's hard eyes fell on Hugh—"can't be that big of a fool. Unless this is his plan to keep himself entertained while Trinity is out catching a killer."

"I have no plans to be *entertained* until Trinity returns." He smirked at Tim. "I will *entertain* myself until then."

Tim chuckled but quickly covered his mouth as if coughing when Millie turned on him.

"This isn't funny. Your daughter is going to be heartbroken—"

"I won't hurt her." He stood. "I won't cheat on her." He took Millie's hand. "I love your daughter and only her."

"Then send the Almighty somewhere else." Millie's eyes softened. "Please, send her away before you crush my daughter. Trinity is strong in many ways, but in this she is vulnerable."

"I can't. Stella has no family. No friends. She has nowhere else to go." Not only was it good for society to see him giving his enemy's granddaughter protection, but he wouldn't feel right abandoning her like everyone else had. He knew all too well how that felt.

"You truly believe that you can live with a young, attractive, single female and nothing will happen, don't you?" Millie studied him.

"Yes, because I'm not going to cheat on Trinity with Stella or anyone else. I don't know what I can say to convince you, so my actions will have to speak for me." He strode toward the door.

"You'll lose her for real." Millie trailed after him. "Trinity won't stand for infidelity."

"He'll be lucky if she doesn't kill him," mumbled Tim.

He stopped at the door, glancing over his shoulder at them. "If I didn't love her, that alone would keep me entertaining myself."

CHAPTER 55: Hugh

Hugh headed to his office and grabbed the maps they'd been looking at before they'd went to the Holstein area. He flipped through them. Wherever Conguise had moved his experiments, it had to be on one of these papers.

He dug through the stack of blueprints until he found the ones for the underground tunnels. He scanned the first one. It was the sewer system for a neighborhood that'd been built a few years ago. He flipped through them, sorting out the older ones.

He spread out the maps on the floor and spent the next several hours comparing the underground tunnels with what was above them. They looked accurate, but something was off. He studied the tunnels near Conguise's lab. None of them led to the forest even though he knew firsthand that they did. He pushed the maps aside and flopped down on the couch. He needed older documents. Ones like the map that was given to Gaar.

He jumped up and grabbed a set of keys that he'd confiscated from Jason's office. These were the master keys to all the rooms in the building, even the ones in the basement. He headed downstairs. He started at the first storage room, wrinkling his nose at the damp, musty smell. Some of these rooms had been shut up for so long that no one knew what was in them.

He spent the remainder of the day searching through dusty, dank rooms but found nothing useful—old journals, trunks of clothes that disintegrated when he touched them, and some laboratory equipment that looked like it'd been made centuries ago.

He stretched, running his hand through his hair. It was late and he was tired, hungry and depressed. He headed for his apartment. He wanted to sit and talk with Trinity. Tell her about his wasted day and listen to her tell him about hers, but that wouldn't happen.

"Where have you been? You're filthy." Rex sat on the chair across from his door.

"Basement. How's the interviewing at the jail going?"

"Not good. Gerald is picky. Why were you in the basement?"

"I'm thinking about fixing up the rooms for Guards and Servants. I know a lot of Servants and Guards slept down there before the war, but this would be different. It wouldn't be squeezing into a corner somewhere. We'd make them cozy. Homes. Do you think they'd like that?"

"Yeah, I do."

"Even the ones who refuse to leave?" He raised his brow at the stubborn Guard.

"They might." Rex's lips twitched.

"But would they use it?" He opened the door to his apartment. "That's the important question."

"Probably."

"Really?" He paused in the doorway.

"Never had a place of my own, and I'd still be here."

"Then pick a room and clean it out." He tossed Rex the keys. He trusted the Guard. "Change the lock on the room you pick and then bring these back to me."

"You're really giving me a room of my own. Here. Not in an apartment blocks away." Rex seemed unsure.

"Yeah. Any of them. There are a ton. Some are full of papers and junk. If you want one of those rooms, put the stuff in the hallway. I need to sort through it before I toss it."

"I-I don't know." Rex stared at the keys, his brown eyes gleaming with excitement.

"Go. Check it out." He patted the Guard's shoulder. "Pick a room and then take what you need from the empty guest chambers to make it a home."

"The guest chambers are...nice."

"Yeah, and they aren't being used, nor will they be. I have no intention of inviting rich Almightys to visit." He smirked. "Most of them hate me anyway."

"But..." Rex stared at the door and then glanced down the hallway.

"I'm going to make a sandwich and then go to the library." He had menus and plans to approve for the fundraising event. The one he no longer wanted to attend. "I'll be there for hours. If you stay here, you'll be protecting an empty room."

"I'll come by when I'm done to make sure you're still in the library."

"I'll be fine."

"Okay and...thanks." Rex didn't move.

"You're welcome, but aren't you going?"

"I'll wait until you leave for the library."

"Of course you will." He shook his head at the Guard's grin.

He'd been going to shower but he'd do that later. He didn't want to make Rex wait any longer than necessary. It still humbled him how little those in the other classes had. He went into his kitchen area and made himself a sandwich from some of the vegetables that Sue had brought.

He grabbed his plate and headed for the door. He stopped, veering over to the liquor cabinet. He poured himself a brandy. Hopefully, it'd help him sleep. Without Trinity to hold, he'd been tossing and turning all night. When he did manage to fall asleep, he had nightmares about her and Jethro, laughing and doing other things. The only way to combat that was to exhaust himself by working.

"Go. Pick a room," he said to Rex as he strode down the hallway to the library. He stopped in the doorway.

Stella sat on the couch reading. She glanced up at him, smiling shyly. "Hi, Hugh."

He grunted a response. He should leave. Millie would be furious if she found him there, but he was an adult. He didn't answer to Millie.

"I'll go." Stella's eyes dimmed as she stood.

There was a loneliness to her voice that tugged at his heart. This girl had lost everything. It wouldn't hurt to sit and talk with her for a bit.

"No, please. I could use some company." He walked into the room.

"Are you sure?"

"Yes." He sat behind the desk, putting plenty of distance between him and Stella.

She smiled slightly and sat back down, keeping the book closed on her lap. He took a bite of his sandwich, the silence hanging uncomfortably between them.

"Did you find what you were looking for?" she asked.

"Why do you think I was looking for something?" His eyes flew to her.

"I didn't mean anything by it." She paled. "It's just that you're dirty and I saw you go downstairs. No one ever goes down there. I've lived my whole life in or around this building and the only ones I ever saw go down there were plumbers."

"Sorry." He smiled sheepishly at her. "I'm still a bit touchy when people ask about my activities." She hadn't meant anything by her question. She'd just been making small talk.

"I imagine being falsely accused and imprisoned would do that to someone." She stared at her hands folded in her lap.

He laughed. She had more spunk than he'd thought. She smiled a bit but still didn't look up at him.

"You don't need to be frightened of me," he said.

She was an adult, in her twenties, but still a child in so many ways. Jason had kept her tucked away and protected, to keep her pure and innocent for her potential husband. It still surprised him that Jason had chosen Jethro for her fiancé.

Yes, Jethro was young and strong, but he didn't seem interested in politics. Of course, those types sometimes made the best leaders, but more often than not they made the best puppets. He took another bite of his sandwich. The only question that remained was why Jethro had agreed to the marriage. Since he wasn't politically motivated, it had to be something else.

"I should go." Stella stood.

"Please, stay." He'd been quiet too long. Trinity would understand him talking to Stella. She knew better than anyone about being lonely. "I could use someone to talk to. My mother-in-law—"

"You're married?" Her blue eyes met his.

"No. Sorry." He cringed. He had to be more careful. "Millie would've been my mother-in-law if Trinity and I hadn't...well..." He had a hard time saying that they broke up. He could if he had to, but he didn't like to say those words. He wasn't superstitious, but he saw no reason to tempt fate by repeating it over and over again.

"I'm sorry. I heard about that. It's never easy. I'm sure."

"Have you ever been in love and lost that person?" His tone was harsher than he'd intended, but her platitudes annoyed him.

"No." She paled even more. "I'm sorry. It seemed like the right thing to say."

"Don't. Okay?"

"Don't what?" She looked like she was ready to bolt from the room.

"Don't say the right thing. Say what you mean. Say what you think. Not what you think I want to hear." That was the problem with this world, with Almightys mostly. They never spoke the truth.

Her eyes narrowed, showing that bit of spirit that Jason hadn't quite been able to squash.

"Go ahead. Say it." He was curious because he truly had no idea what she was thinking.

She shook her head.

"Tell me what you think. I dare you." He leaned forward. "I won't break, and I won't cry. I promise."

"I have nowhere else to go." It was almost a whisper.

"I would never throw you out. You can stay here as long as you like."

"Thank you." She relaxed a bit.

"I am sorry about what happened to you." He wasn't sorry about Jason, but she and her grandmother were innocent of the Supreme Almighty's transgressions.

She remained quiet, but she wanted to speak. It was clear in her eyes.

"Say it," he prodded. For some reason he wanted to help this girl. She'd been used as a pawn her entire life. She needed to take charge and quit being a commodity to be bartered.

"I'd rather not," she said, tight lipped.

"You'll feel better if you do." He should relish her reticence because not one female in his life had ever been quiet about her wants, but instead it was starting to annoy him.

"I doubt that." She stood. "Thank you for letting me stay and for the conversation."

"There you go again, saying what you think you should."

She walked toward the door.

"Do you like being a welcome mat? I know you were raised to do exactly what you were told, but you have the opportunity to change that."

She stopped at the door.

"But only if you want," he said, his voice barely a whisper.

"You think it's that easy." She spun around. "Why don't you change?"

He held back his smile. This girl was at the edge. Another push and she'd be free. "I'm perfect. So why should I change?" He gave her the smuggest look he had.

Her face almost spasmed as she fought to hold back her words.

"Your grandfather would be so proud of you. Standing there, taking it. The perfect Almighty bride. Marry who you're told to marry and let your husband have his affairs. That was your fate. It still is by the way you're acting."

"How dare you." She stormed out of the door and then quickly back inside. "I will not have a marriage like my mother's and my grandmother's. I will not be ignored."

She was actually quite attractive with color in her cheeks and her hands on her hips. He'd have to find a better match for her than Jethro. Although...if Jethro saw her like this, he might be more attracted to her, and if he were attracted to Stella, than he wouldn't be interested in Trinity. Still, Stella needed someone who really cared for her. He'd get to know her a bit better. If he didn't think she and Jethro would suit, he'd find someone else for her. "Feel better?"

"I hate you." She took a deep breath. "But yes, I do."

"Told you so." He laughed.

She spun on her heels and walked out the door.

He finished his drink and grabbed his dishes. When he stood, Millie was standing in the doorway, hands on her hips.

"Don't say a word." He didn't need this right now. He hadn't done anything wrong. "Not...one...word."

He pushed past her and walked quickly back to his suite. This mission couldn't get done fast enough. Not only did he miss Trinity, but he really needed her mother off his back.

CHAPTER 56: Stella

Stella sat at a small café, having lunch with Meesus. The Servant had sent her a note, asking to meet.

"That male over there is watching you." Meesus' voice was soft, but her eyes were far from demure as she stared back at the male.

"Really?" Stella blushed. Before her grandfather's death no one had ever noticed her, except as the quiet accoutrement to her grandparents, and the only looks she'd gotten lately came with whispers and snickers.

"Yes, most definitely."

Stella ran her hand down the front of her new sweater. It was a gorgeous dark blue. Meesus had suggested the color when they'd gone shopping. She'd said it highlighted her eyes and pale skin.

"You are a natural." Meesus smiled.

"A natural what?" She had no idea what the other female meant by that.

"Run your hand down your shirt again. Slowly. Enjoy the feel of the material."

She blushed more but did as the Servant ordered. A few seconds later a young male Almighty walked over to their table.

"Hi." He smiled but his eyes never moved from Stella's chest.

"Hello." She managed to force the word past her tight throat. He was around her age and attractive with light brown hair and blue eyes. The only young male she'd spent any time with had been Jethro, but this guy was more her type—slender and unthreatening.

"Please, join us." Meesus motioned to the chair next to Stella.

He sat, seeming unsure of what to say. She took a sip of her drink and glanced at Meesus, who had a frown in her eyes.

"Tell us. What is your name?" asked Meesus.

"Oh, sorry. Scott."

Meesus gave her a pointed look.

"I'm Stella." It came out barely louder than a whisper.

"What?" He leaned toward her. "Sorry. I didn't hear you."

She grabbed her water and took a sip, hoping it'd clear the tightness in her throat.

"She's Stella and I'm Meesus." The Servant held out her hand, her face softening as his larger hand engulfed hers.

"Nice to meet you," said Scott.

Meesus stared at Stella, her eyes speaking volumes of annoyance as silence settled on their group again. "What do you do for a living, Scott?"

The young man talked about college and working for his father at a clothing manufacturer. Meesus continued to drag information from the young Almighty, the whole time trying to urge Stella to say something.

She wanted to speak, to be witty and sparkling, but she had no idea how to converse with anyone. Her job as the granddaughter of the Supreme Almighty had been to be silent and look proper. As Scott and Meesus chatted, Stella once again disappeared like a pretty picture on the wall—noticed for a moment but then forgotten.

Scott left, promising to meet her again next week at the café, but she was pretty sure he wouldn't show. Why would he unless he wanted to sit in silence?

Meesus handed the waiter the money for their lunch and then stood. She followed the Servant, her head bowed, and her eyes cast downward. She didn't want to see Meesus' disappointment.

"That was a disaster," said Meesus.

"I'm sorry." She choked back her tears.

"Stop looking at your feet. Look at the world." Meesus turned toward her, placing her clawed finger under Stella's chin and raising her head. "You are young. You are an Almighty. And you are pretty. The world is yours, but you have to take it."

"I'm not pretty. I'm invisible."

"Only because you let yourself be." Meesus' eyes softened.

"I don't know how to be any other way." She wanted to be vibrant and alive, but all she knew was silence and obedience.

Meesus took her hand and led her to a bench, pulling Stella down next to her. "Do not be sorry. It is how you were raised, but you need to learn to take what you want. No one will give it to you. Life is cruel and unfair. It is always a fight." Meesus' words were hard and bitter.

"I don't know what to do." She hated how weak she sounded. How weak she was.

"I can help you with this, but you must do what I say. Okay?"

She nodded.

"Good. First, throw away all your old clothes. Only wear what I have bought for you."

"Okay." That'd be easy. She loved her new clothes.

"Second, you must practice talking and flirting."

"How?"

Meesus tapped her lip a moment and then smiled. "You will practice on Hugh."

"Hugh? No, I couldn't." At one time, she'd thought he was the exact kind of male she'd wanted, but that was before last night.

"Yes, he is perfect. He is young, but not too young." Meesus waved her hand. "You will not have to pry conversation from him like that Scott-child." She rolled her eyes and then leaned in closer. "Hugh is also attractive."

Stella felt blood rush to her cheeks. Hugh was very attractive, but he was also a jerk.

"You feel it too." Meesus touched her cheek with a claw. "It's written in the heat on your face. Hugh is a young, virile male, and he is single now." She patted Stella's hand. "He is perfect for you to use to practice flirting. He will only take what you offer."

"I couldn't. I mean, I wouldn't know what to say." She was angry with Hugh, but he'd been right. She had felt better after yelling at him.

"It is just practice, unless you decide you want it to be something more. Talk to him. Be nice, but not too nice." Meesus winked at her. "It is simple. You practice and then you hunt for your mate."

Stella wasn't sure about hunting for her mate, but she'd like someone to talk to. Hugh and Trinity had just broken up, so he was probably lonely too. They could help each other.

CHAPTER 57: Jethro

Jethro stood near the bar with Indy at the Howling Hut, nursing a beer. He had to keep his wits about him. The plan was for him and Trinity to *accidentally* bump into each other and to have a fight. That wouldn't be too difficult to fake since he wanted to shake some sense into her every time he saw her.

"Showtime," whispered Indy as he nudged Jethro.

His gaze drifted to the door as the female he both hated and wanted more than anyone else glided into the bar, her arm looped with Sassy's. Trinity looked good, really good. Her hair hung loose, tumbling over her shoulders in a cascade of reds and browns. Her eyes sparkled with laughter, until they landed on him. For a moment a flare of apprehension and then distaste took over her face.

He nodded and tossed back the rest of his beer. Damn, she was either a good actor or she actually still hated him. He motioned to the bartender for a refill. She had no reason to be angry with him. He was the one who should be mad. He'd tried to save her. He'd trusted her, and she'd drugged him. He'd been willing to give up everything for her, and she'd chosen Hugh. He grabbed his full beer and took a sip. Fighting with her was going to be easy. Keeping himself from strangling her or kissing her was going to be the tough part.

Sassy walked over to him and Indy as Trinity continued to a table. She stopped in front of them, swaying slightly. "You two need to leave."

He turned and leaned against the bar. They hadn't told Sassy anything about their mission. She was drunk way too much and that meant they couldn't trust her to keep her mouth shut. Actually, they were counting on her not being quiet.

"Why is that?" Indy's eyes narrowed. His friend had been trying to watch out for Sassy since Bruno's death, and she'd been nothing but nasty to him. "Do you think there's not enough alcohol for us and you?"

"No." Sassy's lip curled, showing her large canines. "I'm here with Trinity." She glared at Jethro.

"I was here first," he said. "You leave."

"I see you're still as much of a gentleman as ever." Sassy snarled at him.

"I was a gentleman once." He glanced across the club at Trinity who already had two male House Servants talking to her. "I let the female set the pace." He looked back at Sassy. "Ask your *friend* what that got me."

"You got exactly what you deserved." Sassy looked at Indy. "Please, Indy. Go to another bar tonight."

"Maybe we should." Indy turned toward him. "If Hugh's going to show up it'd be better if we weren't here."

"Oh, Hugh won't be..." Sassy clamped her mouth shut.

"You mean to tell me that Hugh isn't chasing after her like always." He stared at Trinity. It wasn't hard to act interested. She fascinated him; she always had. She was a mix of innocence and wildness. She was the forest to him. Freedom and pleasure. Danger and excitement. "Why is that? My *brother* is usually attached to her hip."

"None of your business," said Sassy.

"Okay. Be like that." He pushed away from the bar. "I guess, I'll ask her." He winked at Sassy. "I'm sure she'll be glad to see me. We're old friends."

"Do not go over there." Sassy grabbed his arm. "I'll tell you, but you have to promise to leave."

"Nope, can't do that. I'm meeting a friend here later. One of the female variety. I wouldn't want to leave and ruin her night."

"I'm sure that'd improve her evening." Sassy rolled her eyes.

"No need to be rude." He grinned at her as he waved the bartender over to them. "We're all friends. Right?"

"We're not—"

"I always buy my friends a drink. What are you having?"

"Your usual?" asked the bartender.

"Uhm..." She hesitated a second, her eyes darting to Trinity and then she said, "A double."

"See. I knew we were friends." He tossed some money on the bar and handed the drink to Sassy.

She took a big gulp as if she were dying of thirst. "Just promise to leave Trinity alone."

"Like I said, I'm meeting a friend. She's the jealous type so I think one female will do tonight."

"You're disgusting."

"Just a young male with a healthy appetite."

"Promise." She took another swallow of her drink. Her double was now a single.

"Sure. Why not?" He stopped her from walking away. "As long as you tell me the secret."

"What secret?" She stared at him, her large brown eyes cloudy with alcohol.

"Why my beloved brother isn't sniffing after Trinity tonight."

"Oh. That. It's not really a secret. Everyone will know soon enough." She leaned toward him, lowering her voice. "She broke up with Hugh."

"Did she?" His brows rose as his eyes went back to Trinity. "For good? Or just a spat?"

"For good. I think. She moved in with me."

"That is interesting." He shifted to the side, so he could see Trinity better. "She must be lonely. Sad." He glanced at Indy. "I'm a fun guy, right?"

"You sure are." Indy grinned. "I've seen you brighten up a room just by leaving."

"Shut up." He elbowed his friend in the gut. "You're just jealous because females love me."

"You promised to leave her alone," growled Sassy. "And I expect you to keep your word." She gave him one last glare before walking away.

"But that was before I knew she was available." He grinned as Sassy's back stiffened. He'd counted on the Guard hearing him. Now, all he had to do was wait for the perfect opportunity to join the females and let the anger inside him free.

CHAPTER 58: Jethro

Jethro would rather be whipped again than spend one more minute watching Trinity dance and flirt with male after male. He swore in the last couple of hours, she'd flirted with every male in the place. Right now, she slow danced with a large, handsy Guard. She grabbed his wrist and moved his hand off her butt...again. Jethro wanted to storm over there, tear the guy's arms off and shove them up his...He downed his beer before sliding it forward for a refill.

"You should slow down," said Indy.

"Shut up." He drank half of the next beer. His head spun as he stared at Trinity. He wanted her. She was the one that he always wanted, and she was here. Alone. Without Hugh. Soon she and him would pretend to be a couple. She was his, and that Guard kept touching her. He stood.

Indy grabbed his arm, trying to pull him back down onto the bar stool.

"Let go." He jerked free. He wanted to mate, and he wanted her. "It's time." He strode onto the dance floor.

"Ah, shit." Indy trailed after him. "That Guard is huge."

"Not a problem." He appreciated that Indy always had his back, but he didn't need the Guard's assistance. He could fight a Tracker right now with the way the booze raced through his veins. Trinity belonged to him, and he'd kill anyone who got between them. He grabbed the Guard's arm, stopping the other male's hand from smoothing over her backside. He wanted to tear it from its socket but instead he shoved, sending the Guard stumbling backward.

It took him less than a second to take in his enemies. The Guard had three friends who were watching. By their stance and the hint of testosterone in the air, they'd be more than happy to step in to help their friend.

Indy was behind him, but the Guard was busy keeping Sassy from charging over there. She wouldn't be on Jethro's side either.

"What's your problem?" The Guard shook off the other male who'd blocked his fall.

"Keep your hands off her." The others on the dance floor shifted away and a movement in the shadows caught his eye. It was a small House Servant with vibrant green eyes. That little guy looked familiar but...Ah. It was the Servant who followed Trinity. He could probably count on that kid to help out Trinity, but that wouldn't put him on Jethro's side either.

The Guard stepped up to him until their chests almost touched. The other male was twice his size in girth and a good foot taller than him.

"She's mine," he whispered.

The Guards eyes flared, but the anger only lasted a second before it dimmed. There'd be no fight. The Guard was big but not brave. Jethro's body railed at the denial. He wanted to fight this Guard and his friends, and after he'd beaten them to a pulp, he'd carry off his prize. He glanced at Trinity, but that was a mistake.

She pushed between the Guard and him, and he stared into angry gold eyes.

"I am not yours." Her claws stretched from her fingertips—fully exposed—and her fangs peeked from beneath her upper lip, her anger wafting off of her in waves.

He inhaled deeply, becoming more aroused by the smell because it wasn't just anger. She was female, and she was aware of him as a male. He couldn't stop the smirk from stealing across his lips. "You almost were." He leaned closer. "One more minute or two and I would've been your first. Your last." If they'd mated, he would've never let her go.

Her face tightened so much it looked brittle enough to shatter, and then she slapped him. Hard. Claws out. His head snapped back. He touched his cheek, his fingers sliding through his blood. She was fast. He hadn't seen it coming.

He smiled at her, the scratches pulling across his cheek. "I see my half-brother still hasn't tamed you. Come home with me and I'll show you what a real male can do."

"I hate you." Her voice cracked with anger or tears, maybe a combination of both. "Leave me alone." She stormed away.

Indy let go of Sassy and the two females hurried across the bar and disappeared into the bathroom.

The Guard who'd been dancing with Trinity had moved a couple of steps back and stared at him, a huge grin on his face. "Your next drink is on me." He touched his own cheek, still smiling. "That could've been me. She kept warning me to watch my hands."

"Good advice. If you touch her again, I'll tear your arms off and shove one down your throat and the other up your ass so you can shake your own hand." He walked back to the bar.

Indy chatted with the Guard as they followed him. Indy could make friends with anyone.

"I think she likes you." The Guard ordered a round.

"You have an odd idea of how females act when they like someone," he muttered. "She almost took my face off."

"In my experience females don't get that angry with someone unless they like them." The Guard paid the bartender.

He glanced at the bathroom. Was that possible? There'd definitely been something between them on the other side of Harbor Point. Maybe he'd kidnap her and take her over there again. They could forget everyone else and live there together in the forest.

"Or," said the Guard after taking a long drink. "She could truly hate you. Did you do something to her?"

"Yeah, you could say that," he muttered into his mug.

"Then she hates you." The Guard slapped him on the shoulder.

"That's what I figured." He touched his cheek again and winced slightly at the pain.

The Guard's friends came over and Indy began telling them war stories. Jethro sipped his beer. He wanted to go home and sleep. He should find another female, one that looked like her, but he didn't want a substitute. Not now. Not when her scent lingered in his brain.

Trinity and Sassy came out of the bathroom. They stopped at their table and finished their drinks before heading for the door. Thankfully, his night was almost over. Step one of their plan was accomplished. They'd had a fight. Next, he needed to apologize. She wouldn't forgive him right away, but it'd be the start of a public mending of their relationship.

The two females left, and the little black House Servant followed them outside. The Guard and his friends wandered over to a table full of females. He picked up his drink and stood.

"We should wait a bit." Indy grabbed his arm. "It isn't a good idea to follow her." The Guard said it loudly enough so others would hear. It was all part of their plan.

"I need to apologize." He pulled free and walked to the door.

"Later. Not tonight." Indy followed him.

"My mom always told me to make amends before bed." He opened the door and the scent of Servants hit him in the face. The club had a lot of Servants, but this was a different smell. This was aggression. Anticipation...and fear. He felt it in his bones; someone was hunting Trinity.

CHAPTER 59: Trinity

"Saying I hate Jethro is a huge understatement." Trinity was so mad she trembled as she and Sassy left the Howling Hut.

"Despise. That's the word you need." Sassy stumbled, bumping into Trinity's side.

"That's still not strong enough." She wasn't sure how she was going to pretend to like him when she couldn't even stand being near him.

"Forget about him."

"Don't worry. He's already forgotten." She lied. His words were branded into her mind. Another moment and he would've been her first mate. That would've been a huge mistake. She loved Hugh.

"Great. Then let's go." Sassy grinned as she grabbed Trinity's arm and pulled her toward the alley.

"Why are we going this way?"

"Faster." The streetlights dimmed as they moved between the buildings.

"And you're suddenly in a hurry to get home?" A movement in the shadows caught her eye. It was only Say. She had to stay focused. This area wasn't terrible, but it wasn't necessarily safe for two females either—Sassy stumbled again, and she caught her friend's arm, steadying her—especially when one was drunk.

"Home? We're not going home."

"Not another club." She really wasn't in the mood. She missed Hugh. She'd only gone to the Howling Hut because it was part of the plan. The sooner they infiltrated the black market, the sooner she could save Birdie's family and go home to Hugh.

"Yep. You need to forget about Hugh and the only way to do that is with another male."

"I'm not ready." Her friend should understand that. Sassy was drunk more than she was sober, trying to get through her grief over Bruno.

"You can drink until you are." Sassy took another swallow from the glass she'd snuck out of the bar.

"Doing that isn't..."

Three House Servants glided into view at the end of the alleyway. They were all male, and they moved with lethal intent. She grabbed Sassy's arm, stopping her.

"Hey, watch your claws. That hu..." Sassy's eyes landed on the Servants.

"Let's go back to the club." She kept ahold of Sassy's arm as they backed away. Her other hand caressed the knife at her side. Hopefully, she wouldn't have to use it. They weren't that far from the door.

"I ain't afraid of House Servants." Sassy tried to jerk free from Trinity's grasp.

"We don't need a fight." She tugged on Sassy's arm. If she were alone, she could win a fight against the three without an issue. The problem was that Sassy would never leave her, and that meant at least one of them would attack her friend. At this moment, Sassy could barely walk. There was no way she wouldn't get hurt.

"We can take them. There are only three of them."

She stopped, half-turning as something moved behind her. "Count again."

Another four Servants glided out of the shadows, cutting off their escape.

"Gruntshit." Sassy looked behind them. "I mean, seven isn't that big of a number."

"Big enough." She shifted so she and Sassy were back-to-back. The slight odor of fear mixed with alcohol twirled around her. Sassy was frightened. She didn't blame her, but her friend had never seen her fight. "I can handle most of them. You watch out for yourself," she whispered as she pulled her knife from her sheath.

"Got it." Sassy nodded stiffly.

The Servants moved forward as a group. She'd rather take them on one at a time, but she'd fight the enemy in front of her, just like Gaar and Mirra had taught her. All opponents had flaws...weaknesses. She just needed to find them.

They moved as one. They were focused and deadly, claws out and ready, but they'd make a mistake. Everyone always did. One of the Servants coming from behind them glanced back toward the club. It was the opening she'd needed. She darted forward, slashing with her knife as she passed. The blade danced across his throat.

His mouth opened and his eyes widened as he grasped the wound, but he was too late. He was already dead. His heart thudded, pushing blood out of his neck in spurts. One down, six to go. She leaped, landing on a garbage can as the Servant crumpled to the ground. Too bad she didn't have her spears. She could've taken at least two out with this move instead of just one.

In the next second, they all realized what'd happened and they charged. One grabbed Sassy. She tried to dodge, but she was too drunk to put up much of a fight. He punched her in the face, and she crumpled to the ground.

Trinity bent, prepared to leap off the garbage can and launch herself into the Servant. She wasn't going to let him kill her friend, but he turned and headed toward her. They all did.

She straightened, perched on the garbage can. She really, really missed her spears right now. Gaar had told her not to travel without them, but she'd grown used to city life. Most of the businesses had a no weapons policy. She tightened her grip on her knife. Thankfully, her shirt covered her knife, or she'd be weaponless.

"Take care of him." A tall Servant with jet black hair and brilliant green eyes motioned to the body of the male Trinity had killed.

"Got it." Another Servant with brown hair moved over to the body. He bent, unbuttoning the dead male's shirt before yanking a medallion from around his neck.

She recognized that medallion. "Do you always attack in alleyways?" She stalled for time. She needed an opening but not one of them answered as they spread out, surrounding her. "It seems cowardly to me." She was good, but she couldn't take on six trained Servants at once. Unfortunately, they were as well-trained as the ones who'd attacked her at the shelter. Every motion was calculated and sure. They'd make their move soon. She had to be ready.

Her heart pounded, and she tried to remain calm. She needed to absorb the energy surrounding her. Energy never lied. It'd tell her everything she needed to know if she listened to it. She steadied her breathing as they circled her. They were also waiting for an opening.

The tall one with black hair seemed to be the leader. A slight nod or movement of his hand sent the others to move slower or faster, always keeping the circle around her evenly spaced. He was older than the others, probably in his late thirties but still in his prime. He worried her. The others looked eager, intent. They'd make a mistake in their haste. He looked bored, and that meant he was experienced and confident.

Confidence is its own mistake. Gaar's voice filled her head. *Don't fear, Little One. Fear is your enemy. The rest are only obstacles...* "Yeah," she muttered. "The obstacles between living and dying." She knew the rest of Gaar's saying by heart. "And I'm not done living." Her hand tightened around her knife.

They were males. She was a female. She could distract them. She smiled. Not one of them even noticed. That hurt. She was used to a different response to her smiles, but if she couldn't distract them with her looks, she'd try something else. "You're being cautious. I understand. You probably heard about your friends. The ones at the shelter." The eyes narrowed on a few of them. One's lips even twitched, showing his fangs a bit. This would work. Aggravate them and they'd make a mistake. "I killed them, just like I'm going to kill you."

"You'll die slowly," said the male whose lips had twitched.

"Shut up," said the leader, but it was too late.

When the Servant had threatened her, he'd slowed down a pace. It was a small opening, but it was enough. She leapt, flying between the Servants. Hands grabbed at her, claws out, scratching along her arms and sides. She hit the ground and rolled, leaping to her feet and heading for the wall. In two steps she jumped, hitting the brick and scrambling up it.

"Holy Gruntshit," said one of the Servants. "How's she going up the wall like that?"

Her fingers didn't elongate like Mirra's, but Gaar had taught her to feel for the imperfections in the stone and use them to climb. She wasn't as good as Gaar, but this wall was brick and bumpy. She'd be at the top in no time.

"Leaving your friend behind?" It was the leader's droll tone.

She stilled, hanging on the wall. She'd forgotten about Sassy. She glanced over her shoulder.

The leader had Sassy on her knees, her head tipped back. His sharp claws teased along her throat. "I'm surprised, but I shouldn't be." He smiled sadly. "Rumors and tales are always exaggerated. The lovely Trinity is as pretty as they say but not as brave and courageous." He shook his head. "No one sacrifices themself for their friends. Honor like that doesn't survive in our world." He truly looked sad.

"Don't listen to him, Trin." Sassy's eyes were wide and frightened. "Go. You can kill them later. For me."

She wasn't leaving Sassy, but she wasn't sure what her next step should be. If she attacked, Sassy would be killed. Her only chance, their only chance, was if they let Sassy go.

"Get out of here, you idiot." Sassy's face hardened as tears streamed down her cheeks and she shoved forward, making the Servant's claws push into her throat.

"No." Trinity screamed.

The Servant pulled back his hand, staring at the blood that trickled down Sassy's throat.

"Kill me and get it over with." Sassy jutted out her chin.

"No. Don't. Let her go, and I'll come with you peacefully."

"Apparently, the rumors were true." The leader shoved Sassy to the ground.

"Coward!" Sassy jumped to her feet, charging the Servant.

"No!" She dropped from the wall. "Don't."

The leader's arm flew out, slashing Sassy across the gut. She screamed. Clutching her stomach as she collapsed onto the ground.

"Sassy!" She tried to move forward but the other five Servants surrounded her. She crouched, ready to attack.

"You promised," said the leader.

"You didn't let her go." She had the wall at her back. If she had space for a running start she could climb it again, but she couldn't leave her friend. "Promise you'll send someone to the bar. You can't leave her here. She'll die."

The leader pulled Sassy to her knees by her hair and grasped her throat. "She'll die right now if you don't surrender."

"Go." Sassy's face was pale, and her shirt was covered in blood.

Trinity had no choice. She straightened, letting her hands fall to her sides.

"The knife," said the leader. "Drop it."

She did and two Servants grabbed her arms, pinning them behind her back. The leader let go of Sassy, and she crumpled back to the ground, her breathing rough and unsteady.

He walked over to Trinity. His green eyes searched hers as he ran his hand down her cheek, softly scraping her skin with his claws. "I was wrong. You're selfless and beautiful." He shook his head. "Too bad. The world is no place for someone like you."

"Please," she whispered. "Don't leave her here to die."

"Come." He ignored her plea, heading down the alleyway away from the club.

"No!" She bucked and pulled, struggling in the Servants' grasps. "Send someone to the club. She'll die if we leave her."

The leader continued walking as if she hadn't spoken. Sassy's uneven breathing grew fainter. She never should've trusted him. She'd been a fool, but she'd make him pay. She visualized the leader's eyes going glassy as she twisted her knife in his gut. Now, she needed to make it happen. She lifted her legs and dropped.

"What the..." The two Servants holding her stumbled, their grip loosening for one second as they regained their balance.

She scrambled until her feet were under her and then she lurched to the right, kicking to the left. Her feet connected with a thigh.

"Son-of-a..." yelled the Servant on her left.

The one on her right tumbled to the ground, dragging her with him. She was free. She lashed out with her claws and jumped to her feet. All she needed was another second, but someone grabbed her leg. She kicked at him with her other foot, but another Servant grabbed that ankle, jerking it upward. She fell to the pavement, twisting to try and break free, but soon the other Servants surrounded her. Their hands grabbing her, claws sinking into her flesh as four of them each took one of her limbs.

"I will kill you if she dies." She bucked and fought but it was useless. She should conserve her strength, watch for an opening, but every step, every moment took her farther away from Sassy.

The faint sound of wind moving some of the loose trash teased her ears. Her body tensed, instinctively preparing for Brush-Men, but they lived in the forest not the city. Something large and dark rammed into the Servant who was holding one of her arms. He hit the pavement and in less than a second the Servant who held her other arm followed.

The top half of her body dropped toward the ground. She blocked her face with her arms to protect herself from the fall, but before she hit, her feet were free too. She twisted to break her fall but instead of the jarring impact of hard pavement, she was whooshed into the air. Strong hands grabbed her waist and dropped her onto her feet.

"Run." Jethro shoved her as he turned to fight another Servant. He hadn't killed those that'd been holding her, and they were up, angry and closing in on him. All six of them.

"Sassy." She glanced down the alley. Indy was carrying her friend back toward the club.

"Run," Jethro yelled again as he blocked a swipe from a Servant before punching the male in the chest.

"No." She couldn't leave him. He couldn't fight six trained Servants but before she could move, they attacked as one. She froze, watching as he fought.

He moved in a blur, blocking punches almost before she saw them coming. He was faster than any Almighty she'd ever seen. He was almost as fast as Gaar or Mirra. The leader spun, his clawed fingers flying like a thresher machine. Jethro blocked one hand but the other raked across his chest, blood spilling down his shirt.

"Jethro!" She snapped out of her daze and ran down the alley, grabbing her knife before racing back to his side. "Kill them! Don't just hurt them." She launched herself at the nearest Servant, her knife sliding into his gut. She jerked her arm upward and twisted her wrist before shoving him away to free her weapon. He fell and she spun, slashing at the next one. Her blade ripped across his chest, and he stumbled backward, his hands clutching at his wound.

"Retrieve and fallback," yelled the leader.

One of the three remaining Servants raced to the closest body. There were two others dead besides the one she'd just killed. He yanked the medallion from first one Servant's neck and then the other.

"Stop him," she yelled as she ran toward the male she'd killed.

"Got it." He answered, charging toward the Servant and making him veer to the side.

She bent and grabbed the medallion as Jethro blocked the male's route to her.

"Come!" shouted the leader.

The Servant raced toward his friends. The leader held his arm at an odd angle. He must've hurt it in his fight with Jethro. The Servant wasn't happy, but he nodded slightly before they disappeared down the alleyway.

"What's that?" Jethro stood at her side, panting.

"I don't know, but it must be something important because they always take it from their dead."

CHAPTER 60: Jethro

Jethro almost shoved Trinity into the carriage before he climbed inside. There was a perfectly good street and sidewalk outside the Howling Hut. Only idiots traveled through the dark alleyway instead.

"We need to get her help." Indy sat across from him, cradling Sassy in his arms. The Guard didn't look good. Her eyes were closed and her face pale. She'd lost a lot of blood.

"Dr. Kalper's house. Now!" Jethro leaned out the window and shouted at the Grunts.

"You shouldn't have waited for us." Trinity grabbed Sassy's hand. "Hold on." Her friend didn't even flinch as the carriage lurched forward.

"I wasn't leaving the two of you," said Indy. "You could've been hurt too."

"We would've survived." Trinity glared at Indy. "She might not."

"You don't know you would've survived," argued Indy. "You or Jethro could've been..."

Their argument drifted past him. He'd needed that fight. His blood pulsed fast and strong through his body. He'd battled and killed and now he wanted to mate. His eyes darted to Trinity. His instincts screamed for him to toss her over his shoulder and take her somewhere private where he could lose himself with her for days. Tonight had proven that she belonged with him. She could fight almost as well as he could. She was the only one he wanted, and she was within reach. His hands trembled as he caught a whiff of her. Her scent was strong from the fight. Fear and sweat and female. His female. He gritted his teeth, trying to tamp down his desire. No matter how he felt, this wasn't the time to mate.

She leaned forward, trying to help Indy stop the bleeding. It was a gut wound and it looked bad. Indy was worried. It was clear from his scent and the fear in his eyes. Bruno's dying wish had been for Indy to look out for Sassy. His friend tried but if Sassy died, Indy would believe he'd failed.

He pulled off his shirt, balled it up and nudged Trinity's shoulder. "Use this."

"Thanks." She hesitated a second, her gaze taking in his chest.

He inhaled, flexing his muscles a bit. Was that appreciation in her eyes? Perhaps there was still a chance for the two of them.

"You'll need to disinfect those scratches." She grabbed the shirt from him and pushed it onto Sassy's wound.

So much for that idea.

The carriage stopped. He hopped out and then leaned in, lifting Sassy.

Trinity pushed past him, running to the door and pounding. "Dr. Kalper! We need your help."

"Give her to me," said Indy once he was out of the carriage.

He was going to argue. He was stronger and Sassy wasn't a little Guard but by the look on Indy's face his friend wouldn't listen to reason.

The door opened and Pepper, Kalper's assistant, said, "The doctor's not home."

"Where is he?" asked Trinity.

"Away." The Guard glanced nervously at them, her eyes narrowing when they landed on him.

"Where? We have to find him." Trinity's body trembled. "I'm a friend of the doctor's. I was here the other day. We need your help."

"I told you. He's not here," said Pepper.

"Please. She's going to die if she doesn't get help," begged Trinity.

"He's not here. That's all I can tell you." The Guard slammed the door.

"Where is he?" Trinity yelled and then stopped. She strode back to the carriage, almost seething with anger. "Let's go. We need to take her to my mother." She hopped into the carriage.

"Got it." He took Sassy from his friend, handing her back to the Guard once he was seated. He gave the Grunts the direction before joining the others. Trinity knelt on the floor holding his shirt against Sassy's wound and murmuring soft words to her friend.

The carriage took off at a fast pace, but he wasn't sure it'd be fast enough. They'd jostled her in and out of the carriage, and with that wound her face should be twisted in anguish, but it looked peaceful, like she'd already left this world.

The Grunts skidded to a halt. Carriages lined up along the streets, blocking the Council Building. All the lights were on, and music streamed from inside onto the street.

"Shit." Trinity's eyes met his. "I forgot. It's the party...the benefit. We need to go around to the back." She leaned out the window and gave directions to the Grunts.

It took them a few moments to get around the crowd, but the side entrance was clear of carriages.

Two Guards approached when they stopped. "You can't park here."

Trinity hopped out of the carriage. "I need to see my mother."

"I was told that you didn't live here anymore." One of the Guards frowned, looking into the carriage. "What happened to her?"

Indy slid out from under Sassy and jumped to the street, standing next to Trinity. "Go find your mom."

"Both of you get back into the carriage," said the Guard.

Jethro handed Sassy to Indy, ignoring the council Guard.

"We'll take her to your mom and dad's suite through the back hallways." Indy pushed past the Guards.

"Stop." One of the Guards grabbed Indy's arm.

"She's dying," Indy growled at the other Guard. "You know me. I'd never do anything to hurt Hugh, but if you try to stop me, I...will...kill you. This is Bruno's mate and she's hurt."

The Guard dropped his hold, nodding. "I didn't know who she was." He glanced at the other Guard. "I'll go get Millie."

"I'll find my mother."

"It'll be better for...everyone if I go." The Guard's eyes narrowed on her.

"Better for..." Her voice trailed off. "Oh. Right. Okay."

Jethro wanted to pull her into his arms and protect her from the Guard's anger. Apparently, her leaving Hugh had made the gossip rounds and she hadn't come out the favorite.

"Thank you." Indy strode into the building.

"This way." Trinity led them down numerous hallways. She stopped at a door and entered a keycode on the number pad on the wall. She opened the door. "Follow me."

They entered a spacious apartment.

"Put her on the couch." Trinity moved about the suite, gathering supplies—towels, water, herbs and tinctures of things Jethro couldn't name.

A few minutes later, Millie burst into the apartment, barking commands like a general. "Water. I need water. And towels. Goldenseal."

"Got it. All of it." Trinity pointed at the items she'd laid out on the table near Sassy.

"Good. Good." Millie walked to the couch and began examining the Guard.

He moved out of the way while Indy and Trinity hovered nearby to do whatever Millie requested.

The door opened and Tim stepped inside. He shot Jethro a glare. "Those scratches had better not be from my daughter."

"Unfortunately, not this time." Trinity's father didn't like him, and he enjoyed irking the Servant. "But I still have hope for the future."

"Shut up," snapped Tim.

"Is that the best comeback you have? I'm unimpressed."

"Tim," said Millie, stopping her mate from speaking. "Go get Dr. Kalper."

"Dr. Kalper isn't home," said Trinity. "We went there first."

"Of course not. He's here." Tim turned and left.

Millie forced a liquid of some type down Sassy's throat.

"How bad is she?" Indy clutched Sassy's hand.

"I can't stop the bleeding." Millie sprinkled some more herbs on Sassy's wound.

He swallowed. That wasn't good.

CHAPTER 61: Hugh

"Gracie," Hugh stopped a very rich, older female Almighty as she walked past. "I'm so glad you made it." This was one of the few times tonight he'd said that and had actually meant it.

"Hugh." She gave him a half-hug. "It's so good to see you." Her smile stretched the red arrow birthmark on her cheek, making it quiver like it'd been shot from a bow. "Your mother would be so proud of you."

"Thank you." It was a kind thing to say and probably true, but he still wanted tonight to end. The party was a success, but he was miserable. Trinity should be here at his side. He wanted to proclaim to the world that she was his, and that inequalities between the classes would not be tolerated. Instead, he was here by himself wishing he were somewhere else.

"Your school idea is brilliant," said Gracie. "This should've been done years ago."

"I agree." Ableson walked over to them. "Education for all the classes will help everyone. Think of what talented individuals like Wasee can do with even a little training." He motioned to the Servant at his side.

This was Hugh's cue to introduce them. He'd seen Ableson and Wasee working the floor. He hoped they'd gotten some donations. "Gracie Wentgerd this is Chad Ableson, one of the scientists working on alternative meat products and his friend Wasee who makes prosthetics."

"Really? That is amazing." Gracie smiled at Wasee.

"Wasee is amazing. He saved my life," said Ableson.

"Oh, what happened?" asked Gracie.

With an opening like that, Hugh was pretty sure they already had a check from Gracie. She was a kind-hearted Almighty with a lot of money and few prejudices. It was a shame she'd never had children. The world would be a better place if she had.

"I lost my arm in an accident." Ableson lifted his prosthetic. "Before Wasee made this for me, I was in constant pain. Trying to relearn how to do the simplest tasks didn't seem worth it. I no longer wanted to live. It's so difficult when you lose the ability to do things that you used to do with ease."

Hugh glanced around the crowded ballroom looking for a waiter.

"Trust me," Gracie smiled a bit sadly. "I understand that perfectly. At my age, every day brings a new pain. Too bad Wasee can't make a prosthetic for aging."

"Who knows," said Ableson. "Maybe one day."

"When you do," laughed Gracie. "Let me know. I'll be your first customer."

"Excuse me," Hugh interrupted. "I'm going to go to the bar. Does anyone want a drink?"

"No. Thank you," said Ableson and Wasee.

"None for me." Gracie hugged him again. "It was good seeing you, Hugh."

"You too. We'll talk later." He kissed her cheek and made his way to the bar. "A double," he said to the bartender. He had hours to go before this night ended.

"I was surprised when you allowed me entrance to your grand affair." Kurt Wilson walked up next to him.

Now, he really wished he were somewhere else. He had so much to say to Kurt but had no idea where to start. "I was surprised you'd want to attend. If I'd known, I would've sent you an invitation."

"Why? Because you shot my mother for no reason?"

"Yes." He'd had a reason, but he wasn't going to argue with the other male. "I am sorry that happened."

"It didn't just *happen*. You put a gun to her head and shot her. She wasn't threatening you. She wasn't doing anything but her job."

"And I was ending a war that had already had too many casualties."

Kurt stepped closer. "I don't care about any of them except the last one."

"I'm sure that's true." It made him sick how many Almightys didn't consider anyone or anything unless it affected them personally. He glanced around. They were starting to draw attention. "This isn't the time nor the place to have this discussion. We should talk next week." He had some questions for the Almighty about the prisoners who'd been released.

"I have nothing else to say to you." Kurt's eyes were hard and cold. "I'm just here to make sure that the rest of my family is safe."

"Safe? I have no intention of going after your family."

"Not directly"—his lip curled in a sneer—"but indirectly is another story, isn't it. It is the coward's way."

"Coward?" He was starting to lose his temper. "You mean like falsifying documents to release prisoners so that my half-brother gets murdered in prison?"

"Did someone do that?" Kurt smirked. "I wish I could take credit for it, but I can't."

"Kurt, how are you?" Stella walked up to the bar, inserting herself between them as she placed her empty glass on the counter. "I haven't seen you in a long time."

"Stella." Kurt's face softened. "You look as beautiful as ever. More beautiful actually."

She did. She wore a dark blue dress that brought out her eyes and her hair hung loose except for a clip that pulled some away from her face.

"Thank you." She smiled up at him. "Have you spoken to Francis yet? He has the funniest story about a canoeing accident at the Manor."

"Terbasse's here?" Kurt looked around the room. "I do need to talk to him." He offered his arm as he shot Hugh a glare. "Will you join me?"

"Of course, but you go. I'll be there in a minute. I need to refresh my drink first."

"I'll wa—"

"No." She gave Kurt a gentle push. "Francis was talking about leaving. You know this party is quite tame for his tastes. Go stop him. I'll be there in a minute."

"If you insist." Kurt kissed her hand. "The company here is quite distasteful."

As soon as Kurt strode away, Hugh leaned close to her and whispered, "Thank you."

She picked up her glass that the bartender had refilled and took Hugh's arm, leading him a step away before dropping her hold. "You need to be careful."

"Nothing is going to happen here." The room was filled with Guards, his Guards.

"You need to know your enemies."

"Trust me. I know Kurt Wilson is my enemy." He wasn't an idiot.

"I don't think you do, or maybe you don't know the kind of enemy he is." She touched his arm. "You're used to fighting a war. Politicians never attack from the front. They always come at you from behind with whispers and favors."

"You're right. I am a bit rusty in these kinds of battles."

"I heard what you said about the prisoners. Bette treated her Guards and Servants well. She had many friends on the Council and in the prison. A few years ago she led a committee to improve the living conditions for the prison Guards. If you have enemies there, you need to be very careful."

"You know a lot about Bette."

"I know a lot about everyone who had been in power."

"I bet you do." He needed to have a few chats with Stella. He knew the major players, but he'd been out of the game for a long, long time.

CHAPTER 62: Hugh

"Hugh." Doug Sallers walked up to them. "Stella. How nice to see you again."

"You too, Doug, but I have to run." She sidestepped to avoid his hug and hurried away.

"Okay. Sure. We can catch up later." Doug's eyes roamed her as she made her way through the crowd.

Hugh started to back away. He didn't want to talk with Sallers either, but tonight wasn't his lucky night.

"Great party." Sallers turned to face him.

"Thank you." He stopped trying to sneak away. "I'm glad you were able to make it." He lied.

"It's about time someone did something like this. I've been an advocate of equality for years. I just couldn't say much under the old rule." Doug raised his drink. "To you, Hugh."

"Thank you." He tapped his glass against Doug's. The male was a pompous liar, but he needed the other Almighty's support and money for the new system to succeed. He wasn't a favorite of the old regime. They all knew that he would've killed any one of them to end the war, and he knew that every one of them, including Bette if she'd lived, would put a knife in his back the second he gave them a chance. "I appreciate your support."

"Of course. What you're doing is admirable." Doug stepped closer. "Have you decided on a contractor for the new schools? My brother-in-law has submitted a bid."

"We haven't chosen yet." He wouldn't be picking Sallers' family. They cut more corners than a kid making a paper snowflake.

"Hugh." Sarah, his sister, touched his shoulder. "It's a lovely party."

"It was nice talking to you, Doug, but I need to speak with my sister."

"Of course." Sallers glanced around. "I want to talk with Terbasse anyway."

Hugh would feel badly for Stella but after watching her navigating the crowd tonight, he was pretty sure she could handle Sallers. He turned to his sister and her husband. "Sarah. Sam. I was hoping to get a minute to talk to you." He was glad to see faces he could trust.

"I'll admit"—she lowered her voice as she took his arm—"we were being a bit strategic."

"We thought you could use saving," said Sam.

"You were right." He glanced at Sallers as the Almighty pushed between Terbasse and Wilson to stand next to Stella. "I have never needed saving more."

"Not sure about that." Sam sobered.

"How is the fund raising going?" He changed the subject. His sister and brother-in-law still felt badly about not doing more when he'd been arrested, but there'd been nothing that they could've done without risking their own lives and those of their children.

"Good. Very good," said Sarah. "I'm surprised so many have opened their wallets."

"I'm not." Dave Davies walked up to them. "Hugh and his reforms are all the rage." The other Almighty grinned. "And you know how the rich need to outshine one another."

"Dave." He shook the other Almighty's hand. "Glad you could make it." He really was. He and Davies didn't always agree, but he liked the other Almighty.

"Wouldn't have missed it." Dave glanced around the room. "Everyone who's anyone is here."

"Yep, I invited them all." He'd had no other choice.

"Even some I hadn't expected." Davies eyes fell on Kurt Wilson.

"He showed up. Uninvited."

"I didn't mean Kurt," said Davies.

"Hugh, I've got to go," interrupted Sarah. "I see Vivian Vickers, and she's going to donate."

"She is?" That was surprising. Vivian wasn't a fan of equality. She liked believing she was better than others.

"Yes, she is." Sarah grinned. "I'll make sure of it." Her eyes sparkled. "I learned a few tricks from Mom."

"That you did." He kissed her cheek. "Thank you."

She smiled at him and for a second, he actually felt they were family. He loved her and she loved him, but they'd grown up adversaries due to his unhappiness with their father.

When Sarah and Sam left, he turned to Davies. "So who should I not have invited, according to you?"

"No one." Dave took a sip of his drink. "I was a bit surprised to see Terbasse."

"He's richer than Araldo."

"Yeah. Right."

"He isn't?" He lowered his voice. "I've heard rumors but"—he leaned closer—"should I demand cash instead of a check?"

Davies burst out laughing. "I'd pay to see that. Terbasse's head would explode."

"Probably." He grinned, taking a sip of his drink. "Who else are you surprised to see here?"

"The...others." Dave glanced at him. "Don't get me wrong, I agree with the whole equality thing, but the fact that you invited so many from the other classes—"

"Not inviting them would've sent the wrong message."

"I agree, but I'm surprised that so many of the affluent Almightys deign to rub shoulders with those from the other classes."

"Me too." Most of the guests were Almightys and pompous, but he'd invited some from the other classes. They weren't as rich as the

Almightys, but they had significant influence with the members of their class. He needed money to build the schools so young from all the classes could be educated, but if they didn't have the support from influential members of the other classes, the kids wouldn't come to the schools. This needed to be a group effort.

"How did you manage to get them to come?"

"I have no idea."

"They may have come to see you fail." Dave's eyes met his. "Or suffer. I'm sorry about you and Trinity."

"Yeah. Thanks." He didn't have to fake the tightness in his throat.

"It's tough when things don't work out." Dave's eyes skimmed over the crowd, landing on Kim. "But we move on."

"Are you here with a date?"

"No." Dave grinned sheepishly. "You didn't let me finish. We move on...eventually."

"I'll try to remember that." He laughed.

"What's so funny to make our esteemed leader laugh." Ray walked over to them.

"It's a party." He raised his glass. "Laughter and good times abound."

"Donations are going well, I take it," purred Ray.

"From what I hear, yes."

"I still don't know about mixed groups of students. Educating everyone? Yes, but mixing the classes." Dave shook his head. "I think it'll cause more harm than good."

"At first, maybe, but it's necessary for the future." This new government wouldn't survive unless the classes were united.

"I agree with Hugh." Ray grabbed another drink from a passing waiter.

"Please, enlighten me." Dave smirked at Ray. He wasn't the most non-biased individual, but at least, he spoke with those from the other classes. Many of the Almightys didn't even acknowledge that the others existed.

"It worked in Hugh's army." Ray's eyes hardened. "It should work even better with our young."

"What do you mean?" asked Dave.

"I insisted that teams be made up of members from each group." The other Almighty must not keep up on current events because it'd been explained in detail in Townsend's articles. "They hated it at first, but they learned that each group has unique abilities."

"Oh, I see." Dave took a sip of his drink, but his gaze focused on something across the room.

He turned to see what had captured the Almighty's attention. Jackson and Kim stood talking to Millie and Tim. Millie had insisted on bringing her son for a few hours. Kim played with the baby and even if Jackson hadn't told him, Kim's small, rounded belly would've clued him in on her pregnancy.

"Maybe you're right. Kids only see the good in each other not their differences." Dave sighed slightly.

He felt for the guy. It was hard seeing a female you cared about with someone else. He'd get to experience that soon. When Trinity and Jethro became a fake couple, he'd hear and see it in the papers.

"What age will the young start school?" asked Ray.

Dave tore his eyes away from Kim. "The younger the better. They are so...sweet when they're little."

"They are. Still untarnished by the prejudices of the world." He'd always thought of Davies as a bit of a playboy, but he was pleasantly surprised that the other Almighty had a fondness for children. "I think we should start them around six, but I want to have other classes for the older kids and adults too. It'd be good for everyone to learn to read, write and understand basic math."

"I agree. The Servants are the only class that know how to do all those things, and most have fared okay after the war," said Dave.

"Then you aren't talking to the right ones." Ray scoffed.

"There are less homeless Servants than Guards and let's not even talk about the fate of the Producers after the war," said Dave.

A Guard came to the door and whispered something in Millie's ear. She followed him out of the ballroom.

"That's not true," said Ray. "More Servants have lost their jobs since the war than any of the other classes."

Hugh's brain registered the raised voices, but he couldn't pull his gaze away from the other group. Tim handed the baby to Kim and followed his mate. Something was going on. "Excuse…"

"I think you should check your facts," said Dave.

"My facts?" Ray's voice softened. "You can't possibly mean the misinformation printed in the Almighty's papers, can you?"

"You're both right." He glanced at the doorway where Tim and Millie had been, but this conversation between Dave and Ray could go bad fast. When Ray's voice grew soft, the Servant grew deadly. "The House Servants haven't fared well either."

The tension around Ray's eyes softened a bit.

"Unfortunately, everyone is still finding their way. I'm trying to help in that regard too. The Servants have the skills needed to survive and survive well whereas the other classes do not." He continued before Ray could speak. "The first step is education, but while we're educating, we also have to change the rules. Right now, only an Almighty can get a loan. I'm going to change that."

"You're going after the banks?" Dave wasn't happy about that. A considerable amount of his family business was in banks. "They're private companies. You're going to make them change the way they do business?"

"Yes, and no. They can apply all the same rules, but they can't refuse someone due to class." It wouldn't be easy, but nothing was easy anymore. Tim came back into the ballroom and began searching through the crowd for someone.

"Ahh. What a surprise? Someone talking about Hugh's grand plans for equality." Conguise joined their group.

He wanted to groan. The professor's words were neutral, but the condescending tone was going to push him too far.

"Professor. Glad you could join us." He lied again. He'd rather the professor had spent the night eating something toxic.

"The party is a huge success." Conguise smiled. "I've heard you've had quite a few generous donations for your new education system. It should be enough to build dozens of new schools."

He took a sip of his drink. This was going to be fun. "We'll build a few new schools, but most of the money will go toward modifying the existing ones."

Dave and Ray shifted closer to each other. Their animosity gone in the face of a more interesting battle.

"You can't mean to use our current schools." Conguise gave him a condescending stare.

"I most certainly do." That look would've sent him into weeks of self-doubt when he'd been an intern but that'd been years ago. Years of hard work, betrayal and jail had changed him. "There will be no segregation of the classes. None."

"Of course." Conguise's eyes hardened and then became calculating. "Do you think educating everyone together is fair? How is a ten-year-old Guard going to feel, trying to learn to read when he's placed in a class with five-year-old Almightys and Servants? And what about Producers? How are they going to feel when they can't even grasp the concepts of addition, geography, reading, or history? Concepts that their fellow students in the other classes understand with only minor instruction."

"The classes will be separated by age when they start first grade, but the other grades will be separated by ability."

"So there will be segregation," said Conguise.

"No. Separation by skill is not segregation. Once the child masters a lesson they'll be moved to another class, no matter their genetics."

Tim and Dr. Kalper left the ballroom.

"Excuse me a moment." He walked across the room. Something was up, and he was going to find out what it was.

CHAPTER 63: Hugh

"Don't." Jackson stopped Hugh near the doorway. "It isn't her."

"What's going on?" Someone was hurt. It was the only reason to pull Kalper from the party.

Jackson grabbed his arm and led him aside so they wouldn't be overheard. "There was an issue. Sassy's hurt."

"She was supposed to be with Trinity tonight."

"She was, but Trinity is—"

He pushed past Jackson. He needed to see her.

Jackson followed him into the hallway, grabbing his arm again. "*She* is fine." He paused, smiling at a couple who walked past them. "Trust me. I'd tell you if she weren't."

"I know." He'd do the same for Jackson.

"Good." The Guard let go of his arm. "Stay here. It'll look suspicious if you leave."

"I don't care. I need to see her. Cover for me. I'll only be gone a minute."

"Hugh..."

"If anyone asks, I had to use the restroom." He strode down the hallway toward Millie and Tim's suite. He stopped at the door and tapped. "It's me."

Tim opened the door. "You shouldn't be here."

"Too bad." He stepped inside their apartment and his eyes immediately fell on Trinity. She was unhurt—scared but fine. Jackson had told him, but he'd needed to see her with his own eyes. "How's Sassy?"

"Hugh!" Trinity flew across the room, wrapping her arms around him.

It'd only been a few days since he'd seen her, but it felt like forever. "What happened?"

She pulled back a little, but he didn't move his arms. He'd have to let her go soon enough, but not yet.

"We were attacked in the alley next to the club." She inhaled shakily. "He had his claws against Sassy's throat. I had to surrender. He was going to kill her."

"Surrender?" He reminded himself that she was here, unhurt, in his arms. His heart slowed its panicked pace. "How did you get away?"

"Indy and Jethro." Her eyes darted across the room.

Indy leaned against the wall, watching Sassy. Jethro stood in the corner, arms across his chest...his bloody, bare chest.

"Where's your shirt?"

"He gave it to me for Sassy. To help stop the bleeding." Trinity clutched his arm.

"Oh. Of course." He nodded. "Those cuts look like Servant claws."

"They are. It was Servants who attacked her," said Jethro.

"I have to locate the source of the bleeding." Kalper straightened from examining Sassy. He glanced around the room. "Everyone but Millie needs to leave."

"This way." He kept Trinity's hand in his as he led the group down the back hallways to his suite. No, their suite. She still lived there. This was all pretend.

As soon as he closed the door he grabbed a shirt from a laundry basket on the couch, congratulating himself on not putting them away. This proved that messiness had a purpose. He tossed it to Jethro. "Put this on."

Jethro smirked as he pulled on the T-shirt. It was snug on him, and Jethro wasn't fat. His chest was all muscle. Hugh had to force himself not to look at his own body. He was in shape. Good shape.

Strong and lean, but Jethro was bigger. He must work out a lot to have a body like that...unless it was a side effect of whatever Conguise had mixed with Jethro's genetics.

"Tell me exactly what happened?" Hugh passed around glasses and a bottle of whiskey to everyone before sitting on the couch next to Trinity.

"Sassy and I went to the club. We had a small argument with Jethro, like we planned." Trinity continued, explaining how she and Sassy had left the club and had been attacked in the alley.

He squeezed her hand, the contact the only thing keeping him sane. She'd been in danger, and he'd been entertaining guests. "How did you know she was in trouble? How did you know she was in the alley?"

"I decided that we'd waited long enough after Trinity and Sassy had left. I let everyone hear that I was going to apologize, but when we stepped outside Indy smelled something." Jethro's eyes met Indy's in silent communication.

"What did you smell? I know that club and the alleyways. They reek." The two were keeping something from him, and he needed to know what it was. Trinity's life was at stake.

"Fear." Indy shifted, hiding his uneasiness. "And blood. I was sure that I saw someone dart down the alleyway. I know that Sassy usually travels that way, so I was concerned."

"Sassy doesn't normally go that way," said Trinity.

"She does lately," said Indy. "I'd know. I'm the one who's been trying to keep her safe these last few months."

"Sorry. You're right. I don't really know what Sassy does anymore, but the attackers didn't run."

"I don't know." Indy shrugged. "Maybe it was someone else."

"I suppose it could've been Say," she said.

"He's following you again?" he asked. "I thought he stayed in the forest."

"I don't know where he stayed. He hadn't been around, but he's back."

"Did he try to help you?" He found the little Servant creepy, always following her like a shadow.

"He's too small. He would've gotten hurt." She defended him like always.

"Where did he go?" asked Jethro. "I didn't see him in the alley."

"I don't know." She shrugged. "He comes and goes all the time."

"He could've at least gone to get help when he saw you were being attacked." He liked the little Servant even less than before.

"Maybe he did and that's who Indy saw." She looked at the Guard. "It'd be like him to disappear once he knew help was on the way."

From his recollection, Say would disappear at the first sign of trouble without trying to get help.

"Maybe." Indy shrugged, glancing at Jethro.

There was a knock at the door and then Jackson entered without waiting for a reply. "Hugh, you need to get back to the party. Your absence is being noticed."

"Tell them I'm not feeling well." The last thing he wanted to do was leave.

"Go." Trinity squeezed his hand before pulling hers from his grasp. "The sooner this is done the better."

"Fine." He kissed her. "I hate it when you're right."

"You should be used to it," she teased.

"That's going to take us years." He kissed her again and then stood. "Jackson, let's go. All of you stay here. I'll see you when the party is over."

"On a good note," said Jethro. "There were a few onlookers when we left the alley. Word will be all over that Indy and I saved these two." He grinned. "Now, we don't have to spend weeks pretending to become friends again. We can move pretty fast to the girlfriend-boyfriend part of the plan."

"Yeah, that's great news." He wanted to punch something, preferably his half-brother who was enjoying this way too much. He left with Jethro's laughter following him down the hallway.

CHAPTER 64: Trinity

As soon as the door closed, Trinity turned on Jethro. "You don't have to antagonize him."

"No. I don't *have* to." He smirked.

"You are such an ass." She glared at him, shaking her head.

"You used to find me funny." Jethro shrugged. "I'm sure you will again when we spend more time together."

Indy leaned forward, watching them as if they were the most interesting thing he'd seen in years.

"I doubt that." She headed into the kitchen.

Jethro followed her, leaning against a cabinet by the sink. "Aw, come on." His eyes skimmed down her body and then back up to her face. "As I recall, you quite enjoyed being alone with me the last time."

She clenched her hands at her sides, digging her nails into her palms. *I will not claw his face until there's nothing left but bloody shreds. I will not.* She tried to smile but only managed to curl her lips. "You recall incorrectly. Everything that I...that we did was so I could escape."

"Oh, you mean what happened in my tent." His eyes widened, but his grin belied his surprise. "I was talking about those days we spent together when we were kids." He winked at her. "It's funny that you can't seem to keep your mind off those few moments in my tent when we almost—"

"Shut up." She turned and stormed into her bedroom, slamming the door.

Jethro's laughter followed her. She had to control her temper, or she'd never make it a day, let alone weeks, pretending to be his girlfriend.

She took a deep breath and sat on the edge of the bed. She hated him. He was such a jerk; yet she couldn't dismiss the relief she'd felt when she'd seen him in the alley. He'd come to help her...just like always. Years ago, he'd saved her from Jackson, and she hadn't wanted to admit it, but she believed Indy. Jethro had been going to risk everything to save her from Calvin Folgrant and the Protective Services...until she'd betrayed him.

She took another deep breath. Her heart pounded and her pulse raced, but only because he made her so angry. All she felt for him was gratitude. A small voice whispered that it was more than that. She loved Hugh but she had so many memories of Jethro. She didn't want them or the feelings they brought, but she couldn't wish them away.

She flopped back on the bed. It was going to be a long couple of weeks or however long it took to catch the black-market butcher, and she wasn't sure she'd survive unscathed.

CHAPTER 65: Hugh

Hugh stood by himself, sipping his drink as the minutes ticked by slower than ice formed in the sun. He should be happy. The party was a success but right now he didn't care. He wanted to go back to his room and see Trinity. She'd almost been kidnapped. He could've lost her.

Tim glided across the room toward him, stopping often to chat with friends and even some Almightys. Having been raised by Sarah, Tim was as comfortable here as he was in Ray's warehouse.

How many others here were leading double lives? Ray had let it slip that the black market was run by an Almighty, but he could've been lying. The only thing Hugh knew for certain was that whomever it was had to be wealthy, and those here tonight were the richest of the rich. He studied the guests. He hadn't considered it before, but the likelihood of the leader of the black market being in this room was very high.

Tim stopped in front of him. "Sassy's going to live."

"Thank Araldo." He hadn't looked forward to breaking the news to Townsend if she'd died. Although she didn't live with the reporter anymore, Townsend still considered her his responsibility.

"We need to talk." Tim nodded, his eyes growing darker.

"I know. Later. After everyone leaves."

"Trin...Your three uninvited guests need to leave before someone sees them."

His eyes met Jackson's across the room. He tipped his head toward the door. The Guard frowned but nodded.

"Then we talk now." He and Tim headed for the exit. He didn't want to think about Trinity leaving, but she couldn't stay. It wasn't safe.

Jackson waited in the hallway and the three of them made their way to Hugh's suite of rooms. When they got inside, Indy was dozing on the couch and Jethro was by the window, staring out into the night.

"Where's Trinity?"

"Resting." Jethro nodded toward the bedroom.

He couldn't stop the surge of relief that she'd left Jethro alone. The thought of her and Jethro sitting in here for hours and rekindling their friendship had burrowed into his bones. He went into their bedroom. She was lying on the bed, eyes wide open.

"I heard you were resting." He sat next to her.

"I am. Not sleeping but resting. Thinking." She looked worried.

He bent and kissed her. He couldn't help himself. He'd meant for it to be a warm, comforting kiss but at the first taste of her lips it'd turned into something else. She wrapped her arms around his neck, pulling him closer.

"Don't leave." He kissed her ear. "We'll save Birdie's family and catch the black-market butcher some other way."

"Hugh..." She dropped her arms and sat up.

"I know." He ran his hand through his hair. "I just...Someone is after you."

"I'll be fine." She cupped his face. "I got away from them."

"This time. You might not next time." His words were like sandpaper in his throat.

"I can take care of myself."

"I know that." He grabbed her shoulders. "But you can't take care of yourself and everyone else."

"I—I couldn't leave her."

"I know." His grip tightened. "And that's why you're not safe. You'll never be safe." He hated to push this, but he'd do anything to keep her from being hurt. "You need to stop. We'll find another way."

"No." She touched his cheek. "I will be safe because I won't have to watch out for Sassy."

"What about Jethro?" He watched her closely.

"Don't start that again." Her eyes narrowed. "I told you that there is nothing between us anymore."

She said it with conviction, but he wasn't sure she was being honest with herself. Jethro was attractive, young and her first love. He'd also saved her tonight. That itself was an aphrodisiac, but if he said any of this, they'd fight. "That may be true, but you wouldn't leave him to be killed."

"No, I wouldn't, but I don't think that'll be a problem." Her eyes grew puzzled. "He can fight. I mean, really fight. He's almost as fast as Gaar or Mirra."

"He's that fast?" He'd heard rumors about his abilities in the street fights, but he'd assumed they were mostly exaggerated.

"Yeah. Fast and strong. I've never seen an Almighty move like he does."

He'd tell her about what he'd found in Jethro's blood, if he actually knew something. Right now he had more questions than answers. He didn't need her worrying about that too, and Jethro would never hurt her. Jethro loved her as much as he did and that meant the other Almighty would protect her with his life.

There was a knock on the door. "Are you two coming out?" asked Tim, disgust in his voice.

"We should probably go." He stood.

"If we have to." She took his hand and they walked into the other room.

"Trinity, did you show him?" asked Tim.

"Not yet." She pulled a medallion attached to a long, gold chain from her pocket before sitting on the couch.

"Right. You were busy." Tim smirked as he looked at Jethro. "Better things to do between mates...alone...in a bedroom."

Hugh sat next to her. Tim must hate Jethro more than he'd thought to make innuendos about him and Trinity mating.

"I took this from one of the attackers." Trinity ignored her father and handed him the medallion.

"What is it?" He studied the necklace. It was expensive and well-made. The gold chain was delicate but sturdy. The medallion had a large ornate letter that kind of looked like an A etched into the metal with a spiral symbol circling it.

"I don't know, but I've seen it before," she said.

"When?" He'd never seen anything like it.

"In the alleyway when you were freeing Reese from the Shelter."

"The Servants who attacked you wore this?" Now, he was more than worried.

"Yes." She nodded. "The others retrieved it from their dead."

"They did the same thing tonight, but Trinity stopped them from getting this one." Jethro turned away from the window and faced the room for the first time.

"You helped," she said, her tone a little begrudging.

"A bit." Jethro's lips twitched. "But did it hurt that much for you to admit it?"

"Yes. It did." She fought a smile.

He didn't like this. This was playful. Fun. He took her hand. "You can't go back undercover."

"I have to, and you know it." She wasn't happy, but she didn't pull her hand from his.

"It isn't safe." He took a deep breath. "Let's find out who's after you and then make the decision. I'll show this to Townsend tomorrow."

"Tomorrow?" asked Tim. "Why not tonight?"

"He left."

"Already?" Tim seemed confused. "Why?"

"Because he had somewhere else to go."

"Where?" Tim stared at him expectantly.

The Servant didn't know how to take a hint. "There was a report of an abduction."

"Who? Where?" asked Jackson.

"In the Holstein area."

"I thought Kalper's report on the young Servant proved that this was gang related. No talon marks equal no giant bird-creatures." Jackson looked upward. "Thank Araldo for that."

"It does prove it to me, but not to Townsend." He put the medallion on the table. "So, like I said. I'll show it to him tomorrow and see if he knows anything."

"Let me know what you find," said Trinity. "Until then we'll move forward with the original plan."

"No. It's no longer safe."

"What do you suggest? You and I suddenly make up and then break up again later."

"It happens with couples all the time. Look at Jackson and Kim."

"Hey, don't drag me into this," said Jackson.

"Hugh, I can take care of myself."

"How many did they send the first time?"

She hesitated. "Five."

"And this time?"

"Seven."

"They're going to get to a number you can't handle and then what? Or they'll ambush you. If they want you, they'll keep trying until they get you."

"Exactly," she said. "No matter where I am."

"That's not what I meant."

"But it's true. If they really want me, they'll get me, no matter what."

"I agree with Hugh. You're safer here," said Tim.

"Neither of you wanted me to do this in the first place."

"Because we love you." Tim glanced at Jethro.

"And I love you." She sighed. "I understand you're both worried, but I'm not going to hide while Birdie's family is in danger and some monster is murdering innocent Servants and Producers."

"Give me a couple of days." He ran his hand through his hair. "I'll talk to Townsend and see what he knows."

"We can do that," said Jethro. "It wouldn't look right if she went out immediately after Sassy got hurt."

"That's true." She frowned, looking at Jethro. "Unless I went out to celebrate that she lived."

Hugh watched her closely. She didn't have to be that eager to move on with the plan.

"Yeah, but it won't look weird if you don't." Jethro shrugged. "Plus, we'll move Sassy to my place, and you can come and visit her."

"Why would you move her to your house?" He did not want Trinity spending time at Jethro's house.

"With her injuries she can't stay alone at her place," said Trinity.

"You told me it was a decent area."

"It is. If you're healthy and strong. Sassy isn't either of those right now."

"Townsend would love to have her back at his place," he said.

"She'd drag herself out of there," said Trinity.

"Why is she so against living with Townsend? He and Libby care about her. They treat her like—"

"It's not them. That place reminds her of Bruno, and she...she can't handle it."

"Oh." That he understood, but he still wasn't agreeing to Trinity and Sassy staying at Jethro's. "Okay. Townsend's place is out but so is Jethro's."

"Why?" Jethro gave him a look that clearly said he knew the answer.

There was no way he was admitting the complete truth. "Because it's in the Warehouse District. Servants and Producers were just slaughtered in your neighborhood. If they're stocking up, there are only Grunts, Guards and Stockers left. It's not safe for Sassy."

"Then where should she go?" asked Jethro. "She can't stay here with you because of Trinity, and we've run out of other options."

"There is one other place." He glanced at Jackson who shook his head. "She could stay with Martha, Jackson and Kim." He almost winced at the glare Jackson sent him.

"Fine," said Jethro. "We can take her to Mom's, but my place is closer to the club."

"I'd feel better if she stayed with Jackson and Kim," he said.

"It isn't your call." Trinity had her hands on her hips.

He knew that look all too well, and it was never a good sign.

There was a tap on the door. "It's me. Kim." Jackson opened it and she stepped inside. "Everyone needs to get back to the party, especially Hugh."

"Okay." He stood. "We'll talk later."

"We need to leave," said Jethro. "We have to sneak Sassy out and get her to wherever we're taking her. Dr. Kalper told me to wait to move her until the pain killers had a chance to get into her system. That was almost a half hour ago. She should be ready to travel now."

"We need to get this settled." He wasn't letting them leave without a plan in place. "Talk to Kalper and see if he can give her more pain killers right before we're ready to transport her."

"It is settled," said Trinity.

"Only if you're moving in with Jackson and Kim." His voice raised with his temper.

"That isn't up to you," she said.

"We need to talk." He grabbed her hand.

"No, we don't. I'm not going to have this argument with you again." She jerked away from him. "We'll give you a few days to see what Townsend can find. If he doesn't know anything helpful, we'll move forward like we'd planned before this happened." She turned and walked out of their suite without a backward glance.

CHAPTER 66: Hugh

The rest of the night was miserable. Hugh drank more than he should, but it didn't put him in a better mood. All it did was make his imagination run wild...in vivid detail.

Trinity and Jethro had been pretty friendly but not near as friendly as they were going to be while pretending to be a couple. Pretend. He snorted. It may start that way, but she was kind and loving. Jethro had saved her. She'd loved him once.

"Crap. Stop it. Just stop it." He ran his hand through his hair and tugged. He grabbed his glass and downed his drink. He trusted her...but he didn't trust Jethro, not with her. The boy...Shit. Jethro wasn't a boy any longer. The other male still cared for Trinity. It was as clear as the drink in his hand. He stared at the empty glass and headed toward the bar. It would be as clear as the drink as soon as he had one. He handed the glass to the bartender who immediately filled it.

"You should slow down." Sue walked over to him.

"Why?" He took a large swallow.

She put her arm through his, leading him away from the bar.

"You know there are waiters here." He frowned at her. "They'll bring me another drink."

"Yes." Her brown eyes sparkled with amusement. "But it'll take longer if you're not at the bar." She led him to a table toward the back of the room.

He dropped onto a chair, exhaustion sweeping through him. It was late. The ballroom was almost empty. Soon he could go back to his apartment and sleep. Alone. He took another drink. While his fiancé was with another man.

"Do you really want everyone to think you're a drunk like your father?" Sue sat next to him.

"Ouch." His head snapped in her direction. "That was a low blow." He tipped his drink to her and then finished it, waving a waiter over to their table. "Didn't expect that from you."

"It's what everyone will think." She leaned toward him. "I know you're nothing like him, but these others don't know you."

The waiter took his glass and left.

"What others? Almost everyone is gone."

"Not Conguise." She tipped her head slightly to the right where Conguise stood, talking to Stella.

"Nothing I do will change his opinion of me."

"But he could use your actions to tarnish your reputation with others. We're at a fragile place right now. Don't..."

Dave Davies walked up to the table, holding two glasses and a bottle of whiskey. "May I join you, or is this a private conversation?"

"Sit, please." He pushed out the chair across from him with his foot. "My former Guard likes to lecture me."

"Isn't that a requirement for your Guards?" Dave sat.

"It must be." He laughed.

"Only because we care." Sue wasn't amused.

"Another glass." Dave called to a passing waiter, as he filled the two he had. He handed one to Hugh and the other to Sue.

"Thank you, but I don't drink." She pushed it across the table to Dave.

"You're free now. You should start." Dave smiled at her.

"I've seen how you Almightys behave when drinking." She gave them a look that was usually reserved for mothers to give their naughty children. "I'll pass."

"Suit yourself." Dave held up his drink for a toast. "Congratulations. I'd say that the night was a success."

"It appears so." He tapped his glass against Davies' and then took a sip. He should be thrilled. He'd raised a lot of money and there'd been no altercations between the classes, but his mind kept drifting back to Trinity.

"You're being modest." Dave leaned back in his seat, obviously having had a bit to drink himself. "Can I be honest with you?"

"Always." This should be interesting.

"Oh, I don't know about that. Always would not be a good idea." Dave grinned.

"Why not?"

"I am a businessman."

Hugh laughed and took a drink.

"I like you, Hugh. I didn't think I would, but...I do." Dave finished his drink.

"Glad to hear it." Hugh glanced at Sue. She was as confused and amused as he was.

"I came here tonight hoping there'd be some sort of fight or something." Dave refilled his glass. "You know. Some sort of entertainment."

"That wouldn't have been entertainment." Sue's tone was sharp.

"It would've been for me," said Dave unabashedly.

"To be honest," said Hugh. "I expected some issues."

"But there were none, and for that"—Dave leaned forward—"although I'm disappointed, I am impressed. Not many could've pulled that off." He sat back in his chair, tipping his glass to Hugh before taking a drink.

"I didn't do anything."

"Stop being so freaking modest." Dave waved his hand in the air, almost falling from his chair. "They didn't fight because they respect you." He leaned forward again and lowered his voice. "And let me tell you, there were some in the crowd who tried...really tried...to get reactions from the lower"—his eyes darted to Sue—"other classes."

"You were one of them, I'm sure," said Sue.

"No." Dave shook his head. "I wasn't. I considered it at one point, but..." He shrugged. "For some reason it didn't seem like the right thing to do."

"Because it wasn't." Hugh finished his drink. Great. He'd had near confrontations and instigators, and he'd been too busy thinking about Trinity to even notice.

"Who did try to stir up trouble?" asked Sue.

He glanced at her and then back at Dave. He never would've asked the question because he wouldn't have expected the Almighty to respond honestly, but...now that it was out there...

"Conguise was one of them." Dave lowered his voice again.

"Not surprising." He watched the professor who still talked to Stella. They seemed friendlier than he would've expected. Yes, the professor was an old friend of Jason's, but he'd left her to fend for herself.

"No, not really," said Dave. "Not with your history." He slapped Hugh on the shoulder. "And that's why I'm going to donate more money to your education program."

His eyes flew back to the Almighty. This man was rich, very rich. "How much more?"

"Enough to make renovations to dozens of schools, or to fund new buildings." He filled both glasses. "Whatever you decide. I may even be able to help with finding the locations for the new schools. I own a few properties."

"Thank you. I appreciate that." A few properties were a huge understatement. Jackson wouldn't like Davies hanging around, but they couldn't afford to turn down the offer.

"So what areas were you considering for the new buildings?" asked Dave.

The three sat and talked for hours. Davies had a lot of knowledge about education, having been in different schools during his youth.

"Hugh?" Tim poked his head into the ballroom. "Are you still up?"

"Uh...yeah." He made a face at Davies and then glanced around the room. It was empty except for the two of them and Sue, who was stretched out on some chairs snoring softly.

"You should go to bed," said Tim.

"I will. Later." He took another sip of his drink. He was in no mood to go back to his lonely room. "Why are you up?"

"Because it's morning."

"What?" He glanced at the window where the sun was already rising. "Shit." He hadn't meant to stay up this late.

"I'm going out to get something for breakfast," said Tim. "You want something?"

"No. Thanks though." He looked at Davies.

"Not me." Davies made a face and tossed back the rest of his drink.

"I'll bring you back some bread. It'll soak up all that booze." Tim left.

"If it's going to do that, then I say we have another one."

"No more for me." Dave held his hand over the top of his glass as he stood, wobbling a bit. "I need to sleep."

"Come on. One more." He didn't like begging, but it was better than going back to his suite alone.

"No. I have to go home." Dave shook his head. "We'll go out another night." He grinned. "I know a few females who can help you forget."

"No, that's not...Shit. Am I that obvious?" It helped their plan, but he hated being that pathetic.

"No, of course not...Ah, damn. I said I was going to be honest." Dave slapped him on the shoulder. "Yeah. You are but"—he sat back down, leaning toward him—"I understand. It's hard breaking up with someone you love. But you'll get through this. You'll find someone better."

"There is no one better." He tossed back half of his drink. Araldo, he was a pathetic excuse for a male.

"You feel that way now but..." Dave stood again. "Pour me another one. I'm going to take a piss and when I come back, I'll tell you about some females I know and the things they can do." He grinned. "Before I leave, we're going to have you set up with a date."

"I'm not ready to date." He hollered after Davies as the Almighty walked away.

"Wh-what?" Sue sat up, blinking away her sleep. "What time is it?"

"Late." He pointed at the window. "Or really early."

"You should go to bed." She stood. "I should go to bed."

"You go ahead. Dave and I aren't done drinking." He glanced at her. "I mean talking." He started to refill Dave's glass.

"You've had plenty." She took the almost empty bottle from him. "Dave's coming back."

"I know you're upset about you and Trinity, but you could use this time productively instead of wallowing like a lost baby."

"Ouch." He shook his head. "I always thought you were the kind Guard. One more thing I was wrong about."

"I am kind." She elbowed him in the side. "Buddy would've been a lot worse."

"That's true." He laughed and then sobered. "I miss him."

"Me too." She smiled sadly. "This will pass. She'll come back to you."

"I miss her," he said. Sue had been the only one outside of the group who he'd told. He trusted her completely.

"Use this time to do something important."

"Like I'm not? Setting up schools for everyone and integrating the classes is very important."

"Of course it is, but...Never mind." Her brown eyes filled with tears. "I've said enough. Goodnight."

"What's the matter, Sue?" He grabbed her arm, stopping her from walking away.

"Nothing. It isn't important."

"It is to you."

She shook her head. "You're right. The schools are important."

"Tell me," he said. She was his friend. She'd always been his friend.

"Laddie." The word was a whisper.

It was like a punch to the gut. He'd made her a promise and he hadn't kept it. Not yet. "I'm sorry. I started looking into that but—"

"I understand. You've been busy. I know you'll look into Conguise sometime, but..." She tried to smile but it didn't quite work.

"No, you're right. Laddie and Scar were friends. I made a promise. I'll make that a priority."

"You don't have to." Her words were soft, almost as if she didn't want to say them but felt like she had to.

"I do and I will." He sighed. "I'll have plenty of time now." Not really, but he'd make time.

"You're a good Almighty, Hugh Truent." She smiled again and this time it was real.

"Don't tell anyone else that," he joked.

"Tell anyone what?" Dave pulled out a chair and dropped onto it.

"That it's time for the two of you to go to bed." Sue grabbed the glass from Davies.

"What? No. We were going to..." He looked at Hugh. "What were we going to do?"

"Get you to your carriage." He stood. "Sue's right. I need to sleep."

"Yeah." Davies stood. "Me too."

They left the ballroom and headed for the door. A few Guards and Servants waited in the hallway, trying to hide their yawns.

"Get Mr. Davies' carriage," he said.

"Already at the door," said one of the Servants.

"You have them trained well," said Davies.

The Servant's eyes narrowed, but he didn't say anything.

"They take their *jobs* seriously, and they're the best staff around."

"Of course." Davies seemed to realize that he'd been insulting. "Sorry. I didn't mean anything else."

"Hugh! Hugh!" Tim burst through the doors, his eyes wide and his face pale.

"What's wrong? Did something happen to—"

Sue grabbed his arm, stopping his words.

"No. Something else."

"Is it an attack?"

"You could say that." Tim opened the door and waved him forward.

"Did Beau send word? Did the rebels—"

"Not them." Tim hurried out of the door. "Something else."

"What do you mean by that?" Hugh followed him outside and so did Sue, Dave and the Servants.

The streets were busy with those on their way to work, but no one moved. They all stood as if frozen in place. Carriages were stopped in the middle of the road. Almightys stood half-in and half-out of doorways, and all of them—Guards, Servants, Grunts and Almightys—were looking up.

"What's going..." His words died as a shadow floated across the street. "No." His head tipped back, and his breath froze in his chest as a giant bird-like creature flew overhead. It was large...no bigger than large. This thing was huge. The wingspan had to be at least fifteen or twenty feet as it glided closer, blocking the sun from the street.

CHAPTER 67: Hugh

"Holy Araldo, what has Conguise done now?" Hugh moved his hand from his eyes as the bird-like creature flew overhead.

She stared down at him as she passed, her dark green eyes with golden flecks wide in her tiny face. The gold and black feathers that covered most of her body contrasted with the white ones on her legs which were tucked against her belly. She opened her mouth which looked like it'd gotten stuck transforming from lips to beak. She let out a screech that pierced the air and made the hairs on his neck stand.

The sound of her call broke the trancelike state of those on the street. Screams filled the air as everyone scattered.

"Find cover," he shouted as he dove under a Gruntless parked carriage. The others followed behind him.

"Move." Davies wiggled, nudging everyone as he tried to make room. "My legs are still out there."

"That's your problem for being too tall." Tim elbowed the Almighty, refusing to move.

The creature screeched again, and someone cried out.

"No!" He shimmied backward to get out from under the carriage.

"What are you doing?" Sue grabbed his arm, pulling him back toward cover.

"Let me go." He pried her fingers from his sleeve. "I'm not letting her take someone else."

"Don't be a fool," said Davies. "There's nothing you can do to stop that thing."

"I can't let her..." His friends were right. If she attacked, there'd be nothing he could do except get himself killed. Still, he pulled free and crawled from under the carriage.

"Hugh," yelled Sue. "Don't..."

"Shhh." He leaned against the carriage as silence filled the street. The creature shrieked again as she flew past, her talons, thankfully empty. She disappeared over the next set of buildings.

"What in the name of Araldo was that?" Davies climbed out from under the carriage.

"I have no idea." He glanced at Sue and Tim as they crawled out into the open. He liked Davies but now wasn't the time to talk. "You should get your Grunts home where it's safe."

"Yeah. I don't think I'm coming out again. Ever." Davies shook his head. "You should go inside. I'm going to go on a limb and bet that thing doesn't care enough about you to behave."

"I think you're right."

"I'm going to"—Davies looked around—"we're all going to need an update on this."

"I know." He had no idea what he was going to say.

"This party wasn't what I expected, but it was interesting." Davies headed for his carriage which was now pressed against the building where the Grunts had tried to hide.

"I think you were wrong, and Townsend was right about the Holstein area," said Tim.

"Really? I'm so glad you're here to state the obvious." He couldn't tear his gaze away from the horizon where she'd disappeared. Was she hunting or just glad to be free?

"Why are you still out here? Didn't you see that thing?" Rex grabbed his arm, dragging him into the building. "Are you an idiot? Outside is not a place to be with that...What was that?"

"I don't know, but I'm going to find out." Hugh pulled free. "Go and get Ableson and Gruder. I need to talk to them now!"

He was done letting them pretend that there'd been nothing out of the ordinary about Level Five. One of them knew what this creature was, and he needed answers. Davies was right. Now that everyone had seen this creature, they'd want answers and then they'd want it dead. No, they'd want it dead first.

****

Thanks for reading *Lake of Sins: Machinations and Sacrifices*. I hope you enjoyed the story.

If you liked the story, please leave a review on any of the ebook retailers.

Also, check out my other books. An excerpt from *Chimera Chronicles: Rise of the River Man* is next followed by the Characters section where I list all the characters from the Lake of Sins series.

Sign up for my newsletter

https://lsodea.com/join-the-lake-of-sins-readers-group
Here are some of the perks of being a member of my newsletter

- Fun and entertaining articles delivered to your inbox
- Group Only Giveaways
- Sneak Peeks of illustrations, book covers and stories

https://lsodea.com/join-the-lake-of-sins-readers-group/

FREE: Rise of the River Man

MUTTER WAS IN TROUBLE. No one wanted a Guard like him. He was too big, too strong and too ugly. He stretched out on the concrete floor and winced. His ribs were definitely broken, but he'd fought and won with broken bones in the past. He started coughing. It was this sickness that had cost him the match. He sat up; the coughing subsided. He'd pleaded with Vickers, his Almighty master, not to make him fight but the money had already switched hands. He leaned his head against the bars of the cage. He'd lost the fight and now he'd lose his life.

The door opened and a male Almighty around thirty years old with blond hair entered the room followed by Satcha, the House Servant who ran this establishment. The Guards' Shelter didn't allow visiting at this hour, but Almightys did whatever they wanted. Mutter didn't bother to stand up. He'd learned his lesson. Right after he'd arrived, he'd trimmed his beard and had tried to look pleasant, but it had done no good. Every time that he'd run to the front of the cage and had smiled at the Almightys, he'd smelled the fear on them. Most had tried not to look at him, but he was big and scarred and hard to ignore.

They stopped in front of his cage.

"Ableson, this is the one I told you about," said Satcha. "Looks like he was a fighter. So, he should be used to obeying. I thought he might work for you, but he does have a bad cough."

"Just a little tickle in my throat from this damp, rotten place." He hated Servants. They didn't know when to keep their big mouths shut.

The Almighty remained quiet, his blue eyes never leaving Mutter.

"Come here," said Satcha.

Mutter wanted to stay where he was to annoy the Servant but Guards like him didn't get many chances for a home. He stood slowly, letting the Almighty get used to his size and appearance.

"How old are you?" asked Ableson.

"Not sure. Been around for a while but not too old." That was the safe answer. He had counted nineteen winters but that might be too old or too young. He never could tell what an Almighty wanted.

"By his teeth and body we estimate around twenty-five to thirty years," said Satcha.

Ableson twirled his finger. Mutter understood that signal. Before the fights had started, when the betting happened, he was often sized up by the gamblers. He turned in a circle, giving the Almighty time to study him.

"I'm strong and healthy." That was a lie, but he would be healthy again. He just needed a little time and some food.

"I need an obedient Guard." The Almighty's eyes roamed up and down his frame.

"Won't find one more obedient than me."

"Let's see if that's true." Ableson walked down the aisle. "Is there another Guard who he's close to?"

"Him?" Satcha laughed, following the Almighty. "He's so big and ugly even the other Guards stay away from him."

Ableson stopped in the hallway. "Take this one out."

The Servant opened the cage and slipped a rope over a young Guard's neck. Mutter's chest pinched. Typical. The Almighty's always chose the young ones. His only chance was gone. They would walk out and soon he'd be executed. He started to sit back down, when the three of them stopped in front of his cage.

"Put her in with him," said Ableson.

"Ah, we keep the younger ones separated from the older ones, especially the older males," said Satcha.

The Almighty didn't say a word, but his look was enough. The Servant muttered an apology and opened the door, shoving the young Guard into Mutter's cage.

He glanced at the little Guard who stood as far away from him as possible. She couldn't have been older than nine. She had russet hair and large, frightened, brown eyes.

"Hit her," said Ableson, his tone conversational.

"Wait," said Satcha. "That one's young and attractive. I can find a home for her. Let me get—"

"I'll pay for both." The Almighty's eyes never left Mutter.

Mutter kept his face a mask, but his stomach clenched. He didn't want to do this. He'd fought females before, but they'd all been experienced fighters.

"I need an obedient Guard," repeated Ableson.

The girl trembled in the corner, tears running down her soft, round cheeks. "Please, don't hurt me."

Pleading never changed anyone's mind. He knew the game and it would be her or him. He stared into the girl's scared brown eyes. "Bruised, broken or dead?"

Find out what happens next. https://books2read.com/u/
mZwWPD

Links to all stores are on my website: https://www.lsodea.com

ALL Characters from the Series

Ableson, Chad: An Almighty who used to work with Hugh and Parson at Conguise's lab.

AC: stands for Allied Classes. It is the name used for the rebels. See also: Allied Classes.

Accipitor, Accipitor1: – a creature from Level Five

Adam: A young, male Producer. Trinity's younger brother who was taken when he was three for a "Special List"

Afar: A middle-aged, male House Servant. Is owned by Professor Conguise and works as a butler.

Alice: An Almighty female Hugh once dated.

Allied Classes: Name of the rebels. See also AC

Almightys: The ruling class. They are between five and six feet tall. Generally, have dark hair and white skin.

Arthur: very young, male Producer, House Servant and Almighty. Son to Tim and Millie. Brother to Trinity.

Avions: Small, winged creatures about the size of a loaf of bread. They have feathers and beak but can speak. They are typically very gossipy.

Baggerly, Dr.: an Almighty who makes prosthetics

Barney: An elderly, male House Servant. He works for Professor Conguise

Bell: A Lead Producer. He is Benedictine's favorite and therefore holds much authority in camp. He is the father of Clarabelle and Mirabelle.

Benedictine Remore: A middle aged, male Almighty. He runs the Producer encampment where Trinity lives and the Handler and Tracker camps. He is married to Martha and the father to Jethro and Kim.

Birchwood: Birdie's real name. See also Birdie.

Birdie: A male Avion with brownish-gray feathers. See also Birchwood.

Bitt : A female Grunt. Cack's widowed wife. She serves on the Council.

Blended-Bar: A bar that caters to all classes.

Blue: A young, adult, female Producer.

Bo: An adult male Guard. Lead Guard for the Almightys.

Bob: Hugh's alias when he pretends to be a Guard.

Bradley, Ben: A male Almighty. Assisted Gaar and Mirra with serum.

Bradley, Verly: The Forest Witch. An adult, female Almighty. See also Forest Witch, Verly.

Brennon: An adult, male Guard. Can pick locks faster than anyone.

Brianna: An AC Guard. Works with Bo.

Brick: A Guard in the Protective Services.

Bruno: An adult, male Guard. Very large. Belongs to Townsend.

Buddy: An elderly, male Guard. He belongs to Hugh Truent. He has salt and pepper hair, a beard and is about five foot tall. He was bred for protection, not speed and is solid muscle.

Buster: An old, male Producer who was retired. Taught Millie and Trinity about medicinal herbs.

Butch: A male Lead Producer. Replaces Bell on duty in the guard shack. Is the assigned mate to Tulip.

Callie: A young adult, female House Servant

Captain Calvin Folgrant: An adult, male Almighty. A Captain in the Almightys' armed forces.

Casper: An elderly, male Guard. Belongs to Benedictine. Works with Jackson.

Carla: A female Guard. Belongs to Benedictine. Works with Jackson.

Champfur: A female Almighty who makes dresses.

Chapman: Parson's boss.

Christian: Brother to Harold, husband to Heather and father to Theresa in the story told by Jethro about the Lake of Sins. Also the name given to the River-Man by Trinity.

Christopher: Dave Davies cousin.

Chubs: A Guard. Belongs to Benedictine. Works at the Tracker camp.

Clacker: An Avion. One of Birdie's nephews.

Clarabelle: A female, teenage Producer. Bell's daughter and Mirabelle's sister.

Club Gall: A club for the elite where you can purchase anything you want.

Club Sin: A club for the very elite that is associated with the black market.

Clyde: A fighter. A Guard. Is almost as fast as a Servant.

Coakers: The male Almighty who used to supply Hugh with the serum for the Handlers and Trackers.

Cold Creepers: Reptilian-like creatures, about three feet tall and over six feet long, walk on all fours. They are green, gray or brown in color. They generally hunt in packs.

Con: a young, male Servant

Conguise, Peter, alias the professor: A geneticist. Used to be Hugh Truent's mentor. Daughter was Viola. See also: Professor Peter Conguise.

Council, the: A group of Almightys appointed to rule by the Supreme Almighty and the public.

Coxer, Samantha: An overweight middle-aged council member.

Crosnics Manor: An Almighty estate owned by Dresschew.

Cruck: A male Grunt. Cack's brother

Curtis: An adult, male protection Guard.

Davies, Albert: A male Almighty. Deceased. Had been rich and powerful. Dave Davies' father.

Davies, Dave: An adult, male Almighty.

Dede: An adult, female Servant. Has dark hair. Works as a prostitute at Ray's.

Doma: A young, male House Servant and Almighty mix, mother is Libby. Father is Townsend.

Drakka: An adult male House Servant trained in fighting

Dresschew, Serbian: An Almighty. Owned Crosnics Manor. Deceased.

Duke: An adult male Guard. Member of the Protective Services. Captain Cal's Lead Guard.

Eakers: An Avion

Eela: An adult male House Servant trained in fighting

Emmanuel: A male Handler. Not wild born.

Exhibit: Place where Producers are taken once they are paired to mate, so that they see the dangerous creatures in the forest.

Facility R.: another lab

Fersia: A House Servant. Matilda's daughter.

Forest Witch: An old, female Almighty who lives in the forest and takes in strays.

Gaar: A male Handler. He is the bonded pair to Mirra. See Handler.

Gap: a prison Guard who is in on the business and works for Wickerwood

Gerard: the warden's assistant. A middle-age, male Almighty.

General Hugh Truent Senior: A male Almighty. Deceased. Brilliant military strategist. Raised Little Sarah and Hugh with wife Sarah Truent.

Glareclow Village: A Servant village near the edge of the forest. Barney and Matilda live there.

Glass: A male Guard, prisoner

Reorg this for last name **Gracie Wentgerd** – a very rich older female Almighty.

Graining of Avions: a way to capture Avions.

Gray: a young, male Servant.

Gruder: A scientist who worked on Level Five in Professor Conguise's laboratory.

Guards: Belong to the Almightys. They hunt for the Almightys and protect the Almightys. They vary in size and hair color. Their eyes are usually brown. The males generally wear facial hair.

Great Death: The illness that swept over the earth, killing most humans, all domestic animals and all wild animals larger than a wild turkey.

Grunts: Are large and strong. They are bigger than Producers. They walk on all fours and do not speak. Their purpose is to haul things for the Almightys.

Handler: Predators that bond and help to control Trackers. They are between five and six feet tall but are extremely wide and muscular. They have long arms. See Gaar.

Hap: A male Lead Producer. Hector's son.

Harbor Point: - A large rock wall that extends the length of the world of the Lake of Sins

Harold: Brother to Christian in story told by Jethro about the Lake of Sins.

Heather: Wife to Christian in story told by Jethro about the Lake of Sins.

Hector: A Lead Producer. The section of the fence that he watches borders Troy's section. Hap's father. Hector is very diligent in his duties.

Hester: A female Producer.

Holstein Area: a dangerous area in the city. Lots of gang activity here.

Hopper: A Guard in the Protective Services. He works in the medical tent and is friends with Indy and Jethro.

House Servants: Belong to Almightys. They manage the households and businesses of the Almightys. They are slender in build and short, between four and five feet tall. They have fangs and claws, and their eyes are a vibrant hue.

Howling Hut, The: A Guard's bar located in the Guards' section of the city.

Hugh Truent: A male Almighty. The youngest Almighty to ever be bestowed the title of High. Son of Sarah. Invented the new updated tracking device.

Indy: A Guard in the Protective Services. Jethro's friend.

Jackson: A male Guard. He is the lead Guard to Benedictine. He is also called the hairless Guard because he wears no facial hair. He used to be assigned to protect Benedictine's daughter Kim.

Jar: a bar where the fighters hang out

Jason Dophilez, the Supreme Almighty: A middle-aged Almighty. Rules their government with the Council. He is fat and likes to drink. See also Supreme Almighty (alphabetized by first name since last name is hardly ever used)

JD: young male Servant.

Jeremiah: A teenage, male Producer at the Finishing Camp.

Jethro Remore: A teenage, male Almighty. Son of Benedictine and Martha. Brother to Kim. Befriends Trinity at the Lake of Sins.

Jezzy: A female Producer. Stuart's mate.

Jimmy Smedly: A teenage, male Almighty. A friend of Jethro's.

Jooneen: An adult male House Servant trained in fighting.

Jorge: An elderly, male Guard. He belongs to Professor Conguise.

Kalper, Dr.: An Almighty. He is Sarah Truent's doctor.

Kim Remore: An Almighty. Benedictine and Martha's daughter and Jethro's sister.

Kimmy: A female Guard

King, Dr.: An Almighty. He is Hugh Truent's family doctor.

Laddie: An older, male Guard. Belongs to Professor Conguise. He is a large protection Guard.

Lady-Bird: Accipitor1 nickname

Lazaretto Falls: A large waterfall in the forest.

Lead Producers: A title given to a small set of Producers. They are allowed to carry a club and they interact with Benedictine. They also guard the perimeter of the camp from dangers.

Leelee: A young, female House Servant and Almighty mix, mother is Libby. Father is Townsend.

Leena: A young, female House Servant. A member of the Allied Classes.

Leslie: A young adult, female House Servant with long brown hair and green eyes. Friends with Callie and Miranda. Frequents blended-bars.

Libby: An adult, female House Servant. Townsend is her mate. Mother to Leelee and Doma.

Life: A male Servant in prison who runs one of the Servant gangs

Little Sarah Norable: A middle-aged, female Almighty. Daughter of Sarah Truent and sister to Hugh Truent.

Lola: A female Guard. The madam of a whore house.

Maple: An elderly, female Producer who was retired. Was kind to Trinity.

Martha Remore: A middle-aged, female Almighty. Mother to Jethro and Kim. Wife of Benedictine.

Miles: a male Almighty doctor who worked in the infirmary at the jail.

Millie: A Producer. Trinity's mother. She is the assigned mate to Remy, but actually breeds with Tim.

Matilda: House Servant. Works for Conguise. Barney's mate.

Michael: An Almighty who owns the pub called Michael's Pub

Millie: A Producer. Trinity's mother. She is the assigned mate to Remy, but actually breeds with Tim.

Mirabelle: A teenage, female Producer. Was on the Harvest List last year. Daughter of Bell and sister to Clarabelle. She has one leg shorter than the other.

Meesus: An adult, female House Servant. Manages the prostitutes at Ray's. Was Ray's mate. Very pretty, exotic.

Miranda: A young adult, female House Servant with short, light brown hair. Friends with Leslie and Callie. Frequents blended-bars.

Mirra: A female Tracker. The bonded pair to Gaar. She is brindle with yellow eyes and large teeth. See Tracker.

Mo: An adult, male Guard. Member of the AC. Works with Bo.

Mosquer: a Guard. Manages Clyde.

National Health Assurance Registry System: DNA database. Was supposed to be used to eliminate deformities and illnesses in offspring of all classes and to create better offspring in all classes except Almightys.

Nirankan: A male Tracker. Russet colored. Wild born.

Norable, Sam: A middle-aged, male Almighty. Husband to Little Sarah Truent.

Noreese: An adult, female Handler. Friends with Tatania.

Ott: young, male Grunt

Pab: An adult, male Guard of the AC. Works with Bo.

Parker, Ms.: A middle aged, female Almighty. Nurse by profession. Works for Professor Conguise.

Parra: A male Tracker. He's white and brown. Wild born.

Parson, Steve: An adult, male Almighty. Works in a lab. Used to work for Professor Conguise. Now, goes by Dean Rosenblur.

Peetie: An adult, male Guard.

Pepper: A female Guard. Dr. Kalper's nurse and housekeeper.

Perchies: An Avion. Birdie's niece.

Petarvarius: A male Handler. Wild born.

Petersen: An Almighty who Servants and Guards were spying for the AC.

Phelecks: An adult, male House Servant. Libby's father. Deceased.

Producers: Large boned and strong. They stand between six and eight feet tall. They usually have dark hair and brown eyes. They work in the fields and produce all the food for the other classes.

Professor Peter Conguise: A geneticist. Used to be Hugh Truent's mentor. Daughter was Viola. See also: Conguise.

Protective Services: The Almightys' army.

Quarks, Lawrence: the warden at the prison.

Randy: A male, teenage Producer. Used to be friends with Trinity but now hangs around Clarabelle.

Ranger: A male Guard. Member of the Allied Classes.

Ray: An adult, male House Servant. Has gray hair but is in his prime. Is a childhood friend of Tim's. Runs the Servant section of the city. Was the mate to Meesus.

Released, the: new term used to describe the strays

Reese: A young, female Guard. She belongs to Hugh Truent. She has long, brown hair and is short and thin. She is a cross between a hunting Guard and something else.

Remy: A Producer. Millie's sanctioned mate. He is gay and is Troy's partner.

Rex: An adult, male Guard. Is a member of the Council's Guards and works at the Council Building.

Ritco: Adult, male Stocker. Leader of the Stockers in the Stockers' Village

River-People/River-Men: Fish-like creatures. Can live in or out of water but prefer to be in the water. They can breathe both above and below water. They have scales for skin, sharp teeth. Hunt from below the water and drag their prey under to drown it. Also called Fish-Men. See Christian.

Rocco: One of the Forest Witch's Guards

Rocket: A teenage, male Guard. A stray. Brother to Sassy.

Rosenblur, Dean: The name Steve Parson is now using.

Sallers, Doug: A councilman

Sampson: An adult male Guard. Works at the Howling Hut.

Sarah Truent: An elderly, female Almighty. Mother to Hugh and owner of Tim.

Sassy: An adult, female Guard. Friend of Trinity's. Good at escaping. Brother is Rocket.

Say: Small House Servant who follows Trinity

Scar: An older, female Guard. Belongs to Professor Conguise. She is a protection Guard.

Scott: a young, male Almighty

Scratch: a male Servant in Life's gang

Seepie: A Handler.

Sheno: An Almighty. Was a warden years ago.

Sikka: A female Tracker. She is black and gray. She is wild born.

Silo: a male Guard who worked at Professor Conguise's lab

Sin, The: an elite, private club for black market members

Skeekie: A young Guard. A member of the Allied Classes.

Skippy: An adult, male Guard. Friend of Bruno's. Deceased.

Smedly, Mrs.: A female Almighty. Jimmy's mother.

Sovee: a Guard. A former fighter who now trains fighters. He works for Vickers.

Speck: A Guard in the Protective Services. He's very young.

Stella: Jason's (the Supreme Almighty) granddaughter

Stockers: Short and stout, long muscular arms, usually bald and they are mostly blind with a poor sense of smell, but their hearing is excellent. They are ill tempered and violent.

Stuart: A male Producer. Has been chosen to stay in camp but has not been assigned a mate. Brother to Travis.

Sue: An older, female Guard. She belongs to Hugh Truent. She has long legs. She is a hunting Guard.

Sugar: A female Guard with dark, curly hair

Supreme Almighty: The main ruler of this society along with an appointed Council. Currently, this position is held by Jason Dophilez.

Tammie: A teenage, female Producer at the Finishing Camp.

Tatania: An adult, female Handler. She has long, dark hair, offset by a white streak. Friends with Noreese.

Tee: A young, female House Servant.

Teeko: a male Tracker, Sikka's mate

Terbasse, Francis: rich Almighty male

Theresa: Daughter of Christian and Heather in story told by Jethro about the Lake of Sins.

Timothy (Tim): House Servant. Trinity's father. Millie, a Producer is his mate. He belongs to Sarah, an Almighty.

Tina: A female Producer. Troy's assigned mate.

Titus: A Lead Producer. The section of the fence that he watches borders Troy's section on the opposite side as Hector's. Titus drinks a lot.

Todd: Adult, male Almighty. Assigned to Midtown Shelter.

Tonkers: a male prison Guard who is working with Jethro and Indy to get female companionship into the prison

Townsend: An adult, male Almighty. A reporter. Mate is Libby. Children are Doma and Leelee.

Tracker: A predator. Bonds with a Handler. Stands around ten to twelve-feet tall on its back legs. Can travel on all fours or on two legs. Covered in soft fur which varies in color. Has long sharp claws and teeth. Can find (track) anything. See Mirra.

Travis: A male, teenage Producer. Was on the Harvest List last year. Trinity's only friend.

Trinity: A Producer and a House Servant. Daughter of Millie and Tim.

Trip: A Guard. Belongs to Benedictine. Lead Producer of the Guards at the Tracker camp.

Troy: A male Lead Producer. He is Remy's partner. His assigned mate is Tina.

Trunk: Large male Producer. Tends to be violent.

Tuck: Young, male Servant.

Tulip: A female Producer. Assigned mate is Lead Producer Butch.

Verly: The Forest Witch

Vickers, Vivian: the wife of William Vickers

Vickers, William (Bill) : lawyer involved in black market

Victor, The: A large, adult, male Servant. He works for Ray and Meesus. He is a fighter.

Viola: a female Almighty. Daughter of Professor Peter Conguise and live-in girlfriend of Hugh Truent. She is a scientist and a lifelong friend to Kim Remore.

Wasee: a Servant who makes prosthetics

Wickerwood, Wilt: A male Almighty. Scientist. One of the five who are aware of Gaar and Mirra's existence.

Wilson, Bette: A gray-haired, female council member.

Wilson, Kurt: Bette Wilson's adult son

Let's stay in touch

https://www.instagram.com/author_lsodea/
https://www.tiktok.com/@author_lsodea
https://www.facebook.com/LSODeaAuthor/
Closed Lake of Sins FB Group[1]
https://www.facebook.com/groups/137774923650964/

https://twitter.com/lsodea
Or email at lsodea7@gmail.com

Author Bio

L. S. O'Dea grew up the youngest of seven in a family that uses teasing and tricks as an indication of love (or at least that's what she tells herself). Being five years younger than her closest sibling often made her the unwilling entertainment for her brothers and sisters.

Before she started kindergarten her brothers taught her how to spell her first and middle name—Linda Sue. She was so proud she ran into the kitchen to tell her mother. She stood tall and recited the letters of her name: L-E-M-O-N H-E-A-D.

She's pretty sure she has her siblings to thank for the demons that lurk in her mind, whispering dark and demented stories.

Don't miss out!

Visit the website below and you can sign up to receive emails whenever L. S. O'Dea publishes a new book. There's no charge and no obligation.

https://books2read.com/r/B-A-XJLD-GQUXB

BOOKS 2 READ

Connecting independent readers to independent writers.

Also by L. S. O'Dea

Chimera Chronicles
Rise of the River Man
Feeding Fersia
Breaking the Brush Men
Rage Of Rattus Norvegicus
Leaving Level Five

Lake Of Sins
Lake of Sins: Secrets in Blood
Lake of Sins: Hangman's Army
Lake Of Sins: Betrayed
Whispers From the Past
Machinations and Sacrifices
Lake of Sins: Escape

Standalone
Lake of Sins Series Box Set Books 1-3
Chimera Chronicles
A Demon's Gift